"Now, will you make love to me?"

He'd love nothing better. B~~~~~~~~~~~~~ried about her emot~~~~~~~~~~~~~~~~~~~~with anything like th~~~~~~~~~~~~~~

"Willa, are you ~~~~~~~~~~~~~~~~~you need more time ~~~~~~~~~~~~~~~

Her gaze narrow~~~~~ irritation. He laughed reluctantly. Although the notion of her tearing his clothes off didn't sound half-bad.

"Refill?" he asked her. Now that the moment was upon him, he had no idea how to proceed with her. Yet another first for him. He pressed a full glass into her hand and nudged the bottom of it toward her mouth.

"A little liquid relaxation first, Mr Dawson?"

"Something like that." She was so damned open and forthright. It was disconcerting. Most women were so busy maneuvering into his pants by this point they weren't stopping to talk about his tactics to achieve the same.

"I have faith in you, Gabe."

And there it was. That damned trust of hers. What if he let her down? If she freaked out in the middle of sex and he did the wrong thing? Fear gripped his chest in sharp talons.

"Now what?" she asked.

Now what, indeed.

Vengeance in Texas: Where heroes are made.

A BILLIONAIRE'S REDEMPTION

BY
CINDY DEES

...nia (UK) policy is to use papers that are natural, renewable and
...ble products and made from wood grown in sustainable forests. The
...ng and manufacturing processes conform to the legal environmental
...ions of the country of origin.

...d and bound in Spain

MILLS & BOON

First published in Great Britain 2013
by Mills & Boon, an imprint of Harlequin (UK) Limited,
Eton House, 18-24 Paradise Road, Richmond, Surrey TW9 1SR

© Harlequin Books S.A. 2013

Special thanks and acknowledgement to Cindy Dees for her contribution to the Vengeance in Texas miniseries.

ISBN: 978 0 263 90362 1
ebook ISBN: 978 1 472 00724 7

46-06

Harle
recycl
loggin
regula

Printe
by Bla

Cindy Dees started flying airplanes while sitting in her dad's lap at the age of three and got a pilot's license before she got a driver's license. At age fifteen, she dropped out of high school and left the horse farm in Michigan, where she grew up, to attend the University of Michigan. After earning a degree in Russian and East European studies, she joined the US Air Force and became the youngest female pilot in its history. She flew supersonic jets, VIP airlift and the C-5 Galaxy, the world's largest airplane. During her military career, she traveled to forty countries on five continents, was detained by the KGB and East German secret police, got shot at, flew in the first Gulf War and amassed a lifetime's worth of war stories.

Her hobbies include medieval reenacting, professional Middle Eastern dancing and Japanese gardening.

This RITA® Award-winning author's first book was published in 2002 and since then she has published more than twenty-five bestselling and award-winning novels. She loves to hear from readers and can be contacted at www.cindydees.com.

Thanks to my fellow authors for making this experience such a joy. Y'all are as big-hearted and talented as Texas itself!

Chapter 1

"…We commend the soul of our brother departed, and we commit his body to the ground—earth to earth, ashes to ashes, dust to dust…"

The preacher's voice droned on, but Willa Merris's heart hurt too much for her to hear the rest. Her father, Senator John Merris, was dead. Truly gone. Murdered. And even though his body had been discovered nearly two weeks ago, the finality of it had waited until this exact moment to slam into her like a ton of bricks.

Despair weighed on her until she could hardly breathe. What were she and her mother going to do? He had always been the center of their universe, the two of them pale moons orbiting his brilliant life.

A thud startled her. Her mother had just tossed a tightly balled clod of red Texas clay on top of the casket. The dirt in her own hand was cold and moist, squishing out of her clenched fist. Blinded by tears, Willa tossed her clod of dirt into the hole that contained her father's mortal remains.

She shuddered as dozens of other mourners stepped forward to toss handfuls of dirt on her father's grave. Some of them appeared genuinely sad, but the majority ranged from indifferent to covertly satisfied to bury the bastard. She had no illusions that her father had been a saint. Far from it. He'd been a mean man in a mean business—two mean businesses—a wildcat oilman carving a fortune out of the oil sands of West Texas, and a United States senator, brawling in the halls of Congress.

A comforting arm slipped around her shoulders. She leaned into the embrace for a moment, but then caught a whiff of the aftershave and stiffened. *No. Surely not.* Horror flowed through her. That, and sheer, frozen terror. She glanced up at the sympathetic face of James Ward, the son of her father's longtime business partner.

"Get away from me this second," she cried. "Don't touch me!"

The people around her jolted, shocked by her outburst. She slipped out from under Ward's arm as he stared at her, dumbfounded. Right. Like he didn't know exactly what she was talking about.

Flashes of his big hands tearing her clothes… viciously slapping the fight out of her…shoving her to the floor of her living room…and, oh, God, the pain of his big body slamming into hers over and over. His grunts…the maniacal gleam in his glittering blue eyes… the humiliation and utter degradation of it…

She'd wanted to die. Right there where he'd left her on the floor like some piece of tossed-off garbage. She'd wished desperately to disappear, to just cease to exist. But no such luck. Instead, her father had checked out of his mortal coil and left behind the mess of his life for her to unravel in addition to hers.

"Honey," Ward murmured, "you're overwrought. Let me drive you home. Put you to bed."

Overwrought? Something inside her cracked. She'd show him overwrought! "Get away from me!" she screeched.

Backpedaling from him with her hands outstretched to fend him off, she registered vaguely how everyone had gone stock-still around her. It was as if time had stopped with everyone in funny poses, staring at her slack-jawed as if she'd grown a second head.

"I swear, if you lay a hand on me again, I'll kill you!" she shouted at Ward in rage she didn't even know she had inside her. "Do you hear me? I'll kill you!"

The vignette unfroze all at once with a rush of reaching hands and concerned faces closing in on her like macabre, black-clad clowns. Camera bulbs flashed, cell phones whipped out to arm's length, pointed at her. Even the local news reporter frantically gestured at her cameraman to get all this on film.

Appalled, humiliated and so irrationally furious she scared herself, Willa batted away the hands, shoved through the crowd and broke into a stumbling half run toward her car. The grass and her high-heeled shoes were a lethal combination and she nearly broke her neck before she fetched up hard against her car door breathing heavily. She felt dirty. A driving compulsion to wash away the feel of James Ward's filthy touch overwhelmed her. She had to get home. Take a hot shower. Scrub herself clean.

Willa stabbed at the car's ignition button and nearly ran down the news reporter as she accelerated away from her father's disaster of a funeral, frantic to escape this nightmare from which there was no waking.

Gabe Dawson watched the slender, black-veiled woman race away from John Merris's grave. What was that all about? He hadn't been close enough to hear the commotion, but it had been hard to miss. An angry buzz of gossip hummed around him…something about the senator's daughter threatening to kill someone.…

Quiet little Willa Merris? Alarm blossomed in his gut. Was she in danger? The girl he remembered wouldn't say boo to a mouse. But then, he hadn't seen her in over a decade. She'd been a skinny, awkward teen the last time he'd visited the Merris home. Before his falling out with John Merris. Before the two of them became mortal enemies.

At least Willa's outburst had drawn the attention of the rumormongers away from his arrival at the funeral. As it was, he was sure to be topic number one in the gossip columns for showing up at John Merris's grave. He would probably be accused of coming here to gloat. In point of fact, he hadn't wished the old man dead. Plenty of suffering and failure, yes. But not death.

The preacher mumbled a few more words into the suddenly circuslike atmosphere, but no one was paying attention. Seeming to sense it, the minister cut short and wrapped up the graveside service with unseemly haste. Gabe watched in sardonic amusement as the good ladies of Vengeance, Texas, wasted no time texting and calling their friends to report the latest scandal surrounding the lurid death of John Merris. *Vultures.*

He jolted as a microphone materialized under his nose. "Have you got any comment on Willa Merris's outburst, Mr. Dawson? You're Senator Merris's former business partner, are you not?" a female reporter demanded.

She looked as avidly entertained as the vultures. More so.

"No comment," he growled. He strode away from the woman, but she walk-ran beside him, continuing to shove that damned microphone in front of him.

"What do you have to say about John Merris's murder? Some people are saying you're more pleased than anyone that the senator is dead. Is it true you two had a violent argument just a few weeks ago?"

He stonily ignored the reporter and her sleazy innuendos.

"Is it true that the police have asked you not to leave town, and that you're a person of interest in the senator's murder?"

He stopped at that, turned slowly and gave her the flat, pitiless stare that had earned him his reputation as a hard man among hard men. The reporter recoiled from him with a huff. Smart girl.

"What did you say your name was?" he called after her as she stomped away from him.

She half turned and snapped, "Paula Craddock. KVXT News. Are you going to give me a statement?"

"Nope. Just wanted to know who to sic my lawyers on the next time you harass me."

The journalist's gaze narrowed to a threatening glare.

Yeah, whatever. Better women than she had tried to get a rise out of him over the years. But he wasn't the founder and CEO of a billion-dollar oil conglomerate for nothing. He chewed up and spit out self-serving leeches like her for breakfast.

Meanwhile, the alarm in his gut refused to quiet. What had caused Willa Merris to blow up at her own father's funeral? She and her mother were always the souls of decorum, quiet props in the background of Senator Merris's many public appearances. Willa had been trained practically from birth how not to draw attention to herself. It was unthinkable that she would cause a scene, ever, let alone in public, in front of the press, and most definitely not at a somber occasion like this.

What had gotten into her?

Worry for the unpleasant conversation he had yet to have with young Willa flashed through his head. Maybe he should wait awhile to break his own bad news to her and her mother. But it wasn't like there was ever going to be a good time to tell them John Merris's last, nasty little secret.

He sighed. Lord, this was going to suck. He might as well go find Willa Merris now and make her misery complete.

Chapter 2

No matter how long she stood under the water, nor how hot the water was, Willa never felt entirely clean anymore. But as the shower went from tepid to icy cold, she reluctantly climbed out. She felt like the fragile little handblown glass horse figurine she'd gotten somewhere as a child. At the slightest touch, she was going to shatter into a million knife-sharp pieces.

She'd give anything not to have to face the world for a good, long time. Or better, to leave this place and never, ever come back. But duty drove that rebellious thought back into her subconscious nearly as quickly as it had surfaced. God knew why, but her father had named her executor of his estate, which meant she was trapped in this town for months to come.

The doorbell echoed far away in her parents' mansion. Someone else would get it—Louise, their longtime housekeeper, or maybe Larry Shore, her father's new chief of staff and right-hand man since the old one, Frank Kellerman, wound up in jail for covering up her father's sins.

Despite the ninety-degree weather, an impulse to cover as much skin as possible overcame her. She pulled on a pair of light wool slacks and a long-sleeved cashmere sweater. She skipped her usual French twist and merely pushed her strawberry-blond hair off her face with a simple headband. *My, my. More rebellion, Miss Merris? Leaving your hair down? Scandalous.* Making a wry face at her reflection in the mirror, she put on just enough makeup not to look like a corpse, herself.

A knock on her bedroom door startled her. "Miss Willa. You've got a visitor," Louise announced, her voice laced with heavy disapproval.

Willa allowed herself a mental groan. Decorum dictated that she receive each and every one of the endless stream of her father's business associates offering condolences and, of course, the avid gossip seekers disguised as neighbors and family friends. But the strain of it was getting to her. The constant visitors never gave her a moment's escape from the oppressive grief pervading the house.

If they would all just give her a minute to breathe, to blank her mind and forget everything, maybe she could get her mental feet under her. Start tackling the mountain of decisions piling up around her. She closed her eyes for a moment to gather strength and replied, "Show our visitor into the library. I'll be right down."

She checked her appearance in the mirror and drew up short. She looked...haggard. *Father wouldn't approve at all.* Her train of thought derailed. Her father was dead, and she was no longer obligated to look like a poster child for his endless political campaigns. A surprising and overwhelming sense of relief flooded her. She could go without makeup if she wanted. And wear sloppy T-shirts and jeans. She could say what came to mind without first checking the comment against her father's political platform. So giddy she almost felt ill, she giggled a little hysterically.

Pull it together, girlfriend. There were still a few social boundaries she would not cross. Like not acting properly bereaved at her father's passing.

She hurried down the grand, sweeping staircase to the marble-tiled foyer. Her parents' house was designed for maximum "impress the guests" factor. Personally, she found it gaudy and overbearing. But then, that had been her father. She much preferred her sweet two-bedroom cottage across town by the college.

She opened the oversize walnut doors into the library and stopped cold as she spied her visitor. She would recognize those broad shoulders, that rugged profile, the casual confidence anywhere. *Gabe Dawson.*

It had been years since she'd seen him. A wash of memory heated her cheeks. As a teen, she'd had the mother of all crushes on this man. He had been by far the most handsome and dashing male she'd ever laid eyes on. *And good golly, Miss Molly, he still was.* Of course, he'd never given her the time of day. When he had bothered to speak to her at all back then, it had been to ruffle her hair like she was an amusing puppy, and call her something demeaning like "squirt."

But that had been a long time ago. She wasn't that innocent kid anymore. And he—he wasn't that impetuous, up-and-coming geologist who dared to challenge the established rules for how oil was explored.

He was standing with one elbow propped on the mantel, staring down into the cold, gray ashes of the fireplace. A half-consumed glass of bourbon dangled in his other hand. In this unguarded moment, he looked sad. Worried. Lonely, even.

Her heart went out to him before her conscious mind registered the irony of this man's presence in her father's inner sanctum. Gabe Dawson and John Merris had been like matter and antimatter. Any time they crossed paths, they erupted in a fiery explosion that consumed everything and everyone around them.

She stepped farther into the room, clearing her throat as she did so. Gabe turned sharply to face her with the barely contained energy she remembered. Being in the same room with him was still like standing next to a hurricane.

She registered a few changes, though, as he met her in the middle of the spacious library. His clothes were more expensive, and fit better these days. His hair was shorter but still looked tousled like someone had just run a hand through it. His eyes...oh, my. They were still that dark, mysterious shade of green that looked right through her. Although at the moment, she saw reticence in them.

An urge to stutter and blush like a schoolgirl nearly won out over a lifetime's worth of ingrained manners, but she only fought it off by dint of long years of concealing her true thoughts and feelings.

"Gabe Dawson. What a pleasant surprise," she said smoothly. "Can I get you a refill on your drink? Is it still Kentucky bourbon, neat?"

He waved off the drink offer and set down his glass on a side table. His gaze slid down her body to her toes and back up to her face quickly enough not to be offensive, but with enough thoroughness to send a wave of heat coursing through her—and a shiver of apprehension. He always had skirted the edges of impropriety in the most delicious way. Rhett Butler, move over.

"How are you doing?" he asked, his voice every bit as potent as she remembered. The passing years had given it a richness, a maturity, that tasted good on her tongue. *Oh, my.*

She sank onto the edge of one of the big leather wingback chairs and gestured him into the matching one. He leaned forward in it, propping his elbows on his knees to study at her intently. It was unnerving being the subject of such intense scrutiny. But then he'd always had that effect on her. She restrained an urge to pat her hair and tug at the neck of her sweater. Instead, she folded her hands in her lap and nearly crushed her own fingers.

The monstrous impropriety of his being here occurred to her. How dare he intrude upon her family on this day of mourning and loss? He'd hated her father. Done his damnedest to ruin John Merris. Abruptly, his presence grated like sandpaper on her skin. He had no right to be here.

She gritted her teeth, her training in being polite to everyone in all cases rubbing raw against an urge to scream and rail at this man. Although truth be told, her need to scream at the top of her lungs wasn't all about him. She risked a glance at him, and felt awkward heat bloom in her cheeks. Lord, this man discombobulated her.

She stared down at her tightly twined fingers and very belatedly answered his question. "My mother and I are doing as well as expected after such a shock," she said automatically, for the hundredth time. "Thank you for coming."

"You don't have to put on a show for me, Willa."

Her gaze snapped up to his. "I beg your pardon?"

"I'm not here to pay my condolences. I wouldn't insult you or your mother by pretending to be sad your father is gone."

She leaned back hard, shocked at his bald honesty. This was the deep South. Old-school Texas. People didn't admit to being delighted that their archrival had kicked the bucket. The rules of polite behavior were observed. Leave it to Gabe Dawson to flout even the most basic societal convention.

"I need to speak to you and your mother about a business matter. Is she up to joining us?" he asked.

Minnie Merris had been so doped up on tranquilizers before the funeral, it was a miracle she'd been able to stand. Willa had no doubt her mother had added a handful of sleeping pills to the cocktail of medications by now and was passed out cold in her bed.

"I'm taking care of all business decisions at the moment," she answered smoothly.

"Minnie dumped it all on you, huh?" he asked sympathetically. "She never was much for taking care of herself."

Willa's spine went rigid. He might be absolutely correct, but she didn't need this man pointing out her mother's flaws to her. "If you've come to gloat over our loss, Mr. Dawson, you can leave now."

He threw up his hands apologetically. "I'm sorry. I shouldn't have said that."

Willa noted wryly that he didn't apologize for calling her mother weak and unable to care for herself; he'd merely apologized for saying it aloud. She waited, irritated, as he took a deep breath and gathered his thoughts.

"No matter what your family thinks of me, I am

sorry your father was murdered. Even he didn't deserve an end like that."

She pursed her lips. "Even he? Mr. Dawson, are you bent on offending me?"

He exhaled hard and shoved a hand through his hair, standing it up in a sexy mess all over his head. An urge to reach out and smooth it crossed her palm. She dismissed the impulse with dismay.

He swore under his breath. "I'm going about this all wrong. Please let me start over."

She settled deeper into the embrace of the leather chair, waiting to see where Gabe was taking this. She kind of enjoyed watching him squirm. She'd had to spend most of the past decade listening to her father rant about how this man had stolen Merris Oil's future, and done his best to run her family into the ground. And while her father had been a hothead, prone to making generalizations, he also got things right, sometimes.

"Willa—Miss Merris. I truly am sorry your father has passed away. No matter what our disagreements might have been, I did not wish the man ill personally."

She blinked, studying him anew. His sincerity surprised her. "Thank you," she murmured.

"I do have another reason for coming to see you today beyond expressing my sympathy for your loss."

"Indeed?" Curiosity stirred in the midst of her caution. What on earth could he want here? She flashed back for a second to her teen years when she'd nightly dreamed of him sweeping her into his arms and eloping with her. The absurdity of the notion now almost made her smile. Gabe Dawson was a well-known playboy and self-avowed bachelor. He'd been divorced for many years, in fact. Plenty of time had passed for him to find a wife if he was planning on having another one.

Not the marrying kind, obviously. Just as well. He'd probably be a completely insufferable control freak in a relationship.

She tuned back in to what he was saying so earnestly. "…tried to speak to your father about a sensitive business matter a few weeks ago, but that conversation… didn't go well. Unfortunately, the underlying issue remains unresolved."

A snort escaped her. The way she heard it, the two men had engaged in a violent shouting match that ended with her father throwing a punch at Gabe in the middle of the prestigious and private Petroleum Club in Dallas. What on earth could have provoked her father so horribly? John Merris had been a highly intelligent man, and he knew darn good and well not to make such a scene in the middle of a tough re-election campaign.

Gabe continued doggedly, "As you may recall, I started life as an oil geologist. And as such, I have more than a working knowledge of assessing oil fields."

Her brows knit in a frown. Where was he going with this? Assessing oil fields? "Mr. Dawson, I have nothing to do with the day-to-day operation of Merris Oil. Perhaps you should be having this conversation with Larry Shore. I believe he's going to take over as temporary CEO in my father's place. Or you could speak with the Ward family. They hold a significant minority share in my father's company."

"Please. Hear me out."

She nodded her somewhat confused assent and he continued. "I happen to own the mineral rights to a parcel of land next to Merris Oil's Vacarro Field."

Even she knew what the Vacarro Field was. It was Merris Oil's cash cow—a stretch of oil field about an hour's drive west of Vengeance that churned out millions of barrels of oil each year and was the main source of her family's income.

"Dawson Exploration just completed a survey of the Vacarro II parcel, and it so happens that the seismic data from my land also paints a fairly complete picture of your father's field."

"And?"

"And I took a look at it," he announced heavily.

She frowned. Okay. Seismic data wasn't classified or secret. It wasn't illegal to survey anywhere if a person felt like paying to look at mineral rights they didn't own. When Gabe didn't continue, she said, "I fail to see why you felt obliged to share this with me."

His frown deepened. "I gather, then, that your father didn't speak with you about the state of the Vaccaro Field before his passing?"

"What about it?"

He squeezed his eyes shut. Opened them again and pointed their pained green depths at her. "The field's played out. In another year at most, Merris Oil's Vacarro wells are going to run dry. All of them. Frankly, I'm shocked they're still producing."

Played out? Dry? Blank shock closed in on her, much like it had when she'd gotten the call two weeks ago that John Merris was dead.

Gabe leaned forward and took her hand in his. She supposed hers must be cold, because his fingers felt like a warm, gentle vise around hers. "I don't understand," she whispered.

"The Vacarro Field is done. And the way I hear it, most of Merris Oil's income is derived from that field. Very soon, your family's primary revenue source is going to disappear. I couldn't in good conscience withhold this information from you and your mother if, as I suspected, John failed to share it with you."

The glass horse in her soul did shatter then. It was too much. Every direction she turned, another disaster ambushed her. Any one of them was overwhelming, but in combination, they were drowning her.

First, the completely shocking attack by James Ward. Her father's insistence that she not go to the police, not make a scandal that could kill his chances for re-election, that she cancel all her public appearances until the swelling in her face had gone down and the bruises faded. John Merris had hidden her away like she was the one at fault, and not the victim of a vicious attack.

And then there'd been her father's horrifying and unsolved murder, part of a triple homicide for good-ness' sake, followed by her mother's complete mental collapse. And now this. Her family was teetering on the verge of financial ruin.

Pulling her hand away from his, she folded her arms across her middle and hung on for dear life, so sick to her stomach she thought she might throw up.

How could Gabe do this to her? Why now? Was it some sort of plot by fate to destroy her? Or maybe…a terrible thought occurred to her…maybe this was Gabe's final revenge. He might not have managed to ruin John Merris, but he could finish off the man's family.

Gabe probably couldn't wait to rush right over here, her father's body barely in the ground, to spill this dev-astating news to her. She'd heard he'd been summoned from somewhere halfway around the world when his ex-wife had been reported missing two weeks ago. No one knew if she was dead, too, as part of the murder spree, or maybe kidnapped. Supposedly, he'd been in an all-fired hurry to get back to Vengeance over the news. But concern for the woman he obviously still loved wasn't enough to keep him from gloating over his archenemy's grave.

Her voice barely above a whisper, she said, "I thought better of you, Mr. Dawson. I can't believe you would be so crass as to tell me this on the very day I buried my father. I hope you are happy. Not only did you outlive my father, but now you've gotten to fire the final shot in your feud with him. I guess you win."

Gabe's jaw went slack and he leaped to his feet. Instinctively, she matched the gesture and stood up, which had the effect of bringing them chest to chest. She was nearly five-foot-eight, but he still towered over her.

Her voice gained a little strength. "What have my mother and I ever done to you to deserve you taking your hatred for my father out on her and me in this way?"

"It's not hatred," he sputtered. "I thought you ought to know before you make any major financial decisions…."

Before she realized what he was going to do, he took a quick step forward and wrapped his arms around her. His body was big and strong and so very masculine against hers…and scared the living hell out of her.

She tore away from him in ill-disguised panic and squawked, "I'll thank you, Mr. Dawson, never to darken my family's doorstep again."

His hands fell to his sides and he looked bewildered as she cleared her throat and gathered herself to announce more strongly, "While I have no intention of continuing my father's feud with you, neither will I disrespect his memory by entertaining you any longer under his roof. I'll have to ask you to leave now."

Gabe looked deep into her eyes, and she forced herself not to look away, not to blush, not to reveal her terror at being this close to a man. She noted that her entire body was trembling. She *hated* being this afraid. But Gabe Dawson frightened the living daylights out of her.

"I swear, Willa. I meant no harm. I just thought you ought to know, and there never was going to be a good time to tell you. I'm truly sorry to be the bearer of bad news." With that, he turned and strode out of the library, leaving her standing and staring at nothing.

Was he telling the truth? Was the entire house of cards that was her life about to come crashing down around her and her mother? She'd caught a few whispers of her father pulling a lot of cash out of Merris Oil to make up shortfalls in his campaign fund-raising. If he'd gutted the company and the Vacarro wells weren't going to replenish the coffers, what was she going to do?

She wasn't worried about herself. She had her job as a kindergarten teacher and she lived relatively modestly. But her mother? What would Minnie do? The woman hadn't worked a day in her entire pampered life and wouldn't have the first idea how to rein in her lavish lifestyle. The family name would be ruined. And Lord knew, in a town like Vengeance, Texas, appearances were everything.

Forty miles outside of Dallas, it was a hidden enclave of North Texas's social elite, rife with sprawling ranches and rustic mansions for when folks wanted to "get away" from the Big D. Which was to say, Dallas's bored and rich came to Vengeance to play. Longhorn cattle roamed their pastures and expensive quarter horses stood in their barns. They wore designer cowboy boots and thousand-dollar-a-pair jeans, hosted lavish, catered barbecues and called it the simple life.

She much preferred a classroom full of noisy five-year-olds to the social rat race. However, her father's business and political position made being a mere schoolteacher an impossibility for her. She was expected to make campaign appearances, do the social circuit of parties and fund-raisers, smile in the background of television commercials and never, ever cause a scandal.

Even if the son of an old family friend raped her, she thought bitterly.

The dark-paneled library walls closed in on her all of a sudden, and she hurried out of the room, through the foyer and grand dining room and burst outside through the French doors. The broad, covered patio, with its deeply cushioned sofas, lazily turning ceiling fans, and flat-screen TV mounted high under the eaves mocked her with their casual display of wealth. Wealth that was evaporating even as she stood here.

She ran down the wide steps into the garden—the one thing on earth her mother seemed to truly care about. It was as lush and gorgeous as any botanical garden, with winding walkways through raised beds overflowing with roses and late-season daisies, re-blooming azaleas, and even a few of Willa's favorite gardenias blooming out of season.

How George, the gardener, managed to coax the white, elegant gardenias into bloom for months on end, she had no idea. It probably helped that her mother had built him a commercial quality greenhouse at the back of the nearly two acres of backyard, hidden behind a tall fence covered with Carolina jessamine. The jessamine bloomed in the very earliest spring in a splash of sweet-scented yellow. But even now, a faint hint of its perfume clung to the vines.

What was she going to do? Willa was the executor of her father's estate, much to everyone's surprise, and Larry Shore's immense chagrin. She was supposed to take care of all this, to safeguard it for her mother and for any hypothetical offspring Willa might produce someday. Although at the rate she was going, a boyfriend wasn't in her near future, let alone children.

She sank onto a concrete bench tucked beneath the spreading boughs of a chinquapin oak and hugged her middle, curling in on herself in misery at the thought of dating ever again. She was damaged goods. James Ward might not have taken her virginity, but the bastard had certainly taken her innocence. Her ability to trust men.

The whole world was caving in on her. John Merris was gone, her financial security ruined, her personal life destroyed. She had no one to turn to, nowhere to go, no escape. The vultures were circling, all right.

An inhuman scream, shrill and panicked, shocked her out of her pity party. The noise cut off sharply, which was almost more alarming than the scream itself. Willa jolted to her feet. That sounded like it had come from near the koi pond. She raced toward the far corner of the garden, her heart in her throat. It sounded like a woman had just been murdered. Was her mother okay?

She skidded to a stop as George waved her back. He was bent over something in the rocks above the pond. Water tumbled merrily through the jumble of stones and into the pool below, masking his raspy voice. "Stay back, Miss Willa. You don't wanna see this."

"What is it, George?" she asked frantically.

"Rabbit. Dead."

She frowned, looking around the otherwise serene garden. "How did it die?" There was too much tree cover here for a hawk to have gotten it, and coyotes wouldn't show themselves at this time of day, let alone this close to a human habitation.

"Head's ripped off," he answered shortly. "Nasty piece of work."

There'd been a predator in the garden? Where was it now? This side of the garden was bordered by a forest of nearly ten acres' sprawl. It would be easy to disappear into the trees from here. "Why would some critter sneak into Mom's garden in broad daylight to kill a rabbit?" she demanded. "That makes no sense, whatsoever."

"I dunno, Miss. I'm just sayin' it ain't got a head, and it looks like somethin' tore it clean off. You go on back to the house now, Miss Willa. I'll get a shovel and clean this up."

"You'll hose down the spot? It would upset Mother to see blood."

"Of course," he muttered, frowning down at the mess at his feet.

God, even the safety of her mother's garden had been destroyed! She walked toward the house, her steps getting faster and faster until she broke into a shambling run. She felt eyes staring at her, malevolent and evil. Creeped out beyond belief, she sprinted the rest of the way to the house.

She burst into the kitchen, panting, its pickled pine cabinets and cheery yellow walls incongruous in the face of her terror. She dashed away the tears streaming down her face.

Louise looked up from unloading the dishwasher as Willa came to a stop. "Oh, there you are, Willy girl. The sheriff called a minute ago. He wants you to come down to the station in the morning."

Great. Now what?

Chapter 3

Gabe took a deep breath and reminded himself yet again not to lose his temper. But the young police officer seated across the steel table from him was doing his level best to drive Gabe crazy. This was the third time they'd called him down here to ask him the exact same questions as the first two times he'd been here.

"Tell me one more time, Mr. Dawson, what you and Senator Merris argued about at the Petroleum Club."

He sighed. He knew what they were doing. Get a person to tell the same story three times, and if it changed each time, the person was lying. If it stayed exactly the same, the person was probably telling the truth.

"I went to the club because I knew John Merris would be there. I offered to buy his company from him."

"And that's why he lost his temper and slugged you?"

Gabe shrugged. "More or less. He seemed insulted at the amount I offered him."

"Was it your intent to insult him?"

"I offered him more than a fair price for Merris Oil. He just didn't happen to agree with me on what constituted a fair price."

"And that's why he hit you?"

"I honestly don't know, Officer Radebaugh. You'd have to ask him."

"Senator Merris is dead."

Duh. "I'm aware of that," Gabe replied drily. The cop stared at him, and Gabe didn't bite on the tactic to get him to babble to fill the silence. The stalemate stretched out for close to a minute, ending only when the door to the interrogation room burst open.

"Deputy Green," Gabe said evenly. Green was a good ol' boy who'd been on the Vengeance police force ever since Gabe could remember. He'd hassled Gabe plenty as a teen, but then in fairness to Green, he'd hassled the police plenty back then, too. He was a little surprised Green hadn't been named acting sheriff when Sheriff Peter Burris was found dead next to Senator Merris. The third victim was a young man, recently married, who'd been in town to visit his family. Although rumors were running rampant, no one had figured out yet how the three men—or at least their deaths—were connected.

"Dawson," Green replied as surly as ever.

"Is there anything more I can do to help you with your investigation, gentlemen?" Gabe looked back and forth between the two cops, neither of whom would meet his eyes. They wanted him to be guilty so bad they could taste it, but the poor bastards couldn't figure out for the life of them how to pin the recent murders on him. Particularly since he'd been in Malaysia when his assistant and then the cops called to tell him his ex-wife had been kidnapped. Pretty hard to commit murders when a guy was literally halfway around the world from the victims. As alibis went, it was pretty damned ironclad.

Green finally growled, "Don't leave town, Mr. Dawson."

"Until my ex-wife is found and released, I'm not going anywhere," he declared. He'd been divorced from Melinda for nearly a decade, but she'd been his wife. He still felt responsible for her safety. Of course, she would scoff and call him a Neanderthal for thinking he had to take care of the little woman.

But he couldn't help it. He'd been raised to open doors and hold chairs for ladies, and yes, to look out for their safety. Melinda could just get over it. Although, she pretty much had when she'd divorced him. The old pain of her betrayal of their marriage vows spiked through him again. Damn. He kept thinking it would get better. Hurt less. But it never did.

"If you've got nothing more for me, gentlemen, I've got a company to run." No harm in reminding them he wasn't some local punk from the wrong side of the tracks anymore. Gabe stood up and Radebaugh stood hastily as well, knocking over his chair. Deputy Green looked chagrined as the young cop clumsily righted the chair. Amused, Gabe watched Green beat a retreat.

Officer Radebaugh escorted Gabe into the main station, where a dozen messy, paper-laden desks were huddled. Gabe was startled to spot a familiar pair of slender shoulders and strawberry-blond French twist at the far end of the room. What was Willa Merris doing here? Probably getting an update on the investigation into her father's murder, or maybe answering more questions. Of course, she didn't get hauled into an interrogation room, and treated like a criminal. That pleasure had been reserved for him, apparently.

The cop opened the front door for him, and Gabe recoiled at the crowd of reporters clustered at the bottom of the steps. "What's up with the mob?" he asked his escort.

Radebaugh glanced over his shoulder and then muttered under his breath, "They probably got wind of what Willa Merris is up to."

"What's she up to?" Gabe muttered back, not moving his lips.

"We asked her to come in to answer a few questions, but when she got here, she announced she wanted to file charges against James Ward."

James Ward, as in the golden boy of Vengeance, Texas? Now that John Merris was dead, the Wards were the preeminent family in town, and James was the heir apparent to the family's fortune, power and social position. Not to mention everyone loved the guy. Betting types were picking him to be the successor to John Merris's political career. Gabe had always found Ward a little slimy in that friendly, politician way, but a decent guy, overall.

Surprised, Gabe asked, "What's she charging him with?"

"Assault."

Gabe's jaw dropped. "As in he attacked her?"

"Yup."

Well, that certainly explained the way she'd reacted when he'd tried to hug her yesterday. She'd yanked away like he'd tried to kill her instead of offer a little comfort.

"James Ward?" Gabe couldn't help asking. He'd known the heir to the Ward fortune for most of his life, and he had a hard time believing that the fun-loving, charming young man had an angry side, let alone a violent side. James was always the center of attention and popular with all the girls. "When did this happen?"

"She says it happened a month ago. Not a shred of proof. Sheriff's trying to talk her out of pressing charges because it's gonna boil down to a he said-she said, and she's gonna lose."

"Why's she going to lose?" Gabe asked.

Radebaugh stared at him as if the answer was so obvious, he couldn't believe Gabe had bothered to ask the question. "Because he's a Ward, and her father's dead."

"Since when does justice depend on power or social status?" Gabe snapped.

Irritated, he stomped down the steps and plowed through the phalanx of reporters who knew him well enough after the past two weeks to leave him the hell alone. He climbed into his Cadillac Escalade, grateful for its blacked-out windows. Gripping the steering wheel until his hands ached, he stared ahead at nothing. Willa Merris assaulted? The idea made him so mad he could hardly breathe. She'd been such a sweet kid. So innocent. Why the hell did life have to dump on her all at once like this? Although in his experience, life was rarely fair.

A commotion across the street drew his attention as the mob of reporters rushed up the courthouse steps. He swore as he spotted the source of the ruckus. It was none of his business, and his interference emphatically wouldn't be appreciated. And yet, he leaped out of the vehicle and strode back across the street, swearing every step of the way.

Willa recoiled as a shouting crowd of reporters charged her, microphones brandished like swords. A cacophony of voices crashed into her. "Is it true…James Ward…what proof…publicity stunt?"

How on earth did these jackals already know that she'd filed charges against Ward? Someone in the police station must have leaked it. Wow, that had been fast. And then the gist of the questions registered.

"…provoke him…trying to catch a rich husband… how sexy were your clothes…entrapment…"

They thought she'd tried to get herself raped? Horror poured over her like a waterboarding until she choked and gagged on it. She reeled back from the vicious assault and looked over her shoulder for help from the police. But Deputy Green merely stood in the doorway observing the mauling, his gaze totally impassive.

She tried to shove through the crowd of reporters, but they weren't about to let her slip away. They smelled fresh meat, and the feeding frenzy was on. As the press of sweaty bodies closed in on her, panic and bile rose in the back of her throat. Strangers were banging into her. Touching her. Oh, God. She felt light-headed, and then faint.

Without warning, the crowd parted, and like a dark, avenging angel, a furious Gabe Dawson loomed in front of her. He threw his arm over her shoulders, dragged her up against his side and with his free arm, commenced shoving reporters out of the way like pesky bugs.

He hustled her across the street, shoved her bodily into the passenger seat of his big SUV and slammed the door shut. In seconds, he was in the driver's seat and the vehicle pulling away from the curb. Someone banged on the hood of the SUV and nearly got run down for his trouble.

"You almost hit that reporter!" she exclaimed.

"Sorry. Next time I'll make sure not to miss," he retorted.

She grinned in spite of herself. And the release of tension felt good. Even though the devil himself had rescued her, she wasn't complaining. She didn't want to think about how ugly that mob of reporters could've gotten with her. "Thanks," she murmured.

"No problem. Pissing off journalists is a favorite pastime of mine, and I just took away their new toy."

She nodded and subsided, remembering a conversation with her father once, where he'd confessed to loving sparring with reporters. How could he possibly have relished that kind of attention? She shuddered. The public eye was definitely *not* her cup of tea.

"Where to?" Gabe asked.

"Umm, home, I suppose."

"Your place or your parents'?"

He knew she had her own house in Vengeance? He'd relocated to Dallas nearly a decade ago, and yet he still kept tabs on where she lived? "My parents' house, I suppose. I'm staying there to keep my mother company and help her deal with…everything."

Gabe nodded and pointed his vehicle toward the south side of town. He drove in silence, and she didn't interrupt the quiet that fell between them. What could she say to a man like him, anyway? He was smart and confident and powerful—totally out of her league. And she'd thrown him out of the house less than twenty-four hours ago.

The SUV turned onto the road that led to her parents' estate, and she groaned aloud. Both sides of the tarmac were lined with cars and vans—all brightly painted with the call signs of various radio and television stations.

Gabe accelerated, passing right by her parents' drive-way without slowing down.

"New plan," he announced.

"Back to my place?" she replied glumly.

"Are you kidding? If the press has this place staked out, they'll be crawling all over your house. We were lucky no one spotted us as we drove past, but we may not get that lucky next time."

"Where will I go?" she asked in alarm.

"Relax. I've got it covered."

She frowned. That wasn't an answer. And she didn't like the idea of turning over any more control to this man than she absolutely had to. She knew the type; after all, her father was one of them—rich, arrogant and ac-customed to everyone around them kissing up and doing whatever they were told without question.

But what choice did she have? She'd accused a pillar of local society of a heinous crime, sullied a man's rep-utation and attacked one of the richest and most power-ful families in this part of Texas. Now, the gloves would come off, and the reporters would take whatever pot-shots at her they thought they could land. It would be a free-for-all. She'd seen over the years what the press did to her father at the slightest hint of a juicy story, let alone a full-blown scandal. They attacked like rabid dogs, tearing at every scrap of information and toss-ing it in front of the public no matter what the personal cost to her father or his family. And he'd been a rich, powerful politician with the ability to hurt the report-ers' careers, which had kept the press in check. She was neither rich nor powerful. They'd destroy her.

What had she been thinking, pressing charges against James Ward? It had been a foolish impulse. In-sane. She'd gotten so carried away with the notion that now she could say or do whatever she wanted, that she'd forgotten the consequences the good people of Vengeance, Texas, would level at her.

The SUV rolled smoothly down I-35, its powerful engine devouring the forty miles between Vengeance and Dallas. She frowned as Gabe guided the vehicle into the jungle of modern skyscrapers that was downtown.

"Where are we going?" she finally asked.

"I thought you might like a bite to eat."

Although it was a little early for supper, her stomach was roiling ominously. "I couldn't possibly eat—" she started.

"Nonsense. You're thin as a rail, and I bet you haven't eaten a decent meal in two weeks."

It was kind of him not to mention her father's murder. But Gabe was right. Neither she nor her mother had been able to eat much since John Merris's death. "I'm fine," she mumbled.

"No, you're not. You've had a lousy day and a big scare, and you're pale. You look on the verge of fainting."

"I don't faint!" she retorted indignantly.

He flashed her a brief grin that knocked her indignation into the next county over. "I recall that about you. You're a lot stronger than you look. I'll never forget the way you and that crazy horse of yours ran me into the ground."

He remembered that fox hunt? She'd been seventeen, so that would make it eleven years ago. He'd made some snarky comment about girls not being able to keep up with the boys, and she had bet him a dollar that she would beat him in the annual cross-country race.

"Speaking of which, you still owe me a dollar," she declared.

"Double or nothing at next spring's fox hunt," he retorted jauntily as he guided the car through downtown Dallas.

She made a face. "I haven't ridden a horse since I left for college. I'll just take my winnings and call it good, thank you."

He stopped the car and a valet opened her door for her. Good grief, where were they? She looked up and was shocked to see he'd brought her to the Rosewood Mansion Hotel on Turtle Creek, known locally as simply, The Mansion. Its restaurant was routinely selected as one of the top ten in the world. He handed over the keys and joined her, offering his wool-suited forearm to her.

"This is a bit more than a bite to eat, Gabe."

"How better to tempt a reluctant eater than with the finest food on earth?"

She had to admit that every time she'd ever eaten here the cuisine had been nothing short of exquisite. "I'm not dressed properly—" she started.

"Balderdash," he declared. "I'll get us a private dining room, and no one will see or care what you're wearing."

She couldn't decide whether to ask where he'd learned the word *balderdash* or if The Mansion really had private dining rooms, and ended up merely following him in disbelieving silence.

Of course, a billionaire with more money than sense was clearly the sort of customer who rated a private dining room, which was fine with her tonight. The main dining room was a place where people went to see and be seen. In spite of the city's size, Dallas's elite social stratum was actually a fairly small and tight-knit community where everyone knew everyone else. The last thing she needed was to be seen sharing an intimate meal at The Mansion with her father's archenemy.

The maître d' led them down a small, dim hallway. They passed briefly through the lobby of the hotel proper, and were ushered into a beautifully furnished room that looked like the parlor of a fine European estate. Floor-to-ceiling French doors overlooked a formal rose garden even her mother would envy, and beside the doors sat a linen-covered table set for two.

"Will this be satisfactory, Mr. Dawson?"

"It'll do, thank you."

Willa was startled when Gabe stepped in front of the maître d' to hold her chair for her. She sank into the upholstered Queen Anne chair with a murmur of thanks. Gabe sat down across from her, and suddenly, she was vividly aware of just how frighteningly alone she was with this big, masculine man.

"Would you mind if I were completely frank with you for a moment, Willa?"

"By all means. I always prefer honesty."

"You look a little apprehensive, as if I'm about to leap across the table and devour you." He added wryly, "And if we're being honest, I feel obliged to add that, contrary to your father's opinion of me, I'm not a raving lunatic."

"I'll be the judge of that," she replied tartly, embarrassed that her trepidation showed.

"Hey, I'm the good guy. I rescued you from the press, remember?"

"You're the guy who abandoned my father's oil company and rubbed salt in my family's wounds when he died." She was a little shocked she'd said that. But they *were* being honest with each other.

Gabe planted both elbows on the table and glared

at her. Immediately, fear spiked inside her. Why had she provoked a big, strong man like him? In a similar situation, her father would have started drinking. The old, frozen terror rolled through her. When Daddy was drinking, it was best to hide in her room and not come out. Not get in his way. Not even cross his path.

Who'd have guessed James Ward would turn out to be the very same way? Except now that she thought about it, she didn't remember him drinking that night. What had set him off, then? Had she done something?

She watched with intense relief as Gabe visibly corralled his irritation. Maybe he wasn't like James Ward, after all. James had lost control and never reined himself back in. And she'd been the one to pay the price.

When Gabe finally spoke, his voice was surprisingly calm. "Let's address those accusations one at a time. First, I didn't abandon your father. He fired me from Merris Oil. I showed him what I believed to be an entirely new method of discovering oil, and he declined to invest in my theory."

"I've heard it all before. Believe me." She'd lost count of how many times her father had ranted about Gabe's disloyalty in taking his theories to someone else to profit from.

Gabe shrugged. "I lined up my own investors and proved my theory correct. Your father could've been in on it, but he made a bad business decision. That doesn't make me the villain."

She'd wondered that very thing in private over the years, but in her family's household, nobody would dream of contradicting the word of John Merris. If her father had declared Gabe Dawson a disloyal bastard who'd ripped him off of hundreds of millions of dollars, so it was.

He continued, "And since we're being brutally honest tonight, let me just say your father was not a nice man. His business practices routinely skirted the edge of outright illegality, and he didn't hesitate to crush his competition not only professionally, but personally. He routinely used his political office for his personal advantage and for the good of his private oil business."

"Those are serious allegations."

"Admit it. You know they're not just allegations. They're the truth."

Part of her agreed with Gabe. But loyalty to family and never giving a negative sound bite to anyone had been pounded into her for so long she couldn't bring herself to say it aloud. "I stayed out of my father's business and political affairs. I couldn't comment on his ethics or lack thereof."

Gabe snorted. "Take my word for it. Your old man had the ethics of a junkyard dog."

She sighed and took a sip of ice water. "My father is dead. It no longer matters if he was good or bad, right or wrong."

"I'm glad you feel that way, Willa."

She looked up sharply at the smooth timbre of his voice. He wasn't mocking her, was he? His gaze was dark and direct and didn't waver as she met it with her own startled stare. Nope. Not mocking. It looked like seduction, if anything.

Whoa. Gabe Dawson was putting the moves on her? There must be snowballs flying every which way in Hell at this very moment.

A frisson of delight rippled through her before memory caught up with it. Memory of fear and weakness and helplessness at the hands of a man not so very different from this one. A rich, privileged, handsome man whom women fawned over and society adored.

She stared down at her fingers, twined so tightly in her lap, they ached. A waiter came in to take their orders, but she hadn't even seen a menu. Gabe murmured that they would have whatever was being served at the chef's table tonight.

The waiter left and Gabe sighed. "Will you please talk to me? What are you thinking? I can't read you."

"I was thinking about how society loves you."

That earned her a disbelieving grunt. "Hardly. I have committed not one, but two, unforgivable sins according to your people."

Her people? Hah! They were her mother and father's people, but not hers. She'd tried to break away from high society. To be a normal person. A kindergarten teacher, for goodness' sake. But her father kept forcing her to come back. Insisting on political appearances. And dates with the sons of Dallas's richest and most influential families. It had been nothing short of mortifying.

Gabe continued grimly, "Not only did I have the gall to get rich and not stay on my own side of the social tracks, but then I've repeatedly declined to marry some vacuous, shallow bitch and make her one of the richest women in Dallas."

Amused in spite of herself, Willa tsked. "Scandalous, Mr. Dawson."

He grinned and all but knocked her off her chair with that megawatt smile. His sex appeal had only magnified over the years, and it had been off the charts a decade ago. If only she were more experienced. More savvy about men. Maybe then she wouldn't feel so out of her league around him. It wasn't that their twelve-year age difference was so great, but she'd lived a sheltered, awkward social life. And he… Well, he hadn't.

The waiter brought their first course, and she looked over it at Gabe. "So what have you been up to with your life besides getting filthy rich and shunning the good ladies of Vengeance, Texas?"

"Work, mostly. Exploring for oil has taken me to every corner of the planet. For some reason, oil always seems to come from boiling-hot or freezing-cold places."

"Favorite place you've visited?"

"While looking for oil? Malaysia. While just traveling? Gotta go with Paris."

"Paris, huh? I didn't peg you for a romantic."

That earned her a cynical look. "My ex-wife stripped out what little romance there was in my soul a long time ago."

"Is there any news about her? A ransom note from kidnappers or something?"

Gabe's facial muscles tightened in stress. "No. Nothing."

He clearly cared deeply about his former wife. Willa's natural empathy bubbled up in spite of her reservations about this man, and she reached across the table to lay her hand on top of his. "I'm sorry." But then shocking heat scalded her palm and she jerked her hand away.

"What have you been up to since you grew up?" he asked carefully.

She rolled her eyes. She wasn't a snot-nosed kid anymore, thank you very much. "I graduated from the University of Texas with a degree in elementary education. I'm a kindergarten teacher."

"Kindergarten? So you have a death wish?"

She laughed. "Five-year-olds are actually pretty great

as long as you draw clear boundaries for them and stick to them. I love my job."

"Are you on a leave of absence from teaching right now?"

She sighed. "I am. And the school year was just getting started, too. But there was so much to do to arrange the funeral, and I'm the executor of his estate. I have no idea how I'm going to wade through all the business matters my father left behind. It's a nightmare."

"If there's anything I can do to help, let me know."

It was nice of him to offer, but she didn't trust the man any farther than she could throw him. Still, he'd rescued her from that mob of reporters and was feeding her in rather spectacular fashion. He hadn't once behaved like a slimeball toward her. She supposed she should cut him a little slack.

"After Melinda, you never found another woman who turned your head?" she asked.

"Circling back to my love life, are we?" he murmured, amused. "Nope. I guess she ruined me for any other woman."

The one time Willa had met Professor Melinda Grayson, the woman had intimidated her so badly, Willa had barely been able to form coherent sentences. So, he liked his women aggressive, huh? Count her out, then.

"Actually, no," Gabe commented. "Aggressive isn't my style in women."

Oh, Lord. Had she asked that question aloud? She would just crawl under the table and hide now. Her cheeks fiery hot, she searched frantically for a distraction. "The garden is beautiful."

Gabe looked outside, and she followed suit. Twilight had descended over the rose garden, softening its hues to muted tones of maroon and mauve.

"Shall I open the doors?" he murmured.

She nodded, and he rose gracefully to throw open the double doors. Even wearing jeans and a casual sport jacket, he cut an elegant figure. He must be, what? Forty? The man was in shockingly great shape for his age. His coat bulged with muscle and his face was smooth and youthful. He was going to be one of those incredibly annoying men who looked fantastic at sixty and beyond.

The sound of crickets chirping swirled into the room on the perfume of roses and the day's spent warmth. The light of the twin candles on their table began to take over as night fell around them. The waiter brought the main course—spit-roasted quail, crispy on the outside and juicy on the inside, that literally melted in Willa's mouth. The wine was smooth, her companion smoother, and the combination relaxed her in spite of herself.

For his part, Gabe spent an inordinate amount of time studying her over his meal. Finally, she couldn't resist asking, "Is something wrong?"

"No. It's just strange to see the little girl all grown up. It's like I've walked into a time warp where you aged overnight."

"I got old when you weren't looking, huh?"

It was his turn to roll his eyes. "You are emphatically not old. You're stunning. That's what's got me staring at you. The promise of this kind of beauty was always there, but it's impressive to see it in full bloom. I apologize if I made you uncomfortable."

"Uhh, thank you," she mumbled, flummoxed. He thought she was pretty? Well, then.

"The boys must have been all over you in high school and college," he commented. "Any of them still around?"

Was he actually fishing to find out if she had a boyfriend? Shock made her choke on a sip of water. She eventually recovered enough to croak, "I'm the only kid in my high school who went up to Lover's Point to be alone."

He laughed lightly, disbelievingly even, at her quip. Little did he know how dull her love life had truly been.

She'd taken one ecstatic bite of the most incredibly delicious crème brûlée she'd ever experienced when Gabe's cell phone rang, shattering the quiet between them. She raised her eyebrows at the sappy country tune of his ringtone. Not a romantic, huh? He was such a liar.

"Hello," Gabe said. He frowned, listening in silence for a few seconds and then startled her by saying, "She's right here, sir. Of course, sir."

Who would Gabe Dawson call "sir" in that tone of respect? Even God probably didn't rate that tone of voice from him. She took the phone Gabe held out to her. *"Who is it?"* she mouthed. He merely grinned and wiggled the phone at her. She took it cautiously.

"Hello?" she said even more cautiously. "This is Willa Merris."

"Good evening, Miss Merris. This is Wade Graham. I'm sorry to disturb your evening. My people had quite a time tracking you down."

As in Governor of Texas, Wade Graham? Holy cow. "Uhh, hello, Governor Graham. What can I do for you?"

The governor wasn't of the same political party as her father, and the two men hadn't been close, to her knowledge. It was decent of the man to express his condolences. Except she recalled her mother making some vague reference to having received a sympathy call from the governor last week. Why was the man tracking her down, then?

"I spoke with your father's attorney this morning," the governor explained. "As part of Senator Merris's will, he left a letter expressing his preference for how his senate seat should be disposed of in the event of his death."

"What does this have to do with me, sir?" she asked, confused.

"As you may know, it's not unusual in the event of a senator's untimely demise for the senator's surviving spouse to take the seat until the end of that term."

Horror blossomed in Willa's gut. Her mother was flighty at best, and when she'd been hitting the pills hard, Minnie was barely conscious. Her mother wasn't remotely fit to fill her father's senate seat.

"In a few cases, however, the senator may request that someone else fill the seat. A trusted colleague or staff member, for example."

Larry Shore was going to be thrilled. The guy was ragingly ambitious, and barely containing his fury that John Merris, whose coattails Larry obviously had planned to ride to the top, had had the ill grace to go and get himself murdered. Larry had briefly been a suspect in his boss's murder, but he'd been released on bail and was supposedly no longer a primary suspect.

"...his letter, your father recommended that I appoint you to serve in his stead until a special election can be held. Of course, the regular election is in six weeks, and Congress is in recess so its members can return home to campaign. So, this will be mostly a ceremonial appointment...."

Her? A United States senator? "But, sir," she blurted, interrupting the governor. "I'm a kindergarten teacher."

"Nonetheless, your father thought you were the best

person for the job. He named you in his sealed letter as his choice to finish out his term."

Frantic, she blurted, "But I'm only twenty-eight. You have to be thirty to be a senator."

"I've already spoken to the president. He's given permission under these special circumstances for you to finish out your father's term. The White House Counsel says there have been two senators seated at age twenty-eight in spite of the Constitutional mandate, so there's a precedent."

She didn't know what to say. Shock barely scraped the surface of how she was feeling.

"I'm going to fly up to Dallas tomorrow for a press conference at around noon to make the announcement and formally appoint you. My assistant will give you all the details. You'll need to prepare a brief statement. Given your recent loss, I doubt the press will expect to grill you too hard. Your father's chief of staff can help you draft it."

The line disconnected, and she stared at the cell phone like it was alien technology. A tanned male hand lifted it gently away from her.

"What was that all about?" Gabe asked quietly.

She looked up at him, stunned as the reality began to sink in. "My father requested that I fill his Senate seat until the next election. The governor's going to appoint me to the position tomorrow."

"Congratulations!" Gabe exclaimed.

She frowned. "But I don't want it."

"There'll be nothing to it. You raise your hand, take an oath to uphold and defend the Constitution, and then you sit tight until next January."

"Next January?"

"The election is in November, but your successor

won't be sworn in until next January. You'll get to serve in a lame-duck session of Congress if you want to."

Appalled at the size of the task her father had just thrust upon her, she exclaimed, "But I don't know anything about being a senator!"

Gabe leaned back in his seat and took a sip of brandy. "That's not true. You've lived around a senator for years. You know how to handle yourself in a crowd, and you're smart."

She snorted inelegantly. "And as soon as the national media gloms on to the fact that I accused a man of rape today, the scandal will dwarf my father's murder."

"Rape?" Gabe echoed ominously.

"What did you think I was doing at the police station? You heard the questions the reporters were shouting at me."

"I thought Ward assaulted you. Like he hit you and you fought him off."

"Oh, he did hit. And I did fight," she replied bitterly. "Not that it helped one bit."

"Do you want to talk about it?" he asked seriously.

"Nope." At the end of the day there wasn't much to talk about. She'd been dumb. Trusted someone she'd known for a long time. Let down her defenses. And he'd turned out to be a rapist.

Gabe's eyes narrowed to a deadly glare. "Remind me to show you some self-defense moves," he commented grimly. "There are a few things all women should know about how to take out a bigger, stronger assailant than them."

She studied him with interest. He looked really mad. Why did he give a darn about what happened to her? She was the enemy. "Why are you being so nice to me?"

His spoon stopped in midair. It paused for a long

moment, then reversed course and landed lightly on his plate. "Why wouldn't I be nice to you?"

"Because I'm my father's daughter. And let's be frank. My father hated your guts and went out of his way to cause you trouble. He loved nothing better than making you spitting mad."

The corner of Gabe's mouth quirked up. "The feeling was mutual. I'm gonna miss the old bastard."

She sighed. Was it just her father and Gabe, or were all oil wildcatters this cussed? Maybe someday she'd find a nice, pleasant guy who knew nothing about the oil business to settle down with. These force-of-nature-personality men were so not her thing.

But then a flash of blond, charming James Ward made her blood run cold. Everyone thought he was a nice, pleasant guy, too. He would never hurt a flea, let alone viciously attack a woman, right?

"Are you done with your dessert?" Gabe asked, startling her out of her grim recollections.

"As delicious as this crème brûlée is, that phone call killed my appetite."

"Let's get out of here, then." Gabe came around the table to pull back her chair. The old-fashioned gesture surprised her. The young man she'd known had been brash and unpolished, a kid from the wrong side of the tracks who certainly hadn't held chairs for ladies.

Since when had she become such a snob? So, somewhere along the way, he'd picked up a few points of etiquette. Probably his wife had taught him. Polite behavior did not make the man.

Lord knew James Ward had been plenty polite up until the part where he tried to kiss her and then went crazy on her. She would never forget that strange and violent look that had come into his eyes. He'd tried to kiss her neck and she'd stepped back from him, and he'd done a no-kidding Jekyll and Hyde before her very eyes. It had been, bar none, the scariest thing she'd ever seen.

"Willa? Are you all right?"

She realized that she'd just been standing there like a zombie, staring at nothing. "Sorry. Went wool gathering for a second."

"Good wool?"

Her throat too tight to answer, she shook her head. Gabe held out his forearm to her and waited expectantly until she looped her hand around it. Wow, he really had gone old-school in the past ten years.

He led her out to his SUV, which a valet had pulled around for them, and Gabe handed her into the vehicle. She closed her eyes and let her head fall back against the headrest. A United States senator. Her. The thought just wouldn't compute. Even if the title was purely for appearances and she never did a darned thing, she would still go down in the history books as having served in the United States freaking Senate.

In a few minutes, Gabe slowed his car and turned a corner. Her eyes snapped open to see an underground parking garage. Panic tightened around her chest. "Where are we?" she forced out.

"I keep a place in Dallas for when I have business in town. Since you have to be here for a press conference tomorrow, I figured it would save you hassle to stay in town tonight. And, it has the fringe benefit of foiling those pesky reporters camped out waiting to pounce on you in Vengeance.

"But my clothes are at home—"

"You have power suits befitting a U.S. senator in your closet at home, Ms. Kindergarten Teacher?" he asked skeptically.

"Well, no."

"Exactly. And that means you have to go shopping in the morning. Here, in Dallas. Correct?"

"I guess."

He parked the SUV and came around to open her door. "Then you're staying at my place tonight."

She couldn't argue with the logic of it. But to spend the night at a man's apartment? Alone with him? Fear tightened her entire body.

Gabe Dawson was not James Ward. Not all men were scary monsters who leaped on unsuspecting women. Her brain could believe it, but her gut wasn't even close to convinced. Her brain also said that if she was ever going to have any semblance of a normal life, she was going to have to face, and get over, her fear of being attacked by every man she came into contact with.

Yeah. Her gut wasn't buying that one, either. Besides, her father would croak—

Oh, wait. *She* was Senator Merris now. She could do whatever she darn well pleased, scandal be damned. *Scandal*— She groaned aloud.

Gabe froze in the act of reaching for the elevator button. "What?"

"I filed charges against James Ward today. Now that I'm getting this stupid job, it will be splashed all over the news by tomorrow afternoon."

"Honey, it was splashed all over the news within five minutes of you leaving the police station."

"Yes, but that would've just been the Vengeance newspaper and a few local television stations. Now it'll go national."

"So?" Gabe commented as he ushered her into the elevator.

"So!" she exclaimed. "The media will rake me over the coals!"

"Did you lie to the police? Accuse an innocent man?"

"No."

Gabe took a quick step across the tiny space to loom over her. Abruptly, a wave of danger rolled off him. Who was she kidding? This guy was a whole lot more man than James Ward had ever been, and she hadn't been able to fend off Ward. She wouldn't stand a chance against Gabe if he ever decided to have his way with her. Complete and horrifying vulnerability slammed into her. She was alone and at Gabe Dawson's mercy. Her knees all but knocked together in fear.

His voice was a velvet knife slicing her composure to shreds. "You've got nothing to be ashamed of, Willa. You're the victim. James Ward is the one who ought to be squirming."

He obviously didn't know a blessed thing about shame. It sunk all the way down to a person's bones and poisoned them from the inside out. She risked meeting his dark, angry gaze for a moment but he was too intimidating…and she was too humiliated. She looked away hastily, venturing only, "But the scandal—"

He cut her off sharply. "The scandal will be on his shoulders where it belongs."

She forced herself to shake off the sick feeling gripping her stomach. The two of them were being brutally honest with each other, right? And it wasn't like she was ever going to spend time with Gabe Dawson again. He was years older than she. Compared to him, she was a gawky kid. He dated sexy, sophisticated socialites, and he was her father's archenemy. She couldn't exactly be seen running around with him if she didn't want to be the center of all the gossip in Vengeance for months to come.

"Face facts, Gabe. The press will come after me as hard or harder than they go after James. Women in these situations always have their reputations dragged through the mud. And now, I'm going to drag my father's Senate seat through the mud, too. I owe it to his memory not to do that."

"You don't owe your father a damned thing. He's dead." The elevator dinged and the door slid open to punctuate his forceful statement.

Stunned at the blunt honesty of Gabe's observation, she stared at his back as he stalked off the elevator and crossed a small lobby toward the lone door opening off it. She ought to be furious with him for speaking such a travesty aloud, but a tiny part of her couldn't deny that the man spoke the truth. Her father didn't care anymore about his Senate seat or his precious reputation.

Gabe grasped the long, tubular, metal door handle for several seconds. A red beam of light flashed out of an aperture in the stainless-steel door, startling Willa as it swept across Gabe's face. A click, and the door opened under his hand.

"Latest in biometric scanning," he commented as he threw the door wide for her.

She followed cautiously. Lights went on around them automatically as Gabe moved through the foyer and several steps down into a large living room. The first features she noticed were the floor-to-ceiling glass windows lining the entire far side of the open space. Drawn to the magnificent vista outside, she strolled over to take it in.

The Dallas skyline sprawled at her feet, like a steel meadow full of twinkling white lights. The narrow, modern arch of the Margaret Hunt Hill Bridge glowed white, spanning the Trinity River in the distance. Cool air blew down silently on her from vents overhead, and Willa hugged herself, chilled. As beautiful as it was, the view was distant and impersonal. Cold.

Her politeness as ingrained as always, though, she commented, "Nice view. But don't you feel a little exposed with all these windows?"

"We're on the top floor of one of the tallest buildings in the city, and it's one-way glass. We have complete privacy."

The notion of having complete privacy with him unnerved her more than a little. Thankfully, he moved across the room to a white quartz bar to pour them glasses of ice water. The condo's sleekness complemented his rugged masculinity, its smooth lines standing in stark contrast to his rough edges.

Leave it to Gabe Dawson to own a penthouse at the very pinnacle of this town, symbolically astride Dallas and everything in it. Although, with the amount of money he'd made, she supposed he had pretty literally conquered the town, too.

"Computer, warm whole house two degrees."

"Yes, Mr. Dawson."

Willa glanced over her shoulder at the sultry, female British-accented voice. "Your computer is a girl?"

"Of course."

"And she controls your air conditioner?"

He laughed. "She controls just about everything. Never argues back, either. She's better than any wife."

Willa snorted and refrained from asking the obviously crass question about just what other wifely duties the computer performed for him.

"Computer, lower living-room ambient light to fifty

percent. And how about a little Chopin? Piano nocturnes, I think."

On cue, the lights dimmed to a sexy glow and the haunting strains of a concert piano came out of the walls in perfect surround sound. She whirled in alarm to face Gabe. He'd better not be trying to seduce her! Her fists fell back to her sides when she spotted him sitting on one of the sofas watching her.

"What?" she demanded, to cover her embarrassment at how her fists had flown up like that.

"You're quite a beautiful woman, Willa."

She shrugged, desperately wishing in that moment that she was as ugly as some warty old toad. "Don't compliment me. My parents' genes get all the credit."

He stretched a disconcertingly powerful arm out along the top of the sofa. "It's more than that. Beauty starts inside a woman. It breathes through her skin and shows in her eyes and the way she moves. It surrounds everything she does and everything she is.

"Are you sure it's just not my overpowering perfume you're describing?"

He laughed quietly. "What is that scent, anyway? I know it's floral, but I don't recognize it."

"Gardenia."

"It fits you. It's old-fashioned. Soft. But with a note of mystery."

"It's all of that?" she asked skeptically.

"Definitely."

Dammit, did he have to keep saying things that chipped away at her defenses like that? He was supposed to be a bad guy. Self-serving. Dishonest. Untrustworthy. But the man seated before her was nothing like the villain her father had painted.

She turned back to the window. Gabe let the silence

lie between them and seemed content not to disturb it. As much as she tried to focus on the events of the day, and to gather her thoughts for tomorrow, she couldn't get past her blazing awareness of the man behind her.

This room fit him. It was modern and sophisticated, and frankly, intimidating. She tilted her head and realized she could see his reflection in the dark surface of the glass. He was studying her with shocking intensity.

She spun quickly to face him, but his expression was bland, his eyes masked, by the time she got turned around. A shiver of apprehension chattered up her spine, rattling her bones. Who was this man whose home she was effectively trapped in? Which face that he showed her was the real one? What did she really know about him?

"You know, Gabe, I think I'd be better off just getting a hotel room tonight. If you'll call me a cab, I'll get out of your hair."

He gazed at her for a long time and then finally broke the silence. "That bastard really did a number on you, didn't he? How come your daddy didn't kill him?"

Chapter 4

Gabe hung on to his temper by a thread. Only the undisguised terror on Willa's face had him fighting to rein it in. But still, a need to do violence on her behalf roiled hotly in his gut.

"Kill him?" Willa whispered.

He couldn't tell if it was dismay or hope vibrating painfully in her voice.

He answered roughly, "If someone hurt my little girl, they'd damn well be eating the business end of my shotgun."

She shook her head, and he couldn't contain the beast any longer. He surged to his feet. "Hell, Will. I'll go kill him for you right now if you want."

"No, no. The scandal." Her hands fluttered in the air like the broken wings of a bird.

"When did Ward attack you?" he demanded.

"A month ago."

"A *month?* Why in hell didn't you go to the police before now?" Fury ranged freely through him, heating his extremities until they burned to damage someone. James Ward, specifically.

"The campaign…" she murmured in distress.

Of course. John Merris's precious political campaign. The bastard had failed to protect his baby girl because his damned Senate seat was more important to him than his own family. Hot coals commenced burning their way out of Gabe's gut by slow inches.

"That goddamned sonofabitch," he snarled. "I'll bet he made you stay home until the bruises faded, didn't he?"

Her nod was so small, so stiff and unwilling, that he barely saw it. But it was enough. Gabe strode over to her and swept her into his arms, holding her tight against him. "I take back everything I said. I don't care if he was your father or not, John Merris didn't deserve to live. If he weren't already dead, I'd start by shooting him first."

"Gabe," Willa mumbled from the folds of his dress shirt, "you can't just run around shooting people."

"Why the hell not? This is Texas. I wouldn't be convicted in any court in the state for taking out either man after what they did to you. Juries in this state don't take kindly to people who harm women, children or cops."

Muffled words floated up to him. "You still could go to jail."

"It would be worth it."

"Don't do it on my account. I'll be okay."

"You're not okay," he answered forcefully. "You flinch whenever I touch you, and that haunted look keeps creeping into your eyes. You're scared. Admit it."

She struggled weakly against his arms and he loosened his grip enough for her to lean back and stare up at him. Her blue eyes were huge in her face. Too big. Too scared. Too damned vulnerable. A surge of protectiveness swept over him so hard it almost knocked him off his feet.

"Okay, fine. I'm scared. Is that a crime?"

"Hell, no. So let me get this straight. Ward attacked you. You told your father about it, and he told you to suck it up. To pretend it never happened. Not to cause trouble with his business partner, to save the Merris family reputation and not make waves right before a tight election. Am I right?"

She nodded. Her gaze fell miserably.

"What happened to your clothes? Did your old man take some pictures of your scrapes and bruises or gather some evidence to corroborate your claim later? Or at least to blackmail the bastard with?"

Her lips quirked. "Blackmail, huh? You have a vicious mind, Mr. Dawson."

"You have no idea. At this very moment, I'm trying to choose between several horrible and painful forms of death by slow torture for young James."

A flicker of humor passed through her gaze for just an instant. It was gone almost before he saw it, but it was enough. A spark of the old Willa Merris, the one who'd dared him to a horse race, was still in there. Now all he had to do was find that spark again and nurture it into a flame.

"There's no evidence," she said, disrupting his train of thought. "My father destroyed everything. He took all of my clothes and burned them himself. And I wasn't allowed out of the house until every last scratch and bruise was totally gone."

"Willa, Willa." He sighed. "You're what, twenty-eight-years old? Why did you let your father bully you like that?"

"Because he was John Merris. When did he ever *not* get his way?"

Gabe pursed his lips. "I told him to go to hell, and I'm still standing. In fact, I've done moderately well in spite of John's best efforts to wreck me."

That glint of humor flashed again in her eyes. But he understood her response. John Merris had been known for his frightening temper and razor-sharp tongue that flayed anyone who dared to gainsay him. Even as a teen, he remembered Willa having a talent for fading out of sight and out of mind almost at will. A useful skill for a person who had lived with her father.

"Would you like to see some of the cool tricks my house can do?" he asked her abruptly.

"Uhh, sure."

He gave her a tour of his high-tech apartment ending with the high-definition media wall that took up one entire side of his home theater, projecting everything at life size.

"Wow!" Willa exclaimed. "I'd love to see a Longhorn football game on this monster."

He laughed. She was a sports fan, huh? "You feel like you're on the field with the players. Texas plays Oklahoma State next weekend. You're officially invited to watch it here with me."

"Deal." Her expression was young and happy and warmed his soul. It made him want to pick her up and swing her around, and then make love to her all night long.

Startled, he examined the urge more closely. He had no trouble getting all the sex he wanted; a continuous stream of beautiful women hoping to snare him and his bank account threw themselves at him. But this feeling wasn't just about sex with Willa. He actually liked her. He hadn't *liked* a woman in longer than he cared to think about. In point of fact, he mostly felt contempt for the women who threw themselves into his path.

"You've got a big day tomorrow, Willa. I should let you get some rest."

He showed her to the guest suite and made sure she knew how to operate its various gadgets, including the door locks, before he beat a hasty retreat away from the temptation she represented.

Gabe had seen John Merris's campaign ads on TV where his wife and daughter stood in the background like smiling robots. They'd looked like scary freaks, actually. Gabe had always assumed that the overbearing bastard had stripped their souls clean away. But in spite of her father, Willa Merris wasn't entirely broken.

And in spite of James Ward, too. Gabe's gaze narrowed as he stared up at the ceiling of his bedroom. That boy was going to pay for what he'd done to Willa. It was the least he could do for her. Gabe lay awake long into the night, plotting the destruction of one James Ward.

Willa stared out from the wings of the makeshift stage at the brightly lit podium that the governor would walk out to momentarily, and introduce her as the new junior senator from the great state of Texas.

"You okay?" Gabe murmured beside her.

She nodded, even though it was a lie, and smoothed her new charcoal-gray suit down her front. Gabe had fed her breakfast, helped her write her blessedly short speech and then driven her over to Neiman Marcus an hour before the upscale department store opened.

A personal shopper, makeup artist and hairdresser

had been waiting inside for her. She'd stood like a patient doll while Nieman's efficient staff took care of her, dressing, primping and painting her to perfection for this press conference. And not one bit of it felt real. It was all an elaborate dream. Were it not for Gabe's warm, firm grip on her elbow, she would still be absolutely convinced that none of this was real.

"Remember, Will. You're about to become a United States senator. You have nothing to be ashamed of and everything to be proud of. Of all the people he could've chosen, your father thought highly enough of you to entrust this job to you. And you're going to do great at it."

She smiled ruefully at him, but the expression felt fake and plastic on her face. She was a fraud. And the whole world was about to see it for themselves. "Can I go throw up in the corner now?" she muttered.

Gabe laughed. "Don't bother picturing them all in their underwear. Picture them naked."

"If I can stand up in front of a bunch of five-year-olds and teach, I can talk to these folks," she whispered back. "That's not what I'm scared of."

"What, then?" Gabe asked in concern that was so sweet, she almost forgot she wasn't supposed to trust him.

"They're going to eat me alive about the James Ward thing."

"Screw them," he declared. "Refuse to talk about it and move on with the press conference."

She opened her mouth to retort that the reporters wouldn't give up that easily, but the television camera lights popped on just then with a slight buzzing and a rush of hot, blinding light. Governor Graham walked out from the opposite side of the stage and gripped both sides of the podium as he read from a teleprompter. Too late for her to run away and hide.

"…would like to introduce my choice for the position, Willa Merris, daughter of the late Senator John Merris…"

Her feet stuck to the floor, and were it not for Gabe giving her a smile and a little shove, there was no way on God's green earth she'd have walked out in front of that phalanx of cameras and reporters.

The next few minutes passed in a daze. She held up her right hand, repeated the meaningless sounds that were actually the Congressional Oath of Office and read the strings of words on the piece of paper in front of her on the podium that were her statement of thanks to the governor and her promise to the voters of Texas to do her best to represent them.

And then the governor's press secretary uttered the phrase she'd been dreading worse than facing a firing squad. "Senator Merris will take a few questions, ladies and gentlemen."

The shout that went up was worthy of spectators at a Roman gladiatorial bout. The cacophony held the same avid bloodlust. She recoiled from the aggression of the crowd, stunned at the hostility rolling off the room toward her. Had they all secretly hated her father so much or was this nastiness directed at her, specifically?

She gazed across the sea of faces, looking for anyone who didn't appear openly eager to shred her.

No surprise, her mother hadn't shown up today. Hurt, disappointment and anger swirled inside her. Minnie wasn't a bad person, but forty years with John Merris had broken her. Willa got that. Still, she could've used a little support today from someone who didn't hate her outright.

Larry Shore's face caught her attention. He'd been singularly unhelpful this morning in the scramble to prepare her for this press conference. Truth be told, he'd been of little help to her or her mother since the murder, and no help at all since he got out of jail a few days ago.

At the moment, Larry was leaning against the wall off to one side of the circus, looking so pleased with himself he could bust. Had he given these jackals the scoop on her pressing charges against James Ward? Lord knew Shore was vicious and ambitious enough to pull a stunt like that. He was a chip off her father's old block.

Impatient of waiting for her to call on one of them, the reporters started shouting questions at her. By rights, Shore ought to be up here beside her, telling the journalists to cool it and treat her with proper respect. But he stayed where he was, arms crossed, enjoying the show.

Without warning, a large, male presence materialized beside her. Speaking in a voice that brooked no shenanigans, Gabe growled, "If you all don't pipe down, the senator's not going to be able to answer any of your questions. This is a press conference, not a free-for-all. I'd remind you that Senator Merris has recently lost her father to a shocking and tragic murder, and she doesn't need the likes of you jumping all over her. Do I make myself clear?"

The press pit subsided immediately. Gabe pointed at a reporter from one of the major networks who asked her a harmless enough question about who she planned to endorse in the upcoming election to replace her father. She assured the guy that she would review the candidates thoroughly, and make an announcement in the next week or so.

Another reporter asked whether she planned to go to Washington at all or if her appointment was purely a political favor to her family. She deflected the implied jab by reminding the reporter that the Senate was not in session and reiterated that she would serve in whatever capacity she was called upon over the next several months to the best of her ability.

That answer made Shore scowl. What was up with him, anyway? He'd been her father's flunkie for as long as she could remember. Why was he even here today? He'd been absolutely furious when she'd called him last night to inform him of the governor's appointment. Had he expected the governor to appoint him to her father's vacant Senate seat?

"...verify that you accused the son of a prominent businessman of rape yesterday?"

Her attention snapped back to the brunette woman who'd asked the question. She recognized Paula Craddock from KVXT news. The room went dead silent as dozens of reporters stared at her expectantly, waiting for her answer and sensing the kill.

Honest to goodness, Willa thought she was going to throw up right then and there. Her stomach heaved as all her worst nightmares came true. Even the governor was throwing her a horrified look from the wings of stage left.

She'd been a senator for two whole minutes, and she'd already disgraced the office, disgraced her family and disgraced herself. Shame, hot and acid, bubbled up in the back of her throat all but gagging her.

"Courage, Will," Gabe breathed from behind unmoving lips. "No shame. Chin high."

She took a wobbly breath and answered the reporter, "You're referring to a personal matter that has no bearing on my new position. The events under investigation took place well before my father's death, and I have confidence the truth will come out over time. Until then, I have no comment on it."

"But you're wrecking a good man's reputation and have no evidence to support your wild claims, both of which call into serious question your fitness to hold your father's job," Paula Craddock followed up.

Gabe leaned forward aggressively, but Willa surprised herself by placing a restraining hand on his arm. He yielded the microphone to her reluctantly.

Willa borrowed a page from her teacher's playbook, and looked out across the sea of faces like a chiding parent addressing a room full of unruly five-year-olds. She spoke gently, but with unmistakable steel in her voice. "I said no comment. And I mean no comment. I will never comment on this matter, and I will blacklist any reporter who persists in questioning me about it. Understood?"

A disconcerted murmur rose, and she sagged in relief as the governor's press secretary hustled forward to call an end to the press conference and make a few off-camera wrap-up comments about the governor's schedule for the rest of the day.

Gabe's arm went around her waist as her legs all but gave out from under her. "I told you, you should have eaten more breakfast," he commented. "You're going to look damned silly if you faint after putting them all in their place like that."

She smiled up at him weakly. He told a hotel employee to bring the senator a glass of orange juice, and she remembered at the last second not to look over her shoulder for her father.

One of the governor's aides hustled up to her. "The

governor wanted me to let you know your Secret Service detail will arrive tomorrow. Would you like us to provide you with police protection in the meantime?"

"Heavens, no," she exclaimed. She just wanted her life to remain as close to normal as possible.

The fellow scurried off as a hotel employee arrived with a pitcher of orange juice and poured her a glass of it.

While Gabe watched on, she drank up the refreshing liquid obediently.

"Now what?" he asked.

Now what, indeed.

Chapter 5

Gabe climbed out of his SUV in front of his folks' old place in Vengeance. The neighborhood had changed a lot since he'd been a kid. Back then it had been shabby, bordering on squalid. But sometime in the past decade, the crowd at Darby College had declared this area funky and cool, and had moved in to gentrify the place. Refurbished bungalows with neat paint jobs and new lawns now lined the street.

As for him, he kind of missed the old days. Coming back here used to remind him of where he'd come from. Who he was. Now it felt foreign and fake.

He supposed he should have expected the news crew parked on his front porch, camera and microphone at the ready. He'd been too distracted to spot the white van before. "Paula Craddock, isn't it?" he asked. "What do you want?"

"I hear you're an old family friend of the Merrises.

What do you think of Willa's accusations against James Ward?"

"I think whoever told you I'm a friend of the Merrises was smoking crack," he snapped.

"You were all over Willa Merris today at the press conference. A regular knight in shining armor for her. It looked to me like the two of you are more than friends." She added slyly, "A lot more."

"Climb up out of the gutter onto the curb, Paula. The girl just lost her father, and she's dealing with a ton of crap right now."

"Right. The alleged rape. She didn't look very raped to me."

An image of Willa cringing away from his touch, her eyes big with fear, flashed through his head. "And what exactly does a raped woman look like?" he snarled.

"Some actual evidence might be nice. Even a few cuts and scrapes would lend a little credibility to her story. Assuming she fought back, of course. For all I know, she liked it rough, and is just suffering a case of buyer's remorse."

An urge to bury his fist in the obnoxious woman's face surged through him. Not that punching a reporter would be anything other than a disaster. Instead, he asked smoothly, "Are you sure you're actually human, Ms. Craddock? You have all the compassion of a rock."

The cameraman nearly dropped his camera as he tried unsuccessfully to stifle his laughter. The reporter scowled. Not only was she not getting the sound bite she was looking for, but she seemed to realize she was losing control of this interview.

She pointed the microphone at him again. "Yes, but what do you think of the charges against James Ward? Are you with everyone else in believing that Willa Merris made up this alleged rape in a desperate, and frankly pitiful, attempt to use her father's notoriety to get attention for herself?"

"Is that what everyone else believes?" he asked blandly.

"Absolutely. I gather, then, that you concur?" She shoved the microphone under his nose expectantly.

"I think you're a pushy hack who doesn't give a damn about reporting the truth, and who's looking to claw your way past anyone who gets between you and fame. If we're talking about pitiful and desperate, let's take a closer look at you, shall we?"

The cameraman guffawed with laughter, and Paula growled at the guy to stop filming. She turned on Gabe, glaring venomously. "I can make your life a living hell, you know. I can dig up plenty of dirt on you."

He stepped forward until he was chest-to-chest with the woman. "There's one small flaw with your big threat, darlin'. I don't give a tinker's damn what anyone thinks of me. Say whatever you want about me because I. Don't. Care."

She took an involuntary step backward, and the cameraman made an amused sound behind her. If possible, the reporter's gaze became even more enraged. Gabe brushed by her and stabbed the key in the front door lock.

He half turned and commented casually, "By the way, you're trespassing on private property. I'm going inside and fetching my shotgun. If you're still on my porch when I return, I'll assume you mean me harm and will shoot you where you stand in accordance with Texas homestead laws."

He stepped inside the dim interior and closed the door gently. He did, indeed, cross the living room and take his grandfather's shotgun down from its brackets over the rough-sawed cedar mantel. Gabe had learned long ago never to make any threat he wasn't prepared to follow through on. Otherwise, it made people think you were weak.

He opened the front door, shotgun in hand, and was gratified to see Paula scuttle the rest of the way to the KVXT van in an undignified scramble of legs, microphone wires and stiletto heels. She was still scowling furiously at him as the vehicle peeled away from the curb in a hurry.

No doubt about it, that woman was going to be trouble. But it was nothing he couldn't handle. A billion-dollar bank account gave a man the power to get rid of pests like her. He didn't usually make a practice of throwing his weight around, but he could make an exception for her.

An ugly and unfamiliar feeling crept past his irritation, though. Shocked, he identified it as fear. Obviously, the reporter had set her sights on breaking down Willa's story of being raped. Probably thought she could weasel a Pulitzer out of it for herself. Who cared if she destroyed the life of a victimized young woman who'd just tragically lost her father?

Yup, Paula Craddock was going on the list with James Ward of people to teach a lesson to.

Willa rubbed her eyes and took a sip of the now-cold coffee sitting beside her. She'd been in her father's office for hours, combing through his files on the computer there.

It hurt to go through his private correspondence like this. She could almost hear him saying the things written in his emails and memos. She'd mostly gotten over her disbelief that her father was dead, but the sharp ache of loss still stabbed at her. No matter how big a bastard he might have been, he was still her father. She'd spent the better part of her life trying to please him and had basked in his approval whenever he'd doled out a smidgen of it to her.

Larry Shore had grudgingly handed over the passwords to get into the encrypted portions of her father's machine, and had then departed hastily, leaving her to sort out the jumbled mess for herself. If her father had a system for filing anything, it was certainly eluding her.

A few things about her father's life as a senator were becoming clear, however. He was firmly hooked into the good ol' boy network. Most of what he accomplished was done through under-the-table trades and mutual back-scratching arrangements. Her father didn't appear to have even the slightest sense of ethics or fairness in how he chose to support or oppose various pieces of legislation. It was all about what he could get from someone else.

Although she'd been aware of his horse-trading style, a tiny part of her had hoped he'd had at least some small shred of conscience. That once in a while, he voted on a bill because it was the right thing to do. Instead, she even found an email from him to a junior senator berating the young man for voting with his conscience. Her father's letter closed with a line declaring that conscience had no place in politics.

Was that why her father had been killed? If only the police could make some headway in identifying her father's murderer. Maybe she'd be less jumpy at night and sleep better. Even if all they discovered was why he'd been killed, that would be better than this giant black hole hanging over her family.

She clicked on yet another file and scanned through a mind-numbingly dull list of people to pressure into delaying a vote on something or other having to do with oil companies' right to privacy. It had to do with proposed legislation that would force oil companies to turn over complete lists of the chemical formulas of the liquids they injected into the ground as part of extracting oil and gas from shale rock.

The technique, hydraulic fracturing, commonly called fracking, involved pumping water and a propriety blend of chemicals underground to break up oil and release it from the rock it permeated.

She clicked on the next email, and started as a bright red screen popped up, warning her that the contents were classified. What had Larry said about that? It had been hours ago and her brain was fried. She pulled out the piece of paper she'd scribbled all her father's passwords on and tried the main one that he supposedly used for just about everything. It didn't work. She tried the others, and of course, it was the very last one that caused a new folder to pop up on her screen. It was labeled only Senate CMA.

She clicked on the first file. The letterhead made her frown. Senate Committee on Miscellaneous Affairs? She'd never heard of it. But apparently, her father was a member. She paused in her reading to do an internet search of the term and frowned as a message blinked, "No result matches your search." It must be some sort of secret committee. She wasn't so naive as to think that everything Congress did was known to the public.

She went back to reading. The letter outlined a schedule of meetings for the past year. She noted that more than a few of the closed sessions were actually scheduled for late in the evening. What senate committee started meetings at ten o'clock at night, for good-ness' sake?

Alarmed, she opened the next file. This one outlined an operation by...somebody...a group called Excelsior... to infiltrate Mexico and kill the governor of a Mexican state. Stunned, she read it again. That was definitely what she'd just read. Someone who worked for this se-cret committee was killing government officials of an-other sovereign nation. Last time she checked her civics textbook, that was illegal!

She opened another folder. This one outlined some sort of mission in the Middle East to fund bomb-ings in a country whose regime she recalled hearing the United States didn't like. But that was terrorism! U.S.–sponsored terrorism.

Very afraid, she clicked on the third folder. God only knew what the dozens of remaining folders held. She started to read. Assassination. California. Oh. My. God. Whoever this Excelsior bunch was, they were killing Americans on American soil, too.

Folder after folder gave up its secrets, each more horrifying than the last. For nearly two hours she read about the activities of this secret committee. It created mayhem and death wherever it touched.

Finally, she reached the end of the last file. She leaped up from her father's desk, pacing in agitation. What was she going to do with this information? She couldn't just do nothing. But then that stack of paper-work the governor's assistant had shoved in front of her to sign after the press conference came to mind. Some of it had to do with not revealing classified informa-tion. Was she seriously required to keep her mouth shut about this secret committee and whatever it was up to?

She couldn't do it. Wouldn't do it. Even if she was

prosecuted for revealing classified information, there was no way she would stand by and let something like this go on in her country. Not in her government. Being a United States senator stood for something, and even if she had to throw herself on her sword, she would not sully that institution.

She paused by the French doors opening out onto one side of the back patio. The garden was dark, wreathed in shadows that suddenly looked menacing. The room behind her was dark, lit only by the lamp on her father's desk, and the night seemed to reach right through the window to wrap her in its cold grasp.

Shivering, she rubbed her arms. And that was when she saw it. Flitting through the garden at the edge of her sight. Something ghostly and gray. She swore under her breath. If that was her father coming back to haunt her, she was going to give him a piece of her mind, all right. He'd had no business condoning the shenanigans of that committee. Miscellaneous Activities, indeed.

There it was again. Except this time it wasn't an it. That was a *person* out there. Someone was creeping around in the garden and doing a freakishly good job of blending into the shadows. Stories of hit squads and covert ops teams fresh on her mind, panic ripped through her.

She pressed herself back against the wall beside the window in abrupt fear. Who was out there at this time of night? George, the gardener, went to bed at about nine o'clock, and it was after midnight now. Her mother hadn't even made it downstairs for dinner, and Louise had the night off. Not that the shadow outside looked even remotely female. The intruder was tall and athletically built from what she'd glimpsed.

Willa crept around the margins of the office, hugging the wall, careful to stay out of the line of sight of the windows. She reached the desk and crouched down behind it as she picked up the phone. Quickly, she dialed 9-1-1.

"9-1-1. Please state your emergency."

"This is Willa Merris. There's an intruder in our back garden. A man."

"I'll send a unit over to have a look, Miss Merris... err, Senator. I need you to stay in the house. Is there a room you can lock yourself in?"

"Yes. My bathroom."

"Go there and lock yourself in. Wait for an officer to call through the door and tell you it's all clear."

She hung up the phone and crawled on her hands and knees for the hallway door, staying out of sight of the garden. When she reached the foyer's cavernous darkness, she climbed to her feet and ran for her life. She flew up the stairs, through her bedroom and into her bathroom. She leaned against the locked door, panting in relief in the dark.

Who on earth was in the garden? A reporter looking for a scoop? Some kid just messing around? Or was it more sinister? Someone out to silence her, perhaps? Except she'd barely been a senator for a single day. And everyone knew the appointment was purely a formality until the election could take place. Oh, God. What if it was James Ward out there? Memory of the madness in his eyes shuddered through her. Had he come to take revenge on her for pressing charges? Or even to kill her?

She waited in an agony of suspense for the police. She looked around her bathroom for something to defend herself with and came up with a toilet brush and a can of hair spray. Not exactly inspiring weapons. The mansion creaked and groaned around her, but she swore she detected the stealthy sounds of someone moving around downstairs. Probably just the police. She held her breath to listen more closely.

The faintest whisper of sound came from the other side of the door, in her bedroom, as if someone was breathing very lightly and very carefully only inches away. She was separated from whoever it was by no more than a thin, wooden panel. Why didn't the policeman identify himself? The only possible answer froze Willa in place in sheer, dumb terror. *Because that wasn't a policeman.*

On cue, the faint scream of a siren became audible in the distance, and grew quickly in volume. The police hadn't even arrived yet! Whoever belonged to that thread of breath on the other side of her door was *not* a cop.

Fear for her life roared through her. This went so far beyond any panic she'd ever experienced before, it deserved its own word to describe it. *Death-panic,* maybe.

Her bedroom floor creaked once as if someone had stepped on a loose board, but then silence reigned. So frightened her legs would no longer bear her weight, she slid down the door to sit on the cold tile floor, huddled in a tight little ball as she squeezed her knees to her chest.

Who'd been out there? What had he wanted? Had she nearly died…or worse?

The police were noisy as they stomped around the back of the house and eventually came inside, calling back and forth to each other and clearing rooms as they went.

Finally, an eternity later, a knock on the door at her back made Willa jump a foot in the air. "Miss Merris? This is Deputy Green. You can come out now."

Shakily, she pulled herself to her feet and opened the door. She'd never been so glad to see an armed man in her life. "Thank God you're here. Did you find him?"

"Ma'am, we didn't see any sign of an intruder in the garden. It's as quiet as a sleeping baby out there. Little windy, though. Are you sure you weren't just seeing tree branches swaying?"

"Of course I'm sure. In fact, I heard the intruder just on the other side of this door a few seconds before you got here."

"Miss Merris, the house alarms were turned on and undisturbed when we came in. Nobody's come inside this house tonight but us."

"But I heard him breathing—"

The policeman cut her off politely, but firmly. "Folks' imaginations run wild when they're scared. We see it all the time. But you're safe now. No one was in the house, and frankly, no one looked to have been in the garden. If there was someone back there, it was probably just some kid taking a shortcut home. Why don't you go on to bed, miss. We'll reset the alarm on the way out and make sure the place is all buttoned up."

"Do you know where James Ward is right now? What if it was him? The Ward Ranch backs right up on the other side of the woods behind our property. You need to have someone check on him. See if he's home or not."

"It's the middle of the night. I'm not going to disturb the Ward family at this hour just to satisfy your curiosity—"

Desperate to sound reasonable and calm, she enunciated carefully, "The man raped me. Asking where he is immediately after an intruder came into my home does not constitute idle curiosity, Officer."

"Ma'am, the house is locked up tight and there's no

sign of anyone having been in the house who doesn't belong here."

The Wards and Merrises had been like family forever. Heck, she knew the code for the Ward home's security system. James Ward undoubtedly knew the security code for this house. But she didn't waste her breath trying to change the officer's mind. He'd decided she was imagining things and nothing she said was going to change his opinion.

"...go on to bed, and everything will be fine in the morning," he was saying soothingly.

God, she hated it when people patted her on the hand like this, with a metaphorical "there, there," as if that would make everything better. She wasn't an idiot, and she knew what she'd seen and heard.

The cop wasn't taking no for an answer to the whole go-to-bed thing, and waited expectantly in the hall while she changed into pajamas and a robe. She called out that she was in bed, and the jerk opened the door to poke his head in and see for himself.

"Good night, miss. You just stay in bed and get some sleep. And don't let your imagination run away with you again," he said sternly before closing her bedroom door and heading downstairs. She mumbled a foul name at the closed panel of her door. She was a United States Senator, for goodness' sake, not a naughty five-year-old.

Surely the intruder had nothing to do with those secret files she'd stumbled across. No way could anyone have reacted to her discovery that fast, right? It was just a coincidence.

She'd deal with those tomorrow. But tonight, she was going to try to take Deputy Green's advice and get some sleep.

Huddled under her comforter, she listened to the

sounds of the cops finishing up and leaving. Silence fell over the house. She wasn't crazy, darn it. There had been someone in the garden, and there'd been someone right outside her bathroom door. But no matter how hard she listened for movement, all she heard were the normal sounds of the house itself and an occasional branch banging into her window on a gust of wind.

Damned police. Chased a person off just when things were getting interesting. Willa Merris thought she could hide? Hah. She'd never be safe. If she was so secure in her ivory-tower mansion, then why was her silk blouse right here, right now?

Face buried in her shirt, the intruder drew in a deep whiff of the eggplant-colored silk. That rich floral scent of Willa's swirled up. Intoxicating. Infuriating.

Ride the rage. Ahh, God, it felt good. Down, down, into the abyss, self lost in the fury. Ohh, yes. Come to me, sweet Willa. We'll go down in flames, together....

If she slept at all, it was in short spurts and fitful at best. She'd never been so grateful to see the sun creep through her bedroom window as she was the next morning. She finally slept, then, waking only when Louise knocked on her door to say that the phone was ringing off the hook and Mrs. Merris was worn out dealing with it all.

After saying a short prayer for nothing important to happen on her short watch in the job, Willa dressed and went downstairs to face her first full day as a United States senator.

She stepped into her father's office and frowned. His computer had still been running last night when she'd fled the room. Who'd turned it off? Her mother rarely came in here, and surely the police wouldn't have messed with it. Louise wouldn't dream of touching Mr. Merris's computer, even if the man had been dead for weeks. She was superstitious about such things.

Willa turned it on and, while it booted up, wandered into the kitchen to pour herself a cup of coffee. Her mother was eating lunch with Louise at the kitchen table.

Willa kissed her mother's cheek and asked the house-keeper, "Louise, would it be possible for Marcus to come spend a few days with us?" Louise's son was recently returned from an overseas tour with the marines.

"I don't know. Why do you ask?"

"I'd like to hire him as a security guard. It would be a temporary gig, but I'd feel better if we had a man in the house at night."

Louise grinned. "You mean a big, strong, ex-marine who can chase away the boogeyman?"

Not her, too. Willa sighed in exasperation. Would no one believe her? "I swear, Louise. I saw someone in the garden." She didn't bother trying to convince the woman that the intruder had made it all the way to her bathroom door.

"Honey," her mother murmured, "you're distraught. Maybe you should go away for a few days. Get some rest."

"I don't want to leave you alone, Mom."

Minnie waved a bony hand. "I'll be fine. No one bothers anyone around here. And the police take care of everyone."

Had Minnie forgotten her husband had been *murdered* less than three weeks ago? Willa made eye contact with Louise across the table, and the two women shared a private eye roll. It must be nice to own so much real estate in la-la-land and never have to deal with reality.

"I'll call Marcus," Louise offered.

Willa smiled her thanks and retreated to the office. She set down her mug of coffee and entered the password for the classified files from last night. She moved the mouse to click on—

Where did it go? The file labeled Senate CMA wasn't in the list. Frowning, she checked the file directory. Not there. She tried a search of the hard disk. Nothing. What the heck?

She did a computer-wide file search. Still nothing. The file was gone.

Chapter 6

Okay, she was *not* losing her mind. She hadn't imagined those files last night any more than she'd imagined that breathing outside the bathroom door. She tried every search parameter she could think of, but nothing turned up. All traces of the sinister committee had disappeared.

She picked up the phone and started to dial Larry Shore, but thought better of it partway through dialing. He'd been a complete jerk yesterday at the press conference, and he hadn't been any better here at the house. Instead, she looked in her father's address book and found the number for his Congressional office in Washington, D.C.

"Good afternoon, Senator Merris's office. This is Amber. How may I help you?"

"Hi, Amber. This is, uhh, Senator Merris."

The young aide spluttered, flustered.

"Amber, is there anyone in the office who can tell me about the Senate Committee on Miscellaneous Affairs?"

"Umm, one moment, ma'am."

Willa waited. And waited. Finally, after nearly five minutes, a male voice came on the line. "Hi, Senator Merris. This is Larry Shore's assistant. Committee on Miscellaneous Affairs, you say?"

"That's correct."

"I'm sorry. No such committee exists."

"Would you do me a favor? Crank up my father's computer in his office and go to his private file directory. I'm assuming you have access to it?" At his affirmative noise, she continued, "I'll stay on the line."

In about a minute, Larry's aide said, "Okay, I'm looking at it."

"Start reading the names at Defense Construction Oversight Committee and read down from there." Willa read along on her own computer screen as the aide recited exactly the same list of file names she was looking at. Neither list contained the CMA file.

If a duplicate copy of the missing file had ever existed on her father's Washington, D.C., computer, it had been erased, as well. "Thanks," she said thoughtfully. "That was helpful."

"If there's anything more we can do for you, ma'am, just let us know."

"I will. Thanks again."

On the one hand, she was relieved. The intruder last night probably hadn't been James Ward, after all. However, the man who'd broken into the house had apparently done so with the express purpose of erasing that file. Wow, that had been fast. It spoke of power and reach that boggled her mind.

Furthermore, the intruder probably had a partner in Washington. Which meant there was some larger conspiracy at work here. And based on what she'd read in the missing files, she hesitated to think about how dangerous the owner of that breath on the other side of her door had been.

What were the odds that an intruder had shown up within two hours of her first opening the Committee on Miscellaneous Affairs file and not been connected to the file? And then the file was mysteriously erased overnight? No coincidence was that far-fetched. She stared at the antique reproduction telephone on her father's desk in sudden apprehension. Was it tapped? Was she being watched?

Maybe she was as paranoid as that cop last night thought she was. Maybe she *was* overwrought after James's attack and her father's murder. Maybe Minnie was right. Maybe she needed to get away for a while…

…or maybe she wasn't crazy at all.

On impulse, she unscrewed the cover of the phone's mouthpiece. She had no idea what she was looking at, but she pulled out her cell phone and took several pictures of the guts of the thing from different angles. She screwed the receiver back together and headed for the garage, grabbing her purse on the way out.

"Will you be back for supper, Willy?" Louise called after her.

"Probably not."

"Marcus can come up to Vengeance, but he said you better pay him good if he's gonna have to beat up ghosts."

"I'll pay him a fortune!" she called over her shoulder as she slipped into her little car.

She was relieved to see the mob of reporters had

found other prey today, and wasn't camped in front of the mansion. She wasn't in the mood to deal with their aggression. Following the instructions her onboard navigation system gave her, she headed for a spy shop in a strip mall in north Dallas. It was mostly a gimmick store, but she hoped someone there could help her.

Thankfully, she was the only customer when she walked in to a dizzying display of cameras, microphones, binoculars and unrecognizable electronic gadgets.

"Can I help you?" a middle-aged man asked. He had a crew cut and appeared to be in pretty good shape. Ex-military, maybe? In that tight black T-shirt and camo pants, he certainly cultivated the image.

"I hope so." She pulled out her cell phone and called up the pictures of her father's telephone. "Can you tell me if this has a bug in it?"

The guy took one look at the first picture and replied immediately. "Sure does. Big as day."

Her face felt hot and she was a little light-headed all of a sudden. Her father's—her—phone was tapped? "Can you tell me anything about it?"

"Mind if I transfer these pictures to my computer so I can enlarge and enhance them?"

"Have at it."

The guy hooked her cell phone to a laptop on a workbench behind the counter, and fiddled at the keyboard for several minutes. All of a sudden, he swore, startling her away from a display of stun guns and personal tasers.

"What's wrong?" she asked quickly.

"Where'd you get this picture?" he asked tersely.

"Why?"

"That's a military-grade device. State of the art. I'm

talking brand-new. I didn't know these acoustic bugs were out of prototype testing. They're not available on the open market, yet."

Military? Why would the military bug her? "Which branch of the military does it come from?"

"Hell if I know, lady. Could be CIA, for that matter. But I can tell you one thing—unless you're a high-ranking government official, you should not have a picture of it."

Guilt flashed through her before it occurred to her that she actually was a high-ranking government official. Still, her rushed security clearance wouldn't be processed for at least another week, according to the governor's people.

"Do you sell anything for finding surveillance equipment and disabling it?" she asked.

"You've come to the right place for that…."

An hour later, armed with a bag of nifty electronic gadgets, she guided her car back toward Vengeance. Never in her life had she paid so much attention to the vehicles in her rearview mirror. If she was being tailed she couldn't tell, but that didn't mean much. She was a rank amateur at this cloak-and-dagger stuff.

She dialed her office in Washington, D.C., as she drove and got Amber again.

"Hey, it's me. Willa Merris. I need you to do me a favor and cancel the Secret Service security detail they're assigning to me."

"I don't think that's a good idea, Senator. There are more crazies out there than you might imagine."

She doubted that. She could imagine a whole lot of crazy people right now. Thing was, she had no idea how deep into the government that secret committee's reach extended. Was the Secret Service compromised? Were there sleeper agents inside that agency who were loyal first to that damned committee? Nope, she dared not take a chance on one of the crazies ending up in her own protection detail.

She hung up on Amber's efforts to talk her out of the decision with a repeated order to cancel the security team.

The closer Willa got to home, the more jumpy she became. She couldn't stay at her parents' house one more night. If she was going to die of fright or worse, she wanted to do it in her own bed. She had to assume her house was bugged as well, hence the bag of goodies on the seat beside her.

Thankfully, the press wasn't camped out at her little bungalow. There must have been some new development in the murder case that drew them away temporarily. Whatever it was, she was grateful for the break from media scrutiny.

As she parked her car in the detached garage, it dawned on her that the old Dawson house was only a few blocks away. Not that Gabe ever stayed there anymore. The way she heard it, he'd bought the place, renovated it and stopped by once or twice a year to remind himself of his roots.

Idle speculation was that he planned to make some sort of museum out of it in his old age. "The Birthplace of the Great Gabe Dawson" or something like that. Maybe he planned to charge a few bucks admission to add to his billions.

She carried the bag of electronics into her house and spent the remainder of the afternoon setting up gear that the guy at the store had promised would create static interference and thwart any camera, bug or other surveillance equipment hidden in her home. She stashed the remote control that armed the system in the coffee table in her living room, along with the collection of TV, stereo and DVR remotes she kept in a drawer there.

She didn't turn the system on, though. The guy at the spy store had cautioned her against finding and disabling any surveillance devices. He said it would tip off the bad guys, and furthermore, they would just come back to plant more powerful gear and hide it better next time.

Or worse, they would shift to direct human surveillance, which apparently involved bad guys peering through her windows and using parabolic microphones to listen in on her life. The spy-store guy had said something about them looking through her walls, too, and she'd tuned out at that point. The thought of being that vulnerable and visible was too much for her to contemplate.

She would leave the static generator off until she needed to talk to someone in private. If the bad guys wanted to listen to her cook supper and watch television shows, more power to them.

But as the hour grew late, the prospect of going to bed alone in the dark loomed. She could do this. As long as she wasn't poking around nonexistent files, she wasn't a threat to anyone, right? If they'd wanted to kill her, they'd had their chance to do it last night, right?

The whisper of that light, careful breathing and the faint sound of sirens approaching played through her head over and over as she reluctantly lay down to sleep. She resorted to pulling the covers up entirely over her head when the fear became too much to stand. Then, she'd start to feel foolish and poke her head out once more. She'd emerged from the cocoon of her covers a fourth time, and her alarm clock said it was nearly 2:00 a.m. when she heard a noise.

Not a big noise. A rather innocuous little creak. Except she knew that creak. It was the spot just inside her dining room from the kitchen. A person had to step on the loose floorboard to make it squeak like that. Oh, God. Someone was out there!

She flew out of her bed in sudden terror, grabbed her cell phone from her nightstand, and tore into her bathroom. She closed the door as quietly as she could and locked it carefully. Finally daring to breathe, she eased away from the door and climbed into the bathtub.

She put a towel over her mouth and phone to muffle the sound of her call, dialed the police and whispered in panic, "This is Willa Merris. I'm at my house on Elm Street, and there's an intruder in my home."

"Ma'am, you thought there was an intruder last night, too. Are you sure there's someone in your house? Is it possible your imagination is playing tricks on you?"

They didn't believe her. Someone was right outside, and there was no telling what the intruder had planned for her. She had no time for arguments with skeptical sheriff's deputies.

She disconnected the line, and in panic, dialed Gabe Dawson's cell-phone number.

After three agonizingly slow rings, a gruff, sleepy voice muttered, "'Lo."

"Gabe, it's Willa," she whispered frantically. "There's someone in my house and the police don't believe me. They refuse to come. I didn't know who else to call."

"I'll be right there." He abruptly sounded completely alert. "Where are you right now?"

"The bathtub."

"Stay there. I'm going to be armed and will shoot

anything that moves when I get there. I'll be there in three minutes."

The phone went dead and she pressed herself against the cold porcelain, uncomfortably cramped in her small tub. *Please, please hurry, Gabe.*

Gabe had never moved so fast as he snatched the shotgun off the mantel and tore outside. He leaped into his SUV and roared down the street and around the corner. He probably made it to the curb in front of Willa's place in two minutes, but it felt like two hours. Making no attempt to be quiet or stealthy, he slammed his door and raced up the sidewalk toward her darkened house.

He swore as the front doorknob turned easily under his hand. No way had she left it unlocked like that. Willa was too scared of crap like this not to have double-checked it before she went to bed.

He threw the door open and surged into the front room, shotgun at the ready. He swung the barrel around the room. Clear. He burst into the dining room, which Willa had turned into an office. The place was a shambles, but no one moved in the space. He cleared the kitchen next and moved down the hall toward the back of the house. It looked like two bedrooms and a bathroom back here. He threw open the first door. Bedroom. Clear. He checked the closet fast and then backed out of the room.

Second door was locked. Probably the bathroom where Willa was hiding. She must be scared out of her mind. He moved on to the last door. It was already open and he spun inside aggressively. Nobody there. He heard a sound from the rear of the house and ran for the end of the hall and the door there. He burst onto the back porch in time to see a shadow atop the tall back fence of

Willa's yard. He yanked the gun up fast, but by the time he got it into firing position, the shadow had dropped out of sight on the other side of the fence.

Temptation to chase the intruder and blow a hole in him warred with his need to protect and comfort the terrified woman behind him.

Frustrated, Gabe turned for the house. He went through the place room by room throwing open closets and checking under beds and tables, anywhere a person could hide. Nothing seemed to be missing from the house. Television, stereo, silver and china were all in place. But the computer in the dining room was trashed. It looked like someone had smashed it open with a sledgehammer and pulled out its parts. The intruder had stolen the hard drive, if Gabe had to guess.

He turned on lights as he went, chasing away the shadows. Finally, when he was convinced the house was empty of bad guys, he headed for the locked bathroom door.

"Willa, it's Gabe. The house is clear. You can come out now."

The lock clicked and the door swung open fast. Willa flew out and straight into his arms. He staggered a little as he caught her weight up against him.

"Easy, baby. I've got you now. You're safe."

"Oh, God, Gabe. I heard them, and the police wouldn't believe me. And then there was all that noise like they were ransacking my house, and I was so afraid they were going to kill me, and—" She burst into tears against his chest.

Which he realized abruptly was bare. Her tears were hot and wet against his skin. And he was wearing only a pair of thin, cotton pajama bottoms. Usually, he slept naked. And after that panicked phone call from her, he'd have raced over here in his birthday suit if he hadn't happened to decide to watch a little TV after his shower, and happened to pull on the pajamas.

For her part, she was wearing a skimpy tank top thing that outlined every contour of her perky breasts and taut nipples against his chest. Her waist was narrow, and her hips and tush curved sweetly under his hand as he ran his palm up and down her back to assure himself she was whole and unharmed.

Her arms went around his neck and she all but choked him in her panic and relief. But he didn't care one bit. No woman had clung to him like this in real need for as long as he could remember...no, not ever. And it made him feel ten feet tall.

He released her momentarily with one arm to set aside the shotgun, but then he was holding her again, offering her his strength and safety as she sobbed against his chest. Finally, her tears subsided into wobbly sniffs.

"Better?" he murmured into her fresh-smelling hair.

"What would I have done without you?" Her breath moved softly against his skin as she spoke. "You saved my life."

"I don't think it was as bad as all that. Only thing that jerk killed was your computer."

Willa did a strange thing then. She lurched away from him, pressing her fingers against his lips urgently. He stared down at her, surprised. She pulled out of his arms and headed down the hall toward the living room. He followed, confused.

Wow. Those sassy little shorts showed the entire length of her long, sleek legs and the beginning swell of her tush to massive effect upon his lust. The girl should be a lingerie model with that kind of a body. Who'd have guessed she was put together like that under the boring church-lady suits she wore in her father's campaign ads?

She paused in the doorway of her makeshift office to take in the damage. With her standing in profile to him in that way, he couldn't help noticing the way that thin cotton tank top clung to her high, firm breasts. Oh, yeah. Lingerie model all the way.

She moved on to the living room. He watched, frowning, as she opened a drawer in a coffee table, reached inside, sighed audibly in relief and pulled out a small black box. It looked like an old-fashioned transistor radio. She poked at the buttons on the front of it, and then looked up at him with a tiny smile of triumph.

"There. Now we can talk," she announced.

"What is that?"

"White-noise emitter. It blocks any bugs and causes only static to show up on hidden cameras."

"And you have a white-noise emitter why?" he demanded, alarmed.

"My father's phone is bugged. I figured whoever was watching me at the mansion would watch me here, too. I got this in case I needed to talk in private."

He moved over to her side quickly. Dang, his protective instincts were on overdrive tonight. "You're being bugged and surveilled? By whom?"

"I have no idea." She stared up at him fearfully, her blue eyes dark and scared yet again. God, he hated seeing them like that.

"And you're sure it's you being watched and not just leftover crap from your father?"

"They broke in here and trashed *my* computer, didn't they?"

He sank down beside her on the edge of the couch. "What the hell's going on, Will?"

She took a deep breath and studied him for a minute. Seeming to make some sort of decision, she nodded to herself and began to speak. He listened in disbelief as she described finding a secret folder on her father's computer dealing with a covert Congressional committee doing violent and illegal stuff. His jaw dropped as she described the intruder at the Merris mansion last night and the secret folder's mysterious disappearance in the interim.

"So you think whoever broke into your father's home and deleted or stole that file broke in here tonight, and took the hard drive out of your computer?" he asked as she finished her recitation.

"It seems logical, doesn't it?"

"What the hell was your father involved in? What has the bastard dragged you into?"

"He didn't drag me into anything. Governor Graham did that when he named me to my father's job."

Gabe shook his head. He'd known John Merris was dirty, but he had no idea how dirty. "What was in those files?"

"They were classified. I think I'm not supposed to tell you."

He rolled his eyes. "I'll let you shoot me if I tell anybody else. But we've got to figure out who and what you're up against here, baby."

The endearment slipped out before he even realized he was thinking it. He never called women "baby." Not even in the heat of passion. He made a point of knowing his lovers' names and using them when appropriate. If he'd have ever called Melinda "baby," she'd have bitten his head off. She'd been nothing if not a raging feminist. So unlike the vulnerable and sexy woman shivering on the couch beside him.

"Come here, Willa." He held out his arms to her and was immensely gratified when she crawled into his embrace of her own volition. He leaned back and she cuddled against his chest like a contented kitten. He felt more macho then he had in years. Which wasn't exactly the kind of thing he usually thought about. But she was all woman and seemed to find him all man. It was a heady sensation.

"You're so warm," she murmured against his chest. Her lips moved against his skin as she spoke and his body reacted sharply. He swore mentally. His flimsy pajama bottoms weren't going to leave a thing to the imagination pretty soon.

Desperate to think about something other than steamy, hot sex with this bombshell, he asked, "Do you think the intruders are operatives from this secret senate committee?"

She nodded, her hair sliding silkily against his skin. Lord, that was distracting! "Honey, if you don't stop wiggling, I'm going to embarrass us both. And I know you're a bit…sensitive…about such things right now."

"Oh." A pause as his meaning obviously sunk in. "Oh!" Damned if she didn't settle more firmly against his chest and throw her arm around his waist. "I'm not scared with you here," she whispered.

He about jumped out of his skin as she actually pressed her lips against his sternum, just below his collarbones. Crap. No, not crap. Good that she wasn't terrified of touching a man. But he mustn't think about sex. She felt safe with him? That was progress, right? His brain leaped from thought to thought, disjointed and… oh, God. So horny. Must control himself. *Not gonna happen, buddy.*

"Willa. This isn't going to work. I mean, I do want

to comfort you. I'm glad to hold you. But neither one of us is wearing a lot of clothes, and umm…well, hell. You're incredibly sexy and attractive."

Her hand around his waist moved up his chest and curled around his neck, her fingers playing seductively in the short hairs at the back of his neck.

"Gabe. Look at me."

He stared down at her in distress. He wanted to make love to her right now just about worse than he wanted to breathe.

"I'm not scared of you."

Was she inviting him to… Oh, holy God. No way. He was not going to fall on her like some sex-starved beast. Like James Ward.

"Yeah, well," he retorted gruffly, "I'm scared of me." He squirmed out from under her and surged to his feet. He turned his back fast to hide his arousal from her. No matter what she said, he wasn't going to chance scaring her off men for good.

Arms snaked around his waist from behind, and her delicious chest pressed against his back. He could all but feel the firm globes cupped in his hands. Swelling sweetly into his mouth. He groaned aloud. "I'm trying to be a gentleman, here, dammit. You're not helping, Willa."

"Kiss me, Gabe."

He bolted forward, tearing out of her grasp. "No!" No way was he taking any chances with her. She was still too fragile, too afraid for that. She needed time to recover. To learn to trust men again.

Willa was quiet behind him. Too quiet. Cautiously, he looked over his shoulder at her. And swore. Tears were sliding down her cheeks silently as she stared down at her toes. She looked like a little kid who'd just had her puppy stolen.

He swore aloud as he turned and swept her into his arms. "It's not you, baby. I swear. Believe me, you're just about the sexiest thing I've ever seen. But it's too soon."

She made an impatient sound and shock exploded across his brain. It wasn't too soon for her? Then that must mean...damn...*was it too soon for him?*

Chapter 7

Willa tossed and turned in her bed, so frustrated she could scream. No matter what she'd tried last night, Gabe Dawson flatly refused to kiss her. He kept spouting some drivel about her needing time to learn to trust men again.

Frankly, she expected she would never trust most men. But she did trust him. He'd charged to her rescue three times now. First at the police station when the media mobbed her, then again at the press conference when the reporters had overwhelmed her and most of all, last night.

He'd risked his life to confront a potentially deadly intruder in her house, for goodness' sake. Jerks didn't do heroic stuff like that just to get in some girl's pants.

She punched her pillow, but it was hopelessly bunched and hot beneath her cheek. It figured. The first time she was truly attracted to a man in recent memory, he refused to lay a hand on her, let alone kiss her. After James had beat her up, she'd found herself craving someone to touch her gently. Respectfully. Okay, maybe not so respectfully, but definitely intimately.

At least Gabe didn't think she was a complete troll. Memory of his entirely obvious physical reaction to her last night under his cotton pajama bottoms made her smile in momentary triumph. Temptation to go to him, to cajole and tease him until he couldn't resist her washed over her.

She really shouldn't. It would create a horrible scandal if she dated her dead father's mortal enemy. Not to mention all the divorcées of Vengeance that Gabe had spurned over the years would be out for her blood if she landed him.

But darned if he wasn't everything she'd ever dreamed of in a man. Truth be told, she'd spent most of her teen years, and an embarrassing portion of the years to follow, idly dreaming of him. He'd figured prominently in most of her first sexual fantasies. She'd literally dreamed about him more times than she could count. Hot, explicit dreams where he did all the naughty, forbidden things to her that nice girls weren't supposed to think about or even know about.

She had no doubt he was adventurous enough and confident enough as a lover to fulfill all of those fantasies, and maybe cook up a few that hadn't occurred to her, yet. After all, he wasn't some inexperienced college boy who would fumble his way through the rudiments of sex. If even a tenth of his reputation was rightfully earned, he was an extraordinary lover.

Oh, she'd blushed and pretended not to listen over the years as his various female conquests had kissed and told. But as furious as they'd all been at his unwillingness to marry them, they'd all purred with satisfaction over Gabe Dawson in the bedroom.

Her body humming with need until her nerves jangled, she glanced at her alarm clock. Barely 8:00 a.m. But she couldn't stay in bed one second more. Not without her hands wandering over her body, stirring up even more frustrated fantasies of the man dozing on her living-room sofa. He'd insisted on guarding her through the night, and he'd been equally adamant that he was not going to share her bed.

It had been sweet, really. He'd confessed wryly that a whole squad of intruders could stomp through her house and he would never notice them if he spent the night in the same room with her. Yes, indeed. A little teasing and seduction of the man was just what the doctor ordered.

To that end, she got out of bed and pulled on her shortest shorts, rolled down the elastic waistband below her navel and chose a cropped T-shirt that she usually wore over a tank top. Feeling daring, she skipped both tank top and bra.

She felt a moment's doubt when she checked herself in the mirror, though. The short T-shirt barely covered the lower swell of her breasts. And she never showed this much stomach. At least hers was tanned and toned after a long summer spent in her parents' swimming pool. She brushed her hair until it gleamed over her shoulders and threw on just a touch of mascara and clear lip gloss.

Amused at the notion of putting on makeup to cook breakfast, she opened her bedroom door quietly and peeked down the hall. No movement. She tiptoed to the living room and spent far too long staring down at Gabe sprawled on her couch.

My, my, my, he was pretty. His hair was dark and

tousled against his strong features. His face was an intriguing mixture of rugged and refined—too chiseled to be called pretty, but too elegant to be called rough. Relaxed in sleep, he looked younger. Almost boyish. And so yummy, she could just eat him up.

Acres of muscular chest sprinkled with dark hair drew her gaze, and his legs were powerful beneath his pajama bottoms. Startled at her lack of fear of his obvious sexuality, her mind wasted no time running wild, conjuring possible ways to wake him up. They mostly involved getting naked and pressing herself against his incredible body.

"Like what you see?"

She jumped about a foot in the air at Gabe's husky voice. He'd caught her staring at him like he was her very own ooey, gooey sexual treat.

Fiery heat exploded in her cheeks as she mumbled, "Uhh, yes, actually." Some suave seduction she was off to. She sounded like a bumbling teenager. "Umm, hungry?" she managed to choke out.

"You cooking?" he replied lazily.

Her gaze snapped up to his face at the sexy timbre in his voice. His gaze was sliding down her body with excruciating thoroughness, taking in her skimpy outfit and the assets revealed with laser precision.

That was more like it. "What's your pleasure?" she murmured.

It was his turn for his gaze to snap up to hers.

"Eggs? Pancakes? Steak?" she suggested, a smile hovering at the corners of her mouth.

"All of the above."

"If you want to jump into the shower, go ahead," she suggested. "I'll go have a look in the kitchen and see what I can come up with."

"How about I pop back over to my place to shower? I can grab some clothes that way."

She let her gaze slide down his body and back up. Whoa. He was already wide-awake in more ways than one this morning. "I rather like what you're wearing now."

"Vixen," he muttered, heading for her front door. "I'll be back in twenty minutes. Call if anything happens and you need me between now and then."

Oh, she needed him, all right. The smoky green of his eyes announced that he'd gotten that message loud and clear. But frustratingly, he still seemed determined to do nothing about it. The door closed behind him, and suddenly, her house felt horribly empty. Or maybe it was her who felt his absence so keenly. Yikes. She had it bad for him.

She headed ruefully for the kitchen. She'd always had a thing for Gabe Dawson but had never imagined there was a chance in heck of anything coming of it. Maybe there still wasn't any chance. Maybe she was an idiot to throw herself at him like this. The poor man was just trying to do a decent thing, to keep her safe, and here she was making a complete fool of herself over him.

But if she'd learned nothing else from her father's death, it was that life was too short to waste not going for the things she wanted. How did that saying go? In the end, you don't regret the things you did in life; you regret the things you didn't do. If she didn't try for Gabe, she would regret it for the rest of her life. If he rejected her overtures, so be it. But maybe, just maybe, he'd take her up on her offer.

She kept the conversation light over breakfast and listened with interest as Gabe described some of his more exotic travels over the past few years. But as the meal ended, he pushed his plate back and took control of the conversation.

"What are your plans for today, Madame Senator?"

"I thought I'd add more locks to my doors and windows, maybe invest in a trained attack dog. Is Cujo for sale, do you suppose?" On a more serious note, she added, "Oh, and I've got a charity thing tonight."

"What charity thing?"

"Vengeance Ladies' Auxiliary Annual Ball and Auction. Raises money for some scholarship fund or other."

Gabe made a face. She privately shared the sentiment, but habit prevented her from agreeing aloud. She was all for helping charities, but sending the child of an already wealthy auxiliary member to college tuition-free wasn't exactly her idea of a worthy cause. She would feel better if the money went to a homeless shelter or battered women's support group. She knew first-hand just how hurt and confused and terrified women could feel after being attacked by a man they'd trusted.

"I guess I'll have to dust off my tuxedo, then." Gabe sighed.

"Excuse me?"

"I'm going with you."

Her jaw dropped. Gabe Dawson never showed up at these local charity affairs. He was infamous for his steadfast refusal to participate in the Vengeance social scene. The charity-minded ladies of the auxiliary would dearly love to get their claws into his billions... not only for their pet charities, but also for themselves.

"Why would you subject yourself to such a thing?" she asked, flabbergasted.

"If you think I'm letting you out of my sight any time soon, you're sadly mistaken, Miss Merris."

"But the break-ins only happen at night. You must

need to rest after all the excitement last night. And you do have a life of your own. A company to run. I'll be fine."

"You're not fine," he disagreed. He didn't raise his voice or sound in any way angry, but he made it clear he wasn't standing for any arguments. Her father could be stubborn the same way. She'd never bothered to fight with him, but she tried with Gabe, anyway. "Aren't you worried about what people will say if you finally show up at one of these events? They're going to expect you to donate a lot of money to their cause."

He shrugged. "I don't care what anyone says, and I'll give my money to whomever I please. Though their little scholarship fund for one of their own isn't high on my list of worthwhile charities."

"You have a list?" she asked in surprise.

He looked abruptly uncomfortable. "Yes, actually."

She planted her elbows on the table, fascinated. Gabe Dawson did charity work? "Do tell."

"I support a women and children's shelter in Dallas. And I fund a food bank for senior citizens. It's also a pet food bank so the elderly won't feed their pets their own food and go hungry themselves. Oh, and I built the Vengeance library building."

That raised her brows. The anonymous donor was widely thought to have been her father, and John Merris had let people make the assumption without correcting them.

"Why a library?" she asked curiously.

"Books gave me an escape from the bad times in my life. And they showed me there was a big, wide world out there waiting to be experienced." He shrugged. "They taught me to dream bigger than Vengeance."

Huh. Who'd have guessed Gabe Dawson was a closet bookworm?

He continued, "Of course, I build schools in every place Dawson Exploration drills in for oil. They're pretty well publicized, though. My company's PR people have a field day with those projects."

"Why schools?"

"I figure if we're removing one natural resource from an area, we should replace it with a more valuable one. And what's more valuable than education?"

"Hey, I'm a teacher. You're singing to the choir."

"And then I own an elephant sanctuary."

"Elephants?" she exclaimed.

"We rescue them from zoos and circuses, mostly. And give elderly elephants somewhere to retire in peace. We help them form family bonds. For many of them, it's the first time they've ever been with another elephant. Did you know they make friends with each other and are inseparable from their BFFs?"

Willa studied Gabe's face with interest. He was animated and happy when talking about the elephants and books and his schools. The guy truly cared about his various causes. This wasn't the coldhearted shark she'd grown up hearing vilified by everyone in Vengeance.

"Since when did you become such an avid philanthropist?" she asked.

"It takes having money to give it away. Melinda got me started, I suppose. Even before I made my first million, she was railing at me to give back to society."

"She railed at you?"

He smiled wryly. "On a good day. On the bad days, I'd describe it as simple screaming."

"Is that what broke up your marriage?"

He frowned. "It was a combination of things. I was

traveling so much, and she was so involved with building her career. I'd like to say we grew apart, but I don't honestly think we ever had all that much in common to begin with. She's a hardcore feminist, and I'm…not."

Willa reared back in mock horror. "You're not one of those 'women belong barefoot and in the kitchen' types, are you?"

He grinned. "I like my women naked and in the bedroom, thanks."

Her cheeks heated up, but she pressed the point. "What do you mean, you're not a feminist?"

"Don't get me wrong. I think women should get equal pay for equal work, and with a few exceptions for jobs requiring heavy physical labor, I think women can do just about everything men can, and just as well."

"But?"

He sighed. "But, Melinda thought she should be in control of our marriage, and I happen to think the man should have a say at home. Or at least have equality."

"Women should cook and clean and men should drink beer and watch sports?"

He laughed. "Not at all. I cook very well, thank you. And I can do my own laundry and scrub a toilet if it comes to it."

She scoffed. "When's the last time you scrubbed a toilet?"

He shot her a chagrined smile. "Not since my bank account topped a billion. Still, I stand by the point I'm trying to make. Melinda wanted to make all the financial decisions, even though I was the one with business experience and decent money sense. She wanted to schedule all our free time to support her career and never mine." As Willa opened her mouth to protest that women should be part of those decisions in a marriage,

Gabe waved a hand to stop her so he could add, "And she wanted to be in charge in the bedroom."

Ahh. Willa could see where a man like Gabe might balk at that. He was definitely a take-charge sort. She'd never even kissed the guy, and she could tell he would want to call the shots in bed. Personally, the notion made her feel fluttery and a little weak in the knees.

"What time does the rubber backstabbing and blood-letting begin tonight?" he asked with certain resignation.

"Seven."

"I'll pick you up at seven-thirty." She frowned, confused, and he clarified. "They won't serve dinner until at least eight, and I can only take so much judgment and condemnation before they get on my nerves."

"No one will—"

He cut her off gently. "Mark my words. Tonight will be a nightmare."

Not if she had anything to say about it.

"I do have one request, though."

She looked up sharply at the serious tone in his voice. "What's that?"

"Wear something people will notice you in."

Her eyebrows shot up. "Don't want me to ruin your reputation for dating hot chicks, huh?"

"Not at all. I could never stand seeing you in the back of your father's campaign ads looking like a mouse and blending in with the wallpaper. You're a beautiful, sexy woman, and you're Senator Merris now. It's time for people to notice you."

Wow. That was really perceptive of him. Her father had always demanded that she and her mother dress ultraconservatively, and in colors and styles that wouldn't call attention to themselves. She had more beige, boring dresses than she cared to count. Maybe this afternoon she'd burn them all.

And maybe this afternoon she should go shopping for the sexiest dress she could find, and spend the rest of the day making herself irresistibly gorgeous for this man who actually seemed to *see* her.

To that end, she stood her ground and insisted he go home to catch a nap and get a little work done. As soon as his SUV turned the corner and disappeared from sight, she headed for her own car and drove back to Dallas. She made a beeline for Nieman Marcus and its amazing personal shoppers. She'd never even looked for the sort of gown she had in mind for tonight and wanted to get it just right.

Sure enough, a lovely woman named Chloe found her the perfect dress, sexy but classy, and entirely grown-up. Willa was sick and tired of being John Merris's quiet, conservative, proper daughter who never drew attention to herself. For once, she wanted to draw a whole lot of attention to herself. At least from one man in particular.

As Willa stood in front of her bathroom mirror, carefully applying her makeup, she felt like Cinderella transforming into a princess for a night. Although the rollers all over her head did look rather silly. She always wore her hair up in a bun or pulled back in a low ponytail, but not tonight. She was turning over a new leaf. Willa Merris was coming out of her father's shadow for Gabe.

Her courage faltered momentarily when she put on the gown. Its sweep of copper satin down her body in a formfitting drape was more revealing than she remembered from the store. The dress's boatneck swept across her collarbones, but then swooped down her back, baring her spine—almost all the way down to her buttocks.

No, she was not going to chicken out. The dress was exquisite and she looked smashing in it, if she did say so herself. She hadn't been dressed particularly sexy the night James Ward attacked her, so it wasn't like dressing like this was going to put her in particular danger of a repeat assault.

Ropes of crystal tied across her upper back to hold the dress on her shoulders, their ends falling in a sexy shimmer down her bare back. The skirt had a slit that rose nearly to her right hip. It was simple, stunning and by far the sexiest thing she'd ever worn. Carefully, she took her hair down and sprayed its lush waves as they fell over her shoulders. The effect was retro, harkening back to 1940s movie stars. In keeping with that theme, she applied bright red lipstick that made her fair skin look like velvet cream.

The doorbell rang promptly at seven-thirty, and she quickly slipped on crystal-encrusted mules that added several inches to her height. She threw on a silk wrap, grabbed her clutch and opened the door. Gabe's fist froze in midair as he reached for the door to knock.

His gaze slid down the smooth satin, taking in every curve and every inch of leg peeking through the high slit. His voice deep and a little rougher than usual, he commented, "I approve."

"You're looking pretty sharp yourself, Mr. Dawson." He wore a tuxedo like he'd been born to it. Although she supposed it wasn't the wealth a man was born to but the confidence within him that made a tuxedo work.

He held out his forearm to her and she took it shyly. He led her down the front walk to his Escalade, and helped her into the passenger's seat. Her slit gaped open, and her entire right leg was revealed before she snatched at the copper satin.

But his hand got to the edge of the skirt first, and he gently draped the sleek fabric across her leg, his fingertips trailing fleetingly down the length of her inner thigh. She looked up at him, shocked and thrilled at the intimacy of his touch, but then the door slammed shut and he was gone.

His door opened and he slid into the seat. They were silent for the short ride to the college campus and its grand ballroom where the dinner, dance and charity auction were to be held.

Valets parked vehicles out front, and she and Gabe blended into the trickle of people moving into the venue. She took a deep breath and let it out carefully.

"Nervous?" he asked her, sounding surprised. "Haven't you done a thousand of these things?"

"Yes, but always as John Merris's daughter. Never as myself."

"Well, then. Here's to the coming out of Willa Merris. And in case I don't get a chance to say so later, it's an honor to escort a woman as stunning as you."

"I could say the same for you, Gabe. You cut quite a dashing figure in that tux. Thank you for doing this for me. I know how you hate these things. Any number of your, umm, former companions, have mentioned that they can never get you to go out to big social functions."

He laughed heartily. "Former companions, huh? You mean the ring-hunting sharks trying to rope me into marriage, or at least hoping to be seen by every other ring-hunting shark in town as having landed the elusive Gabe Dawson fish?"

"Exactly." She laughed. "Do you need help fending them off? I could always put out the word that you've decided to become gay and swear off women for good."

He grinned. "In the first place, that wouldn't slow

them down because it's my money they're after and not me. And in the second place, no one on earth would believe I'm gay as long as I'm with a woman as sexy as you."

Her jaw sagged.

"What?" Gabe responded in quick alarm, pausing at the top of the long row of steps leading down into the ballroom. "I didn't mean to make you uncomfortable after—"

She turned to face him and pressed her fingers against his lips. "Don't apologize. No one's ever called me sexy before. That's all."

"Are you kidding?" he burst out.

"I don't exactly run around in slinky gowns with X-rated underwear and my hair down and wearing come-hither makeup that often."

"X-rated—" he broke off sharply, and his arm immediately went around her waist protectively. He happened to slip his hand under her wrap as he did so, and his warm palm slid across her bare skin. A strange look crossed his face. "I think I'd better see the back of your dress before I let you take that shawl thing off."

On cue, a bellboy stepped forward and reached for her shoulders to remove the wrap. Gabe glared the kid off, though, and stepped behind her to lift away the garment himself.

"Sweet baby Jesus," he breathed.

She looked over her shoulder in quick alarm. "Is something wrong with my dress?"

"I'm only going to have to snarl off every man in the room tonight. Wouldn't be surprised if I end up having to fight a damned duel over you," he grumbled.

A slow smile spread across her face. "You like it?"

"Merciful God, woman. I've never seen anything like it. I can't take my eyes off you."

"Thank you," she whispered, more grateful than she could express at his gratifying reaction. It was just the confidence boost she needed to face the lion's den of Vengeance society.

They started down the steps once more, Gabe's arm firmly wrapped around her waist. "Good thing I box a couple of times a week," he muttered in her ear. "I have a feeling I may need a solid right hook before the night is out."

She leaned in close to murmur back, "Why's that?"

"Because every damn man in the place is staring at you like they'd like to eat you up."

She glanced up at the crowd closing in around them. Good grief, he was right. She was so used to being invisible, to trailing along in her father's wake and picking up the spare bits of attention thrown her way as a matter of courtesy, that this concentrated attention by everyone was badly intimidating.

She might have shrunk back from it or even turned around and left were it not for Gabe's arm anchoring her at his side and lending her strength.

Jacquelyn Carver, chairwoman of the charity fundraiser committee closed in on her and Gabe like a guided missile. "Why, Gabe Dawson. To what do we owe this pleasant surprise?"

Willa's teeth ached to grind together at the syrupy purr the woman aimed in Gabe's direction.

He answered drily, "I'm merely attending as Senator Merris's escort."

"Senator—" Jacquelyn looked over Willa's shoulder as if searching for John Merris. "Oh. Of course. Why, yes. Willa, congratulations on your appointment. It must have come as quite a shock."

"Why do you say that?" Gabe asked immediately and a little aggressively.

"Well, everyone thought Larry Shore would be named…" Apparently, it dawned on Jacquelyn a little late that Willa might take offense at not having been on the short list to replace her father.

Willa took pity as the woman's face turned red. After all, she was on Gabe Dawson's arm tonight; she could afford to be generous. "I was more surprised than anyone when the governor called me, Jackie. But it wasn't like I could say no to my father's last request."

"Will you go to Washington?" the woman asked hopefully.

"The police have asked me not to leave town." As Willa watched avid curiosity about the charges she'd made against James Ward cross Jackie's face, Willa added drily, "It's in case I can help with my father's murder investigation and the kidnapping of Gabe's ex-wife."

Jackie turned to Gabe, placing a solicitous hand on his arm. "You poor man. You must be so distraught over that. Such an impressive and brilliant woman, your wife."

"*Ex*-wife," Gabe retorted.

"Why, yes. Of course," Jackie gushed.

Willa's gaze narrowed. So that was how it was going to be, huh? The good ladies of Vengeance were going to snipe at Gabe for being out in public while his ex-wife was missing, and they were going to come after her for trying to replace Melinda Dawson. She supposed that was better than turning on her for charging James Ward with rape.

But then another woman strolled up, this time landing a snide barb about Willa certainly having come out of mourning in a big way. As that particular cat strolled away, Willa said to Gabe, "Did they expect me to show up in widow's weeds like it's the nineteenth century?"

Gabe answered smoothly, "They're jealous. Take it for the compliment it is."

She smiled warmly at him. "Good point."

"We can always leave if you'd rather not face the cats and their claws."

"I'm no coward," she retorted. "And I've got to face them sometime. I may as well get it out of the way tonight, when I've got this beautiful dress and a knight in shining armor to defend my honor."

"That's the spirit. I rather like the sound of Sir Gabriel."

"Gabriel? That's your real name?"

"Gabriel Michael."

"Your parents went for the whole archangel theme, huh?"

"Fat lot of good it did them to name me after angels," he retorted. "I'm anything but."

The idea of him being a dark and dangerous bad boy turned her on more than she could believe. As far as she knew, she didn't react in any overt way to the thought, but Gabe leaned down to whisper in her ear, "Hold that thought for later, baby."

Her toes curled into tight little buds of lust in her shoes. "Can we leave now?" she asked hopefully.

He laughed quietly. "But the upstanding citizens of this fine town aren't done skewering the two of us yet. You wouldn't want to deprive them of their righteous pleasure, would you?"

Chapter 8

Dinner was served, and Willa spent the next hour dealing with plates and food and drinks and not spilling anything on her gorgeous gown or otherwise making an idiot of herself. But then the tables were cleared and, while the auction was set up onstage, the guests were free to mingle again.

Apparently, the wine with dinner had kicked in or some unspoken signal she wasn't aware of passed between the members of the ladies' auxiliary as everyone left the tables. Or maybe it was Gabe excusing himself for a moment to visit the restroom. But the second Willa was alone, the barracudas closed in on her.

"You've got some nerve showing your face around here after what you did to James Ward."

"Just because you got your father's job doesn't give you the right to destroy a sweet, innocent man like James who never did anything to you."

"You lying, pathetic bitch. How dare you accuse James Ward of laying a finger on you! And then you show up with a sleazeball like Gabe Dawson?"

"Who'd have guessed you were such a slut? Your father must be rolling over in his grave."

They came at her so fast and from so many directions she had no hope at all of addressing any of their vicious attacks. And frankly, she had no idea what to say to any of them. Never in her life had anyone spoken to her like this. She was absolutely speechless over the hatred and jealousy in their voices. Had they always hated her this much? Had it only been her father's power that held them at bay? Or was all this venom directed specifically at her?

And then a voice she recognized all too well separated itself from the others.

"What are you doing here? And dressed like that. I'm appalled, Willa Merris. Not to mention your choice of escorts. Gabe Dawson? Are you intentionally trying to rub your family's nose in the slime that boy crawled out of?"

Willa whipped around to face that voice. "Mother? I didn't know you were planning to come to this event. You should have told me."

"And when did I have a chance? You've been too busy running around accusing nice boys of horrible crimes and grabbing at your father's wealth and position. If you think you're going to rob me blind, you've another think coming, young lady. I'll fight you. I'll get my own lawyers, and I'll see to it you don't get a penny of your father's estate."

Willa's jaw dropped in complete shock. What was this? She didn't want her father's money...what little of it there was, if Gabe was telling the truth about the

Vacarro wells. "I don't want Father's money, and I certainly don't want to steal anything from you."

Her mother ignored her and spewed, "You've disgraced our family. Splashing private business all over the news with your crazy accusations. Then trying to take over Merris Oil, and stealing your father's senate seat. And look at you. You look like a cheap whore."

Her mother's eyes were overbright, maybe even a bit maniacal, as she pointed an accusing finger at Willa. And Minnie's voice had risen enough that a number of people beyond the cluster of attacking women had turned to listen.

Willa spoke in an urgent undertone. "Mother, this isn't the place to have this conversation."

"Where else are we going to have it?" Minnie screeched. "You're too busy shacking up with the man who tried to ruin your father. You traitorous little slut—"

A sharp voice cut across Minnie's tirade. "That will be enough." Gabe's arm went around Willa's shoulders, and he pulled her tight against his side.

"Who are you to—" Jackie Carver started.

Gabe glared around the circle of women furiously enough to quiet them all. "Minnie, you know better than to mix alcohol and your medications. You're going to regret everything you said in the morning, but at least you've got an excuse for your atrocious behavior. As for the rest of you, what's your excuse for acting like white-trash gossips?"

Shocked silence was his only answer.

He spoke grimly. "Senator Merris didn't ask for her father to be murdered, nor did she ask to be brutally attacked. I've seen the evidence, and there's no question she's telling the truth about Ward. I also happened to be present when the governor called her to inform her of her father's request to appoint Willa to his senate seat in the event of his death. That was entirely John Merris's doing, not Willa's. The lot of you should be ashamed of yourselves for acting like a pack of gutter jackals."

And with that scornful observation, he hustled Willa past the staring women and toward the exit. By the time they reached the long staircase, she'd started to shiver, and by the time they reached the top of the stairs, she was shaking uncontrollably. *Her own mother? What poison had people been spouting in Minnie's ear to make her turn on her daughter like that?*

"Just a little farther, baby," he murmured. "Be strong for me."

A valet held out her wrap, and Gabe grabbed it with his free hand without ever breaking stride as he hurried her to the door.

As they stepped outside, a shockingly bright light illuminated, making Willa lurch against Gabe's side. A female voice called from the darkness beyond the spotlight, "There she is! Senator Merris, what do you have to say about the health hazards of oil fracking?"

Gabe swore under his breath beside her, then muttered to her, "That's Paula Craddock. Don't answer."

"Thanks. I had that one figured out," Willa muttered back. Why were an investigative reporter and a camera crew waiting outside this non-political fund-raiser?

As if the reporter's call had been a cue, a crowd of people rushed forward to line the sidewalk Willa and Gabe had to traverse to reach the curb and his vehicle. There were maybe thirty people, but they all wielded cardboard signs and commenced chanting loudly, "Stop the freaking fracking!"

The signs were lurid, claiming that fracking killed

kids, that oil companies were satanic and that the government had been bought off by frackers. At the end of the gauntlet of protesters waited Paula Craddock, microphone in hand.

"Looks like you're going to have to make a statement," Gabe mumbled. "Want me to handle this?"

"Are they here to yell at you because you own an oil company or to yell at me because I'm a politician?" she responded.

"Since no one knew I was coming to this shindig, and I wasn't on the guest list, I'm guessing they came for the good senator. But I can tell Paula to go suck an egg if you'd like."

"That's okay." She threw him a wry look as they ducked under the waving signs. "I lived in the shadow of my father for a long time. I learned a thing or two about handling hostile reporters and angry mobs."

"Are you saying your old man had a talent for attracting both?" Gabe retorted drily.

She snorted in amusement. "Perchance."

"Senator Merris, your father used his position to protect oil companies from taking any responsibility for the environmental and health carnage of fracking in Texas. Do you plan to do the same?"

"Congress is not in session at the moment, and no major legislation will come up for a vote regarding fracking between now and next January, so I'm not going to have an opportunity to take any stand on the matter. But thank you for asking. I'm so glad you came to cover the Annual Scholarship Ball and Auction. Let me take you inside and introduce you to the event chairwoman. Her name is Jacquelyn Carver. She'll be thrilled to meet you and tell you all about the event."

Willa took the reporter by the arm and gestured for

the cameraman to come along. She kept up a steady stream of commentary about the Ladies' Auxiliary and their charity work, and gave the reporter no chance to get a word in edgewise. It was a tactic straight out of her father's playbook. Before Ms. Craddock knew what was happening, Willa had handed her off to Jackie Carver, who would no doubt talk the reporter's ear off.

Willa turned away from the camera and flummoxed journalist in relief. And there was Gabe, only a few feet away, waiting watchfully.

"Shall we be on our way again?" he asked.

"Let's."

This time when they went back outside, the picketers weren't as loud or aggressive with their sign waving. Willa stopped in front of a woman whose poster showed a very sick little girl lying in what looked like a hospital bed.

"Tell me about your daughter," Willa asked gently.

The woman told a tale of respiratory problems and mystery symptoms, and a frustrating failure by doctors to find a source of the girl's serious illness. Willa pressed her business card into the woman's surprised hand. "Call me tomorrow. I'll have my staff help you get access to medical research specialists. If fracking is making your daughter sick, I want to know."

The crowd nearby went silent, apparently stunned that she gave a darn.

"Do you have a leader or representative of some kind?" Willa raised her voice to ask the group at large.

An imposing man in a black suit coat, jeans and black cowboy boots stepped forward. "That would be me, I suppose."

She gave him a card, as well. "Call me. I want to hear more about what all of you are experiencing."

"Uhh, okay. Sure," the man replied, obviously more than a little suspicious. But the crowd's ire seemed diffused and they called farewells to her as Gabe handed her into the SUV.

The Escalade pulled away from the curb before he asked, "Are you really going to talk to those people?"

"Yes. The way I understand government to work, I'm the representative of the people. It's hard to represent them if I don't know what worries them."

"A noble—and naive—sentiment. If you were to hold your father's office for more than a few weeks, the lobbyists and political-action committees would change your mind soon enough, I expect."

"I'm not so sure about that," she replied. "I read a number of my father's notes, and I have no lofty illusions about how deals get done in Washington. In my mind, the key to being a decent congresswoman is to plan on serving only one term in congress and spending that entire time voting the will of one's constituents and one's conscience."

Gabe laughed. "If only."

She sighed. "It's not like I'm going to get a chance to make a difference in the few months I've got in this job."

"You've still got the power to endorse a candidate and make a few statements and press releases. The question is, what things matter to you? What do you want to tackle in the time you have?"

She studied him with interest. That was an excellent question. And no one had ever asked it of her before. What did matter to her? For her entire life, John Merris had dictated what was important to her and her mother. He'd coached them in how to answer any political or opinion questions to mirror his platforms. It had always been about him.

"I don't even know which political party I would support if I had the choice," she said in wonder.

Gabe glanced over at her in surprise. "Well, then, you've got some homework to do, kiddo. Your father's political party expects you to endorse their replacement candidate for him by next week."

She sighed. "I should be teaching a bunch of kids their numbers and letters and colors this week. Instead, I'm embroiled in politics and my father's murder, people breaking into my house and a criminal investigation against James Ward. And if the women at the ball were correct, I've apparently sprouted horns and a forked tail, too."

"You don't actually care what those bleached-blonde bitches think, do you?" Gabe asked scornfully.

If only she had his tough hide. But no one had ever turned on her like that before, and it had been hurtful and humiliating. And her mother…

"Someone must have given my mother uppers to get her to that ball. She's been nearly catatonic since my father died."

"It sounded like someone fed her a bunch of lies, too. You do know not to take personally anything she said, right? She looked completely whacked-out on amphetamines or better."

"You think?" Willa asked hopefully.

"I know."

"How?"

"An ex-girlfriend with a drug habit."

She replied lightly, "Why, Gabe Dawson. I don't know whether to be more surprised that you dated a druggie or that you actually stuck around long enough with any one woman to consider her a girlfriend."

"What the hell do the GCBs of Vengeance say about me?" he exclaimed.

"GCBs?"

"Good Christian, uhh, Belles," he answered sourly.

She smiled. "Well, they say you're quite a lover. But that you refuse to talk about marriage, and get thoroughly surly if the subject even comes up. Common wisdom is that you never got over your wife dumping you and that you still carry a torch for her."

Gabe said nothing.

"Comments? Rebuttals?" Willa asked lightly.

"No comment."

Rats. She'd really love to know how he actually felt about Melinda Grayson. Did he still have a thing for his ex-wife? It would explain a lot about him. Like why he'd hightailed it back to Vengeance when the police told him Melinda had gone missing, and why he'd never remarried. Was she tilting at windmills to even fantasize about a relationship between the two of them? Would she want way more from him than he could ever give her?

"Aww, c'mon, Gabe. Give me something, here," she cajoled teasingly. "I was straight with you."

"Fine." He sighed. "I *am* an excellent lover."

She laughed, not only in amusement, but also to hide the way her stomach was suddenly jumping with nervous anticipation. What she wouldn't give to see for herself. "What about your ex-wife? Do you still have feelings for her?"

"Melinda was—is—a force of nature. You either get sucked into her orbit or she chews you up and spits you out. Making it to the inner circle of her universe was a big accomplishment for me back then. But I couldn't honestly tell you if I ever got to know the real woman or not. The one I was married to was impressive in just about every way. But she didn't go much for feelings. We never talked about things like love or insecurity or need."

Wow. That sounded cold and, frankly, unappealing.

Gabe continued, "Do I have feelings regarding her? Of course. Worry. A sense of unresolved differences. Abandonment. She bailed on me before, and as selfish as it might seem, I feel like she has bailed out on me again." He added in a rush, "I know the police think she was kidnapped, and this disappearance isn't her fault. And I feel as guilty as hell for feeling like she's left me again. So the answer to your question is yes. I still have plenty of feelings toward my ex-wife."

Complicated ones. That might or might not include romantic feelings like love and desire to reunite. He'd neatly avoided talking about those in his outburst.

"What do the police know about her kidnapping?"

"Shockingly little. Her housekeeper arrived one morning, and Melinda was just gone. There were no signs of a struggle in her house or office. Her car was still parked in the garage, her keys and briefcase and laptop sitting on the kitchen counter. Her syllabus and lecture notes for the semester were on her desk."

Willa shuddered. It sounded a lot like her father's murder—a life interrupted completely without warning.

Gabe continued, "The only unusual thing the police found was a grocery list in Melinda's handwriting. It stopped in the middle of a word. Maybe the phone rang or someone came to the door, or someone snuck up on her from behind and grabbed her. It's a mystery."

"And there were no witnesses or anyone with any more information?" she asked.

"No one legitimate has come forward in spite of the hundred-thousand-dollar reward I put up, and there have been no ransom demands."

"Is there a chance—" Willa broke off. "No, never mind."

"Go ahead. Say it."

Willa winced. "Is there a chance she was murdered, too? She did disappear right about the same time my father and those other men were killed."

Gabe went very still. "I would be lying if I said it wasn't possible. But I can't think that way." His voice gathered force. "I won't think that way. She's alive. I'm standing by that until I have positive proof to the contrary."

Willa felt like he'd just stuck a knife in her gut. He did still love his ex-wife. But she couldn't exactly blame him for revealing it. After all, she was the one who'd brought up the subject of Melinda's possible murder. And in all fairness, if she'd been kidnapped and was alone and terrified, she'd be desperate for her family and friends to continue fighting to find her, to continue believing she was alive, to continue their efforts to rescue her.

"Is there anything I can do to help find her?" Willa asked soberly.

Gabe looked over at her in genuine surprise. "No, but thanks for the offer. That's kind of you."

Willa frowned. "You say that like you thought I was wishing Melinda would turn up dead."

His answer was surprisingly bitter. "Let's just say neither she nor I were ever embraced by the scions of Southern society in this corner of the world."

"What does that have to do with me?"

They were stopped at a red light, and Gabe stared across the vehicle at her in open shock. "You do realize that you are as blue-blooded an insider to the halls of old-school power in Texas as they come, don't you?"

She blinked at him, uncomprehending.

"You're the daughter of one of the richest and most powerful men in Texas for the past thirty years or so. And you're beautiful and single, to boot. There have to have been young men falling all over themselves to marry you since you got out of school."

"If there have, they've been invisible," she retorted. Not for lack of her father constantly throwing her at every son of some powerful, old-money family or another from Dallas. It was just that none of the boys had ever called back. It was as if they'd taken her out as a favor to her father. But once they'd met her, they'd moved on quickly to greener pastures. Heck, her father had set up the date with James Ward.

The light turned green, and Gabe accelerated before demanding, "Tell me you're lying."

"I'm serious, Gabe. My social life has hovered between life support and dead pretty much forever."

"That's not possible," he announced. "A woman as beautiful and intelligent and charming as you?"

How embarrassing was this, having to confess that no one had ever wanted to date the shy, awkward daughter of a scary man? "It's not like I've ever run around looking like this before. And after the reaction I got tonight, I'm not going to try it again any time soon."

Her own mother had called her a whore and a slut, for goodness' sake. Tears welled up in her eyes to recall it. She'd thought this dress was beautiful, and for once in her life, she'd felt pretty. And the way Gabe's eyes had lit up when she'd opened the front door—she'd thought that maybe he'd found her pretty, too.

Speaking of Gabe, she risked a sideways glance at him. His jaw was set, and if she wasn't mistaken, muscles in his neck were tensed in irritation. Was he mad she wasn't the social catch he'd thought she was? Had he expected that with her on his arm, people wouldn't treat him like dirt for once? She sincerely wished she'd been able to give him the social acceptability he seemed to crave beneath his I-don't-care attitude. But instead of lifting him up, apparently, she'd succeeded in dragging them both down.

How could a simple charity ball have gone so horribly wrong?

The Escalade turned into a driveway she didn't recognize. It led to a garage behind a small craftsman bungalow near Darby College. "Is this your place?" she asked. She'd known his childhood home was somewhere in this neighborhood, but she'd never seen it before.

"Yup." He got out of the Cadillac and came around to open her door for her in grim silence. Grim enough that she decided not to ask just now why he'd brought her here. She followed him up the wide steps to a gracious porch and waited while he unlocked the front door.

"Don't call the place cute," he growled as he stepped inside. "I despise cute."

She stepped into a living room as masculine as any room she'd ever seen. Flagstone floors, cedar paneling, oversize leather furniture and a massive fieldstone fireplace dominated the space. "There's nothing remotely cute about this room," she assured him. "I'd call it rustic or comfortable or perfect for its owner. Or I might even say that Ralph Lauren would approve. But I would not call it cute."

He grunted in what she thought might be thanks as he moved swiftly through the room and disappeared down a hall. At a loss, she waited inside the front door, unsure of what to do with herself. Lights went on in other parts of the house.

"We're alone," he announced as he swept back into the room. As masculine as it was all by itself, the room seemed bigger, more alive, with him in it. It was as if he wore the space like a favorite pair of old blue jeans. He untied his bow tie and let it hang around his neck as he unbuttoned his collar. His neck was tanned and powerful, and yet again she was struck by how strong and forceful a man he was.

Every ounce of awkwardness and shyness she'd ever experienced flooded her as she stood there. She ought to say something sophisticated and smart, and all she could do was stare at him. God help her if she was drooling. If she'd ever thought she was woman enough to seduce Gabe Dawson, she knew, positively knew, in that instant that she was completely out of her league. She would never be woman enough for Gabe Dawson.

Chapter 9

The sight of Willa Merris in his living room, blushing like a nervous schoolgirl, brought Gabe to a complete halt. He could stand there and look at her all night long and never tire of the sight. She was the soul of innocence and oozed sex appeal all at the same time.

He'd never gone much for younger women, but he couldn't ever remember desiring any woman the way he wanted her right now. He wanted to debauch her, to tease her and teach her, to take her innocence for himself and unleash all the simmering sensuality she didn't even know she had within her.

If only he was a dozen years younger. He'd give anything to have her think of him as someone other than a safe uncle. This morning, when she'd sashayed out of her bedroom in that sassy little T-shirt and skimpy shorts, he'd thought maybe she was flirting with him. And then that backless dress…

But who was he kidding? At the moment, she looked on the verge of bursting into tears, or maybe bolting altogether. She might need reassurance that she was still desirable after Ward's attack on her, but she didn't want him, personally. Hell, for all he knew, Willa Merris was looking for a father figure. Lord knew her old man had failed her miserably in that department.

"Can I get you something to drink?" he asked her in resignation.

"Umm, why am I here?" she responded.

"So I can protect you from whoever seems determined to break in to wherever you're staying?"

Shock registered on her face. Didn't want to spend the night with him, huh? It might have been okay once, in Dallas, where no one would catch her and she had an entire suite to herself. But heaven forbid that she get caught with him in Vengeance. Had she honestly not known just how giant a pariah he was among her friends and associates?

He hated himself for wanting her to want him, and he hated himself for lying to her about why he'd brought her here. But hey. In for a penny, in for a pound. He added another lie on top of the first.

"Not to mention, Paula Craddock is gunning for you. She told me so herself. And after you sicced Jacquelyn Carver on her, she's going to be madder than ever at you. I figure she'll hang out at your house or your mother's looking for you. If, for some reason, she comes sniffing around here, she and my shotgun have an appointment to get better acquainted."

Willa's musical laughter made him look up sharply from the whiskey he was pouring for himself. "Can I be there to see that?" she asked.

"Sure."

"Promise?"

"Scout's honor." He poured her a glass of Licor 43, a Spanish liqueur that women told him tasted like chocolate-chip cookie dough. Personally, it was too sweet for him. But over the years, he'd dubbed it "Liquid Panty Remover."

"Kick off your shoes if you want. Get comfortable." He carried the drink to her, and enjoyed how her face lit up when she tasted it. She sank onto one of the matching leather sofas while he lit the fire already laid in the fireplace.

He spoke wryly over his shoulder as he fanned the fledgling flames. "I'd turn on some music, but I wouldn't want you to think this was some cheesy seduction scene."

"Of course not," she answered quickly. Too quickly.

He sat down on the other end of the couch and studied her carefully. "I can't read you. What are you thinking?"

Her cheeks went crimson. "Umm, nothing."

"In my not inconsiderable experience with women, when they tell you nothing's wrong, something's always wrong. And they're never thinking *nothing*. What's up?"

Suddenly, his shoes appeared to interest her more than just about anything else in the world. Genuinely worried now, he reached out to tip up her chin with his finger. "Willa?"

"I can't begin to thank you for all you've done for me. Goodness knows, you don't owe me or my family anything. I truly am grateful."

"But?"

"Is there a but?" she half whispered.

"I don't know. You tell me."

"But I don't expect all of this from you. You don't have to seduce me as a pity case."

"A pity case!" he exclaimed.

"It's sweet of you to feel sorry for me, but I don't expect you to fix me. It's my responsibility to get over what James Ward did, and I'm not going to force that on anyone, certainly not on you after everything else you've already done for me."

"Force— Willa, you're not forcing anything on me, and certainly not yourself. In case you hadn't noticed, I'm quite a bit bigger and stronger than you. Not to mention, nobody has made me do anything I didn't want to for a number of years now."

She sagged beside him. She ought to be relieved by his declaration, but for some reason, she looked… crestfallen.

"Do you *want* me to seduce you?" Normally, he wouldn't be so blunt with a woman. He knew the signals well enough to recognize if a woman wanted to sleep with him or not. The problem with Willa, though, was she was giving him mixed, and contradictory, signals.

She definitely was attracted to him. And when he'd seen that dress at her front door earlier, he'd been pretty damned sure she wanted to sleep with him. But then those women—and her own mother, the bitch—had shredded her, and it was as if he'd brought an entirely different woman home from the party than the one he'd taken. This one looked like a lost little girl. Or worse, like the robot from behind her father's shoulder at campaign appearances.

"You haven't answered my question," he said to the side of her averted face.

"I can't," she said in a muffled voice.

"Why not? It's okay to say you don't know what you

want, or not now, or hell, no. But please be honest with me." Not that he had any business pointing fingers at anyone for being less than truthful. He wanted her in his bed so bad he could taste it.

"I can't answer because—" she took a deep breath and continued in a small voice "—because if I said I did want you to seduce me, you'd do it to be a gentleman and not because you actually wanted to."

He laughed heartily. "Honey, if I seduce you, it most certainly won't be out of any sense of duty. And I don't necessarily promise to be a gentleman about it."

Her gaze snuck up to his for an instant before sliding away. She tossed back a large gulp of her liqueur and coughed as it burned a path down her throat. He reached over to pound her back until she could breathe again.

So. Willa Merris was interested, but too insecure to admit it. He could work with that. He could definitely work with that.

He plucked the empty glass out of her fingers and took it over to the bar to refill it. When he returned, he was pleased to see that she had kicked off her shoes. He passed her the drink and lifted her feet onto his thigh to massage them. In moments, she was making little moaning sounds of pleasure that just about drove him out of his mind.

"So, we're agreed, then," he said in a businesslike tone. "Seduction is the order of the day."

Another gulp and another cough. But she conspicuously failed to disagree with him. The fire crackled, and its golden light painted Willa's exquisite features with glistening fairy dust.

"You've got me at a disadvantage," he murmured.

She looked up at him, her blue eyes big and wide and questioning.

"You're arguably the most beautiful woman I've ever seen, but if I tell you that, you'll think it's a cheesy pick-up line."

"I wouldn't believe you if you said it, anyway," she answered lightly. "I've seen a bunch of the women you go out with. You have sophisticated taste. I'm not in that league at all."

"That's the point. You're different. You're…real."

She laughed painfully. "A real mess."

"Everyone's got baggage. And most of yours isn't of your making. For tonight, could you try to set it aside?"

"I'd love nothing better than to do that." She sighed. "But I don't know how."

"You just need a distraction to take your mind off things."

"Like what?"

Lord, she asked that so innocently. Like she truly didn't know what he meant. An urge to be the one to show her what was possible between a man and a woman surged through him. "Dance with me."

"What? Here?"

"I never got to dance with you at the ball. I owe you one."

Smiling, she set her glass down and rose to her feet. He relished her slenderness as he drew her into his arms in front of the fireplace.

"Shouldn't there be some music?" she asked. "Can't you just tell the house to turn something on?"

He smiled down at her. "No computers here. This is my anti-technology hideaway."

"This house is so different from your penthouse. And yet, it fits you as well as that place does. It's like each one reflects a side of your personality." She swayed lightly in his arms and he imagined what she would feel like wrapped around him.

"So, tell me, Gabe. Do you have any other houses that reflect some other part of you?"

"I have a beach house in Northern California. It's all glass and stone. It's about the ocean and the sound of the waves crashing on the rocks."

"What part of you does it reflect?"

He gazed down at her candidly. "My wild and primal side that connects with nature."

"I think I might like to see that place."

Her face was turned up to his, and her lips glistened softly. She so wanted to be kissed. But did he dare? Once he started kissing her, he doubted his ability to stop. Thing was, he had no idea how traumatized she was nor how to proceed with finding out.

"Say the word, and I'll take you there," he murmured.

Her eyes widened, and he belatedly realized the double entendre implicit in his comment. "I'm sorry, Will. I don't mean to come on so strong. I know you're scared, and God knows I don't want to make it worse. You're going to have to tell me what you want and don't want."

"What are you talking about?" She was looking up at him like he'd grown a second head.

"The attack, of course. You flinch every time a man touches you, and every now and then you get this rabbit-about-to-get-eaten look in your eyes."

She huffed in what sounded like displeasure. "But I've already told you, I'm not scared of you."

Chagrin tore through him, hot and acid. Right. He was some old guy who posed no threat to her. A favorite uncle. *Damn* it. His arms fell away from her and she took an alarmed step forward and grabbed his lapels.

"What's wrong? What did I say?" she cried out

softly. "Crud. I'm so bad at this. I always mess this up. They always go away and never call again. I'm such a klutz—"

He cut her off. "What the hell are you talking about?"

"Men. I'm no good at relationships. I'm a complete freak—"

"Stop." He stared down at her in shock. "Willa. You're so beautiful it hurts to look at you. You're intelligent. Sweet. Interesting to talk to. And sexy. God, woman. You're so hot I can barely think straight around you. If men are running away from you, it's because they're so intimidated by you. They don't think they're good enough for you. Hell, I don't think I'm good enough for you."

She stared at him blankly. Like she hadn't heard a word he said. Or maybe like she heard but didn't believe a word of it.

"I'm serious, Willa. You're extraordinary. You keep saying I'm out of your league, but honey, it's the other way around. I'm a cynical, selfish, forty-year-old oil man with enough money to buy sex, but with no real friends. I'm a hard-ass businessman most of the time, and a workaholic to boot."

"Anything else?" she asked.

He glared at her obvious skepticism. "I'm serious."

"Okay. But if you'll forgive me for saying so, you left a few qualities off your list."

"Like what?"

"You're a gentleman at heart. You've rescued me more times than I can count. You've been decent to me when my family has been nothing but rotten to you over the years. You run a retirement home for elephants, for goodness' sake. How many men can say that?"

Elephants? She was bringing those up now?

Her palms slid slowly up his lapels to grasp the ends of his bow tie. She tugged him close and he yielded reluctantly to the pressure.

"Gabe," she whispered achingly, "I want you to make love to me, even if it is pity sex on your part. I know it'll be a one-night stand. I have no illusions about how you operate. But I've wanted you ever since I can remember, and tonight, I just don't care about anything else."

He stared down at her in shock. "You've wanted me for how long?" he asked slowly.

"Since I was about sixteen," she confessed, her cheeks starting to turn a dull red.

"But why?"

"C'mon, Gabe. You know how sexy a man you are. You know women crawl all over you not only for your money, but because you're so attractive. And since when is forty old? You take great care of your health. And frankly, after women experience a few twenty-something guys with no clue what they're doing, surely you can understand why women would much prefer a man who knows his way around a woman. You do know your way around a woman, don't you?" she asked in quick dismay.

"Yes," he answered drily. "I do."

"Well, there you have it. You're a hunk and a hot catch. *Now,* will you make love to me?"

He'd love nothing better. But he was still worried about her emotional scars. He'd never dealt with anything like that before. "Willa, are you sure you're ready for this? Do you need more time to trust me?"

Her gaze narrowed in irritation. "I'm trying really hard to be brave and bold here. To get past…well, to get past my past. If you don't quit asking me that, I'm going to have to tear your clothes off and have my wicked way with you. And to be honest, that notion scares me half to death. Besides, you've already said you like to be in charge in the bedroom."

He laughed reluctantly. Although her tearing his clothes off didn't sound half-bad. "Refill?" he asked her. Now that the moment was upon him, he had no idea how to proceed with her. Yet another first for him. He laughed ruefully. "You do manage to mess with my head, Will."

"I'm sorry."

"Oh, don't apologize. It's…interesting. You keep me on my toes." He pressed a full glass into her hand and nudged the bottom of it toward her mouth.

"A little liquid relaxation first, Mr. Dawson?"

"Something like that." She was so damned open and forthright. She would talk about anything, apparently. It was disconcerting. Most women were so busy maneuvering into his pants by this point, they weren't stopping to talk about his tactics to achieve the same.

She gazed up at him artlessly. He'd swear she was a virgin if he didn't know better. "Ward wasn't your first, was he?" Gabe asked carefully.

She made a face. "Thankfully, no. But truth be told, no guy has ever impressed me tremendously."

"I'm supposed to impress you?" He laughed. "A tall order."

"I have faith in you, Gabe."

And there it was. That damned trust of hers. What if he let her down? If she freaked out in the middle of sex and he did the wrong thing? Fear gripped his chest in sharp talons.

"Now what?" she asked.

Now what, indeed.

Chapter 10

Deal struck, sex forthcoming. All of a sudden, Willa was more scared than the first time she'd done the deed with a sweaty frat boy in college whose face she could barely remember and name she couldn't recall. But this was Gabe Dawson. The object of her lustful desires for most of her sexually aware life.

Thankfully, it wasn't the kind of scarred-and-damaged scared she'd feared would wreck the rest of her sex life. It was the butterflies-of-anticipation, so-nervous-she-could-barf, please-God-let-her-not-embarrass-herself kind of scared.

"How are we going to do this?" she asked nervously. "Do you want me to take off my dress?"

Gabe smiled. "No, Willa. Breathe. I'm not going to fall on you like some ravenous beast. We've got all night. And frankly, if the vibe's not right tonight, we can get around to it some other time. Relax, already."

"Relax? I'm not sure I know what that is."

His smile widened. "Hungry? Thirsty?"

"Umm, no." What was he doing? He led her over to the couch and eased her down onto it. He took off his tuxedo jacket, tossed it over the back of a chair and sprawled casually beside her. He kicked off his shoes and propped his feet up on the stone hearth. His right arm stretched out across the back of the sofa toward her, and with his left hand, he nursed his whiskey.

Perplexed, she propped her bare feet up beside his.

"Nice toes," he commented.

She wiggled the digits in question, enjoying the little flowers painted on her freshly manicured toes. They even had a tiny crystal glued in the center of each flower. They *were* cute. "Foot fetish?" she asked conversationally.

He laughed quietly. "Not especially. But I confess to enjoying every part of a woman. Fascinating creatures, you are."

The fire hissed quietly, and the dance of flames between the logs soothed her.

"So how did your first day as a senator go?" he asked.

"Not too bad, considering. No one has tried to kill me yet, and I was only partially flayed alive at that party."

"I'm sorry about that. I shouldn't have left you alone. I knew they'd jump you, but I didn't think they'd go for the jugular so fast. Vicious bunch of hyenas."

"Can I quote you on that?"

"Absolutely. What's on your agenda for tomorrow?"

She studied him quizzically. "Why do you ask?"

"Far be it for me to tell you what to do…" he trailed off.

"Go ahead."

"You might want to take a look at the candidates to fill your father's slot in the upcoming election."

"Do you have a favorite?"

He shrugged evasively.

She turned to face him. "Who do you like?"

"Your father's opponent. I've donated a fair bit of money to his campaign."

She laughed, genuinely amused. "I should've known."

"You're not mad at me?"

It was her turn to shrug. "It's just politics. For all I know, I may endorse the guy, too."

Gabe stared, shocked. "You'd turn on your father's political party?"

"If I don't like their platform, I will."

"And I thought I was a rebel. Your father created a monster when he gave you his job."

"I've spent my whole life living in his shadow. I'm sick and tired of it. I'm stepping out into the light."

He reached up to smooth a strand of hair back from her cheek. "Just be careful, okay? Life in the spotlight can get rough."

"What do you mean?"

"Not only does everyone see the good things you do, but your mistakes are out there for the whole world to see. It takes a tough hide to deal with the negative stuff that comes with fame."

"You mean like crazy stalkers breaking into your home?" she asked soberly.

"Among other things. The press delights in crucifying public figures."

"I believe I got that memo already," she replied drily.

He sighed, his fingers trailing through the ends of her hair. "I suppose you're more prepared than most for the storm that's headed your way. You've watched your father live in it for years." He laid his palm at the base of her neck as if contemplating the pulse fluttering there beneath his touch. He added reflectively, "Although I suppose you've been caught in the edges of that storm long enough to know what you're getting into, don't you? You're so much stronger than you look."

She tilted her head. "Do I come across as weak? A victim?"

He frowned, his hand going still on her skin. "Why do you ask that?"

"I read online that women who are raped often give off signals that they're weak and would make easy victims."

"Christ, Will. The bastard wouldn't even let you talk to a live counselor?" Gabe's voice was abruptly harsh. Furious. She didn't need to ask which bastard he was referring to. That would be John Merris.

"It's okay. I read up on it. I understand how I feel and why I feel that way. And I know what I have to do to put it behind me. I'll be okay, no problem."

Gabe's jaw rippled, and there was abruptly a faint tremor in the hand on her neck. "It's not that easy, Willa. This is going to take time. I swear, I'd kill him myself if he was still alive."

She put a soothing hand on his cheek, forcing him to open his tightly shut eyes and look at her. "Gabe. I appreciate your protective urges. But I'm a grown-up. I can take care of myself."

"Like when that guy broke in to your mom's house? Or when the police wouldn't come to your place last night?" he snapped.

Her hand fell into her lap. Was he right? Was she doomed to be taken advantage of and picked on for the rest of her life because she was too wimpy and afraid to stand up for herself? Would she always have to depend on other people to charge in to her rescue when she got in over her head?

Big hands came up to either side of her face. Tilted her unwilling gaze up to meet the color of the deepest, most mysterious forest. "I'm sorry. I just worry about you. I want everything in your life to be safe and wonderful and perfect."

A frown knit her brows. "But why? I'm nothing to you."

He leaned forward slowly, his gaze never leaving hers. His voice was a bare whisper of sound across her skin. "Because I've wanted to make love to you since you were a teenager."

She inhaled in sharp surprise, but the gasp was cut off by his lips touching hers. His mouth was warm and resilient, featherlight against hers, a mere brush of sensation.

"Really?" she whispered.

"I thought I was a pervert for lusting after you, barely legal." His lips brushed across hers again. "You were like a newborn colt, all long legs and the promise of elegance to come. The beauty you have now was all there, but just starting to unfold. It was mesmerizing."

"But you always called me those stupid kid names."

He laughed against her lips, a warm breath of whiskey into her mouth that tasted so good she went weak at the knees. "I did that to remind myself that you were way too young for me."

"I wanted you, too," she confessed softly.

"I know. That's why I had to work so hard to stay away from you. I was the adult. It was my responsibility to do the right thing by you."

She drew back slightly to stare up at him. He'd been looking out for her all those years ago? "I had no idea…."

"Of course not. I didn't want you to know."

She tilted her head forward, resting her forehead against his chin. "If only I'd known."

"What would you have done? Defied your father? Run away from home to sleep with me? Ruined your reputation and your life for me? I couldn't let you do that, Will. You were destined for bigger things than a kid from the wrong side of the tracks."

"Do you really think I'm such a snob?"

He kissed her forehead, her temple, her cheekbone. "I think you're a miracle."

How could she not melt a little at that? Her arms went around his neck and she scooted forward until she was practically sitting in his lap. His hand plunged into her hair, drawing her up against him as he really kissed her then.

His lips were firm and confident, possessing her mouth completely. He surged up over her, drawing her the rest of the way into his lap. His hand slid under her hair and started a long, slow journey down her bare back. Shivers radiated outward from his palm as it counted her vertebrae one by one.

He reached the small of her back, but his hand didn't stop. Lower, and lower still, his fingers moved, easing inside the seam of her dress. She moaned a little as his finger hooked in the edge of the skimpy thong the sales lady had sworn was the only lingerie she could wear under this gown. A single finger slipped into the upper cleft of her buttocks, and she all but came undone then and there.

Her entire body went languid and warm, flowing

against him like sun-drenched honey. She kissed the side of his neck, groaning as his finger retreated and then advanced once more.

"Are you okay?" he asked carefully.

"Mmm-hmm," she murmured against his collarbone.

"Need more time?"

She blinked her eyes open, struggling to focus on his face through the haze of lust enveloping her. He looked…worried. Cautious. *Crap.* She didn't want cautious.

"Gabe, there is something I do need."

His hands retreated from her body instantly. "Anything."

"I need you to forget for a while what's happened to me in my recent past. If you treat me like I'm psychologically damaged and am going to break if you take the slightest misstep, how am I going to put that out of my mind?"

He started to open his mouth, but she talked quickly to get out what she had to say before she lost her courage. "I need you to make love to me like I'm a real woman. Like you want me. I need you not to hold back. Ravish me. Take everything you want from me. Show me what it means to be your woman."

He looked positively thunderstruck. "Are you sure?" he choked out.

"I've never been more sure of anything in my life." She'd also never been more scared. This was it. She was going for everything she'd ever imagined getting from him. Reaching for her dream. *Please, please, let him not freak out and run screaming from me.*

By infinitesimally slow degrees, a smile formed on his lovely mouth and spread until it encompassed his entire face. His eyes glowed hotly, and his jaw rippled with sudden tension. "All right, then," he breathed.

Her heart leaped into her throat. She had no idea what she'd just unleashed, and she was a little intimidated at the notion of finding out, but she'd already jumped off the cliff and was in free fall now. She might as well enjoy the flight.

"Now, where were we?" she said softly. She leaned forward to kiss the taut muscles of his neck, and let her palms slide up the contours of his chest under the fine linen of his shirt. She raised up to nibble his earlobe and swirl her tongue around his ear while she got to work on the collar studs of his shirt.

Cuff links and studs fell with metallic clinks to the floor and she peeled his shirt away with reverence as she unveiled a gorgeous display of pecs and abs. The man was in stellar shape. He must work out for hours and hours each week to have built a physique like that.

"Good grief, you're amazing," she mumbled against his collarbone as she leaned forward to taste all that delicious brawn.

"You ain't seen nothin' yet," he muttered.

She laughed against his skin, pushing him back onto the cushions so she could explore him more thoroughly. To his credit, he was in no rush and let her take her time learning the feel of his smooth, tanned skin and hard muscles. The man had no body fat. A network of veins lay just beneath his skin, testament to how fit he was. He might not have the bulk of a hardcore body builder, but he certainly had the definition of one.

"Talk to me, Willa. What are you thinking and feeling right now?"

Surprised by the question, she chuckled ruefully.

"I'm trying hard not to think about how unworthy I am of a man like you. You're a freaking god."

That brought him up off the cushions, reversing their positions quickly until she was pressed deep into the leather sofa and he loomed over her. "I hate to be the one to break the news, but you're breathtaking. You may have hidden behind those old lady suits and drab makeup all these years, but the butterfly has broken free of her cocoon, baby."

She smiled up at him skeptically. If lavishly complimenting the women he was making love to was part of his arsenal, far be it for her to disagree with him. She had told him not to hold back, after all. And he did make her feel kind of pretty.

He slid off the sofa, kneeling beside her as his hands and mouth wandered over smooth copper satin. His mouth closed on the peak of her breast through the skimpy fabric. She arched up into him, shocked at how violently aroused she was when he nipped at her flesh through the gown. It teetered right on the edge between pleasure and pain. For just a moment a bolt of fear pierced her desire, but then a single thought washed through her. *This is Gabe. I'm safe.* She relaxed once more and let the lust he provoked rage through her, unchecked.

She reached for him to return the favor, but his fingers snagged hers and he pulled her hands high up over her head, her arms outstretched. "Lay the backs of your hands on the arm of the couch, baby. And don't move them. Keep them there. Understand?"

She nodded, too aroused to trust her voice. And as his hands skimmed down her body to cup her privates, she began to understand. The slit in her skirt gave his hot hand convenient access to the juncture of her thighs.

He simultaneously kissed her into oblivion and slipped his hand between her legs, which were too weak with desire to do anything but give way beneath his touch.

Slipping under the skimpy lace thong, his fingers played upon her raging desire like a concert piano, and then she fully understood his order not to move her hands. She writhed beneath his touch, trapped by her promise, helpless to stop the need ripping through her and possessing no will to stop it, anyway.

He lifted her hips briefly to push her satin skirt up and out of the way, baring her entire lower body to him. Self-conscious, she squirmed, but he merely pushed her thighs apart and leaned forward to kiss her more intimately than anyone ever had before. His mouth was warm and wet and drove her completely out of her mind. Whatever embarrassment she'd felt was incinerated by the heat he generated deep within her desperately clenching body.

"Let it go for me," he muttered against her throbbing flesh. His tongue swirled across her, and she lurched in shock as her entire body clenched and then exploded with an electric tingle that shot from her core to every extremity on a violent spasm of pleasure. *What in the world was that?* Holy cow. Was *that* what all the fuss was about? How—in her admittedly not that frequent sexual encounters over the years—had she missed *that*?

"Wow," she gasped. "Do that again!"

Gabe laughed against her inner thigh. "My pleasure, ma'am." His mouth closed on her again, and in mere seconds, her swollen flesh was tightening, the explosion building deep within her, growing, growing, until she cried out her release on a shudder of ecstasy that swept through her like chain lightning. She fell back against the leather, panting.

"Still with me?" Gabe asked against her belly.

"Coming back down to earth slowly," she replied, more than a little dazed.

"Mmm. That's how I like my women."

"Boneless and stunned?"

"Stunned?" he questioned.

"I've never, umm, well, just wow," she mumbled, abruptly embarrassed at how green she really was at this sex stuff.

"Never done that or never reacted like that?" he asked, lifting up on one elbow beside her to look down at her.

Her face exploded into fiery heat that could only be the mother of all blushes. "Neither," she confessed.

"That was your first orgasm?" he exclaimed.

She squeezed her eyes shut in mortification. If possible, her face heated up a few more degrees Kelvin.

And then his mouth was on her forehead, kissing her face all over as his fingertips caressed her body lightly through the satin gown. "Wanna do it again?" he murmured against the corner of her mouth.

"Yes!" she blurted.

He laughed richly. "You women have all the luck. You get to have as many of those as you want until you fall unconscious of exhaustion."

She couldn't help but reply, "That sounds absolutely amazing."

He laughed again. "Sex till complete exhaustion it is."

He pushed up off the sofa and reached down for her hands, still plastered to the arm of his sofa. He lifted her to her feet, and she was shocked at how wobbly her legs were. His hands took bunches of satin at her hips and raised the gown up over her head, blatantly skimming his palms over her curves as he went.

He stepped back for a moment to stare at her standing there in just the thong. With a smile, he moved close once more to hook a finger under the lingerie and whisk it down her body, as well.

"Better," he murmured. "The firelight looks even sexier than that dress on your skin."

And with those words, he banished any shame or self-consciousness she might have been feeling. He was still wearing his tuxedo trousers, with a satin stripe down their sides, emphasizing the length and power of his thighs. She reached for his waistband and he grinned down at her as she hooked both pants and briefs and stripped them off him.

He was more than ready for her and she, too, stepped back to take a long look at him. The firelight made him look like a savage, strong and wild and untamed. And yet, he was beautiful, too. Someone ought to carve a statue of him and put it in a museum.

"You okay?" he murmured.

She gazed up into his eyes. "I'm fine. I keep telling you I feel perfectly safe with you."

"Maybe you shouldn't," he muttered half under his breath.

"Why not?"

He looked over his shoulder into the fire before admitting, "Because of some of the things I want to do to you, Miss Merris."

"Show me?"

His gaze snapped back to hers, blazing more brightly than the fire. "Are you sure?"

"You promised to make me go unconscious of exhaustion," she reminded him.

Who knew a gaze so dark could burn so bright? It seared into her, promising exhaustion and more. He stepped forward, swept her into his arms, and burned the night down around her.

Willa woke to a weight across her middle. Even in sleep, Gabe had a possessive árm thrown across her, claiming her as his. She took in the morning light in his bedroom, which was as rustic and comfortable as the rest of the bungalow. Funny how this place was as much a part of Gabe as his high-tech condo in Dallas.

She took inventory of her body, which felt unfamiliar to her. She'd had no idea it was capable of the excesses of pleasure to which Gabe had brought it last night. This morning she felt limp. A little achy here and there, but overall, glorious. No wonder women raved about him in the bedroom. Not that she planned to add to the gossip about him any time soon.

What the other women had failed to mention was how sweet and funny and considerate he could also be. Yes, he'd demanded everything she had to give to him and had not allowed her to hide any part of herself from him. But he'd never made her feel anything other than special and beautiful and sexy. He'd fundamentally changed how she viewed herself. Her body. Her sensuality. For the first time in her life, she felt like a woman.

He stirred, his arm tightening around her, pulling her closer against his side. His mouth moved lazily in her hair. "Morning," he mumbled.

She turned into him, looping her arms around his neck. "Good morning, indeed," she murmured back.

His eyes opened and a smile gleamed in them. "You're even more beautiful the morning after. Women the planet over would kill to look like you with no makeup on, and their hair tousled around them like that."

She smiled up at him with a new confidence she'd never had before. Not until Gabe Dawson had loved her. "I bet you say that to all the girls."

His visage went surprisingly serious. "Actually, I've never said that to a woman before. And I meant it when I said it to you."

Warmth unfolded low in her belly that had nothing to do with lust. "You really are a special man. Thank you so much for last night."

A crack of laughter escaped him. "Honey, that's my line. I'm the one who should be thanking you. Hell, I should be doing it on bended knee with dozens of roses in my arms."

"I prefer gardenias. Roses are too sweet and over-whelming for me."

"Duly noted." He kissed the tip of her nose and rolled over onto his back, taking her with him by virtue of his arm around her shoulders. "What shall we do today?" he asked reflectively.

"Don't you have an empire to run?"

He shrugged beneath her ear. "It'll run itself for a few days."

Since when did he blow off his company for a woman? The way she heard it, he took business calls in the middle of sex. Although, having experienced his total focus firsthand, she had to question the quality of the woman's lovemaking who'd reported that salacious little tidbit about him. Nonetheless, he had a solid repu-tation as a workaholic.

She was definitely on board with the notion of spend-ing the day in bed with him. She couldn't get enough of him. And not just the sex. Just being skin-to-skin with him like this renewed her spirit. Healed her wounded soul. She felt like a woman again, cherished and whole. They lay there for several minutes of relaxed quiet, which was another thing she loved about him. He didn't feel a compulsion to fill the silences with meaningless noise.

But then the ring of a telephone shattered the quiet. He reached out to pick up his cell phone and look at the incoming number. He swore quietly and put the phone to his ear. "Dawson, here."

She snuggled against his side, relishing his heat and strength as his fingers twined lazily in her hair. All of a sudden, his entire body tensed.

"What?" he burst out. "When?" A pause. "I'll be there in ten minutes."

She sat up in alarm beside him. "What's wrong?"

"The police got a video of my wife."

His wife. He called Melinda his wife. Not his exwife. Willa rolled away from him and climbed out of his bed hastily, all but running for the living room and the scanty protection of her clothing. *He'd called her his wife.*

Chapter 11

Gabe leaped into jeans and a shirt and was relieved to see Willa dressed in her gown and waiting by the door when he came out of his bedroom.

"I'll drop you off at your place on my way to the police station," he told her.

She nodded, and followed obediently as he rushed out the front door. He opened her door impatiently, nearly slamming it on her skirt in his haste. The short ride to her house was silent.

He pulled up to the curb out front and she said only, "I hope Melinda's all right."

"Me, too," he bit out.

He peeled away from the curb without watching Willa to her front door. It was nine in the morning, after all. The bad guys were only coming after her at night.

Thankfully, Vengeance was a small town and no destination was more than a few minutes away. He pulled up outside the police department and was not surprised to see reporters camped out on the front steps. If he were the new sheriff, his first order of business would be to plug the leak in the Vengeance police force.

Girding himself to face the grilling, he stepped out of his Escalade and was immediately assaulted by a chorus of shouted questions.

He raised his voice to be heard over the cacophony. "I don't know anything. I have no comment, and I'm sure you already know as much or more than I do." That brought a few dry chuckles from the press. Yup, definitely an informant in the building.

He elbowed aside a newcomer to the Vengeance coverage who hadn't learned to stay the hell out of his way yet, and jogged up the steps to city hall and the police department inside.

Officer Radebaugh met him just inside the door. The young cop struck him as clumsy but well-meaning, and not entirely incompetent at his job. Gabe nodded at the officer. "How's Melinda? How much does the kidnapper want?"

"There's no ransom demand. Would you like to see the video?"

Duh. "Of course."

"We've got a video set up in the conference room. An analyst from the FBI is looking at it now."

Gabe followed the cop down a short hall to a dim room dominated by a long conference table, disordered chairs and an old-fashioned roll-down screen at one end of the room. A laptop projected a currently still image up on the wall. Gabe stopped, shocked.

Melinda sat in a wooden chair, her short blond hair disheveled, her arms restrained behind her back in some unseen manner. Although her ankles weren't visible, her posture indicated that they were tied to the chair, as well. The collar of her blouse was torn, and she looked haggard. A lurid bruise lit up her left eye. She looked like she hadn't bathed or slept in days.

Radebaugh spoke from behind Gabe. "This is Professor Grayson's husband."

An attractive brunette woman looked up briefly from her contemplation of the still image, then went right back to her study. "I'm Agent Delaney. Play the video from the beginning, Green," the woman ordered absently.

Deputy Green made a face at the woman's back as he hit a button on the laptop sitting in front of him on the table.

Gabe watched the video of Melinda intently. Her voice was as assertive as ever as she said, or maybe read, "My name is Melinda Grayson. I am alive and being held against my will. I am unharmed as of now, and as long as the police call off their search for me, I will remain that way. Further instructions will be forthcoming that, if followed to the letter, will ultimately result in my release."

The video stopped.

"That's it?" Gabe exclaimed.

"Yup," Radebaugh answered.

The FBI analyst turned abruptly. "Would you say the syntax of that speech was similar to your wife's typical patterns of sentence construction and inflection?"

Gabe blinked, startled at the question. "Are you asking if that sounded like Melinda?"

"Yes," Agent Delaney replied impatiently.

He considered it briefly. "That sounded exactly like Melinda. If someone told her to say that she was unharmed and instructions would follow, that would be pretty much exactly how she would say it."

The analyst tapped a front tooth with a long, manicured fingernail. "Then why the explicit statement that she is being held against her will? It's a strange assertion to add into this sort of communication. Of course she's being held against her will. We can see that she's tied to a chair." Delaney frowned and then added, "Dr. Grayson strikes me as an extremely intelligent person who takes pride in her intellect."

"You would be correct," Gabe replied drily.

"Then it would not be her style to make such a blatantly obvious observation?" the analyst asked tersely.

"She's generally scornful of people who state the obvious," Gabe answered, frowning. Now that the agent mentioned it, that had been a weird thing for Melinda to say.

"Watch it again, Mr. Grayson. Does anything else stand out to you?"

He would have corrected Agent Delaney's mistake about his name, but the tape started to play again. He perched on the edge of the conference table to watch it more closely.

"Again, please," he murmured.

After about three more times through it, the analyst asked, "Anything?"

"Well," he answered slowly, "it seems a little strange how forceful she sounds. Don't get me wrong. She's nothing if not an assertive woman. But I would have expected her to sound a little more...cowed...by the experience of being kidnapped and held against her will. She's not accustomed to much of anything happening against her will."

Of course, maybe he'd been spending too much time

around sweet, gentle Willa Merris. By comparison, Melinda was about as soft and feminine as a Mack Truck. As soon as the thought crossed his mind, though, he felt bad about it. He shouldn't compare the two women. They were as different as night and day. And he owed Melinda a certain loyalty. They'd been married once, after all.

He added, "Maybe Melinda is playing some sort of head game with her captors. It would be her style to manipulate them as much as possible. Could she be signaling us as to what she's doing?"

Lord knew Melinda had played plenty of head games with him during their short marriage. When he'd finally gotten wise and started calling her out on it, she'd poo-pooed his anger, saying it was part of her job as a sociologist to experiment on the people around her. They'd had quite a fight over it, as he recalled, with him insisting he didn't want to be her lab rat, and her railing that he was being oversensitive and childish.

Most of their fights had come down to that. He'd never been enough man for her, not smart enough, not mature enough, not intellectual enough to satisfy her. He'd spent their entire marriage feeling wholly inadequate, and scrambling to play catch up with the meteoric rise of her career.

Even now, when he was a billionaire for crying out loud, Melinda accused him of being a slave to the almighty dollar and of not having achieved anything of real importance. Not like her—author of multiple books, famous lecturer, professor, intellectual and sought-after commentator.

Agent Delaney tilted her head thoughtfully. "Does she have enough psychological training to attempt to manipulate her captor or captors?"

Gabe snorted. "The woman's brilliant. And her favorite hobby is messing with people."

"It's an interesting theory, Mr. Grayson."

Gabe pointedly ignored Deputy Green's smirk as the FBI agent called him by the wrong name again.

The woman distracted Gabe by asking, "You used the plural, captors, when referring to whoever kidnapped your wife. Why is that?"

"I just assumed..." he trailed off. "You'd have to know Melinda to understand. She's a formidable woman. The idea of a single person overwhelming her and kidnapping her just doesn't seem plausible. It would have to be several people."

"She's a fighter?" Delaney asked.

"That's one way to describe her," Gabe replied. "Combative. Aggressive. Self-confident to a fault. She wouldn't go down without a fight."

"And yet," the analyst commented speculatively, "not a thing was out of place in her home. Not a chair overturned, not a pencil on the floor. Nothing whatsoever to indicate that there was any kind of struggle."

Gabe nodded. "I know. That part baffles me, too. It makes no sense at all that someone just walked in, knocked her out and was able to drag her out of her home without leaving a single sign behind."

"Can you think of anyone she might have left home with willingly? Perhaps not realizing she was being kidnapped?" the agent pressed.

"I've been over this and over this with the police," Gabe answered on a sigh. "I can't think of anyone. But then, I don't know any of her students or colleagues. I'm fairly out of touch with her life these days."

"And why's that?"

Deputy Green snorted behind Gabe. *Jackass.* "Because we've been divorced for nearly ten years."

Agent Delaney, to her credit, looked chagrined. "My mistake. You seemed so invested in her safety when you came in here...." The woman turned back to the screen without finishing the observation. Uncomfortable silence filled the room.

Deputy Green commented snidely, "Guess we know who wore the pants in that relationship."

Gabe's jaw tightened until he thought he was going to crack a molar. He had no illusions that Melinda had tried to wear the pants in the marriage and that had been one of the reasons it broke up. He'd wanted a partnership with her, not to follow her around like a pet puppy.

But it wasn't as simple as walking away from her. She knew exactly how to get her hooks into people, and she'd buried hers deep in his psyche. Hell, it was part of why he refused to remarry. He never wanted to be that vulnerable to—or victimized by—another human being again.

Gabe turned his back on Green and murmured to Officer Radebaugh, "Keep me in the loop, okay?"

"Of course," the young officer replied, startled.

Gabe beat a retreat before he put his fist through Deputy Green's smirk.

He scowled his way through the reporters who, for once, seemed to catch a clue to leave him the hell alone. Either that, or their source inside the police station was so good, they didn't need to bother him for details about Melinda's tape.

When he got home, he took an overdue shower, which finally cooled down his temper. He wasn't normally a particularly volatile person, but with both Willa and Melinda under serious threat, the strain had put him on edge.

Melinda had insisted that they have an amicable divorce, which in her world meant the two of them stayed in touch and occasionally went out to some event or other together. Given how vicious she could turn in an instant, it was easier to go out with her a few times a year than to make an active enemy of her.

And it wasn't like he'd been a perfect husband. He'd been the one to go haring off to the far corners of the world in search of oil. She might have traveled a lot, but at least she'd stayed mostly on the same continent. Although truth be told, it was easy to be in the same room with Melinda and feel a million miles away from her. When she was working on an academic project, she'd never had time or attention for anything or anyone else.

He made himself a bite to eat, and strolled out into his living room at loose ends since he'd planned to spend the day with Willa. But the phone call from the police had put a kink in that plan. He called her, but Willa's cell phone went immediately to voice mail.

He sighed. As a senator, she might not necessarily pick up her own messages. Hence, he left a generic message thanking her for last night and hoping they could do it again soon. It wasn't the one he'd have liked to leave for her, telling her that she'd blown him away, he couldn't get enough of her and would she please consent to spending many, many nights in his bed forthwith.

He watched the news, returned a few phone calls from the office and found himself pacing his living room impatiently in under an hour. He tried Willa's number again. Still no answer. Damn. Sometimes he really hated dating busy women with careers that took precedence over him.

His rational self rolled its eyes at his selfishness, but his emotional side acknowledged that Melinda had done a number on him that he was now taking out on Willa. It wasn't Will's fault she'd been named to her father's senate seat.

He would like to call again, but he didn't want to make her feel like he was stalking her. She'd already had one too many creeps in her life. He glanced at his watch, frustrated. How much longer until he could reasonably call her again?

Willa stared at her cell phone in dismay. That was the fifth call today from Gabe. He was now calling her every hour on the hour, and his messages were getting steadily more urgent and taking on a tone of worry for her safety. She couldn't avoid him forever, although she'd really love to. When Louise called, a strange note in her voice, and asked if Willa could swing by the big house, she jumped on the request.

The mansion was in an uproar when she arrived. Her mother was sobbing at the kitchen table, Louise was hovering over Minnie and wringing her hands, Louise's son, Marcus, was striding around the garden with a shotgun and George was nowhere to be seen.

Willa couldn't get a straight answer out of either of the women in the kitchen as to what was going on, other than it was just horrible and who would do such a thing? At a loss, Willa headed out for the backyard. Marcus wasn't in view, but she caught sight of George's broad-brimmed straw hat and headed for it.

"What's going on?" she asked the older man.

"Never seen anything like it, ma'am. Dead animals keep showing up in the garden. First it was that rabbit. Then a cat, and today a deer. All of them have their heads cut off. Or more accurately, torn off."

"Have you called the police?" Willa gasped.

"They think it's a bobcat or a coyote."

"A coyote wouldn't take down a deer and tear its head off."

"That's what I told the cops, but they wouldn't listen to me. City slickers don't know nuthin' about coyotes. It would take a pack of 'em to bring down a buck, and they'd eat it if they killed it. And there wasn't a single mark on the rest of the carcass. Coyote would've hamstrung something big like that. Torn out its throat maybe, but not taken its entire head."

A chill crept up Willa's spine and icy goose bumps raised on her arms. Who on earth would kill animals in such a gruesome fashion, not to mention dump them in her mother's garden? Minnie didn't have any enemies. It had to be directed at her father or her. Except John Merris was dead. *Which left...*Willa gulped...*her.*

A cackle escaped while looking through the lenses of the high-powered binoculars. Willa Merris looked worried. She was good and scared now, wasn't she? Bitch. The Merrises were done messing with other people. High time they learned what it felt like when someone else played games with their lives. Come after other people, would they? Set up other folks, would they?

Suffering. Willa Merris needed to suffer pain. And fear. No, she needed to feel terror. She'd scream with it. Lust surged at the thought of her screaming. Tie her up. But no gag—gotta hear the bitch scream. A thin blade, maybe. Sharp. Lots of little cuts. Tiny rivers of blood striping her white skin. Pretty pattern. Ahh, the agony. The panic. The sweet smell of it.

An orgasm exploded without warning and practically knocked the binoculars loose. Dammit! Loss of control like that was bad. Bitch would pay for that, too. She'd pay for everything....

For once, Willa was grateful for the mini-pharmacy on the nightstand beside her mother's bed. It had taken plentiful dosing with tranquilizers and sleeping pills to get her mother calmed down and resting quietly. Apparently, it had been Minnie who discovered the mutilated deer in her garden, and the shock had been too much for her already fragile state of mind.

Enough was enough. Willa called a private security company in Dallas, and hired a team of guards to come out to the mansion immediately. The half-dozen men who showed up in an hour were big, quiet and competent-looking. They swept the entire property, established a security perimeter—whatever that was— and commenced setting up cameras, motion detectors and who knew what else in and around the house.

They also advised Willa to stay in the mansion until further notice. Something to do with minimizing exposure and consolidating assets. She wasn't thrilled to be back in the mansion, but she was relieved to have a tall, muscular bodyguard nearby at all times. Her security and her mother's were restored. If only Gabe Dawson was so easy to deal with.

He'd continued to call every hour on the hour, but there was no way she was talking to him. His wife, indeed. If he was still that invested in Melinda Grayson, the two of them were welcome to each other. She admitted to herself reluctantly that she might be hiding behind her anger to mask the hurt she actually felt at being second-best to his ex-wife. No wonder all the women who slept with Gabe declared him unmarriageable material. They were right.

And she was a big ol' fool. She'd known what kind of man he was when she fell into his bed, and she'd deluded herself into thinking they could have more. But he was one tiger who wasn't about to change his stripes for anybody. Her best bet was to cut her losses and move on.

But move on to what? Who else would ever measure up to him? She'd been sweet on him forever. If she was being honest with herself, she would admit that she'd measured every guy she'd ever dated against him. And they'd all come up lacking. It was one of the main reasons why she'd never found a guy she could really commit to emotionally. None of them were Gabe.

Except now that she'd had him, however briefly, it was time to accept that having no man at all was better than having Gabe Dawson.

Thankfully, the dossiers on all the candidates in the upcoming elections that she'd asked her father's—her—staff in Washington to compile came across the fax in her father's office shortly after dinner. She desperately needed the distraction, but felt a little guilty at the size of the stack that finally printed out. The staff had to have worked frantically all day to have pulled so much information together so fast. She emailed them a message of heartfelt thanks for their hard work and settled down in the library to read the briefings.

A commotion at the front door around ten o'clock interrupted her concentration as she sorted the candidates into possible-yes, undecided and definite-no piles. One of the bodyguards stuck his head into the room. "Guy at the door named Gabe Dawson. Says he's your boyfriend. Wants to see you."

"Tell him I'm not available."

"Roger, ma'am." The guy backed out and closed the door behind him.

Wow. That had been easy. She should keep a couple of giant bouncer types around more often to get rid of people she didn't want to deal with.

It didn't take long for her cell phone to ring. She didn't even bother looking at it. She knew who was calling. Gabe. The phone even sounded angry as it rang. She let his call go to voice mail before she reluctantly listened to what he had to say.

"Seriously, Willa? You're going to hide behind a bunch of thugs? What the hell did I do to you? I thought we had something great going. But I guess I was wrong." The earlier worry was gone from his voice, replaced by cold fury.

Remorse speared through her. Had she overreacted this morning? Had he merely spoken thoughtlessly in his worry for his ex-wife? It wasn't a bad thing that he still cared about Melinda's safety, was it? Maybe all it meant was that he was a decent man who would worry about anyone in the position Melinda was in. For all Willa knew, Gabe was the closest thing to family Melinda had.

Okay, she felt bad now for siccing the bodyguards on Gabe. But the fact remained, he wasn't a marrying kind of man and never would be. Sleeping with him had been great. Epic, in fact. But at the end of the day, she wanted more. And more was something Gabe Dawson couldn't and wouldn't give her.

Chapter 12

Willa narrowed her choices for possible candidates to endorse down to two men. But without meeting them and personally gauging their ethics and morals, she wasn't willing to throw the powerful Merris name behind either man. Those cynical letters on her father's computer fresh in her mind, she was determined not to send a business-as-usual politician to Washington if she could help it.

She had to admit that having a congressional staff was handy. Amber assured her it would be no problem to set up meetings with the two candidates. In fact, the girl gently assured Willa both men would leap at the chance to speak with her. She was Senator Merris now. She kept forgetting.

The first candidate, a man named Kevin Mc Conahhay, stopped by the mansion on his way to a campaign appearance in Denton. She winced as his garishly painted campaign bus pulled up in front of the Merris mansion. People were going to assume she'd already endorsed the guy. His politics were actually fairly close to her father's, although McConahhay was spending more time talking about himself than any actual issues.

From the moment he rounded the corner into the library, she didn't like the guy. It didn't help matters that his first words were a booming, "So here's the little lady keeping my seat in Washington warm for me."

He was a good ol' boy all the way. Not that all good ol' boys were all bad. But this one left a decidedly sour taste in her mouth. He just assumed that, as the candidate her father's party had hastily chosen to replace John Merris, her endorsement was in the bag. He talked so much about himself and his extensive connections to the oil industry that he barely allowed her to get a word in edgewise. No question about it, he would operate in Washington the exact same way her father had—playing lobbyists off against each other, trading favors under the table and getting as rich as possible while in office.

The second candidate, a man named Thomas Montoya, was in Dallas campaigning, and rightfully surprised that the daughter of his political rival was calling him. He immediately invited her to attend a fund-raising dinner he was having tonight. Wary of her presence being construed as an endorsement, she only agreed to meet him for coffee before the meal. But the fact that he didn't once refer to her as a little lady went into the definite plus column for him.

She dressed in the power suit the folks at Nieman Marcus had fixed her up with, and two of the security men drove her down to Dallas in a big black SUV that she had no doubt was armored and bulletproof. It would have been cool if she didn't actually need the protection.

Montoya's fund-raiser was in a big hotel downtown. Her ride pulled up at the loading dock out back, and one of the guards whisked her into a thoroughly unglamorous service elevator for the ride to the twentieth floor where Montoya was apparently waiting for her.

She stepped into a generic hotel suite, where Montoya, and a lovely but quiet woman who turned out to be his wife, stood and introduced themselves. Willa was struck by how the wife immediately faded into the woodwork, serving coffee with a smile, murmuring a few pleasantries and then moving to the far end of the room.

A few weeks ago, that had been her. Willa shuddered in recollection at how it had felt to have people constantly looking right through her as if she wasn't there. She made a point of looking the wife in the eye and speaking directly to her. The wife smiled with a gratitude that broke Willa's heart. It was a hard life being the significant other of a politician.

She turned her attention to Montoya. He was quiet and thoughtful, clearly versed in the issues and highly intelligent. But the clincher for her was his response when she commented, "I have to say, my fear with you is that the special-interest groups will eat you alive when you get to Washington."

Quiet steel entered Montoya's voice and his eyes flashed with determination. "Unless we send people to Washington who are willing to say no to the same old way of doing business, who are willing to vote against lining their own pockets, who are willing *not* to be re-elected, how will we ever fix the problem?"

She laughed ruefully. "You're singing to the choir, Tom. So you're truly willing to be a one-term senator?"

"I fully expect to be a one-termer. I have a successful law practice back here in Texas, and frankly, it's going to be a real inconvenience to my firm and my family for me to spend six years in Washington."

"Well, Tom, you've got my endorsement. How would your campaign manager like me to announce it?"

Montoya stared at her in shock. "But I was running against your father."

"And doing a fine job of it, too. He was scared stiff you were going to beat him." She shrugged. "I happen to agree with you. And I happen to believe in acting according to my conscience, not my father's."

"I'm honored to get your nod." He added wryly, "You're a brave woman. I wouldn't want to face the flak you're going to take for abandoning your father's party."

Now that he mentioned it, she supposed there would be hell to pay for switching sides, particularly at the last minute like this. Good thing she had that team of bruisers to protect her.

The campaign manager was jubilant, and suggested that Willa stay for the fund-raiser and announce her endorsement there. It made sense. The press would be there in force, as would many prominent and wealthy supporters of Montoya's.

Willa made a point of chatting with Mrs. Montoya, who turned out to be a highly educated intellectual in her own right, while they waited in the wings for the fund-raiser to begin, and the crowd to be whipped into a proper frenzy before Tom Montoya was introduced. Willa knew the drill well and ignored the roar of the crowd. Tom went out and the screams and chants grew deafening.

Then it was her turn to be introduced. The crowd went wild when she announced her endorsement. She sat down at the head table in the place of honor hastily arranged for her, and looked out across the room at a sea of dark, unrecognizable silhouettes. She couldn't see a thing with all the spotlights pointed at her. The meal passed in a fog.

Circulating in the crowd afterward was surreal. She was used to being the one who listened respectfully and nodded politely while everyone else talked, but tonight, people wanted to hear what she had to say. The main question was why the party switch? She eventually got her explanation down by rote and recited it pretty much automatically.

But then a voice came out of the sea of faces that shocked her into stillness.

"Tell me, Senator. Why did you feel obliged to wreck my life and ruin my reputation with your groundless accusations?"

She whipped around to face James Ward. His nostrils flared sharply as if he was incensed that she would dare to face him. A few days ago, she might have wilted and slunk away from him, but no more. She was done being the eternal wallflower and always backing down.

"What are you doing here?" she demanded.

"Supporting Tom Montoya's campaign."

He leaned in close to her and she flinched in spite of herself as his pupils expanded until his eyes were entirely black. He muttered menacingly, "You'd better drop those stupid charges. You're the one who looks crazy, not me."

She looked crazy? He was the one who had turned into a maniac and attacked her!

His gaze raked up and down her scornfully, and his

voice dropped into an entirely creepy whisper. "Still playing the vestal virgin. We both know what a lie that is, don't we? Uppity bitch. Pretending to be better than everyone else…"

She reared back in horror, but ran into the impervious wall of tuxedoes around them. *Trapped.* She was trapped!

Her voice shaking, she inched back as far as the press of people around them would allow, and tried to reason with him. "James, this is not the time or place to talk about what happened. I'm sure both of our lawyers would advise not to speak to each other at all."

His shoulders hunched forward and his hands flexed and unflexed in angry fists. His entire body tensed as if he wanted desperately to spring at her in violence. "Afraid I'll get another shot at you? Afraid you'll like it too much? That everyone will find out just what a hot little slut you are—"

She cut him off sharply. "You're never getting another shot at me, James. Do you hear me? *Never.*" She backed away a few more steps, breathing hard, her limbs begging her to turn and run for her life.

Apparently, their little confrontation was finally drawing the attention of the people around them. Or maybe it was just that Willa was backing into total strangers and tromping on their feet with total disregard. Out of the corner of her eye, she noted a commotion headed their way. Crud. She was about to fan the flames of scandal already surrounding her and James Ward. Intense need to avoid a press fiasco and diffuse this confrontation warred with her instinct to confront this bastard and not let him cow her any longer.

James shook his head briefly and stood up straighter, relaxing both fists and his aggressive posture. The transformation was shocking. He was suddenly back to being the charming, urbane scion of Dallas society that everyone knew and loved.

"Willa. I have to say I'm shocked to see you here," he said conversationally. "What do I have to say to convince you to drop those ridiculous charges against me? We both know nothing happened that night."

The gall of the man! As soon as he knew he had an audience, he completely changed his tune! The ease and completeness with which he transformed was chilling. If he could turn on the charm like that in court, she was in big trouble. What jury would believe that this pleasant, attractive man housed the monster she'd just glimpsed?

Belatedly, she ground out from behind clenched teeth, "You call rape and violent assault nothing?" She forced herself to look him in the eye and was stunned to see what looked like genuine confusion there. What had happened to the furious, threatening man of moments before?

Confused and more afraid than she'd been since the night of the assault, she said with disgust, "It took a week for the swelling in my face to go down, and longer for the bruises and other injuries to heal. And you dare to call that nothing?"

The crowd around them was jostling now. The gossips were no doubt angling closer to hear this juicy little exchange.

James spoke a little more loudly, no doubt for the benefit of the wagging ears around them. "I would never hit a woman. And I certainly would never force myself on one."

She was so shocked, a feather could have knocked her over. The bastard actually sounded sincere. And that was when the fury came upon her. So angry she could hardly keep her fists still at her sides, she gritted out, "How long did it take you to perfect that injured innocent routine? Are you practicing it to deliver it to a jury?"

His wide blue eyes gazed at her, injured. "Willa, I would *never* lay a finger on you. Why would you make up such a horrible lie? What did I ever do to you? I only asked you out in the first place as a favor to your father. I wasn't interested in you in that way at all. Why in the world would you go to the police with a cockamamie tale that no one believes? Are you that desperate for attention? Maybe you should talk to someone, honey. A counselor or something."

The bright lights of a television camera crew were closing in on the two of them, and she had time only to grind out, "You and I both know what happened, and you know I'm telling the truth."

He had the nerve to look at her in what could only be described as utter bewilderment. If she didn't have firsthand memory of his attack, she might wonder herself if she hadn't lost her mind.

So that was how it was going to be, huh? She saw now exactly what his defense in front of a jury was going to be. He was going to paste on that wounded look and swear on a stack of bibles that he'd never touched her. Cold dread settled over her. He might just get away with it, too. His act really was convincing.

No surprise, Paula Craddock was the reporter in front of the camera when it pulled up beside the two of them. The woman looked back and forth at Willa and James Ward as eagerly as a dog begging for a bone. "Well, what have we here?" she drawled. "Lover's spat, perhaps?"

James took the initiative, turning those innocent blue eyes of his to the camera. "We were never lovers. I categorically deny ever laying a hand on this woman, let alone doing any of the things she has accused me of. My momma and daddy raised me never, ever to harm a woman."

"So, you're calling Miss Merris a liar?" Paula purred.

"As sad as it makes me to say it," James answered soberly, "I am."

The fist that shot out of the darkness beyond the camera's blinding light connected with Ward's jaw solidly, snapping his head back and laying the guy out flat on the floor. The camera light wobbled and then fell to the floor as something or someone jostled the cameraman in the eruption of chaos to follow. The camera light went off. Paula Craddock added to the chaos by yelling at her cameraman to get the damned film rolling because he was missing all the good stuff.

As the spotlight went dark, Willa abruptly was able to see Ward's attacker. Gabe Dawson stood there, flexing his right hand as he glared down at Ward on the floor. James struggled up to an elbow, and Gabe snarled, "Stay down unless you want me to break your jaw next time."

Ward subsided.

Willa's bodyguards muscled through the mob to her then, and just as she made eye contact with Gabe, her mouth opening to thank him for defending her honor like that, the two bodyguards each grabbed one of her elbows and practically lifted her off her feet. They hauled her out of the room at a near run and didn't stop until they'd rushed her through the hotel kitchen, out the loading dock and into the SUV, which promptly sped away from the hotel.

She didn't even get a chance to speak to Gabe, darn it. If only she'd known he would be here. Maybe she could have found him and apologized for overreacting yesterday. She supposed she shouldn't have been surprised that he had backed her father's opponent in the election.

Chagrin rolled through her that he had come to her rescue, even after she'd shunned him and acted like a jealous, immature idiot.

The SUV had made it about halfway back to Vengeance when she couldn't stand it any longer. She leaned forward and said to the driver, "Could you take me back to Dallas?"

"Back to the fund-raiser?" the guy exclaimed. "I can't recommend that, ma'am. The press will tear you up."

"Not back to the fund-raiser. To a private residence. A penthouse with crazy security."

If the driver knew who lived at the address she gave him, he made no comment on it. The SUV exited Hwy 35E and turned around. In a few minutes, the skyline of Dallas loomed in the distance like a beacon beckoning her home.

Showing up at Gabe's place unannounced could turn out disastrously. For all she knew, he might want nothing to do with her. She wouldn't blame him if he didn't. The anger in his voice message last night still rang in her ears.

But then, why would he punch James Ward tonight for calling her a liar? Did he or didn't he like her? She hated the confusion roiling in her gut. If nothing else, seeing Gabe tonight should clear that up one way or the other. She hoped.

The SUV pulled up in front of the posh apartment

building, and a sudden attack of nerves turned her gut to jelly. Sheesh. She wasn't some thirteen-year-old knocking on a boy's door for the first time. Although in point of fact, this was the first time she'd ever knocked on any male's front door. They had always come to her house to pick her up. She had definitely lived too sheltered a life, and it was high time to rectify that.

She pushed the button beside Gabe's nameplate in the lobby. *Please be home. Please be home.*

Without warning, a deep voice came out of the intercom. "Willa? What the hell are you doing here?"

"How did you know it was me?" she blurted, startled.

"Lobby cam."

Of course. This was his techno-toy place. "Can I come up? We need to talk."

"Do we?" he asked cryptically.

Was he going to make her beg? She supposed he had the right after she'd been such a jerk yesterday. But to have to apologize over the intercom, in front of her bodyguard…

A buzzer startled her. "Enter the number 4-9-2-7-5 on the key pad in the elevator and it'll give you access to the penthouse," Gabe directed.

"Up in a sec," she replied gratefully.

She turned to the bodyguard. "Would you freak out if I asked you to stay down here?"

"No, ma'am. I'm familiar with this building and its security system. You'll be safe. We'll wait in the car until you're ready to leave. If you decide to stay the night, text me and we'll take off. Just let us know what time you want a pickup tomorrow."

Thankfully, the arrival of the elevator saved her from having to answer that. Her face must be scarlet if the heat in her cheeks was any indication. The bodyguard stepped inside, looked around the conveyance briefly, and held the door impassively for her as she stepped inside and keyed in the code.

"Good night, ma'am," he said emotionlessly.

The guy said that like he expected her to spend the night. She did have to admit, the idea of making love with Gabe again made her breath come short and her heart pound disconcertingly.

The elevator ride was far too short as she tried to regain her composure and give herself a pep talk. No matter how many times she told herself this would be okay, she didn't believe it as she knocked timidly on Gabe's completely intimidating, stainless-steel front door.

Without warning, the door swung open beneath her knuckles, and Gabe loomed in front of her, scowling darkly. He gestured silently with the whiskey bottle in his left hand for her to enter the lion's den. She took a deep breath and stepped inside.

Chapter 13

Gabe didn't know whether to be relieved or infuriated that Willa had shown up on his doorstep like this. He'd planned to spend the evening tying on a good, old-fashioned drunk. To hell with everyone who said a guy shouldn't drink alone. Besides, he had plenty of ghosts to keep him company. The ghost of John Merris, the father he'd never had and whose standards he'd never quite managed to live up to. The ghost of Melinda, another person he'd never been quite good enough for.

What the hell did a man have to do to win their approval? He'd made a billion bucks with the sweat of his own brow, for God's sake. Wasn't that good enough for them? What the hell was the use of having all that money if it didn't impress anyone? Maybe he should give it all away. Maybe that would impress them.

He snorted as he eyed Willa's sexy little tush sashaying toward his living room ahead of him. John would call him a damned fool if he gave away his billions. Melinda might be momentarily impressed, but he knew all too well she wouldn't stay that way for long. She would probably bust his balls for not giving the money away to the right cause.

"Drink?" he asked Willa.

She perched on the edge of his sofa in her linen church-lady suit, straight out of the political fund-raiser fashion catalog. He much preferred the hot copper number from two nights ago. She hadn't looked like some damned virgin in the backless gown. But in this modest getup, he felt dirty for even contemplating sex with her.

Not to mention the damned outfit made her look about fourteen years old and playing dress-up in her mother's clothes. He had a flashback to when he'd first known her, and how guilty he'd felt about the lecherous thoughts she had inspired in him back then. Since when had he become a dirty old man? He had no business sleeping with someone her age. She ought to be out finding some nice young man her age to settle down with, not wasting her time with an old bastard like him.

"Are you drunk?" she asked when he stumbled on the edge of an area rug.

"Yes. Yes, I am."

She nodded knowingly. "Be careful. Whiskey makes for some interesting true confessions."

"Confess something to me so I'm not laying out my guts all by myself," he retorted.

"I've imagined doing some very kinky things with you in bed, over the years."

He stared disbelievingly, shocked out of his buzz. "No way."

"Way," she replied matter-of-factly. "I fantasized about sleeping with you pretty much all the way through high school. And truth be told, through college, too. You thoroughly messed up my social life."

Son of a— Who'd have guessed? Sweet little Willa Merris had harbored naughty thoughts of an older man? Tsk, tsk.

"Drink?" he asked her.

"No, thanks." She said that like she could use a little liquid courage. But hey. If she didn't want it, that was her call.

He made his way to the wet bar where he pulled out a double old-fashioned glass, stabbed it into the ice maker and poured a few fingers of whiskey over the ice. Damned women. Made a man drink politely. Out of a glass instead of straight out of the bottle. He carried his whiskey over to the sofas and sank down cautiously on the one opposite Willa.

"Why are you here?" he asked baldly. He winced at the lack of subtlety in his voice. If he wanted to remain rational, he'd probably had enough to drink.

"To apologize for yesterday. For refusing to take your calls. I overreacted."

"To what?"

"To you calling Melinda your wife."

He frowned, confused. *Huh?* "I'm drawing a blank here. Help me out. What the hell are you talking about?"

"When the police called to tell you they had a video, you called her your wife. Not your ex-wife."

He rolled his eyes. "That's what had your panties in a wad?" he exclaimed. "The cop on the phone called Melinda my wife and it was easier not to bother correcting him. The FBI analyst made the same mistake, too."

"What analyst?" Willa asked. She added in quick concern, "Is Melinda all right?"

She sounded like she genuinely gave a damn about

Melinda's safety. He knew plenty of women who would have secretly been rooting for his ex to die horribly, and clear the way for them. Not that Melinda was actually in the way…

…Right? It had been years since they divorced. He was over her, even if he hadn't gotten into any serious relationships since then. He'd been too busy getting rich and letting the money fill his bed with beautiful women to get serious with anyone. No need to settle down. He had all the time in the world to do the whole commitment and marriage thing. Except now he'd blasted past age forty and his window of opportunity was starting to close. What if he never found the perfect woman? Was he doomed to live out his old age alone and bitter?

Damn, he'd forgotten how maudlin whiskey could make a man. The young beauty seated across from him was certainly ripe for the picking. She would make some man a hell of a wife. She was sweet and smart and a lady in public. And in private, she was another story, entirely. His body stirred with lust at the memory of the wildcat she'd been in his arms two nights ago. Once she had let go of her inhibitions, she'd been all the woman a man could ask for and more. He had to admit, it had made him feel damned good that he'd been the one to unlock her sensual side like that.

At the moment, her lips were pursed, her arms folded across her middle and her legs crossed primly at the ankles. Her body language screamed that she wasn't even remotely thinking about sex right now. She was probably wallowing in disapproving thoughts of how he was going to hell for getting drunk.

"I don't care if I go to hell for indulging in a little whiskey," he announced.

She shrugged, apparently unfazed. "I've seen worse.

Besides, I wouldn't call you actually drunk. You're only mildly buzzed. You might have a headache in the morning if you don't drink a little water before bed, but that's about the extent of it."

Now where would John Merris's shockingly sheltered daughter learn to gauge a drunk so accurately? "John Merris was a drinker?" he asked, stunned.

"More often and more heavily than you might think," she replied grimly.

Well, hell. Now he felt bad for drinking in front of her. He set his glass down on the coffee table in sudden distaste. "Why did you get all upset over me calling Melinda my wife?"

That brought spots of color to her already pink cheeks. "I was in bed with you for goodness' sake. Why do you think it upset me?"

"Enlighten me."

"I like you."

Ooooh-kay. "And?"

She huffed. "And I was jealous. I was mad at the thought that you still have deep feelings for her and think of her as your wife, not your ex-wife."

He frowned. *Did* he still think of Melinda as his wife? He tried to imagine her sleeping with another man to see how he would react. Not only did no anger or hurt stir in his gut, but he couldn't even conjure up an image of Melinda with any man. All that came to mind was some poor schmuck on his knees in front of her while she wore a latex jumpsuit and snapped a crop against her boot.

Maybe that was what broke them up. He'd refused to be her lackey the way she wanted him to be. He'd insisted on being his own man, heaven forbid.

Thank God Willa wasn't that kind of woman. She'd

liked it when he took charge in bed. The simmering lust in his loins heated up a little more.

"Look, Gabe. I think it's decent of you to still care for Melinda. It dawned on me last night that she may not have any other family to look out for her. She's a human being, after all, and it's not her fault some nut job kidnapped her. The fact that you put up the reward money and you've been pushing the cops so hard to find her is noble."

Noble or sycophantic? Had he let go of his obsession with pleasing Melinda or hadn't he? When John Merris had rejected him, had he been so needy that he'd turned to the next impossible-to-please control freak he could find? The thought sickened him vaguely. He was his own man, dammit. Had been for years. But who'd have guessed those ancient apron strings would be so hard to cut? He ought to walk away from Melinda and let her stew in whatever mess she'd landed in.

But Willa was right. Melinda was a human being. He couldn't turn his back on her in her time of need. It was common decency to see this thing through.

Surprised at Willa's altruism, he replied, "It's good of you to understand. She and I haven't had anything between us since long before we divorced. But she's got no one else. Her brother's her only living family, and he's in jail for the rest of his life. I didn't have a choice but to step up and help out."

He was a cad for taking credit for such noble motives. But the way Willa's eyes softened and warmed toward him, how could he not do it? He'd do just about anything to make her look at him like he was some kind of hero.

"And about tonight," she said softly, snapping his attention sharply back to her, "thanks."

"You're not mad at me for punching Ward?" Melinda

would have had a fit and called him a Neanderthal for acting out on his violent impulses.

"Mad?" she exclaimed. "I'm just grateful I was there to see it! I wish I could do the same."

"You can. You just need to learn how to make a proper fist and put your weight behind it." Inspired, he stood up. "I'll show you now."

Across town, her nemesis stewed. Funny, but Willa didn't even know she had a nemesis. But she would, soon enough. That was a promise.

Willa Merris would get hers, all right. That bitch thought she could sic her toy boy on decent, upstanding members of the community and get away with it? Someone needed to take her down a peg or two. Hell, knock her off the damn pegboard.

Uppity bitch.

Pain would be hers. Panic. Suffering. Death.

Definitely a knife. Peel her skin like an orange.

Gabe was mesmerized as Willa smiled up at him and rose to her feet. He led her over by the windows where there was open space for them to maneuver.

"Rule number one," he lectured, "never stick your thumb inside your fist. Curl your fingers and keep your thumb outside your fist so you don't break it."

She nodded in concentration, getting into the spirit of the thing, and rolled her fists into experimental balls.

"Rule number two," he said, warming to his subject, "keep your fist aligned with your arm bones. If you cock your wrist and really put force into your punch, you'll break your wrist."

He showed her how to punch her left palm with her right fist to get the feel of how the energy traveled down her arm. After a minute, she nodded and held up two credible fists in front of her.

"And now to put your weight behind it." He showed her how to punch off her back foot, leveraging her entire body weight into the thing. She didn't get it right away, though, and he moved behind her, put his arms around her and guided her body through a slow-motion punch.

She felt so good in his arms, he could barely focus on the task at hand, though. And she smelled good, too. That intoxicating gardenia scent of hers swirled around her. It made him think of southern belles and hot, lazy summer nights. And sex. Smoking-hot, mind-blowing, toe-curling sex with a lady turned wildcat.

She relaxed back against him, her body going limpid in his arms. Memory of that body by turns taut and boneless against his surged through him. His head lowered and his mouth found the shell of her ear. She inhaled on a sexy little gasp as his lips brushed across it. Her hips rocked back, pressing against his exquisitely uncomfortable groin. He groaned under his breath as lust pounded through him.

She turned in his arms, and suddenly the prim-and-proper lady gave way to the siren. She kissed him so deeply his head spun, promising delights that would beggar the mind. And he had just enough whiskey in his system to ignore the little voice in his head warning that the two of them still had things to work out before they fell into the sack again.

He didn't have to drag her up against him. She was already there, pressing herself into him, her arms twining around his neck as if she couldn't get enough of him. His hands slipped under her linen suit, shoving the pesky thing off her shoulders. The white silk of her entirely too prudish blouse at least had the good grace to cling enticingly to her curves. He cupped her breast through the sleek fabric and she moaned softly, arching into him even harder.

He didn't deserve her. He ought to let her go. She was young and had her whole life ahead of her. And he was a half-drunk old man who had no business taking advantage of her. Not to mention she'd had an upsetting encounter with James Ward just a few hours ago. She needed time to recover, and any half-considerate bastard would keep his hands off her tonight. But damned if he could stop himself.

He did promise himself to go slow with her. To be gentle and let her call the shots. It was a flimsy compromise between his conscience and his lust, but it was the best his impaired judgment could manage under the circumstances.

He untied the annoying bow at her neck and worked his way down the row of buttons that guarded her virtue like tiny, plastic sentinels. The silk fell away beneath his fingers, and he inhaled sharply at the fragile lace bra that came into sight. The naughty beneath the nice of it made his knees go a little weak. Or maybe it was just all the blood pooling in his groin that made him light-headed.

Willa returned the favor and unbuttoned his shirt with gratifying haste. He'd already shed his jacket and tie when he got home. He led her toward the sofas as they mutually stripped each other, he dragging her skinny skirt down over her hips while she fumbled at his trousers eagerly.

He groaned as her hand dipped inside his briefs, clasping him boldly and fanning the inferno that was his desire. She bumped into the back of the sofa, and he kissed her deeply, invading her mouth with his tongue the way he wanted to invade the rest of her body. Her hands shoved impatiently at his remaining clothing, and he stepped out of the puddle of wool. He eased her sexy little panties down and cupped her core, all but scorching his fingers on her eager heat.

She whispered hotly in his ear of how badly she wanted him and her fingers squeezed his flesh until he nearly exploded. His jaw dropped when she turned around in his arms and bent slightly over the back of the sofa. She gave him a smile and a come-hither look over her shoulder that brought a disbelieving grin to his face. Apparently, the lady had given way to the wildcat.

Gripping her hips, he guided her gently back and onto him, letting her find the perfect fit. She groaned his name aloud as he filled her tight heat, seeking the core of her desire. She rocked against him experimentally, and he savored the elegant curve of her spine as she arched backward into him.

"More," she murmured.

As the lady requested. He pressed deeper into her by slow degrees, gritting his teeth as she slid up and down his length, wet and hot. He ventured farther and farther until she finally went still around him.

"You all right?" he managed to grind out, straining for all he was worth not to slam into her mindlessly. He felt her internal muscles relax and adjust to accommodate him, and then she was gripping him again, her body pulsing so sweetly around his, he nearly lost it then and there.

"Oh, yes," she gasped. "I'm fine. More than fine. Fantastic."

He moved slowly, worried about hurting her in this position that gave him such deep access to her body.

She wiggled impatiently against him, silently demanding more. He loosed the reins on his lust a tiny bit.

"Please, Gabe. Don't make me beg."

"For what, baby?"

"For all of you. I want it all. Now. Please…" She ended on a keening moan that was so sexy he couldn't stop his hips from rocking forward, from pushing to the hilt within her. Checking himself sharply, he withdrew partway and eased forward carefully once more.

"Again," she panted.

"Faster," she begged.

"Harder," she demanded.

And he complied, dammit. How could he not? All his best intentions to be gentle with her went right out the window as she planted her hands on the sofa cushions and opened herself entirely to him, sobbing out her pleasure as he finally let go, pounding mindlessly into her, lost in her body and their mutual lust and the completeness with which she gave herself to him.

She arched up off the leather, shuddering around him as she cried his name out loud. Her orgasm went on and on, one spasm folding into the next until she destroyed what little control he had left. His own orgasm ripped through him like thunder and lightning. He shouted her name hoarsely, gripping her hips to his until their bodies were all but fused together. She shuddered out the final throes of her massive orgasm as he collapsed against her, covering her body protectively with his.

"You've killed me, woman," he panted in her ear.

"Then we've died and gone to heaven," she panted back.

He eased out of her limp body and lifted her in his arms, carrying her back to his bed. Next time, dammit, he *would* be gentle with her.

Except there shouldn't *be* a next time. Any way he cut it, having sex with her was a mistake. She deserved more. He couldn't give her what she needed, and continuing to have sex with her was selfish on his part, and potentially destructive to her. The last thing he wanted to do was hurt her. She'd already been hurt far too much already. It was clear she had a crush on him, and taking advantage of it made him the worst kind of cad.

Except he liked her, too. A lot. Too much, in fact. Was it wrong for the two of them to indulge in the private fantasy they'd both held for all these years? Maybe it was a good thing they'd scratched the itch between them. Maybe it would give them closure and allow them both to move on with their lives. Right?

Who the hell was he trying to kid? He'd seen her, he'd wanted her, he'd taken her. He was a first-class son of a bitch who ought to be thrown in the deepest circle of hell for taking advantage of a sweet, innocent young woman. End of discussion.

He lay her down in his bed, drew the covers up over her sleepy, relaxed body, kissed her gently on the brow with a murmured promise to come back soon and walked out on her.

Chapter 14

Willa opened her eyes and disorientation slammed into her. Where was she? In a moment, recollection came. Gabe's bed. And last night…

A smile curved her lips. She stretched luxuriously under the soft cotton sheet, feeling better than she had in years. That man sure knew how to make her feel like a woman. An attractive, sexy, relaxed one.

She got out of bed and availed herself of his super-high-tech bathroom. It was kind of fun to watch the news on the plasma screen in the shower, and the full body dryer was amazing. Dozens of jets blew warm air at her, and in a matter of seconds, she was entirely dry. No shivering, dripping race to towel herself off this morning, no sirree.

Her clothes were nowhere to be seen in Gabe's bedroom. If she was certain he would be alone in his living room and not using that video teleconferencing phone he'd shown her the last time she was here, she wouldn't mind prancing out into the condo naked. But as it was, she raided his walk-in closet and found a T-shirt and gym shorts in the built-in drawers that opened silently at a touch. Too cool.

She padded, barefoot, out into the condo. It was silent and still. "Gabe?" she called out.

Nothing. Huh.

"Computer?" she tried experimentally. "Where is Gabe?"

The British sexpot intoned on cue, "Mr. Dawson is not in this residence."

Not here? "Computer, when did he leave?"

"Mr. Dawson left the residence at 12:10 a.m. this morning."

That was right after he'd tucked her into bed so sweetly last night! The sunlight streaming in through the huge windows dimmed a little. He'd left her?

And then it dawned on her. He must have been looking out for her reputation. He'd known she had bodyguards waiting downstairs. He'd left so they wouldn't think the two of them had done…well, what the two of them had, in fact, done. What a gentleman. The sun regained its brilliance. She dressed and cooked herself breakfast with the help of the computer, who ably told her the location of everything she needed in the kitchen to fry up some eggs, make toast and brew a small pot of coffee.

She ate slowly in hopes of Gabe rejoining her, but he didn't, and like it or not, she had work to do today. A quick text to her bodyguards got an immediate response that they would be out front in ten minutes. She washed up after herself in the kitchen, donned her pumps and headed out.

She exited the elevator in the building's lobby, and winced mentally. If she didn't know any better, she'd think Paula Craddock was stalking her. Worse, the woman had spotted her coming off the elevator. Backing into the conveyance would look cowardly and earn the reporter's ire. Willa sighed and stepped forward, pasting on a smile.

"Good morning, Miss Craddock, What brings you to this neck of the woods this morning?"

"You, of course. Did you and Gabe Dawson spend the night together?"

Willa was abjectly grateful to Gabe that she could look the reporter steadily in the eye and answer honestly, "Of course not! He was kind enough to let me spend the night at his condo because of how late it was when I finished my business in Dallas. But he wasn't here." She added hastily when the reporter opened her mouth to pounce on that, "And I have no idea where he did spend the night, Miss Craddock. You would have to ask him that."

She expected he'd driven to his little house in Vengeance, but she wasn't about to help out the journalist.

Paula recovered quickly. "Do you have any statement regarding your shocking endorsement of your father's opponent?"

"Is it shocking? I wasn't aware of that," Willa replied mildly.

"You abandoned your own party and your family's long tradition of supporting the same party. People are calling it a posthumous slap in your father's face."

Willa smiled sweetly around her clenched teeth. "My father left his office to me to do with as I see fit. He trusted my judgment. Of course, if he were alive, I would have given him my full support. But in my father's absence I made a rational, serious, thoughtful choice of who to endorse based on all the available information. Isn't that what a United States senator is supposed to do?"

Paula mumbled something about supposing that was true. Thankfully, as the woman held out her microphone once more, Willa spotted the big black SUV and her driver pulling up at the curb.

"I'm sorry, Paula. There's my ride. I'm afraid I have to go. It's been lovely chatting with you."

About as lovely as a bad case of jungle rot. Willa smiled warmly at the second bodyguard who jumped out of the SUV and came inside to escort her to the vehicle.

She muttered under her breath to him, "Your timing is exquisite."

"We aim to please, ma'am."

The SUV whisked her back to Vengeance and the guards deposited her in her father's office in the mansion. Today she planned to tackle Merris Oil. She had no intention of involving herself directly in the business, but she'd inherited her father's seat on the board of directors, and given Gabe's dire predictions regarding the company's future, she felt a driving need to educate herself as quickly and thoroughly as possible on the oil business.

Her father's correspondence pertaining to Merris Oil was a mess. Without an efficient congressional staff to keep him marginally organized, his records were a disaster. Willa spent much of the afternoon simply sorting paperwork into piles. Clearly, John Merris had never heard of a thing called a filing system.

She spent close to an hour on the phone with some vice president at Merris Oil trying to get him to tell her whether Merris Oil was or wasn't oil fracking, and never did get a straight answer from the guy. He seemed to think that, based on her gender, she was incapable of comprehending the possible variations on the process, nor could her delicate sensibilities handle hearing about the pros and cons of doing it as a company. She was thoroughly frustrated when she gave up, hung up and took a break to eat.

She grabbed a quick bite of supper in the kitchen with Louise. Apparently, Minnie was out to dinner with friends. Willa was delighted to see her mother rejoining the human race. For a while there, she'd been really worried about her mother's ability to recover from the shock of John Merris's murder.

She went back to work, plowing through various Merris Oil reports and making frequent visits to the internet to read about different oil-drilling techniques. She had just dived into the daunting pile of financial reports when she heard a lot of female voices in the front hall.

Seizing on any excuse to avoid the profit-and-loss statements, she stepped out into the foyer, folder in hand, to say hello to her mother and thank whoever'd managed to peel Minnie out of her bed.

Willa recognized all of the dozen women, who were of an age with her mother, and longtime friends of the Merris family. "Hi, Mom. Ladies. Did you have a nice dinner?"

Minnie turned to her, and Willa's smile froze. Her mother's eyes were bloodshot and Minnie wove a little as she completed the turn.

"There she is," Minnie said acidly. "My loving, sweet, *loyal* daughter. You just couldn't wait to stick a knife in your father's back, could you, you ungrateful little bitch?"

Oh, no. Minnie was on the warpath again. She steeled herself not to overreact and said evenly, "Father's dead and buried, Mom."

"At the rate you're going, you'll be burying me before long, too, young lady. You'd just love that, wouldn't you? And then you can have all of this for yourself."

She knew her mother was drowning in a cocktail of booze and medications, *knew* Minnie didn't know what she was saying and wouldn't remember it tomorrow. But a little voice in the back of Willa's head whispered that maybe this was really how her mother did feel about her. Had the liquor and drugs brought out long-hidden truths about Minnie's real feelings?

Lord knew Willa had suppressed a whole lot of anger and resentment of her own toward her father over the years. But she'd always thought of Minnie as her silent ally in the suffering and self-effacement. Had Minnie seen her as the enemy all along?

"Why, look," Minnie said with saccharine viciousness. "She's already perusing Merris Oil's financials. Calculating how much you can take your father's company for while you're bankrupting me?"

Willa was vaguely aware of all the women but one staring fixedly at various paintings and floor tiles as they tried not to witness this family's dirty laundry.

But Roseanne Ward was paying avid attention to the exchange. She piped up now. "I told you she'd come after you, too, Minnie. She turned on my James and now she's doing the same to you. You've been harboring a viper to your breast, you poor thing."

Willa stared at the woman in sudden comprehension.

So, Roseanne was the source of the poison in Minnie's fuddled mind.

And the woman wasn't done spewing venom, yet. "Why, she's driven my poor boy nearly to distraction. He can't sleep or eat, he's having terrible headaches and anxiety attacks. And there she stands, as cool as a cucumber, not giving so much as a never mind about the suffering she's causing him. Not to mention the grief and pain she's causing her own mother."

"Let me guess," Willa said pleasantly. "Tonight's little outing was your idea."

Roseanne's back went rigid. "Indeed, it was. You're far too busy running around like some cheap whore with your father's enemies to pay any attention to your poor grieving mother. Some daughter you are."

The barb hurt. Particularly because Willa had to admit there might be a little truth to it. She'd been so overwhelmed since her father's death that she probably hadn't been spending enough time with Minnie. But after days and days of sitting beside her mother's bed while the woman slept off her tranquilizers and antidepressants, there hadn't seemed to be much point. And then the avalanche of details involved in planning a funeral, dealing with her father's will, answering the hundreds of sympathy notes…and then Gabe…

She turned to Minnie. "Roseanne's absolutely right. I haven't been spending enough time with you. I'm so sorry. Tomorrow—"

"No more lies!" Minnie screeched. "Get out of my house! This is *my* house. Not yours!"

The outburst brought Louise hurrying out of the kitchen in alarm. A pair of the bodyguards peered over the housekeeper's shoulder, also alarmed.

Willa stared at her mother in dismay. Minnie was kicking her out? Really?

"Go!" Minnie screamed.

Everyone froze. The other ladies, Louise and the two bodyguards stared back and forth between Minnie and Willa in appalled shock.

It took every ounce of the training John Merris had pounded into her never to show weakness and never to give in to emotion to say calmly, "If that's what you want, Mother. Of course I'll return to my own home. Right away."

She walked across the foyer, her back feeling like an icicle, rigid, heavy and on the verge of shattering. She vaguely heard the bodyguards politely shoving through the crowd of buzzing women behind her. Without stopping to wait for them, she made her way to her little car parked at the edge of the driveway, grateful that it wasn't blocked in by the big Cadillacs her mother's posse had been driving.

Willa started the car, her fingers so numb they didn't even feel the keys, and headed down the driveway. There was some sort of commotion behind her—shouting and lots of movement. The bodyguards were waving their arms frantically in her direction, but she ignored them. The tears were starting to come now, and she really didn't need a couple of guys hovering over her while she cried them out. It looked like the guards' SUVs were blocked in by the line of Cadillacs. All the better. She needed to be alone. To lick her wounds and try to figure out what she'd done to make her mother hate her so much.

In that moment, she felt more alone than she had in her entire life. Apparently, when John Merris was shot, she'd lost not only her father, but also her mother. A sob escaped her. Tears flowed freely down her cheeks now and she dashed at them trying to see the road.

Darkness had fallen, and lightning flickered faintly on the horizon. She judged that it would be a few hours before the storms came, and frankly, she didn't want to go home right now. Her bodyguards would head there first in search of her. Lover's Point was the peak of a giant bluff west of town that kids parked on and made out in their cars. It looked over the western part of the county, and she'd always found it a peaceful place. She guided her car up the winding tar and gravel road. Trees closed in around her car and then started to give way to limestone outcroppings jutting up out of the rolling hills.

Of course, she'd never been up here in a car with a boy in high school. She hadn't ever been one of the cool girls who got invited to have awkward sex in the backs of cars. And fear of her father had kept the mean boys from trying to get into her pants for the sake of winning some stupid bet.

In retrospect, she probably hadn't been missing out on nearly as much as she'd thought she had in high school. Gabe had been well worth the wait…. Gabe. She desperately needed to hear his voice all of a sudden. To be reassured that her mother loved her and wasn't in her right mind at the moment. She just needed to know that someone, anyone, gave a damn about her.

She picked up her cell phone and dialed his number. It rang a half-dozen times and then kicked over to his voice mail.

A pair of headlights came up behind her on the twisty road, moving fast. That had better not be her bodyguards. She really wanted to be alone. Gabe's recorded voice urged her to leave a message, and the ubiquitous beep sounded.

"Hey, Gabe. It's me. Thanks for last night. It turned out to be a good thing that you left the apartment when you did. Our favorite reporter was waiting in the lobby for me this morning. I swear, that woman has it in for me."

The headlights pulled closer and Willa noticed in relief that the vehicle was not a big, black, sleek SUV, but rather a white van. Probably some kids heading up to the point to have sex in their shaggin' wagon.

"At any rate," she continued, "my mom was on a tear tonight and threw me out of her house. I think Roseanne Ward is the one putting ideas in Mom's head that I'm trying to steal her money and ruin her. Call me. I miss you."

She put the phone down on the seat beside her and concentrated on the progressively narrower and more treacherous road. Near the summit now, it switched back hard next to a massive drop-off. A wide valley stretched away into the distance hundreds of feet below her. It was Willa's least favorite part of the drive. She clutched the wheel tightly and slowed cautiously as she approached the turn.

A tremendous impact made her scream aloud as the van behind her slammed into her. Willa fought her fishtailing car back under control, tires squealing as she hit the brakes. Another bone-jarring impact shoved her car partially off the pavement. She stood on her brake pedal for all she was worth, locking up the tires completely. But the van revved behind her, using its superior weight and horsepower to shove her closer to that ominous expanse of blackness.

What the heck was wrong with that driver? Willa

shouted at him to stop regardless of the fact that the driver couldn't hear her.

Her remaining tires hit the gravel shoulder and she abruptly lost all traction. Her little car lurched forward and the hood pitched down and out of sight. Her seat tilted forward violently as the car went over the edge.

Willa only had time to scream, "Nooooooo!"

Chapter 15

Gabe got out of a mind-numbingly long staff meeting that had turned into a dinner meeting, it had run so long. He'd been neglecting his company badly the past few days, and several major decisions had stacked up waiting for him.

He listened in shock to his voice mail as Willa praised him for abandoning her last night. How in the hell had she turned the most despicable thing he'd ever done into some sort of favor to her? Guilt tangled in his gut as she called him smart and thoughtful, when, in fact, he'd been a selfish jackass. He never should have made love to her last night. And once he had, he shouldn't have left her like some coward. He should have faced the music this morning and broken things off with her face-to-face. Like a man.

He headed wearily back toward Vengeance. Normally, he'd spend the night in Dallas close to his corporate offices, but the memory of Willa in his bed and in his arms was too fresh. Too painful. He'd never wanted a woman so bad in his life. The hell of it was that she was eager and willing to have him, too.

He so shouldn't have taken her. She was twelve years younger than he, the daughter of his archenemy, and everyone was already giving her hell for spending time with him. If word got out that the two of them were having a torrid affair, Willa's friends and neighbors would crucify her outright. He couldn't take them all away from her. She'd lived in Vengeance her entire life. Everyone she knew and loved was there. The good people of Vengeance would shun her completely if she got involved with him. For her happiness, he owed it to her to suck up his own desires and stay the hell away from her.

If only she hadn't led such a sheltered life in such a small town. If she had known anyone outside of Vengeance, had any friends who didn't come from the town's inner circle of moneyed elite, if she'd had ties to anything at all outside of Vengeance, he could have thrown caution to the wind and continued his relationship with her.

He passed a hand across his face, tired beyond belief. He hadn't slept a wink last night and he'd been going hard all day at the office. He felt every one of his forty years keenly tonight. Yet another reason to set Willa free. She was still in her twenties. Plenty young enough to find herself a great guy, settle down and have some kids. The family and normalcy she craved.

Funny how his wealth and extravagant lifestyle were the exact opposite of what she wanted. He'd always assumed that if he got rich enough, he could have any woman he desired. Who'd have guessed it would drive away the one woman he really did want? Another day, the irony might have amused him darkly, but tonight it just pissed him off.

His cell phone rang, and he didn't recognize the number on his vehicle display. Why would some security company call him at this hour? It was too late for solicitors to be bothering him. Annoyed, he answered the call.

"Dawson, here."

"Sorry to bother you, sir. I'm calling from Elite Security Services. We're currently working for Senator Merris, and we've got a little problem. We were hoping you could help us."

At the mention of Willa's name, Gabe's blood ran cold. "What's wrong?" he snapped. His foot levered downward on the accelerator and the Cadillac leaped forward. Toward Willa.

"We've lost the senator."

"*Lost* her? How the hell did that happen?"

"There was some sort of altercation between the senator and her mother. Senator Merris left her mother's home rather abruptly and my men were unable to follow her. Their cars were blocked in. By the time they got out, she was gone."

A hum of alarm set up shop low in his gut. Something was wrong. Very wrong. "How long ago did she leave the Merris mansion? You've checked her place?"

"She disappeared approximately two hours ago. Her house was the first place we checked. I've got a team waiting there now in case she shows up. We were hoping she might be with you."

"I've been in business meetings all day. Let me check my condo. I'll call you back in a minute."

Gabe quickly dialed the phone number to his downtown pad and waited impatiently through the recorded message. "Computer, this is Gabe."

"Good evening, Mr. Dawson. What can I do for you?"

"Is there anyone in my apartment?"

"No, sir. Your residence is currently unoccupied."

"What time did Willa leave this morning?"

"She left at 9:31 a.m., sir. She exited the elevator at the lobby level of the building."

Dammit. "Thank you, computer. Text my cell phone if anyone arrives at my apartment."

"Of course, sir. Shall I prepare a hot bath for you?"

"No." Gabe wasted no time on niceties with the machine and hung up on it. He dialed back the security firm. "She's not at my place in Dallas," he announced. "Have you checked my house in Vengeance?"

"Second place we checked, sir."

He didn't know whether to be relieved that Willa's security team knew her behavior so well, or chagrined that the two of them hadn't done a better job of hiding their liaison. Gabe frowned. That hum in his gut was turning into a full-blown chorus of wrongness. "Can't you guys track her cell phone or something?"

"Only law-enforcement authorities can legally access cell-phone signals."

"Then do it illegally!" he exclaimed. "I'll take responsibility for it if you get caught."

"With all due respect, sir, we wouldn't get caught. My men are very good."

"Then do it, already. Call me back when you get a location on her." He was still about a half hour out of Vengeance. His foot pressed down on the gas even harder. "I'll be in Vengeance in twenty minutes."

"We should have her signal isolated by then," the security man said briskly.

He bloody well hoped so. He was going to start hurting people if they didn't find Willa, and soon. He pulled up in front of his house in eighteen minutes. By what miracle he'd managed to avoid any speed traps or the vigilant Vengeance police force, he couldn't say.

He charged into his house, shouting, "Willa? Are you here?"

Only the echo of his worried voice answered him. He swore freely and dialed the security company again. "Where is she?" he asked without bothering to identify himself.

"We lost her signal west of Vengeance."

"What do you mean, lost it?"

"The signal stopped. She must have turned off her phone."

He sat down heavily on his sofa. Why would Willa run away like this? It was totally unlike her. Not only was she not a rebel by nature, but she had nowhere to go. To his knowledge, she didn't know anyone in the next county over. Her whole life centered around Vengeance, Texas.

Where was she headed? It was possible she'd headed for the Vacarro oil field, which was about seventy miles west of Vengeance, but surely she knew better than to go to an oil drilling operation by herself. They were dangerous places if a person didn't know their way around an oil rig.

There wasn't anything else west of Vengeance but farms and grazing land for hundreds of miles. Was she just driving around randomly? Working things out in her head? He'd been known to do that from time to time. Although it didn't particularly seem to be her style. Worried, he paced his living room and did his best to ignore the fat lady bellowing a veritable opera of alarm in his gut.

C'mon, Willa. Come home to me. At least call me.

Although, why should she? Despite her effort to put a happy spin on it, fact was, he'd abandoned her last night. He'd been the worst sort of cad and walked out on her after making love to her. She deserved so much better than that. Than him. Was that why she had run? Was this his fault? He swore at himself. How could it not be his fault?

If she was out there somewhere, alone and upset, he owed it to her to find her and make it better. He grabbed his car keys and headed out to his truck. Texas was a big place, but he'd find her somehow. And when he did, he owed her an epic apology.

He headed west toward the hilly area where the security firm had last pinged her cell phone. A series of deep valleys and high bluffs ran north-south through the western part of the county. His geologist's trained eye identified it as ancient river erosion. Cell-phone coverage in the area was terrible. If she'd gone there, she might not have turned her phone off at all. She could've simply lost a cellular signal. The rift ran for nearly fifty miles north and south of Vengeance. She could be anywhere in it. Determination to find her anyway steeled his jaw as he pointed his truck at the area.

The sun had dipped below the west rim of the first valley already, and deep shadows striped the road. Tall deciduous trees, protected down in the valley from Texas's vicious winds, crowded the asphalt and created a mysterious emerald ambience all around him. He could see Willa coming to a place like this to find comfort.

The security man had mentioned she and her mother

had had a fight. Gabe sincerely hoped it hadn't been over him. Yet another cross for him to bear if he'd come between Willa and her mother.

He'd just topped the rim and was starting down into the next gully when his cell phone rang. He was impressed that he still had coverage out here and snatched it up hopefully. "Willa?"

"No, sir. This is Agent Delaney of the FBI. We have news regarding your wife."

He really wished they'd quit calling Melinda that. "What news?" he asked quickly.

"We've found Dr. Grayson. An operation earlier this evening to liberate her from her captor was successful."

A week ago, that news would have made him the happiest man alive. But now, he could barely spare attention for the news in the midst of his panic over Willa.

The FBI agent was speaking again. "If you would like to meet me at Vengeance Hospital, that is where your Dr. Grayson is being taken."

"She's hurt? How badly?"

"I don't have that information."

Dammit. He really wanted to stay out here and look for Willa. But Melinda could be seriously injured and traumatized. He weighed Willa being alone and upset against Melinda definitely hurt and traumatized. Heavily, he turned his truck around and headed back toward town.

As the valley retreated in his rearview mirror, he murmured, "I'll be back for you, baby. I promise."

Willa blinked, but her eyes weren't working properly. Everything was unfocused in shades of gray around her. Like it was getting dark. Or maybe she was dying. She became aware of pain. Too many places on her body hurt to list, and they all blended into an overwhelming ache that made it hard to think. She was too sleepy to concentrate and figure it all out.

A sound came from nearby. Deep. Braying. Like someone laughing. A laughing hyena. Except those lived in Africa, right? Why was her brain so muddy? Oddly, the sound seemed to be coming from above her. How was that possible? Did birds laugh? Where was she?

Her car. Except it was tilted all crazily on its side. Toward the passenger door. A mat of leaves covered the windows. A big tree branch was sticking into the car like it had grown through the glass. Strange dream.

Her weight hung in the too-tight seat belt and shoulder harness. Hurt. And there was a floppy white bag draped all over her front. She shoved at it, shocked at how feebly her hands moved. Sticky. Her hands were sticky. Curious, she examined her palms. Something black and wet was smeared all over them.

What happened?

Gabe would know. He knew everything. Her mouth tried to form his name. To say it aloud. If she could just say his name, he would appear and rescue her. He always did. But no sound came out of her mouth, and her chest hurt from the exertion. Instead, she wished hard for him to come for her, to take care of her. He always looked out for her. He was so good to her.

Something warm leaked out of her eye and trickled down her cheek. She missed him so much when he wasn't with her. As if a piece of her was missing. Was this what love felt like? It was sweetness and pain, joy and sorrow all rolled into one. It would be lovely if only it didn't hurt so much. The pain was starting to come in waves now, each one a little worse than the one before.

That crazy laughter echoed from above her again as she drifted away on a cloud of peaceful darkness that carried away all the pain. All the confusion. Everything.

Chaos reigned as Gabe parked in the hospital's car lot. News trucks were jockeying for position by the emergency-room entrance. Deputy Green was doing his best—and failing—to force the vans back from the hospital doors. A crowd of bystanders had gathered, but for the moment, the Vengeance fire department seemed to have them contained behind wooden sawhorse barriers.

When he hopped out of his SUV, a chorus of shouts went up. The reporters had spotted him. They sounded like a flock of geese. He ignored them as he shoved through the crowd, and Deputy Green waved him through the barricades.

The emergency room was relatively quiet after outside. He spotted the FBI analyst who'd watched Melinda's videotape and who'd called him.

"Any news?" he asked her tersely.

"Ambulance brought her in a few minutes ago. None of her injuries appear serious."

"How is she emotionally?" Now there was a question he'd never thought to hear himself ask about Melinda Grayson.

Agent Delaney shrugged. "Haven't had a chance to speak with her yet. Medics said she was lucid but upset."

He winced. Melinda *upset* equated in his mind to her having a screaming hissy fit. Surely, the FBI analyst didn't mean the word that way. "Can I see her?"

"As soon as the doctors are done treating her." She added a shade too innocently, "Dr. Grayson asked that you be with her during her debriefing."

"She did?" Gabe blurted.

"You sound surprised," Delaney commented mildly.

"She's usually so strong and independent. It's not like her to want support from anyone. Being kidnapped must have been a hell of an ordeal for her to ask for me like that."

He waited impatiently; glad he was here for Melinda, but fretting over Willa. He called the security company and was frustrated that they'd heard nothing from Willa. Problem was the security team was Dallas based. They didn't know the local area and weren't being the slightest bit efficient in searching the western part of the county for her. He'd do a much better job of it if he could just get out of here.

But then guilt at the notion of abandoning Melinda, who'd been through an obviously terrible experience, assailed him, and the cycle of relief, fretting, worry and guilt repeated itself. He felt like he was being torn in two, and it sucked.

The weird part was that he didn't even particularly like Melinda. She was charismatic, though, and once she had her claws in someone's head, she didn't let go. It had taken Willa coming along for him to realize how psychologically tied he still was to Melinda.

An urge to turn around and walk out of the emergency room came over him. To hell with Melinda. She was a grown woman and could take care of herself. Lord knew she'd never needed him or anyone else over the years. Willa, on the other hand, could use a friend. Her life had gone to hell in a handbasket, and not one bit of it had been her doing.

He stood up, determined to follow his heart and go find Willa when a male voice said from behind him, "Mr. Dawson?"

He turned to face a physician in a white lab coat.

Spatters of blood on the coat sent a hot wave of guilt through Gabe's gut. "How is she?" he asked quickly.

"Come with me."

Agent Delaney fell in beside the two men as they strode through a pair of swinging doors. A brightly lit hallway with all the usual medical clutter lining it stretched away from them. The doctor led Gabe to the first door on the left.

Gabe stepped inside, his heart in his throat.

Melinda was sitting up in bed, her arms speckled by Band-Aids, a small piece of tape across her right cheekbone and a bandage around her right knuckles. She had a fading black eye and a little puffiness along her jaw. But all in all, she didn't look half-bad. She did, however, look royally pissed off. He knew that narrow-eyed glare she was firing at the nurse all too well.

She looked up at the visitors, spotted Gabe and burst into tears. Honest-to-God wetness issuing from her eyes and running down her cheeks. Never, ever had he seen Melinda Grayson shed a tear before. The woman had sat stony-faced through her own father's funeral, for God's sake. Yet here she was, bawling theatrically.

She held both hands out to him in a gesture reminiscent of a toddler, and he lurched forward, shaken. Melinda Grayson wanted to be held? The end of the world must be upon them!

He perched on the edge of the high bed and gathered her into his arms. She stiffened against him, but her arms still went jerkily around him. Frankly, after the way Willa cuddled against him all soft and sweet, this was like hugging a cold, wet fish.

But as soon as the thought crossed his mind, he banished it. Melinda was hurt and scared and probably exhausted, and she surely deserved better from him.

"Dr. Grayson, what can you tell me about your kidnapper?" Agent Delaney asked.

Gabe looked up sharply. "You didn't catch the bastard?"

"Please don't interrupt, sir, or I'll have to ask you to leave."

Melinda's arms tightened hard around him. Damn, that woman was strong for someone who'd been tied to a chair for the past few weeks. "I never saw him. He kept me blindfolded all the time."

"What about when that video of you was filmed? Did you see him then? Or even a silhouette? How tall was he? What kind of build did he have? Race? Coloring? Anything?" the agent persisted.

Melinda shook her head. "There was just the camera on a tripod. He told me what to say from another room."

Agent Delaney pounced on that. "So he *did* script that video for you."

Melinda's gaze narrowed fractionally. Had Gabe not been inches away from her and not been so very familiar with her, he probably wouldn't have seen it. Now why did the agent's statement irritate Melinda like that?

"No, no. He just told me when to talk."

"Did he ever say anything about Senator John Merris, Sheriff Burris or a young man named David Reed?"

"No. Why?"

"All three men were murdered at about the same time you were kidnapped, ma'am."

Melinda did the strangest thing then. She burst into tears. No kidding. Wet stuff on her cheeks, sobbing hysterically, tears. Gabe was flabbergasted. The Iron Maiden knew how to cry? Wow. She must be a whole lot more messed up than she'd been showing initially.

The questioning paused until she could collect herself, but then continued onward, albeit more gently after Melinda's breakdown. And so it went. Agent Delaney pressed for details, and Melinda steadfastly denied knowing anything significant about the kidnapper. No matter what questions the FBI agent asked, no useful information was forthcoming from his ex-wife.

Although, every now and then, Melinda would tense slightly or give away some tiny facial expression of anger. But all the while, she clung to him like a pitifully scared child. When the agent suggested a polygraph test, Melinda burst into loud tears once more and buried her face against his chest. He'd never seen her act even remotely like this before. She was definitely a lot more rattled than he'd expected.

When Melinda's crying bout refused to wind down, Agent Delaney gave up with a visible sigh, and retreated from the room. The moment she left, Melinda's tantrum eased.

"It's okay, Mel," he soothed her. "No one's going to make you take a polygraph. You're the victim here. They're just trying to catch your kidnapper and were hoping you could help."

"Well, I can't!" she exclaimed, pushing away from him. She turned her ire on the nurse. "Get me some damned painkillers, already."

"I'm sorry, ma'am. The doctor will have to prescribe those."

"Well, what's he waiting for? The Second Coming?" Melinda snapped.

This was more like her. Funny how he'd forgotten how nasty Melinda could be. Maybe he'd been around it for so long he'd gotten numb to it. Willa would never dream of being so mean to anyone— *Stop it. Stop comparing the two women!*

The nurse answered Melinda with thin patience, "The FBI asked that you not be medicated until they'd had a chance to speak with you."

"Clearly, they've spoken with me. So get that damned doctor in here to do his damned job."

Yup. Melinda was back to her usual bitchy, domineering self.

Agent Delaney poked her head back into the room just then. "Oh. I forgot to ask earlier. Did your captor have any sort of an accent in his voice?"

Melinda sagged against Gabe immediately. He caught her weight in surprise as she answered tiredly, "No. None. Midwest neutral."

"Thanks." Agent Delaney smiled pleasantly as she backed out of the room.

Melinda sat back up and snapped at the nurse. "Now, get me that doctor."

Thoroughly confused, Gabe stood up. "Let me go see if I can find him for you." The nurse threw him a grateful look. Little did she know he was escaping as much as he was trying to help out.

Agent Delaney was lounging against the opposite wall of the hallway, and straightened up to walk beside him as he headed for the nurses' station. "Interesting woman, your wife."

"*Ex*-wife."

"She always that big a drama queen?"

Gabe stopped and turned to face the agent as he considered her question. He answered slowly, "Yes. But not in that way. I've never seen her cry in all the years I've known her. And she's not usually so..."

"Erratic?" Agent Delaney supplied.

"Actually, I was thinking more along the lines of touchy-feely."

"She's quite an actress, your *ex*-wife. What drew you to her in the first place?"

An actress? That was an interesting observation. But it hadn't been what attracted him to Melinda. He explained, "She's shockingly charismatic. Tends to disapprove of you when you meet her. Makes you want to earn her approval."

"Which she always withholds just a little," the agent added blandly.

He nodded. "I suppose it's her way of tying people to her. I always figured she was more insecure than she wanted to let on. Afraid people would abandon her. Her mother abandoned the family. She's pretty estranged from her siblings."

"Mmm," Agent Delaney said noncommittally.

"Is there anything else I can do for you?" he asked her, impatient to get back to the business of finding Willa.

"Not right now. You've been more helpful than you know," the FBI analyst replied. "I'll call you if I have any more questions."

He stopped briefly at the nurses' station to relay Melinda's request that the doctor prescribe her some painkillers, and then he headed out quickly. Whether he was running from Melinda or toward Willa, he couldn't rightly tell. Both, maybe.

It was fully dark by the time he got back to the last known location of Willa's GPS. The spot was just inside the rim of the main canyon of the complex of gullies and valleys. His geologist's eye envisioned the ancient earthquake that had torn this series of giant cracks in the generally flat landscape. Probably a secondary fault related to the massive New Madrid fault that had created the Mississippi River basin.

Willa had been heading west the last time her signal pinged off a cell tower. He thought about what lay west of him. The network of narrow, winding roads that would be treacherous after dark. Willa had been in her little car, which meant she wouldn't have ventured onto the more isolated tracks that crisscrossed these valleys. Most of them led to deer hunting stands and took a high-clearance, four-wheel drive truck to traverse. She had to have stuck to the main roads...of which there weren't many out here.

About a mile ahead, this particular road forked. The right branch went due west up over the next ridge, and the left one turned south and wound up to the top of a high bluff overlooking the entire canyon complex. It was a hangout for teens to drink and make out.

Abrupt memory jogged his brain. Willa had commented once that she was the only person who went up to Lover's Point for the view. Was it possible? Had she gone up there to be alone and think? He vaguely recalled it being a beautiful spot; although, unlike Willa, his reasons for going up there as a teen had never included the view.

He guided his SUV over the ridge and toward the fork in the road. He veered left and started up the winding asphalt strip. He slowed cautiously as the curves became sharper, the road became steeper and the dropoffs grew steeper and closer to the edge of the road.

A cloud bank drifted over the new moon and darkness pressed in on him and his SUV. All that existed was a short strip of asphalt in his headlights. He turned on the Cadillac's snazzy halogen high beams to better illuminate the road ahead. And that was probably why he spotted the faint skid marks, black slashed on the dark gray pavement.

A little voice in the back of his head shouted, *no no no no no!* He stopped the SUV and jumped out, his heart in his throat. He approached the precipice cautiously, and nothing but air stretched away from him. But when he reached the edge and peered down, he saw that the broken limestone cliff wasn't completely vertical. Not far below the road, a stand of scrubby saplings clung to the steep slope. And wedged among them was a small car, resting on its side.

He almost leaped down the slope before his brain kicked in. Rope. He needed rope. Racing back to the Escalade, he set its emergency brake and fished in the back of the SUV for the tow rope he had stowed somewhere. He spotted the bright yellow nylon as thick around as his thumb and snatched it out. Quickly, he lashed one end of it to the hitch in the rear bumper and looped the other end around his body.

Using the rope to slow his descent, he slipped and slid down the nasty incline. *Please be alive. Please, please be alive,* he begged Willa silently.

He groaned as he made out a white face through the spiderweb of cracked glass that was the windshield. "Willa!" he shouted.

The figure inside the car didn't move. Horrendous dread clutched at him. She couldn't be dead. He'd just found her, dammit! He couldn't lose her!

He slipped and slid to the car, which actually was resting mostly on all four tires. It was tilted onto its side by the severity of the slope. Tree branches poked through the passenger window and roof, skewering the tiny car like a shish kebab. A deflated air bag hung from the steering wheel, and another smaller one from over the driver's side door, partially obscuring Willa. He yanked at the door, but it didn't open. Given how badly the entire frame of the car was bent, he doubted it would budge.

In through the windshield, then. He eased left toward the hood of the car. Bracing himself on a tree trunk, he kicked at the windshield. As badly damaged as the tempered glass was, it bent inward but didn't give way. He jammed his heel into the thing again, and this time it shattered into millions of little pieces. Using his bare hands, he ripped away the remaining bits of glass.

His heart stopped as he glimpsed Willa. She was as white as a ghost and slumped in her seat belt like a rag doll. *Oh, God.* He lunged forward, reaching for her throat. *Have a pulse. Have a pulse. Have a pulse.*

There. A faint bump against his fingertip under her skin. *Alive!*

He put his weight on the edge of the window frame to reach for the seat belt release and the entire car lurched ominously. He froze, swearing. The trees that her car rested upon were perilously small saplings, and they were bent over badly under the weight of the car. He noted with dread that there were no more trees beyond them. The cliff dropped off more sharply beyond this one spot that the tree roots held tenuously in place.

He eased his weight more gently onto the car frame and the trees creaked ominously. Swearing, he reached under Willa for her seat belt. It was twisted, and with her entire body weight resting on it, not about to release. He reached into his back pocket and pulled out his trusty Swiss Army knife. Opening the main blade quickly, he sawed at the nylon webbing holding Willa in place.

While he did so, he visually checked her for obvious wounds or broken bones. There was a fair bit of dried blood on her face, but he'd seen enough facial cuts around the oil rigs to know they bled a lot. None of her limbs looked to be lying unnaturally, or bent where they shouldn't be. Internal injuries would be the real killer, of course. But a tiny spark of hope lit in his gut.

The seat belt gave way all at once and Willa nearly fell out the passenger window before he could grab her under the armpits. The car jerked hard and one of the saplings snapped in half. Crap. With that tree gone, it would throw all that much more weight on the remaining trees. They could all fail at any second.

He backed out of the car fast, relieved to get his weight on the ground, as steep and slippery as it was. He dragged Willa awkwardly through the windshield. Her shirt tore on a piece of metal and the loud tearing sound startled him.

She stirred faintly, and flapped her arms feebly. He nearly lost his grip on her as the car lurched again, the sapling under the engine cracking and giving way in slow motion.

Crap, crap, crap. Sitting on his rear end on the steep slope, he dragged Willa up and over the engine block of her ruined car. Another sapling gave way with a loud, sudden crack like a gunshot.

Hugging Willa against him, he lay down entirely, her body on top of his. He was able to let go of her long enough to lash the rope around her, looping it under her armpits in a makeshift navy loop. The car shifted beside them, rolling slowly onto its roof as branches snapped one by one in a stately progression toward oblivion.

He pushed against the loose shale with his heels, moving himself and Willa a few inches up the steep slope. Again. A few more inches. He grabbed the rope above Willa's head with one hand and heaved hard as he pushed with his feet. That gained them a full foot.

The car flipped over quickly below them then. It rolled from its roof onto the passenger side, perched there for a breathless moment, and then plunged over the edge, swallowed by the yawning abyss below.

Crashing noises followed by ominous silence marked the end of Willa's car. The cliff loomed above them, and only a thin length of nylon stood between the two of them and the same fate as her car.

It was a tortuously slow journey up the cliff. Stones rolled out from under his feet and dug into his back painfully as he made his way back up the slope with Willa sprawled on top of him. His arms ached, then burned like fire, then went numb and heavy under the strain of hauling both of them up the mountain, inch by agonizing inch.

It gave him plenty of time to think about what would have happened to her if he hadn't come back to look for her again. Plenty of time to ponder his life without Willa, with only a hole in his heart where she used to live. Plenty of time to make peace with the fact that he loved this woman, age difference or not, parentage or not, social status or not. And most important of all, whether or not she returned his feelings.

He had given her his love without any expectation of payment in kind, and the notion shocked him. Was this that selflessness people talked about when the subject of true love came up? He'd always rolled his eyes at those sappy souls. Love was about bargaining like everything else in life.

Lord knew it had been a coldly calculated deal between him and Melinda. I help your career, you help mine. I boost your social standing, you boost my image. It had been purely a business deal between them, but they'd both been either too jaded or too damned ignorant of what love was to know they hadn't gotten it right at all. Hell, in retrospect, he doubted Melinda had ever loved anyone in her entire life. For that matter, neither had he. Until now.

He grunted and groaned, straining for every inch of progress up that damned cliff, carrying Willa along with him. As painful as it was.

They had almost reached the top when she roused again.

Disoriented, she tried to push up to her hands and knees and succeeded in causing a mini-avalanche that slid them a dozen heart-stopping feet back down the cliff before he was able to dig in hard enough with his heels to stop the plunge toward death.

"Don't move," he grunted as he gripped her tightly against him with both arms. She struggled weakly and he tried again to get through to her. "Willa. It's Gabe. I've got you. I need you to relax and trust me. Let me do all the work."

Whether she heard him or not, he couldn't tell. But she subsided against him once more and he went back to work climbing that damned cliff bit by painful bit.

Finally, his head cleared the slope. He pushed once more and his shoulders reached the edge of the road. One more big push and he was able to roll onto his side, laying Willa on the road's shoulder. Breathing hard, he dragged himself up one last time by the rope and landed on the flat road beside Willa. Panting, he pushed to his feet. His arms were in so much pain, he barely registered the gravel grinding into his palms and scraping them raw.

Exhausted, he summoned the strength to lift Willa in his arms. He laid her in the back of the SUV, climbed in the vehicle and carefully U-turned on the narrow road to point it down the mountain. Driving as fast as he dared, he headed back to Vengeance Hospital.

Most of the news crews had left, along with the fire department and their barricades. He pulled up in front of the emergency-room door and raced around to the back of the Escalade. He picked up Willa, who was still unconscious, and hurried into the emergency room with her.

The same nurse Melinda had snapped at took one look at the two of them and ordered, "This way."

He followed her into the examining room across the hall from Melinda's and laid Willa on the bed there. He wasn't surprised as another nurse and the doctor who'd treated Melinda shoved him aside. But he was surprised as a third nurse took him by the arm and led him into the next room.

"She's the one who's hurt. Not me," he protested.

"Have you looked at yourself in a mirror?" she asked.

"No."

"How does your back feel?"

Now that she mentioned it, his back did burn a bit. "I guess it hurts a little."

"What happened to you? It looks like a mountain lion attacked you."

Oh. All of a sudden, his entire body felt like raw hamburger. "That would be the stones, I suppose. I had to carry Willa up a cliff. It was so steep I had to lie on my back and push us up the slope."

"I'm going to cut off your shirt, Mr. Dawson. And then I'm going to clean out your cuts and see if any of them need stitches. This might sting a little."

He yelped as the nurse's idea of a little sting hit his skin. Acid wouldn't have hurt much more, he reflected as he tried to distract himself from the fire on his back. The next several minutes were spent in grim silence while the nurse worked, and he gasped periodically.

Finally, she announced, "All done. Mostly scratches and contusions. It's going to be uncomfortable for a few days, but it should heal up. I'll have the doc come take a look at you when he's done with the young woman."

"How is she?"

"Now, how would I know?" the nurse asked gently. "I've been in here the whole time taking care of you."

"Could you check for me? Is she going to be all right?"

"Are you family?"

"Might as well be. She's got no one else. Well, technically, her mother's alive, but that woman's less than useless right now. Her mom's the reason she was out driving on that dangerous road, anyway."

The nurse left without comment and he swore under his breath, agonizing. Willa had to be okay. She *had* to. He prayed hard then, making every bargain with God he could think of if He would just save Willa's life.

The nurse poked her head back in a few minutes later. "Since you're not family I can't say anything, but if you were family, I'd tell you your friend is alive."

"What else would you tell me?" he asked anxiously.

"She hit her head. Concussion. Going to have to spend a day or two here for observation at a minimum. She's gone for an MRI to rule out any internal injuries, but initial indications don't show anything life threatening. She's regained consciousness. Is asking for you. As soon as she's done getting scanned, you can see her."

Gabe jumped up off the edge of the bed and gave the nurse a big hug.

"Easy, there," she exclaimed. "I just got your bleeding stopped. Don't make me clean you up twice."

He let go and stepped back sheepishly.

"By the way, your ex-wife has been moved to a room. The doctor wanted to release her, but she made such a stink about it that he finally gave in. What a bi—" the nurse broke off. "Uhh, interesting woman, your wife."

He replied blandly, "She can be quite a bitch, too."

The nurse smiled broadly at him. "There's a big pile of paperwork out front for you to fill out when you have a moment."

He nodded, and spent the next half hour filling out the required insurance forms and questionnaires on himself and Willa. He indicated that he would pay for any medical costs her insurance didn't cover.

He glanced at the big clock on the wall. Nearly eleven o'clock. If he was lucky, Melinda would be asleep by now, and this obligatory sympathy visit would be short and sweet.

Nonetheless, he got directions and headed up to the third floor where Melinda's room was. He stopped by the nurses' station to inquire about her, but a screech of fury from her room answered the question of whether or not she was asleep.

The duty nurse glared up at him in exasperation.

"Horse tranquilizers might shut her up," he commented drily.

"Or a ball-peen hammer," the woman snapped back.

They broke into simultaneous smiles. Gabe murmured, "Could you tell her I stopped by to ask about her…after she went to sleep?"

"Gabe? Is that you?" Melinda called out from her room.

Drat.

"Busted," the nurse whispered sympathetically.

"If there's any word on Willa Merris, will you come rescue me?"

The nurse nodded conspiratorially. Steeling himself to endure one of Melinda's patented tirades, he stepped into her room. But his heart was in another part of the building entirely.

Chapter 16

Willa started as she opened her eyes and was surrounded by nothing but white. Had she *died?* "Where am I?" she asked experimentally.

A disembodied voice answered, "You're in an MRI machine, Miss Merris. Please don't move. We're almost done."

"I'm alive, then?"

"Very much so."

That was good, at any rate. "How did I get here?"

"An orderly wheeled you down here on a gurney."

"No. I mean to the hospital."

"Mr. Dawson brought you in."

So, she hadn't imagined that dream of him cradling her with his body and climbing out of hell with her. Except it hadn't been hell. It had been outside, though. She remembered feeling a breeze on her skin. And the acrid taste of limestone dust.

Something bad had happened…. She tried to remember, but only snatches came back to her. Strange laughter echoing around her. Someone pushing her. No, not her. She frowned and tried hard to remember. Her car. Someone pushed her car.

Abruptly, memory exploded of standing on her brake pedal with all her strength while her little car slid over the edge of a cliff on the way to Lover's Point.

"Oh!" she exclaimed. She tried to sit up, but something restrained her.

"Please, ma'am. Don't move."

"Someone tried to kill me. I remember now!"

A pause. "Who?"

"I don't know. A car. No. A van."

"A van tried to kill you?" the voice asked doubtfully.

"Well, obviously not the van itself. Someone in a van. It hit me and then pushed me off the road."

"I'll notify the police, ma'am. But please lie still."

She subsided, impatient for the stupid MRI to end. "Where's Gabe?"

"Mr. Dawson?"

"Yes, yes," she answered impatiently.

"He's waiting for you. You can see him as soon as you're done."

And just like that, everything was all right. She was alive. Gabe was alive. He'd saved her like he always did, and he was nearby. Her knight in shining armor. Warm, soft, joyous feelings flooded her. This *so* had to be love. She loved him. Overwhelmed and overjoyed at the notion, she relaxed until a technician came to wheel her out of the MRI machine.

Her first words were, "Can I see him now? Can I see Gabe?"

"I'll tell the doctor you're asking for him."

But she was wheeled into a room and hooked up to a bunch of machines, and still there was no sign of him.

A new doctor came in and announced, "Your MRI looks good. There don't appear to be any serious internal injuries. I think we can safely say you're going to make a full recovery." He shined a bright flashlight into both of her eyes and added, "We're going to keep you here for observation overnight, though, because you hit your head and were unconscious for an extended period of time. It's just a precaution. Is there anyone we should notify?"

A deep voice said from the doorway, "Consider me notified, doctor."

Her heart leaped, and she smiled at Gabe. Even through the bright spots dancing in front of her eyes from the doctor's flashlight, Gabe was beautiful. His jaw had a long scratch on it, and he was moving carefully, but he was still her Gabe.

She held out her arms to him and he brushed past the doctor to gather her in his embrace. Tears of joy overflowed her eyes.

"Hey, no need to cry, baby. You're going to be fine," Gabe murmured into her hair.

"I'm not sad," she whispered back. "I'm happy. To see you and to be alive. I knew you'd save me."

His arms tightened around her. He spoke over her head. "Does she get a clean bill of health besides the knock on her noggin, doc?"

"Yes, sir."

His arms tightened even more, but she didn't care one bit that he was squeezing the stuffing out of her. For a while there, she'd been pretty sure she wasn't getting off that mountain alive. The doctor slipped out of the room, for which she was entirely grateful. There was something she needed to tell Gabe, and she darned well didn't want an audience when she did it.

She hesitated, nervous, and opted for a circuitous approach to the topic on her mind. "I thought I was done for up there."

"God, Will. I'm so sorry I didn't get to you sooner. I was no more than a mile away when I had to turn around and go back to town. If only I had known you were out there—" He buried his face in her hair and took a shaky breath.

Why did he have to return to town? She would normally have asked, but she didn't want to get sidetracked. "I had a little while to think about my life in between bouts of unconsciousness."

"Reach any conclusions?" he asked.

"Actually, yes. I realized how much I trust you. And depend on you. I think of you as my knight in shining armor."

He laughed a little, sounded embarrassed. "Well, maybe I'm an old knight in dented and tarnished armor." He added teasingly, "To heck with a horse. I charge to rescue in a Cadillac."

"Nonetheless, you saved my life. I can never thank you enough."

"Willa, if something had happened to you—" He didn't finish the sentence. After a moment he said soberly, "Believe me, saving you was as much for my benefit as yours. If something bad had happened to you…" he tried again. Still no conclusion to that thought other than his arms crushing her until she squeaked for air.

"What I'm trying to say, Gabe, is that I think I lo—"

A commotion at the door stopped her on the verge of declaring her love for him. Gabe looked up sharply at the same time he leaned over her protectively. Two large, black-shirted men barged into the room in a rush. Her security guards. The poor guys looked nearly as frazzled and glad to see her alive as Gabe had.

And speaking of Gabe, he glared past her at the two men. "Yeah," he said grimly, "you're fired."

"Gabe!" she exclaimed.

"Baby, you almost died tonight. You shouldn't have been on that road alone and upset. You wouldn't have gone over the edge, otherwise."

"Uhh, actually, I would have," she said in a small voice.

All three men stared at her. "What do you mean?" Gabe asked ominously.

"There was a van. It pushed me off the road. Well, it hit me first. Rear-ended me. And I hit my brakes. That's when it pushed me over the edge."

"As in it hit you a second time?" Gabe exclaimed.

"No. As in it drove up behind me, put its bumper against mine and the driver stood on the gas until he shoved me off the edge of the road.

The two security men all but jumped down her throat. "What did the van look like? Did you get a license plate? What did the driver look like?" At a terse nod from Gabe, their cell phones came out and both men talked fast into them.

When the guards came up for air, she said wryly, "I guess my guards are rehired, then?"

Gabe nodded reluctantly, but added to the men, "Just so we're clear, gentlemen. One strike and you're out. No more screwups."

"Roger that, Mr. Dawson," the taller of the two men agreed.

The security team went through their questions again, more slowly this time. She described the van as best she could, which wasn't actually in much detail. She hadn't seen the driver at all, nor had she spotted a license plate before it was plastered against her rear bumper.

As their questions wound down, she added slowly, "I have this weird memory of laughter. At least I think it was laughter." She described the maniacal sound echoing around her as she lay in her mangled car.

Gabe and the security men exchanged significant looks. "Okay, Willa. It's time to tell us about every enemy you have. Anyone who might have any reason to harm you," Gabe said gently.

She frowned. "I don't have any enemies."

"That's not exactly true," Gabe responded soberly. "There's James Ward, for one. He's pretty pissed off at you."

She winced. "I think his mother is madder than he is."

Gabe nodded at the guard who was taking notes on a tablet computer. "Good point. Roseanne Ward goes on the list, too."

The second guard asked encouragingly, "Who has given you a dirty look recently or said something nasty to you or hated something you've done?"

Willa sighed. "Just about everybody."

"Like who?" the guy prompted.

Willa went through the past several days in her mind. "Jacquelyn Carver from the charity ball. Those anti-fracking protestors outside the ball. My dad's right-hand man, Larry Shore."

"When was he nasty to you?" Gabe blurted in surprise.

"He was furious that the governor appointed me to my father's position and not him," Willa replied.

Gabe nodded as she continued building her list. "That reporter, Paula Craddock, seems to have it in for me. Oh, and the guy from my dad's political party who thought I was going to endorse him to replace my father in the senate race." She added reluctantly, "And my mother. She's convinced I'm trying to rob her blind."

"Then there's the six-hundred-pound gorilla in the corner you're ignoring," Gabe commented drily.

She blinked at him in surprise. "I don't understand."

"Have you forgotten about that secret committee your dad served on?"

"You think government agents might be trying to kill me because I found out about them?" she exclaimed.

"Possibly."

She frowned. "But wouldn't they have succeeded by now?"

"Honey, somebody pushed your car off a cliff tonight. I'd say they came damned close to succeeding, wouldn't you?"

He was right.

One of the guards piped up. "What government agency, specifically, is trying to kill the senator?"

Willa cut off Gabe when he would have answered. "It's classified. I'm not allowed to talk about it."

"With all due respect, ma'am, every one of the men at Elite Security is ex-Special Forces. We all have high-level security clearances." When she hesitated, the guard added, "We also have tons of back channel contacts in the government. Maybe we can run interference for you. Call off the dogs, as it were."

She looked over at Gabe, and he nodded to her. Quickly, she filled in the men on what she'd seen on her father's computer before it had all been erased and/or stolen. When she was finished, one of the guards let out a low whistle.

The second guard nodded. "That explains why you wouldn't accept Secret Service protection. We were wondering about that. You didn't know who to trust inside the government, did you? Are the break-ins at your mother's home and your place related to this committee?"

She shrugged, but thought better of the movement as her body protested achily. Oh, man. She was going to be one sore puppy tomorrow. She answered, "I don't see how the break-ins can't be related. The timing is pretty suspicious, and both break-ins targeted my computers."

The guards traded grim looks. "We're going to be increasing your security detail, ma'am, and we're going to be packing substantially more heat."

"What does that mean?" she asked.

"We'll be more heavily armed. Your security protocols are going to be quite a bit tighter from here on out. We apologize in advance for the inconvenience."

She was flummoxed when Gabe rolled his eyes. Apparently, he had a good idea what the guy was talking about. Personally, she was clueless. But she liked the sound of it. If she'd learned nothing else tonight, it was that she *really* didn't want to die. She'd just found Gabe, darn it! Speaking of which, she still hadn't gotten around to telling him she loved him.

"Is there anything else, gentlemen?" she asked, being sure to let weariness creep into her voice. It was a cheap ploy, but she really wanted to be alone with Gabe.

"No, ma'am. We'll have men posted outside your door around the clock and outside below your window. If you need anything from us or sense any threat whatsoever, give a shout out."

"Okay." She sighed. Sheesh. She was on the third floor, and they were still going to put a guy under her window?

The guards stepped outside, and she waited for the door to close behind them. "Thanks for not firing them," she told Gabe. "It wasn't their fault I ran out on them."

"Next time, no matter how upset you are or how much you just want to be alone, wait for your security team. Okay?"

"I promise." Jeez. She wasn't a five-year-old. Now that she understood the magnitude of the threat to her life, she wasn't about to ditch her guards again.

"As I was saying before the guys interrupted us," she started, "I realized something important while I was waiting to die."

Gabe winced, and moved swiftly to gather her in his arms again. She was distracted when his mouth touched hers tentatively. As soon as it became clear that she was not caused pain by it, he deepened the kiss swiftly. It felt so good to be with him like this, tasting him, merging a part of herself with him, melting into him.

She would never get enough of him. She'd wanted him for so long, and to have him now, like this, was nothing short of a miracle. He kissed her voraciously, as if he needed to reassure himself in this way that she was alive and essentially unharmed. She was glad to provide him with the proof.

Finally, he came up for air and she dragged in an unsteady breath.

"You were saying?" he murmured against her lips.

"Mmm. What? Oh. Yes. As I was saying—"

The door swung open behind Gabe, banging into the wall. "Mr. Daws—" A nurse started. "Oh! I'm sorry."

Gabe sighed against her temple and half turned to face the nurse. "You wanted me?"

"Yes. Your wife is demanding to know where you are. The FBI wants to question her again and she refuses to talk to them until you're there."

"Melinda's here?" Willa gasped. "They found her? Is she all right?"

Gabe went stiff against her. "Yes. She was rescued earlier this evening and she's fine. Well, actually, she's acting damned erratic. But physically, she's okay."

"Oh," Willa said in a small voice. "I'm glad she's all right. If she needs you, by all means, you should go to her."

"But—" Gabe started.

A beautiful brunette woman stuck her head in through the door just then. "There you are, Mr. Dawson. If you could come with me, I need to speak with Dr. Grayson, and she's being a wee bit uncooperative."

"A wee bit?" the nurse snorted. "She threatened to kill that cop."

Willa glanced at Gabe in surprise. He muttered, "Deputy Green. I hope she does kill him. It would be a good riddance."

Willa forced a smile even though her heart was shattering. "Go. She needs you. I've got my guards and I'll be okay."

On cue, one of the security guards stepped into the room. "I'll be stationed in here until Mr. Dawson or another family member returns. You're not to be alone at any time, Senator."

"Not even when I'm sleeping?"

"No, ma'am."

Seriously? The ramifications of super-tight security

were suddenly dawning on her. She hated being hovered over constantly.

"I'll be back in a flash," Gabe whispered to her as he leaned down to kiss her cheek. "Rest until I get back. Okay?"

"Okay," she replied. Now that he mentioned it, she was feeling sleepy. Dead tired, in fact.

The door closed behind Gabe as he joined the gorgeous brunette. "Who was the pretty one?" she asked her guard.

"Agent Delaney. FBI. Her credentials were legit. Nobody gets in here without us checking them out, ma'am."

FBI, huh? Must be one of the agents on Melinda Grayson's case. His ex-wife's rescue must have been the reason Gabe turned around and went back to town earlier. Had he been out looking for her before? She asked the guard drowsily, "Did Gabe know I took off from my mother's house?"

"Yes, ma'am. He was the first person we called when you didn't go straight back to your place."

Mystery solved. Embarrassed that her guards knew so much about her and Gabe, she subsided. A thread of jealousy tangled into a messy little knot in her stomach. It was clear that Melinda and Gabe still shared a strong connection despite how long they'd been divorced.

More devastated than she cared to admit, Willa rolled gingerly onto her side and pulled the covers up over her ear. Thank goodness she hadn't gotten a chance to blurt out a declaration of undying love to him earlier. She would've looked like a complete idiot.

It wasn't her place to give Gabe an ultimatum. The

ex-wife or her. Besides, it looked like he'd already chosen. Melinda Grayson snapped her fingers, and Gabe still jumped for her.

Chapter 17

Gabe had just about had it with Melinda and her bizarre antics. The whole clinging, crying, I'm-so-weak-and-in-need-of-saving female act from her was wearing very thin with him.

Willa could cry and cling to him and even call him her knight in shining armor, and it made him feel like a conquering hero. He knew without question that underneath her soft exterior was a brave, strong woman. And yet, she still needed him and was willing to depend on him. Unlike Melinda, who'd never needed anyone in her life and scorned any female who did "need a man."

Willa had faced down the disapproval and outright condemnation of literally everyone she knew with quiet grace over the past week. She'd stood up to her attacker, James Ward, at great personal cost, and she'd stepped into her father's shoes without batting an eyelash.

Melinda was frankly just being mean. The good

news was it appeared that Agent Delaney was on to his ex's tactics. She blandly ignored Melinda's tears and pleas that it was all too upsetting to think about, and pushed her relentlessly for details. Melinda might have finally met her match. Although truth be told, he'd stack Willa up against Melinda any day and bet on Willa to win.

Willa's strength was quiet. Unassuming. Deep within her. It wasn't something she needed to put on display, and she had no need to prove she was tougher than everyone else. Unlike Melinda, who apparently felt an overwhelming need to bully everyone around her. Funny how he'd never perceived it as bullying before, but that was ultimately what it was. Thank goodness Willa had come along to make him see his ex's true colors. Who knew how long it would have been, if ever, before he would have caught on to Melinda without Willa's shining example.

Funny how he thought he'd been running around rescuing Willa, when all along, she'd been rescuing him.

Finally, an exasperated Agent Delaney left Melinda's room. On cue, Melinda's waterworks and hand wringing stopped cold.

"Better now?" Gabe asked drily. He felt bad as soon as the sarcasm left his mouth. The woman had been kidnapped and traumatized. She had a right to be messed up. Just because he'd rather be with someone else was no reason to be nasty with her.

She answered stiffly, "The local police will be here in the morning to question me. I need you to be here for that."

Insecurity and Melinda Grayson went together like hot sparks and dynamite. What in the hell was going on with her? "What's the deal, Melinda? Why all the theatrics with the authorities?"

"Like they're going to take me seriously any other way?"

"Since when doesn't everyone take you seriously?" he snorted.

She threw him a rare, startled look. It dissolved into a thoughtful expression, and he took advantage of her distraction to say, "I have to go."

"Where are you off to in such a rush?" she snapped.

"We're not married anymore, Melinda. That's frankly none of your business."

"A woman, then. One of your usual bimbos?" she sneered.

Like he planned to share the intimate details of his love life with her? He clenched his jaw against the angry retort struggling to escape his mouth and turned to leave.

Behind him, she commented snidely, "Face it, Gabe, you're never going to find happiness with a woman. You never have quite been able to give them what they really need."

He paused. Looked back over his shoulder. Smiled. "Thank you for that note of derision. It was exactly what I needed from you." He nodded pleasantly. He had indeed meant the comment sincerely. She was making it easy for him to cut whatever remaining emotional ties lingered between them. And it felt good. Really good.

Melinda's ability to snare people in her web and hold them there was truly extraordinary. She was a master at manipulating people, and had just demonstrated her uncanny ability to put her finger on people's Achilles' heels and exploit them to her own advantage. He would be forever grateful to Willa for proving Melinda wrong.

It felt like a ten-ton weight had lifted off his chest now that he no longer believed the crap his ex-wife spouted at him about his inadequacies with relationships. He was finally free of her web.

More power to Melinda and her head games. She may have survived a horrific ordeal, but he was done with her.

The bitch was alive? Not possible! Her car went off the cliff!

Noooooo! The scream echoed off the vehicle's interior. Fists pounded the steering wheel until blood came. Crimson. Mesmerizing. Beautiful. It should have been her blood. Willa Merris's blood. It would be her blood soon. Very soon. Speculative eyes studied the security guard lounging against the stucco wall of the hospital. A hundred to one that one of the windows above the guy was her room.

There were ways to get around security guards, though. A giggle escaped at how easy it really was to fool them. The giggle turned into laughter and the laughter to hysteria. Oh, yes. Little Willa would pay for surviving, most of all.

Gabe tossed and turned most of the night, fretting over Willa. It was enlightening how his worried thoughts never once turned to his ex-wife. No question about it. He was slam-dunk, plumb-tuckered in love with Willa Merris. A goner. And nothing had ever felt half this great in his entire life.

Melinda would no doubt accuse him of having a midlife crisis. Part of him replied that if she was right, bring it on. But most of him knew without a doubt the accusation would not be true. His emotional growth had frozen in his late twenties when he'd gotten tangled up with Melinda. Willa had set him free and got him moving forward again. Finally.

When light finally began to show dully around the curtains, he threw on jogging clothes and went for a run to work off some of the residual stress of nearly losing Willa last night. It was a cloudy, threatening morning with heavy gray clouds scudding low across the sky. He'd gone several brisk miles and circled back to his house when he spotted the white news van parked in front of it. Paula Craddock got out as he approached.

"Don't you ever give up?" he asked her.

"Never. I always get my story."

"What story are you after this time?"

"What's going on between you and Willa Merris?"

"I thought you were a hard news reporter. Isn't that a little too gossip-column for you? What happened? Did you get demoted to the society page?"

"Avoiding the question, are we? Then am I to assume you two are having an affair?"

"I believe one of the parties in a relationship has to be married for it to qualify as an affair, Ms. Craddock."

"I'm going to report that you two are an item," she threatened.

He shrugged. "You can report whatever you want. Just remember my attorneys will hold you to the strictest interpretation of what constitutes slander or libel."

He'd had enough of her, and jogged up his sidewalk to his front door. She called after him, "I always get my story, Gabe. You can't stop me."

Whatever. He slammed the door on her threats and took a quick shower. He grabbed a bagel on his way out the door and was relieved that the news van had disappeared by the time he pulled out of his driveway in the

Escalade. He drove to the hospital eager to see Willa. He felt like a twenty-year-old kid in love for the first time.

Come to think of it, this was the first time he'd ever really been in love. Melinda had fascinated him and posed an irresistible challenge, but he'd never felt this bubbling-over joy and complete sense of rightness before. Part of him wanted to shout his love to the rooftops, and another part had gone entirely still and quiet. At peace. It was miraculous.

He headed for the third floor of the hospital and was satisfied to see the security guard at Willa's door nod alertly at him as he stepped out of the elevator. He stopped at the nurses' station and asked, "Is Willa awake yet? How was her night?"

"She's still sleeping, sir. I just came on duty, but I can check her chart for you. The night doctor and doctor coming on shift should be starting their rounds momentarily and will wake her up. You can ask Dr. Pitts how she did last night. He was her on-call physician."

Gabe was amused that the nurse pointedly told him nothing about Melinda. But then, he had just as pointedly not asked. He spotted a pair of doctors in white lab coats coming down the hall and headed for them to check on Willa's condition.

"Early for you to be here, Mr. Dawson," the one with the name Felix Pitts, M.D., embroidered over his pocket said.

"I was worried about my girl. She was pretty rattled last night. Did she sleep all right?"

"Like a baby. Assuming her condition doesn't change throughout the day today, we ought to be able to release her later. Will she be coming home with you? We'll want someone with her to monitor her condition for a few days."

"I hope she'll come home with me. I plan to ask her to marry me. Almost losing her has shown me just how deeply I care for her."

"Congratulations, Mr. Dawson," Pitts said warmly.

Gabe took a step toward Willa's room to peek in on her when a door across the hall swung open. Melinda gushed, "Gabe? Oh, my God. You want to marry me? That's incredible! I knew you'd never gotten over me. I never got over you, either. Of course I'll marry you again. This time for good. This time let's have a big, gaudy wedding to make up for that dinky little thing we had last time."

He stared at her, speechless. She thought he wanted to marry her? She'd never gotten over him? Huh?

The elevator slid open behind him, and Agent Delaney and the new sheriff stepped out of it. "Oh, good. You're awake," Agent Delaney said to Melinda. "Glad to see you're here, Mr. Dawson. Saves us any more theatrics like last night's."

Melinda's eyes narrowed at the FBI agent as she abruptly sagged against Gabe, forcing him to catch her body weight, lest she fall over.

"Why don't we take this into Dr. Grayson's room?" the sheriff suggested.

Cursing under his breath, Gabe was herded into Melinda's room, his ex clinging to him like a barnacle, to endure another session of Weird Melinda Interrogation. He cast a longing look over his shoulder at Willa's room before the door shut behind him.

Willa stared up at the ceiling of her room in utter shock. Gabe had proposed to Melinda? And she'd accepted? That didn't make any sense, but she'd heard it with her own ears. No mistake about it.

Nothing in Willa's life had prepared her for this sense of free fall. It was as if the entire planet had dropped away from beneath her feet. She was rushing through space toward oblivion and there was nothing to hold on to. No safety. No Gabe. Just blackness and falling. She'd been a fool to think that his attention was anything more than pity and guilt over what happened.

Sick to her stomach, she curled into a fetal ball, in too much agony even to cry. She breathed in jerky gasps as grief ripped her in two and then in two again, over and over until she was torn into tiny, scattered shreds.

He loved Melinda Grayson. Was going to re-marry his ex-wife.

Her life was over. No one was who they seemed. Not her father, her mother, the "good ladies" of her parents' social circle, James Ward…or Gabe.

She'd lain there for several minutes when the phone next to her bed rang, causing her to jump sky-high. Automatically, she reached for it, pulling the old-fashioned plastic receiver to her ear.

"Hello?" she managed to croak.

A raspy voice, obviously disguised or altered in some way, said, "Get away from your security guards. Meet me at your house in an hour."

"Who is this?" she mumbled.

The caller ignored her question. "One hour," the caller added.

"Or else what?" she asked, past really caring.

"Or else I'll start killing your students. One by one, I'll strangle the life out of their little bodies. And I'll make them scream first. Lovely screams of pain and terror. The animals in your garden were all right…but to kill a child by slow degrees…" The caller let out a groan of nearly sexual pleasure.

Willa's eyes went wide with revulsion and fright. The caller could have threatened her mother, or even Gabe. Those would have been the obvious choices. But no. Innocent five-year-olds who barely knew her were at risk. Yes, indeed, the caller knew her very well to harm kids if she didn't comply.

"Don't believe me? Let's listen to one of your little brats cry, shall we?"

She heard a sharp crack like a palm across a cheek, followed by the wails of what sounded like a small child. Her blood froze in her veins at the sound. *This monster had one of her kids?*

The children of Vengeance hadn't done anything to anybody. The school year had been barely two weeks old when her father had died and she'd had to take a leave of absence. The sounds of crying in the background turned her gut to jelly.

She *had* to save that child. She ought to call the police, but what was the point? They didn't believe anything she said anyway. Not to mention that unlike most of the guys on the force, she had no one to go home to. No family. She would be no great loss to anyone.

Frankly, she didn't much care if she lived or died right now. Losing Gabe on top of everything else was the last straw. Her spirit was broken. She was finished. She couldn't take any more. She was sick of being a pawn, sick of being jerked around by other people. No, she would personally deal with this bastard once and for all.

"Don't hurt that poor baby," she pleaded in a whisper, eyeing the security guard who was watching her now from over by the door. "It may take me a little while longer than that to get there, but I'll be there. I promise."

The phone clicked and a dial tone buzzed in her ear.

Crud. How was she supposed to get away from the brute squad hovering over her like protective bears? Panic made her jumpy, and a need to bolt and run for home threatened to overwhelm her at any second. She felt like she might throw up. *Hang on, sweetie. I'll come save you. I'll figure out a way.*

She lay there for several minutes racking her brain for an escape plan, but to no avail. Gabe had surrounded her with too much effective protection.

If she was going to take care of this mess herself, she had to ditch them, too. Besides, they'd gotten all chummy with Gabe since she disappeared yesterday. Was there no one at all whom she could trust? Her gut answered with a resounding no.

In the meantime, that poor child was depending on her. Panic and despair clawed at her. But then, her door swung open, and a pair of doctors stepped inside. Inspiration struck. She didn't know much about medicine, but she figured faking double vision and a terrible headache, oh, and drowsiness, would alarm them enough to run some more tests.

Sure enough, it worked like a charm. After about one minute of examining her, one of the doctors ordered her taken down to the imaging department for an emergency MRI.

An orderly pushed her in a wheelchair while her two inside-the-hospital bodyguards walked alongside. The guards had to stay outside of the MRI area and the orderly pushed her through a pair of swinging doors. One hurdle crossed; inside guards ditched. Now, to get out of here and somehow dodge the outdoor contingent of security.

She asked for a restroom visit before she went into the MRI machine and a female technician was happy to let her go. Thankfully, the bathroom had a window. It was small and fairly high, but as soon as she was alone, Willa climbed up on the counter and slid it open. It would be tight, but she could make it. And this side of the building was not the one her room had opened out onto. Hopefully, Gabe hadn't insisted on exterior guards on every side of the darned building. Scrambling awkwardly, she fell through the small window, mooning a bunch of birds that flew up, squawking, as she hit the grass.

Grabbing at the back of the gown to cover her bare backside, and crouching low, she darted out into the parking lot, ducking behind cars for cover. Rain threatened in the pregnant clouds overhead, but so far none had started falling. Thankfully, she lived only a dozen blocks from the hospital. Running barefoot was painful, but it wasn't like she had any choice. And it felt good to move. Her instincts had been screaming at her to do exactly this ever since that phone call came in.

A nut ball was hurting an innocent five-year-old, and she was the child's only hope. It was up to her to stop it from happening. Spurred by that knowledge, her feet flew across pavement and grass like the wind.

It was still early, and the streets were mostly empty. She alternated between jumping behind shrubs and racing along the sidewalk like she always went for a morning run in a hospital gown. If anyone had been watching her, they'd have surely thought she'd lost her mind. She just hoped she could reach her house before someone called the police on the lunatic woman running down the street.

She figured she had five to ten minutes before the MRI technician went looking for her, and notified her guards that she'd gone missing. Feeling the pressing weight of the ticking clock, she sprinted the last block to her house and ran around back to fetch the spare key hidden in her messy garage.

She burst into the house. "Hello?" she called. "Are you here? I came like you wanted."

Silence was her only answer. Where was the caller? Where was that poor baby? She'd made it home in under an hour. Now what?

Frantic, she went to her bedroom and dressed quickly in jeans, a T-shirt and running shoes. She ought to call the police, but then the sound of that slap and the wails that followed stopped her. This was her fault. Her problem to solve. Not the police's. She paced, wringing her hands. Her security guards would be here any second looking for her. She couldn't let them find her, but the caller obviously planned to contact her here next.

She jumped about a foot in the air when her phone rang. She pounced on the receiver. "Hello?"

"I can't come to your house. Those thugs of yours might spot me. Meet me at the Darby College Bell Tower in ten minutes."

"But I don't have a car," she replied, feeling dense.

"Don't you have a bicycle? Run for all I care. But get there."

How did the caller know she had a bike? "You have to let that child go. I won't cooperate unless you promise."

"Fine," the caller snapped. "I don't want the brat, anyway. It's you I want. You and I are taking a little trip."

"Where are we going?"

"Where else? To where you and your damned family ruined me. The Vacarro Field, bitch. A fitting ending for the Merrises, don't you think?"

Huh? The line went dead and a dial tone resumed in her ear. Confused, she nonetheless ran for the garage and her bicycle. Even with wheels, getting to the bell tower in ten minutes would be close. Not to mention her security team would likely show up here at any second and prevent her from saving that child. They hadn't heard the fury in the caller's voice, the sick pleasure at the thought of causing pain. They didn't realize that her caller was dead serious. But she did. Oh, how she did.

She yanked her bike off its hooks in the garage and headed through her backyard. At least it would blend in on the campus and be hard to spot in the crowd of students pedaling to their eight o'clock classes. The bike had the added advantage of letting her go cross-country and not having to stick to streets that were no doubt already crawling with freaked-out security guards.

Eyes watering from fear and from the wind whipping past her face as she pedaled for that poor baby's life, she managed to reach the edge of the campus. She guided the bike toward the broad, grassy park surrounding the tall brick clock tower in the middle of campus.

A few fat raindrops splatted onto the pavement around her. What else could go wrong today? She was about to get drenched. As the reality of facing the psychopath at the other end of the phone in person loomed, common sense finally began to kick in. Or maybe that was panicked survival mode kicking in. She overrode the impulse by reminding herself that a child's life hung in the balance. Her life was worth nothing in the face of that. If she had to sacrifice herself to save an innocent, so be it.

Still, meeting this person on her own was unquestionably stupid. She had no skill at talking down a deranged lunatic. She should have called the police. Told her guards. Gotten some sort of backup. But the sound of crying echoed in her ears, and spurred her onward despite her doubts. She'd figure out something.

Now what? She was almost to the bell tower. One more street to cross, then she'd have to get off her bike and walk it across the grass to the base of the bell tower.

And then she spotted it. A beat-up white van parked at the curb to her left. It started to roll forward directly toward her. The driver had seen her. Desperation and a very belated sense of fear for her life finally penetrated the fog that had enveloped her since she'd heard Melinda Grayson accept Gabe's proposal in the hall outside her room.

The van pulled up beside her. She wasn't getting in that thing unless the driver turned that child loose this instant. The passenger door swung open and she stared into the maw at the familiar face.

"Get in," the driver snapped.

"Let the kid go," she retorted.

The driver laughed and tossed a tape recorder outside at her feet. While she stared in shock, the driver clapped once, in loud imitation of slapping someone, and then let out a perfect rendition of a small child wailing in pain and fear.

She'd been tricked? Willa took a step away from the door.

"Ah, ah, ah. Not so fast, Willa." The small black circle of a pistol barrel came into view, pointed directly at her. She stared in horror at the promise of death staring at her. "Get in the van. Now."

Everyone knew never to get in a car with a criminal. It was infinitely smarter to get shot in a public place where medical help and police would be summoned rapidly than it was to allow oneself to be taken someplace isolated where the kidnapper could torture and kill at their leisure and there was no hope at all of rescue.

Thing was, Gabe didn't love her. He was going to marry Melinda. This person could still kidnap and kill her students at some later date, and Willa firmly believed the threat. Her or the kids? She had nothing left to live for, and the children had their entire lives in front of them. It was a no-brainer.

"If I go with you, you have to give me your solemn promise that you'll never hurt any of my students. That you'll leave them completely alone. Promise?"

"Fine. Whatever. I promise." The driver looked around outside nervously. "Now get in."

She stepped off her bike, laid it down on the grass and slid into the passenger seat. The van pulled away from the curb.

Chapter 18

Gabe started when one of Willa's security guards burst into Melinda's room. One look at the man's tense face, and Gabe dumped Melinda unceremoniously on the bed and strode toward the door, ignoring her squawk of outrage.

"What now?" he bit out as he and the guard headed out into the hall.

The guard broke into a run and Gabe's alarm climbed. This guy panicked was not a good sign. As they raced for the exit, the guard reported in snatches, "She ran. Got a call in her room. Went pale. My guy was suspicious. Doctors came in just then and sent her for an emergency MRI. Guard figured she was sick. She went to the restroom, climbed out the window and disappeared. We need you to go to her house. See if anything's out of place or missing. Some clue as to where she's gone."

"Why her house?" Gabe asked as he jumped in the passenger side of the guy's black SUV.

The vehicle peeled out of the parking lot in an aggressive move that had him grabbing the armrest as the guard answered, "She was wearing a hospital gown. She needed clothes. If she's running, she needs money. Women rarely flee without stuff—a change of clothing, makeup, a purse."

Gabe nodded and didn't further distract the grim man from concentrating on his driving. The SUV screeched to a halt in Willa's driveway in about two minutes flat.

"Take the front," the guard ordered as he tore around back.

Gabe leaped the front steps and pounded on the front door, shouting, "Willa! Let me in!"

Nothing. But a few seconds later, he heard the sound of shattering glass, and moments later the guard let him in the front door. "Not here," the guy announced. "Hospital gown's on the floor of her bedroom, so she was here."

Gabe raced through the house looking for something, anything, that would tell him where Willa had gone. A quick circuit of the cottage brought him back to the living room in frantic frustration. The guard was talking fast into his cell phone. He identified himself as Cade McGrath, the team lead on the Merris job.

Gabe scanned the cozy room. A faint scent of gardenias drifted to him and nearly brought him to his knees. Where the hell was she? What made her run? Fear for her safety roared through him. As sure as he was standing here, something was terribly wrong with her. He felt it in his bones.

His gaze landed on the remote control that turned

on her white-noise system. Had the bastards from that secret government program snatched her to silence her about their shenanigans? Icy terror flowed through his veins at the thought of Willa in the hands of cold-blooded killers. She'd been so afraid of them. They'd been tapping her phone, for God's sake....

He leaped for Willa's telephone, which lay on the coffee table beside the white-noise controller. He snapped at the guard, "If someone was bugging this phone, would they hear me talking into it if I didn't dial a number?"

"Probably not," McGrath answered, frowning. "It would be an automated recording system activated when a call came in or went out. The recordings would typically be reviewed later. If there's a direct surveillance op running, there may be a couple of guys sitting in a vacant house across the street beside the recording device. In that case, they would listen to the calls in real time."

Gabe punched in the first phone number he could think of—his apartment. He waited impatiently until his computer picked up. Then he spoke loudly and clearly, "I know you guys are bugging Willa's phone. The senator has been kidnapped and her life is in danger. If it was *not* you guys who took her, I need you to pick up this line right now."

He paused, but no one came on the line. He continued grimly, "If it was you guys who took her, I swear I'm going to blow your little program sky-high. By tonight, I'll have you sons of bitches splashed all over the national news. Willa told me all about you, and I remember enough names and places of your operations and killings to make your lives a living hell—"

A male voice spoke abruptly in his ear. "Is this Mr. Dawson?"

"Yes, it is. Who is this?"

"We did not kidnap Senator Merris. What do I have to do to convince you not to reveal our existence? I assure you, it's a matter of national security."

"Whether or not you add to or take away from national security is a discussion for another time," Gabe snapped. "What I need right now is for you to tell me if any calls have come in to this phone number in the past half hour."

"One call, Mr. Dawson."

"Do you have a recording of it?"

"We do."

"I need to know who called Willa and exactly what was said."

"The recording hasn't been reviewed and transcribed, yet. I will have to pull up the actual recording. This will take a moment."

Gabe waited impatiently and caught the thunderstruck look Cade McGrath was throwing him. He murmured at the guard, "Have you got weapons in your vehicle?"

"Of course."

Gabe nodded, and the anonymous voice was back in his ear. "It'll be quickest if I play the recording for you."

Gabe put the receiver on speakerphone so McGrath could hear, too. They listened in dismay at the electronically altered voice. A child had been kidnapped to force her cooperation? No surprise, Willa was throwing herself on her sword to save the kid. Then the caller mentioned the Vacarro Field. Gabe and McGrath looked at

each other in relief. That was where they'd find Willa.
If they were in time.

"Let's go," Gabe bit out.

Willa looked over at James Ward, who was staring
grimly at the winding road ahead through a pounding
rain. His route today was slightly different than hers
yesterday, but the road was still steep and winding,
made even more treacherous by the rain. He was driving like a madman through the arroyos and canyons
where he'd nearly succeeded in killing her last night.

Oh, wait. He *was* a madman.

Lord, Willa must be terrified. To have the horror
repeat itself like this, for her attacker to get hold of
her *again*—it must be every victim's worst nightmare.

"James, do you want me to drop the charges against
you? Is that what this is all about? Because if you want,
I'll do it. My life has moved on, and I've gotten past
what happened between us."

"You think dropping the charges removes the stain
on my reputation?" he snarled.

"If you're worried about your reputation, why are you
kidnapping me? This won't help matters, you know," she
said reasonably. "Why don't we just go back to town,
get a cup of coffee and talk this over?"

He glanced over at her, and she recoiled from the flat,
blank, almost reptilian quality to his eyes. She asked
carefully, "How are you feeling, James?"

"Head hurts," he whined in a weirdly childlike voice.
"Pain won't stop. Brain's exploding from the inside out.
Keep telling them. But they won't believe me. Damned
head's splitting in two."

"Do you want to pull over and rest a little? I can drive you to a drugstore. Get you some pain relievers."

"All your fault," he mumbled. The van swerved dangerously close to the edge of a steep drop-off and she let out a little squeal of fear as he jerked the van back onto the road.

She thought fast. Headaches. Stress, maybe? Lack of sleep? Were they associated with mental illness, maybe? She had to keep him talking. Get him to reveal what was really going on with him. Figure out a way to diffuse his unreasoning rage.

He drove on in silence. His foot must be mashed down on the accelerator all the way to the floor. The only thing keeping them from tearing along this road like a bat out of hell was undoubtedly the steepness of the grade and the van's underpowered engine. But as it was, they careened around every curve, and it felt like they were going to skid out and plunge over the edge of the road to their deaths at any second.

Terrified beyond the ability to speak, Willa clung to the armrest and braced her feet against the floorboards, praying for all she was worth just to make it to the Vacarro Field alive.

Finally, they topped the highest of the ridges and the road began to go downhill. Thankfully, on this side of the canyon, the road's curves were gentler and finally straightened out completely. The van picked up speed and tore along the asphalt road at nearly a hundred miles per hour.

When her heart came down out of her throat enough to speak, she asked, "What's so significant about the Vacarro Field to you?"

He glanced over, and the van careened to the right. "Eyes on the road!" she blurted.

He sneered. "Damned schoolteacher. So self-righteous. Willa Merris, goody two-shoes. So charitable and noble. Giving up wealth to teach goddamned brats."

"I don't teach because it's noble. I do it because I love kids. I love teaching."

"Bitch."

"We were talking about the Vacarro Field," she prompted, trying to steer his erratic thoughts back to the topic at hand.

"Son of a bitch thought he'd screw us good, didn't he?"

"My father?" she guessed. Most times when someone got called an SOB around her, he'd been the recipient of the epithet.

"Tried to buy us out. Rob us blind. And my old man was gonna do it, too. But my mother wouldn't let him. Good thing, or the bastard would have succeeded."

"My father tried to buy the Ward interest in the Vacarro wells?" This was the first she'd heard of that.

"Tried to steal 'em, more like."

"Why do you say that?"

"Offered about a tenth of what they're worth." He mumbled incoherently under his breath for a few seconds and then his words became clear again. "Gotta have that money. Save my ass. Debts. Bad investments. Not my fault. Who'd a' thunk those calls would get exercised. Damned bankers…"

She frowned, confused. "If you were in financial trouble, why didn't your family take my father's offer and pay off your debts?"

"Oh, that's what you'd have liked, isn't it?" James exploded. "Screw us when we're down. That's how you Merrises operate. But I screwed you, instead!" He laughed wildly, and Willa recoiled from him. Well, at least she knew now why James had raped her. He was getting even with her father. She supposed that was better than James having actually had it in for her.

"God, that smell…" James said in a singsong voice that trailed off like an old woman drifting off to sleep midsentence.

Startled, she glanced over at him. "What smell?"

"Sweet. Ahh, God. My head," he moaned. He took both hands off the steering wheel to grasp his head in both hands. Willa dived across the space between them to grab the wheel as the van drifted left out of its lane and toward the opposite shoulder of the road at a hundred miles per hour.

"James!" she cried. "Focus."

He inhaled loudly and deeply through his nose as she lay half across him, frantically steering the vehicle. This time his voice was a preternaturally deep growl. "Gonna make you bleed. Peel you like a grape. Make you scream."

What the heck was going on with him? It was as if he was inhabited by two people. And right now the crazy, violent one had firm control of him. He shoved her away and took the wheel once more. She sat up cautiously, watching him like a hawk. He seemed to be in control of himself and the vehicle once more.

"Have you ever been diagnosed as schizophrenic?" she asked conversationally.

He snorted with laughter. "Think I'm crazy? Yeah. Me, too. Been telling them something's wrong with my head. Mommy dearest says it's stress. That you damned Merrises are out to wreck my life. Maybe she's right…" He trailed off into another bout of mumbling.

Oh, yeah. He was off his rocker, all right.

She leaned forward ostensibly to retie her shoe, but

out of the corner of her eye, she tried to spot his gun. There. Holster on his left hip. A surreptitious glance over her shoulder into the back of the van revealed a big assault rifle with a sniper's scope attached, a shotgun and at least thirty boxes of ammunition. It looked like he was planning for the last stand of the Alamo. A large nylon gym bag bulged in the back, too. No telling what was inside that puppy. Maybe his tools of torture. Her flesh cringed at what he might have in mind to do to her this time.

And this time Gabe wouldn't be coming to her rescue. He'd made his choice, and it had not been her. She was on her own. A sense of futility and hopelessness swept over her. What did it matter what James did to her? Maybe it wouldn't be such a bad thing if she died. It wasn't like anyone would miss her.

Her chest felt like it had a big empty hole in it where her heart had been. The grief of losing the first and only man she'd ever loved was simply too much to bear. Maybe her last thoughts would be of him. Of how happy he'd made her when she'd thought they were together. It would be a nice way to go out. She made a silent promise to herself to keep him in mind when the end came.

She wondered idly what her father's last thought had been. She blurted abruptly, "Did you kill my father?"

"No!"

His answer was quick and startled. Spontaneous. He wasn't lying. Purely to make conversation and keep that maniacal emptiness from creeping back into James's eyes, she asked, "Who do you suppose did kill my father?"

He shrugged and she continued, "I could see my dad being in cahoots with Sheriff Burris over something, and the two of them getting themselves killed together.

But that third victim. The young guy from out of state. I just can't see how he fits in with the other two murders."

"Don't know. Don't care. Just glad the bastard's dead." His voice slipped a notch into madness. "I hope he suffered a lot."

"You mentioned the animals in my mother's garden. Do you rip their heads off?" she asked on a hunch.

He looked away guiltily. "Don't know nothin'. Don't know how I got there. Don't remember…"

Was he having blackouts? Committing violent acts while out of his right mind? Maybe suffering from a multiple-personality disorder?

She subsided, out of ideas for what to talk about with him for the moment.

"You're going to suffer, you know," he said matter-of-factly. "Sins of the father, and all. You get to pay. My head's going to start hurting and you'll end up just like those critters."

With her head torn off? Horror filled her throat with acid bile. "So this is all about my father?" she forced herself to ask calmly. "You're admitting that I never did anything to you?"

"Hah! Uppity bitch. Always so perfect and unattainable. No one was good enough to kiss the bottoms of your shoes. Spurned us all. Nobody in Vengeance good enough for Miss High-and-Mighty."

What? She was nothing of the sort. She was shy and awkward and uncomfortable in her own skin. "Is that how everyone saw me?" she asked him in surprise.

"We called you the ice princess."

"And there I was, hoping it was just that everyone was scared to death of my father," she replied wryly.

James looked over at her, and she thought she saw…

something…in his pale gaze. A hint of sanity. For just an instant. Maybe there was hope for reaching him yet.

The van began to slow and she looked up to see the distinctive shape of an oil derrick interrupting the flat line of the open plain on their left. The Vacarro Field. It stretched across thousands of acres of prime oil land, and this was just the first corner of it. There was an entire airfield tucked in the middle of the property, in fact. No less than twenty massive oil-drilling platforms spread across the property in an east-west line that followed the oil below.

James turned the van onto a dirt road winding into the property. A trail of dust marked their passage. It hadn't rained out here.

They approached the first towering steel structure. The huge, rotating hammer head of the pump was parked at the four-o'clock position.

"How come the well's not pumping?" James asked.

"I have no idea. Maybe it's down for maintenance."

The road led them another mile or so to another well, which also was still and silent. "What the hell?" James growled. "You shut the field down to squeeze my family dry, didn't you? Bitch!" he exclaimed.

The van picked up speed and bumped across the rough track, deeper into the massive isolation of the Texas plains. The road ended at the airfield, which sported a half-dozen large hangars. Willa didn't remember those from the last time she'd been out here. But then, it had been years since she'd visited the oil field with her father. He'd been on a press junket, as she recalled. Trotting journalists out here to crow about domestic oil production being the future of America.

Heat devils made the air over the long asphalt airstrip waver. Indian summer must be here. It couldn't be much past 10:00 a.m., and it already felt well over ninety degrees.

James stopped the van, and the pistol came out of its holster to point at her. He walked around front, the weapon trained on her the whole time. He yanked her door open. "Get out. This is where the road ends for you."

He stepped close and grabbed her by the arm. Oddly, he froze, nostrils flaring. "Pain and suffering, blood and agony," he crooned to her. "Gonna kill the little Merris girl. Slowly. Hours and hours of screaming." He groaned in pleasure. She glanced down involuntarily and was appalled to see a telltale bulge in his pants. Shuddering, she stumbled as he yanked at her arm, dragging her forward.

She was done praying for her life. Now she only prayed that her death would be fast.

Chapter 19

Gabe was glad McGrath was at the wheel as they drove the treacherous roads through the pass where Willa had almost died last night. The guy was clearly a trained offensive driver and flung the SUV around the vicious curves like a Formula One racer.

They came out of the worst of the terrain and the big SUV picked up speed, devouring the road like a hungry beast. "Faster," he urged anyway.

"I'm flooring it, Dawson. Just topped one-forty."

They had to get to her in time. Willa had to be all right. He was going to strangle her when he caught up with her, but she'd damned well better be alive when he did it. *Hang on, baby.*

"The Vacarro Field is just ahead, isn't it?" McGrath asked.

"Yes. On the left. There's an unmarked turnoff that leads into the field maybe a mile from here. Next road into the field is about five miles ahead. Bastard could've taken either road in."

The SUV slowed. A faint cloud of dust hung over the road in front of them, and McGrath murmured, "Guess that answers that." He guided the vehicle onto the dirt track and stopped it.

"What are you doing?" Gabe demanded.

"We're going into a hostage situation. We can't just barge in there, guns blazing, without knowing what we're up against. Not if we want Miss Merris to come out of this alive."

McGrath hopped out and went around to the tailgate, and Gabe did the same. The guard rummaged in a black nylon bag and passed him a pair of field binoculars. "Can you handle a gun?"

"Hell, yes," Gabe replied.

McGrath passed him a large-gauge shotgun and a box of shells, which he took grimly. He stuffed his pockets with shells and climbed back into the SUV. They continued slowly, with him gazing ahead through the binoculars.

"Anything?" the guard asked.

"Trail of dust. They've passed this way recently."

"What's up ahead?"

Gabe thought back urgently to his years working as an oil geologist for Merris Oil. It had been over a decade since he'd been out here. "Vacarro Four and Five wells. Then an airstrip. Then the road veers south and into some hillier country. Wells Two, Three and Eight are on this track out that way."

"Any buildings out here?"

"There are trailers by each of the operating wells." He hadn't been surprised to see Vacarro One shut down behind them. The oil below it was gone. There'd been no trailer parked beside the second well, either, which meant it was probably capped off for good, too.

"Any buildings at the airfield?" McGrath asked.

"Not the last time I was out here. But that was ten years ago or more."

"We'll drive by it if we stay on this road, right?"

"Correct."

They proceeded in grim silence, the guard navigating the rough track and him watching ahead for any sign of movement. A cluster of low bumps ahead marred the horizon. "Buildings," he muttered. "Merris must have built some hangars out here."

"Why would he do that?" McGrath queried. "It's not like anyone's going to permanently store an airplane out here. And if the weather's going to get bad, wouldn't a pilot just fly the plane out ahead of it?"

"You'd think. I have no idea why Merris built hangars out here."

"Describe the buildings to me," McGrath ordered.

"Metal and steel construction. New-looking. Big. Maybe a hundred feet wide. Longer than that. They might be for storing drilling equipment, but no operator in their right mind lets drilling rigs sit around rusting. You lease them out and keep them making you money." He frowned as something else strange came into focus. "There are cameras mounted on the corners of the buildings. High up."

"Security cameras?"

"Exactly."

McGrath stopped the SUV in a hollow, the airfield and its odd buildings temporarily out of sight. He tried his phone and cursed when he failed to get coverage. "More of my guys will be here shortly. I was hoping to update them, but that'll have to wait until they get here. You and I don't have enough fire power to clear such large spaces ourselves, anyway."

"So you expect us to just sit here and wait?" Gabe demanded incredulously.

"Yup."

"But what if Willa's inside one of those right now, being tortured…or worse?"

"I know you're worried, but I can't recommend charging in there. The object is to get her out alive."

Gabe's gut screamed at him to take action now. "How long until your men get here?"

"Fifteen, maybe twenty minutes."

No way could he wait that long. "I'm going in," he announced. "You can come with me or wait. Whatever you like."

"You could get her killed!"

"My gut's telling me she'll die if I don't go in. And I got to where I am today by listening to my gut. It's never steered me wrong before."

"Are you willing to bet Willa Merris's life on it?"

He looked at the guard for several long seconds, considering. "Yeah. I am."

McGrath sighed. "All right. I guess we're going in. A few ground rules, then…"

He listened carefully as the guard set up a few simple rules for which direction Gabe would and wouldn't shoot his shotgun, established several hand signals and told Gabe in no uncertain terms to stay behind him and out of the line of fire.

They scrambled through the thick clumps of side-oats and bluestem grass, batting away the swarms of tiny black flies that rose up around them. As they drew close to the airfield, they crouched low and proceeded more slowly. Impatience gnawed at him until he thought he was going to leap up and make a run for the first building.

McGrath circled wide to the left of the first building and they approached it from behind. As they drifted farther left, Gabe jolted. A white van was parked between the first and second hangars.

A female cry made Gabe jump straight up in the air. He took a quick step forward, but a powerful arm grabbed him around the chest from behind as he would have bolted.

"Don't panic," McGrath ground out in his ear. "She's alive. If he hasn't already shot her, the bastard's planning to play with her for a while."

Gabe cursed violently under his breath. "Don't expect me to stand here and let her be tortured while I listen on. Ain't happening, buddy."

McGrath stared at him grimly, then whispered in resignation, "Fine. I'll check out the building on the right. You take a look in through the windows at the left one. If you see Willa or her captor, don't go in. Come get me. Got it?"

Gabe nodded impatiently as Willa cried out again. McGrath took off in a low, crouching jog, and he did the same. The weight of the shotgun in his hands felt impatient. Demanded justice. He seriously wanted to shoot the bastard who was making Willa cry out like that.

He plastered himself against the side of the building next to one of the dusty windows. Cautiously, he eased forward toward the lower corner of the window until he could peek inside the structure. His blood ran cold. Willa was tied to a chair, and a tall silhouette stood directly behind her, a weapon held to the side of her head.

A sinister voice floated out to him immediately.

"There you are, Gabe Dawson. I knew you'd come for your little whore. Why don't you join us?"

Crap, crap, crap. McGrath was nowhere in sight. He yelled out loudly and prayed the security man heard him, "Okay. I'm coming in."

He ran around to the door in the front of the building. It was sandwiched between two large garage-style doors. It squeaked as he opened it. No chance of sneaking up on the bastard, then.

He paused inside the dim interior while his eyes adjusted to the shadows.

"Gabe?" Willa asked wonderingly. "What are you doing here? Aren't you going to marry Melinda?"

"What?" he asked incredulously. "I love you. I'd never marry her!"

"But I heard her accept your proposal—"

"Shut up." The man behind Willa struck her in the temple with the weapon in his hand. Her head snapped sideways and she groaned, sagging in her ropes.

Gabe lurched forward involuntarily.

"Now, now. Gabey-poo. Come any closer and I'll shoot her. And then I'll just have to play with you, instead."

He thought he recognized that voice. "James? James Ward?"

"Come closer. Slowly. Drop the shotgun. Hands on top of your head."

Gabe did as ordered. He was alarmed to see a trickle of blood running down the side of Willa's face. Her eyes were closed and she looked out cold. And Ward, he looked possessed. Crazy didn't begin to cover the madness in his eyes. It distorted his whole face. It was as if the man had been consumed by a monster. He looked straight out of a bad horror movie. Except that was real blood and a real gun and Willa tied to that chair.

He walked forward, his eyes glued to Willa's captor. As much as he'd like to check Willa for breathing or movement, he dared not look away from Ward. At least the gun had turned away from her and was now pointed at him.

"So glad you came, Dawson. Now I can really make the bitch suffer. I'm so damned sick of listening to her talk to you like you're here. Going on about how she loves you and is so grateful you showed her a glimpse of love and made her life complete before she died. Makes a guy want to puke."

Gabe stared, stunned. Willa loved him? He made her life complete? He jerked his attention back to Ward. How to draw the guy away from Willa? McGrath had to be outside by now, assault rifle trained on Ward. Why hadn't he taken the shot? The only reasonable explanation was that his shot was blocked by Willa.

"That's close enough. Stop," Ward snapped.

Gabe did as ordered, his mind racing. He had to distract Ward. Get him to move far enough away from Willa to give McGrath a clear shot.

"Can't you ever pick on someone your own size, Jimmy? You always did have a thing for picking on the kids littler than you."

Ward made a growling sound. His free hand drifted to the side of his head, pressing against it as if he had a headache. Gabe used his distraction to move a step to his right. He had to get Ward to shift position.

Ward cried like he was in pain, and Gabe slid another foot to his right. "Stop that, dammit!" Ward shouted. He turned a bit to his left to train his gun on Gabe.

There. The shot was clear. Why wasn't McGrath taking it, dammit?

Ward devolved into incoherent shouting that sounded like a combination of random words and animalistic sounds. Holy crap, the guy was completely unhinged!

Where was McGrath? Had something happened to him? Did Ward have an accomplice? Panic shot through Gabe. Were he and Willa on their own with this madman?

As the seconds ticked past, and Ward's tirade wound down without a shot coming from McGrath, sick realization came over Gabe. He had no backup. Willa's life depended entirely on him. And he was too far away to jump Ward, and armed only with his wits.

"Tell you what, Jimmy. If you'll cut Willa loose, I'll let you tie me up and do whatever you want to me." His gaze strayed involuntarily to the array of knives, pliers, jumper cables and other implements of torture laid out on the floor behind Willa.

"How about I keep her tied up, tie you up, too, and torture you both? It'll be so romantic. You can see each other suffer in the name of love." He used his free hand to rub his crotch.

Gabe was sickened by the depravity that had taken over James Ward.

"Go over there. Get that chair. Set it down in front of the bitch princess. Oh, yes. This is going to be fun." When Gabe didn't move immediately, the pistol swung back toward Willa, this time pointed at the top of her left thigh.

Reluctantly, Gabe did as he was told and fetched the chair. It was old and made of solid wood. Heavy. Wouldn't make for a bad weapon if he could get within range to swing it at Ward. But with that gun pointed at

Willa, that wasn't a possibility. As he approached within a dozen feet of Willa and James, Ward slid back behind her, using her as a shield.

Gabe was shocked when Willa's right eye cracked open slowly. She looked up at him, and then she winked at him! She was awake? Exultation shot through him at just knowing she was conscious and with him. He saw her feet shift slightly within her bonds, both tennis shoes planted firmly on the floor.

"That's close enough," Ward warned. "Put the chair down. Hands behind your back—"

Willa and her chair flew backward without warning, slamming into Ward. The guy staggered backward and Gabe lunged forward. The pistol came up and he threw the chair up in front of himself. A gunshot exploded and the chair was all but torn out of his hands as a bullet slammed into it.

Gabe used the momentum to throw the chair at Ward, following it with his body as he laid a flying tackle on the madman. The pistol slammed incredibly painfully into his shoulder as he grappled with Ward. Gabe got an elbow between them and threw it with all his strength into the guy's face. Elbow bone connected with nose bone with a crunching noise.

Something large rolled toward them. Willa, still tied to the broken remains of the chair. No! She had to get away!

Ward was unbelievably strong, and Gabe hung on to the guy's gun-carrying wrist with all his strength. But inch by inch, the muzzle of the weapon was being forced down toward him. Another few inches and Ward would be able to blow his face off.

"Get up, Willa! Run!" Gabe shouted.

But she rolled again, carrying her even closer to him

and Ward. One of her feet came free of the tangle of wood and rope, and kicked out. Ward swore viciously. She must have connected with some part of him. Another kick and the gun wavered, moving away from Gabe's face.

Up close, Ward's eyes were one of the scariest things Gabe had ever seen. No sign of a human being remained within them. He grunted as he grappled with the monster, "Get out of here, Willa! Go, dammit! Save yourself!"

Several more kicks in rapid succession were her only answer. Her attack distracted Ward enough that Gabe was able to get the upper hand on the gun wrist again and force it back up over Ward's head, blessedly pointing well away from Willa.

His arms were starting to tire, however, and Ward was showing no signs of weakening in his insanity.

Both of Ward's arms were stretched high over his head now. In desperation, Gabe dropped one hand away from Ward's wrist and smashed his fist into Ward's broken nose as hard as he could. The guy screamed and dropped the gun, grabbing at his face.

Gabe scrambled off him and leaped for the gun. He snatched it up while Ward screamed curses, but he wasn't fast enough. Ward rolled to his knees and got an arm around Willa's throat by the time Gabe turned, brandishing the pistol. Ward laughed, a hyena-like bray that made his blood run cold.

"Take the shot," Willa begged. "I trust you."

"Are you sure?" Gabe asked her gently.

"I'm sure. I love you."

Gabe took careful aim and squeezed the trigger.

Chapter 20

Willa felt James tense as Gabe aimed the pistol. Ward was going to throw her in front of the shot. But she was okay with that. Once she was dead, Gabe would kill this monster. Gabe would be safe, and her students would be safe. Funny how, when she loved a person, she was willing to sacrifice herself for them, no questions asked. No one had ever told her that was part of love. Live and learn.

Or in her case, learn and die.

A pair of gunshots exploded deafeningly, one so close after the other that she barely could tell them apart. Warmth and wetness exploded across her face as the impact jolted her. But she didn't feel anything else. That was nice. She'd hoped death would be like this. Peaceful. Painless.

But then sounds intruded on the moment. Commotion. Someone—no. Many someones—rushed toward her. Man-shaped shadows shouting. Hands grabbing at her. Tearing ropes and broken wood away from her. Really. She didn't care if they buried her still tied to the chair she'd died in.

"Willa? Can you hear me?"

The voice was familiar. Beloved. Gabe. Oh, no. He hadn't died, too, had he? "Are you coming with me?" she asked tentatively. "We can go to Heaven together. I was hoping you'd survive. I'm sorry I couldn't save you."

"Honey, what are you talking about? Open your eyes."

She thought they already were open. She concentrated on her eyelids and was surprised that they moved. Gabe's beautiful, worried face swam in front of her.

"It's all right," she murmured. "I'm not in any pain. This isn't so bad, really."

"Baby, you're alive. I didn't shoot you. I shot James in the face. I knew he would move at the last second, so I shot wide the first time, and then, after he'd jerked in reaction, I adjusted and took the second shot."

"What?" She blinked up at him, not understanding.

"James is dead. You're alive. We're both alive. You're safe now."

Hands, many hands, lifted her to her feet. But then Gabe's arms went around her, crushing her against him and suddenly, her world righted itself. This was home. She knew where she was now.

"Oh, God, I thought you were going to die," she sobbed against his chest. "And James was going to kill my students—"

"Shhh. It's all over now. He's not going to hurt anyone else. I've got you."

"Don't ever let me go, Gabe," she whispered.

"I'm not planning on it, baby."

From the safety of his embrace, she looked around at the dozen men around them. They wore all-black, military-style clothes and were toting all kinds of fancy gear and guns. She didn't recognize any of them. These weren't her security guards.

"Who are you?" she asked the nearest one of the strange men.

"That's a damned good question," Cade McGrath, the leader of her security team, growled from across the space.

She glanced over at Cade, surprised to see him restrained in plastic handcuffs and guarded by two of the black-clad men.

A man who looked to be in his mid-thirties stepped forward. "Senator Merris?"

"Yes. That's me," she answered cautiously.

"Your father leased this facility to us some months ago. We've been using the Vacarro Operations base to launch various, umm, missions, south of the border. I'm afraid this is a highly classified military operation."

"You're from the Committee for Miscellaneous Affairs, aren't you?" she exclaimed.

The man's eyes narrowed. "You were never supposed to find out about that."

Gabe piped up. "John Merris was reporting the payments from you guys as income from his oil wells, wasn't he?"

"I don't know," the spokesman answered. "I suppose he could have done that."

"I knew it!" Gabe exclaimed. "There was no way this field was still producing any oil. I couldn't figure out where the income was coming from."

"So we're not fracking for natural gas and poisoning the locals?" Willa asked.

"There's no drilling of any kind happening on this property, ma'am," the man answered.

Well, that was a relief. She would hate to think Merris Oil had made anyone sick.

"We're going to need you and Mr. Dawson and Mr. McGrath to sign security statements agreeing not to reveal anything you saw here today."

"What about him?" Willa asked, forcing herself to look toward the covered lump that was James Ward's remains.

"We'll turn his body over to the coroner. The ballistics analysis will show Mr. Ward was shot with his own weapon. Mr. Dawson, in fact, rescued you single-handedly, and your statements to the police never have to reflect that we were here. After you and Mr. Dawson talk to the police, I'm sure they'll rule that the shooting was a clear case of self-defense."

The next few minutes were a whirl of activity as she and Gabe and McGrath were hustled out of the hangar and driven to McGrath's SUV. James Ward's body was laid in the back of their vehicle. It was creepy riding back to town with a dead man in the back, but true to his word, Gabe kept an arm around her and kept her plastered to his side all the way back to Vengeance. A pair of similarly black and powerful SUVs accompanied them back to Vengeance and the police station. But as McGrath parked in the back of the building, the two SUVs disappeared.

For once, the press wasn't hovering vulturelike, sniffing for a story. She and Gabe had to be separated to give their statements as to what had happened, and the whole time she felt bereft, like part of her was missing. After she finished that, she had to sign an inch-high stack of papers dealing with not revealing classified information on pretty much pain of death.

The sheriff surprised her by stepping into the little interrogation room in person as she was finishing up. He said quietly, "I thought you might be interested to know what the preliminary examination of Mr. Ward's body has shown."

"The coroner's already done an autopsy?"

"Not yet. He has started it, though. First thing he did was x-ray Mr. Ward's head. Had to locate the bullet to know where to dig, I mean, do surgery, to remove it."

She made a face as he continued hastily, "At any rate, it turns out Mr. Ward had a sizable brain tumor. Right in the middle of his head near something called the amygdala or something like that. Doc says it's the smell center of the brain. Did Ward say anything to you about smelling strange things?"

"No, but now that you mention it, every time he caught a whiff of my gardenia perfume he went crazy."

"Doc said the right scents might have triggered violent, psychotic episodes in Ward."

Thunderstruck, she thought back to all the times James had become violent around her, starting with the sexual assault. Every time, she'd been wearing her gardenia perfume, and every time, he'd been plenty close enough to smell it.

The sheriff held her chair as she stood up, stunned. "You were mighty lucky, ma'am. Next time, call the police. Civilians shouldn't tangle with criminals on their own."

"Believe me, I never plan to do something so crazy again," she replied fervently. "And I will most certainly leave it to the police if there is a next time!"

She stepped out of the interrogation room and was immediately swept into Gabe's arms. "You okay?" he murmured.

"Yes. You?"

"Right as rain. Let's get out of here."

Someone had brought Gabe's SUV over to the police station while they were making their statements, and the sheriff handed Gabe the keys as they stepped out into the main room.

"Ready to face the press?" she asked as they approached the front doors.

"Stick with me, kid. I'll show you how to scare them off."

True to his word, he put on a ferocious scowl that dared anyone to get in his way and they swept past the crowd of shouting reporters without incident. He closed her in the Escalade and guided the vehicle away from the curb. She was surprised when he didn't point the SUV toward anywhere that either of them called home. In fact, he headed out toward the west side of town once more.

"Where are we going?" she asked in alarm. She had no wish to revisit the scene of James's death.

Gabe merely smiled enigmatically at her. "Relax. You're gonna like it."

She trusted him. As they wound into the canyons, she let the rugged beauty of the Texas landscape wash over her. It was rough country. But tough. Like her and Gabe. They'd survived an ordeal that would have broken someone with less courage. With less to live for.

She smiled as Gabe turned the Escalade into the scenic overlook the local kids called Lover's Point.

"I thought for once you might like to come up here

for more than the view. Wanna make out?" he asked gruffly.

"With you? Always."

"About Melinda. I was talking about you with the doctors when I said I loved you. She misunderstood and barged out to spout all that crap about marrying me. I'm totally over her," he finished adamantly. "You've got to believe me."

"What about that other part you told the doctors. That you were planning to propose?"

"Well. About that." He got out of the car and came around to open her door for her. He escorted her to the front of the car where a towering thunderhead blocked the sun. It was backlit in shades of lavender and gray, with a corona of sunbeams bursting outward in all directions like the promise of a new day.

"Are you sure I'm not too old for you, Willa?"

She rolled her eyes. "It's not like you're a hundred years old, Gabe."

He laughed and knelt on one knee in front of her. "Then, if you will have this old wreck, would you make me the happiest man on earth and do me the honor of becoming my wife?"

Her heart expanded as big as the Texas sky and filled with as many colors of joy. "Oh, yes, Gabe. I will. I definitely will."

* * * * *

"Feeling better?" he whispered, the movement of his mouth tickling her lips.

Heat flowed like lava through her entire body. Out to her fingertips and toes and back, swirling through her until it settled in her core. She bit her cheek to keep from moaning with pleasure.

"I feel wonderful," she answered breathlessly.

He lifted his head slightly. When she raised her gaze, she saw his firm, wide mouth soften. Was he about to kiss her? Really kiss her? Right here in the middle of running from people who were trying to kill them?

She should say something. Should stop this. Because all they were doing was seeking comfort in a dangerous situation.

The men who wanted to kill her were dangerous, but so was Harte. And right now, she wasn't sure who frightened her most.

STAR WITNESS

BY
MALLORY KANE

First published in Great Britain 2013
by Mills & Boon, an imprint of Harlequin (UK) Limited,
Eton House, 18-24 Paradise Road, Richmond, Surrey TW9 1SR

© Rickey R. Mallory 2013

ISBN: 978 0 263 90362 1
ebook ISBN: 978 1 472 00725 4

46-0613

Harlequin (UK) policy is to use papers that are natural, renewable and recyclable products and made from wood grown in sustainable forests. The logging and manufacturing processes conform to the legal environmental regulations of the country of origin.

Printed and bound in Spain
by Blackprint CPI, Barcelona

Mallory Kane has two very good reasons for loving reading and writing. Her mother was a librarian, who taught her to love and respect books as a precious resource. Her father could hold listeners spellbound for hours with his stories. He was always her biggest fan.

She loves romantic suspense with dangerous heroes and dauntless heroines, and enjoys tossing in a bit of her medical knowledge for an extra dose of intrigue. After twenty-five books published, Mallory is still amazed and thrilled that she actually gets to make up stories for a living.

Mallory lives in Tennessee with her computer-genius husband and three exceptionally intelligent cats. She enjoys hearing from readers. You can write her at mallory@mallorykane.com.

To Michael, for always.

Chapter One

Harte Delancey always felt like such a wimpy kid around his older brothers—probably because that's how they treated him.

He looked up from the grill where steaks were sizzling. Lucas and Ethan were tossing long spiraling passes to each other in the football-field-sized backyard of their parents' Chef Voleur home. If Travis were here instead of overseas somewhere, he'd be out there too.

Harte preferred more solitary forms of exercise—running, backpacking and biking. He chuckled wryly and flipped the steaks as Lucas made a spectacular leap and snagged the football out of the air.

"Steaks ready in five," he called out as his mom brought a big bowl of her famous buttermilk ranch potato salad from the outdoor kitchen to the already laden table. Lucas's wife, Angela, followed her carrying a massive casserole of baked beans.

"Everything looks great," Harte said.

"I hope so," Betty Carole Delancey said in her self-deprecating way. "The tomatoes don't look very good."

He eyed the plump, bright red slices with amusement. "If they were any better, the *Times-Picayune* would be on the story. What do you think, Dad?" he asked his father, Robert, who sat in his wheelchair watching Lucas and Ethan.

Harte's dad turned his head slightly. "Everything good," he said haltingly. It had been fourteen years since the massive stroke had left him partially paralyzed and unable to speak. With his wife's help, he'd relearned how to talk.

Lucas and Ethan washed up at the sink, arguing about who had the more accurate throwing arm. Then Lucas kissed Angela on the cheek before sitting down beside her. Ethan grabbed the chair opposite the two of them.

Harte took the last T-bone off the grill and set the platter down in the middle of the table. He sat between Lucas and their mother.

"Want to play a game of three-team touch later, Mr. Prosecutor?" Lucas asked as he tousled Harte's hair. Harte ducked but not in time. "Or should I call you *Monsieur* Chef?" he mused, stabbing a steak with his fork and holding it up for inspection.

"After you eat all that and can't move? Sure." Harte was used to Lucas ribbing him about his choice of career and his cooking.

Lucas was a detective with the New Orleans Police Department, as was Ethan, and Travis, an Army Special Forces operative, was stationed overseas. It was a sore spot with all three of them that their youngest brother had broken tradition and studied law.

As if reading his thoughts, his mom said, "I was hoping we'd hear something from Travis this week."

"What's it been—six months since you last spoke

with him?" Ethan asked, then washed a bite of steak down with iced tea.

"September," his dad said.

"That's right, darling," his mom said as she cut his steak into bite-sized pieces for her husband. "It's been seven months."

Harte saw Lucas and Ethan exchange a glance. He knew what they were thinking. It chafed them that their mother was so solicitous and gentle with her husband. Neither one—especially Lucas—had ever forgiven their dad for his drunken rages and punishing fists. It didn't matter to them that Robert's stroke had rendered him a docile wraith of his former self.

At that moment, the patio door opened. It was Cara Lynn, smiling and dressed in a casual floral dress that sported all the pastel colors of spring. Not that the north shore of Lake Pontchartrain in Louisiana ever saw spring…or fall for that matter. The weather was generally either hot and humid or chilly and wet.

Still, the sun seemed to shine brighter when their only sister and Harte's closest sibling was around.

"What a gorgeous day to have dinner outside," she said as she rounded the table, giving everyone a quick kiss, then sat.

"Nice of you to grace us with your presence," Ethan said, cutting into his steak.

Cara Lynn made a face at him. "I'm showing twelve pieces at the New Orleans Fiber Arts Show in just over a month," she said, "and I've got finish work to do on five of them. You probably won't see me again until after the show."

Harte's mother sighed as she set two loaves of French

bread on the table. "That's why I try to have these din-
ners as often as possible. Everyone's so busy these
days."

"Speaking of which," Harte said, "the court date in
the Freeman Canto murder case has been moved up.
The judge will hear opening arguments on Tuesday."

"Tuesday?" Lucas said. "Five days from now? That
seems sudden. Didn't you just take over the case a couple of months ago?"

"And they were talking about putting it on the docket
for June. But now defense counsel Felix Drury has to
have open-heart surgery, and the judge didn't want to
put off the case another three or four months while he
recuperates."

"Maybe you'll get lucky and Drury will plead his
client, or at least try to wrap up the case early," Ethan
said. "I've testified in a case or two where *Jury* Drury
was defense counsel. He treats the jury like his own
personal fan club. Plays to them and draws out his arguments. Plus, doesn't he love to file motions for ac-
quittal?"

"Yes, he does. The D.A. got the notification about
the new trial date around one-thirty today, and before
three there were two defense motions on his desk."
Harte speared a bite of steak. "So that means I probably won't have time to breathe until the trial is over,
starting tonight." Just as he finished speaking, his cell
phone rang.

His dad grunted. "Dang things," he mumbled.

Harte glanced at the display and excused himself
from the table. "Got to take this," he apologized as he
walked to the other end of the patio.

"Delancey? It's Mahoney," Detective Tom Mahoney said unnecessarily. The gruff detective didn't like cell phones any more than Harte's dad did. "Got a problem."

"What kind of problem?" Harte asked, smothering a sigh. Mahoney was an excellent detective, but he had a very broad definition of *problem*.

"Your witness in the Canto case was almost run down a little while ago."

Harte's scalp burned. "Dani? What happened? Is she all right?" He blinked away a disturbing vision of Public Defender Danielle Canto's exquisite body crumpled on the highway.

"Yep. A vehicle nearly sideswiped her on the sidewalk leading up to her house. Doubt it was an accident. The damn car left tracks in the grass—and skid marks—looks like it didn't even try to slow down—"

"Tom! What about Dani?" Harte broke in.

"She's okay. But real shaken up. Has a few scrapes and bruises from throwing herself up onto the porch, though," Mahoney assured him. "That saved her. The front steps are nothing but toothpicks now."

"I'll be right there."

"No need to rush," Mahoney said. "The excitement's over now."

"Well, it may not be the last of it. Did you hear that the Canto case has been moved up? It's due to start Tuesday."

"Hmph. That explains a lot. That car had to be sent by Yeoman. He doesn't want Ms. Canto testifying against him."

Harte agreed. Ernest Yeoman was an importer and distributor who supplied goods to all the Hasty Marts in the Southeast. He had long been suspected of dealing in contraband, specifically drugs, through his import business. "Please tell me you've got evidence that ties him to this."

Mahoney cleared his throat. "Can't say. We picked up some headlight glass fragments and paint chips where the vehicle sideswiped the porch. We'll see if the lab can match it up with a make and model."

"Where's Dani now?" Harte asked. "Did she have to go to the hospital? I want to talk to her. Find out what happened."

"She's at home. We've got her statement. You can read it as soon as it's typed up."

Harte was already fishing in his jeans for his car keys. "You left her by herself?"

"I told her to go to a hotel or a friend's house until we could arrange something, but she's about as stubborn as her granddaddy always was. I've arranged for a cruiser to drive by hourly through the night."

"Good. I'll head over there as soon as I find a judge. The hourly drive-by is great for tonight. But I'm getting an order of protection. I'm not taking any chances with my star witness."

THE BOTTLE RATTLED against the glass shelf of the refrigerator as Danielle Canto pulled it out. Her hands were shaking. She tightened her fist around the cold green glass with a disgusted huff. Her hands never shook.

But today was a special occasion, she thought wryly. She'd felt the brush of hot steel and the prickle of splintered wood against the backs of her calves just before she'd managed to leap up onto the front porch of her grandfather's home. She barely remembered doing it, but it had to be a new high-jump record. The wooden porch was at least four feet off the ground.

She'd hit the porch hard and rolled, bruising her thigh, scraping her knees and elbows and hurting her wrist. She'd rolled up to her haunches immediately, but between her aching muscles and the panic that had hitched her breath, she hadn't gotten the license plate. By the time she'd taken a deep breath and managed to focus, all she'd been able to see was the car's back fender as it screamed away in a shower of stones and mud.

She'd grabbed her phone and called 911, and waited without moving until they got there. She hadn't even considered inspecting the damage to the steps and the four-by-fours that supported the porch. Maybe she should check now, but that would involve getting a flashlight and going around from the back door to the front, not to mention the trauma of seeing how much damage the car had done to the porch. No. She didn't want to know—not tonight.

After grilling her for twenty minutes to squeeze out every detail she could give him about the incident, Detective Mahoney had guessed that the car had been sent by Ernest Yeoman. She shuddered. Could Yeoman be that stupid, or maybe that arrogant, to think that he could scare her into refusing to testify? A horrible thought occurred to her. What if whoever was driving that car had been sent, not to scare her, but to kill her?

She squared her shoulders. Whatever the reason for the attack, it was time for her to take action. She wasn't her grandfather's granddaughter for nothing. Freeman

Canto had taught her to take care of herself. She looked at the bottle of Chardonnay still clutched in her fist, then set it carefully on the granite countertop. Right now she needed a means of self-defense more than a drink. She held up her hand. It would not be shaky long.

Stalking to the bedroom closet, she took down the metal box from the top shelf and unlocked it. Inside was the lock-pick kit her granddad had given her for her tenth birthday.

"Never know when you might need to get through a door," he'd said.

The small leather case felt familiar in her hand and reminded her of the hours she'd spent picking every lock in the house, again and again. She didn't remember when she'd stopped carrying the small kit. Probably about the same time she started wearing lipstick and noticing boys. Well, she'd be carrying it now.

With a sad little smile, she set the case on the dresser, then carefully lifted out the other object in the box. Her grandfather's gun, a SIG Sauer. She wrapped her hand around the grip. The cold metal felt good against her palm. She supported her right hand with her left, the way Granddad had taught her, and slid her forefinger over the trigger.

She'd never shot anyone, hopefully never would, but tonight she was thankful that he'd taught her how to take care of herself.

She handled the weapon quickly and expertly, ejecting, checking and reinserting the seventeen-round magazine. Then she grabbed the second loaded magazine from the box. Sighting over the barrel, she nodded slightly. She wouldn't go anywhere unarmed until the trial was over. Next time somebody tried to run her down, she'd take him out—or his tires at least.

She took the gun, the extra magazine and the lock-pick kit to the foyer and put them in her voluminous purse, then hefted the bag to her shoulder for a quick test of its weight before setting it back on the table. She felt much safer with her granddad's things so close. Now she could relax. As soon as she double-checked all the locks. After a quick round through the house, she headed back to the kitchen.

Her hands had stopped shaking while she concentrated on cleaning and checking the SIG, but as she picked up the corkscrew to open the Chardonnay, they started quivering again. It took a couple of tries to remove the cork, but finally, she was able to pour the chilled Chardonnay with only a little clanking of glass against glass.

Holding the glass high, she said, "To you, Granddad. The bastards who killed you will rot in prison if I have anything to say about it." She took a long swallow and shuddered.

Grabbing the bottle, Dani walked to her bedroom, kicked off her high heels and frowned at the long scrape that marred the red leather of the right shoe. "Great," she sighed, and flopped onto the bed.

Outside, she heard a faraway rumbling of thunder. She shivered. She didn't like storms. They scared her. Her dad had died in a tornado when she was only seven. Until that awful night last year when her granddad was murdered, storms had been the only thing that scared her.

That night, she'd learned that home did not always

represent safety, that faceless monsters could murder a man without conscience and that as strong and capable as she'd always thought she was, she'd been helpless to save her granddad. But at least Ernest Yeoman, the man who she was convinced was behind her granddad's murder, would soon be brought to trial.

According to Harte Delancey, the prosecutor who'd been assigned to her case, the D.A. was practically salivating at the chance to get his hands on the suspected drug smuggler. Yeoman had long been suspected of using his import business to smuggle contraband and drugs into the country through the Port of New Orleans. He was also rumored to have friends in the legislature. Some rumors had even suggested that Freeman Canto was one of those friends.

Dani felt the determination that had sustained her since the night her grandfather had died rise inside her, pushing away the fear. She was not going to let Yeoman or anyone else frighten her away, no matter how serious the threats. Nobody would smear her granddad's name if she had anything to say about it.

She held her glass up in a salute. "I'm fighting for you, Granddad," she whispered, her throat tightening. Just as she brought the glass to her lips, something made her stop dead still.

What had she heard? Footsteps maybe, in front of the house? Or had the rain that had been threatening all day finally gotten here? Holding her breath, she listened. There it was again. That was *not* rain. It was footsteps.

She didn't move a muscle. The rhythm and the muffled crunch ruled out the raccoons that toppled her garbage can at least once a week. Raccoons didn't make that much noise. This varmint was human. Her pulse skittered as the footsteps crunched on the gravel driveway.

It could be one of the police officers or the crime scene unit, taking more pictures before the rain got too bad. But that was doubtful. Detective Mahoney would have called her, knowing how shaken she was.

Whoever was out there wasn't sneaking, but he wasn't tromping either. She listened as he rounded the house and came up onto the back stoop.

Dani tensed, but to her surprise, everything went quiet. She set her wineglass down and prepared to get up, angry at herself for her apprehension. She was *not* going to let Ernest Yeoman make her feel unsafe inside her own home.

Finally, a staccato rapping echoed through the house. Although she half expected the knock, she still jumped. She slipped off the bed and tiptoed down the hall to the front foyer. She worried her lip between her front teeth as she eased the gun out of her purse. Drawing courage from the heft of the weapon in her hand, she stepped into the kitchen, gun at the ready.

The silhouette of a man was outlined on the window shade of the back door. The dark figure's shape didn't look ominous, but it didn't have the reassuring outline of a police officer's uniform and hat either. Nor was he wearing the cap and jacket of a crime scene tech.

She eased closer until she was about ten feet from the door. Raising the gun, she thumbed off the safety. Just as the silhouetted man lifted a hand to knock again, she snapped, "Who is it?"

The hand stopped in midair.

"Get away from my door!" she yelled in a loud, commanding voice. "Now!"

"Dani, it's Harte. Just checking on you."

Her pulse slowed as relief coursed through her. It was Harte Delancey. *Great.* She rolled her eyes. *Thanks, Mahoney.* She should have known he'd call the prosecutor who'd been assigned Yeoman's case three months ago. "Go away. I'm fine," she said irritably. "Go study your briefs or something."

The shadow shifted and she saw his head shake. "Yeah, ha-ha. I never heard that one before." He spread his hands, palms out. "Come on, Dani. Open up. I'm not armed."

She shook her head in exasperation. "Well, I am," she retorted. "Now go away. I'm not dressed."

"Sure you are," he said. "I can see your outline through the glass."

Muttering some unladylike words, Dani slid the bolt and unlocked the back door. As she turned the knob, she braced herself for the sight of him. As much as he irritated her, she couldn't deny that he was easy on the eyes, which made her very *uneasy* all over.

But when she swung the door wide, she was stunned. The Harte Delancey she was used to seeing was slickly handsome, from his perfect dark hair and expensive suit to his blindingly polished shoes.

But this was no slick prosecutor who stood in front of her now. His hair was tousled and flopped over his forehead. He was wearing a T-shirt and jeans. Dani did a double take.

The T-shirt was a worn and much-washed New Orleans Jazz Festival shirt from several years ago. The fabric stretched across his chest and shoulders and draped loosely over faded, very nicely fitting jeans.

She swallowed. Suits did not do Harte Delancey justice.

Harte cleared his throat and Dani realized she was staring at his—jeans. Her gaze snapped to his, her face burning with embarrassment. And there in his expression was the polished prosecutor she was used to seeing. His dark eyes were filled with mischief, and a familiar, knowing smile curved his lips.

She glared at him. "What are you doing here?" she asked, letting her gaze sweep downward and back up.

He pushed his fingers through his hair, dislodging droplets of rain. "Can I come in?"

She rolled her eyes. "Oh, sure. Why not? After you went to all the trouble to sneak around my house."

"Sneaking? I wasn't sneaking. I couldn't very well come to the front door like civilized folks." He assessed her. "Are you all right?"

She shrugged. "I'm fine."

"You don't look fine. Are you hurt?"

She shook her head, suddenly feeling a lump growing at the back of her throat. Swallowing hard, she straightened. "I was just—thinking about my granddad."

Harte's brow furrowed and his snapping dark eyes softened. He started to speak, but Dani cut him off.

"I guess Mahoney told you what happened."

"Where did you get that gun?" he asked. "You shouldn't—"

He stopped when she lifted her chin. Then she realized she was still holding the weapon. She clicked on the safety and set it down on the counter. "I have a license," she said defensively.

He visibly relaxed. "Seriously, Dani. Did the EMTs check you out? Make sure you didn't break something?"

"I didn't break anything. The driver broke my porch." She had to suppress the urge to press her palm against her tightening chest. She just wanted to go to bed and pull the covers over her head. "What's the matter, Mr. Prosecutor? Afraid you're going to lose your star witness? I can guarantee you I will be there to testify. These *accidents* are nothing more than an inconvenience."

He shook his head, and his smile faded. "I'm positive I won't lose my witness." He pulled a folded piece of paper from the back pocket of his jeans and held it up between two long, sturdy fingers.

Her stomach sank to her toes. "Oh no. No, no, no," she said, shaking her head. "You didn't," she grated through clenched teeth. "Come on, Harte. Tell me that's not—" She reached for it, but he held it over his head. If she'd had on her four-inch platform heels, she might have been able to snag it, but she was barefoot, and therefore at least six inches shorter than he.

"It's an order of protection—" he started.

"No!" she broke in. "You are not sticking me in some airless bedbug-ridden hovel for weeks."

"It won't be weeks, and hopefully it won't be bedbug-ridden or airless." There was a definite tone of amusement in his voice. "In fact, you ought to love it. It's a bed-and-breakfast in a Victorian house in the Lower Garden District."

Dani crossed her arms. "I won't go. The public defender's office is shorthanded as it is. I have cases and trial dates."

"Your cases are more important to you than your safety?" he shot back. "Than your *life?*"

She blinked. "My life?" she echoed. "I object. Assuming facts not in evidence."

He shook his head. "Mahoney told me about the car, and I saw what's left of your porch steps. If that vehicle had hit you, you'd be nothing more than a smudge on the sidewalk."

Chapter Two

"Ouch!" Dani said, cringing at Harte's words. "A smudge. Great. Thanks for that image."

"Come on, Dani. Another public defender can be appointed to take your cases until this trial is over. You are in danger and no, I'm not just worried about my case. I'm worried about you."

Dani sniffed. "Better watch out. Con Delancey will haunt you for consorting with the enemy."

He shot her an exasperated glance. "Our grandparents' feud is ancient history. And it was probably just for show anyhow."

"I can believe Con Delancey was posturing, but my grandfather always fought for what he believed in. That's why he was—" She swallowed. Why were her emotions so near the surface tonight? Even as the question flitted through her mind, she knew the answer was obvious. Because she'd almost been run down by a car.

Harte held up his hands, palms out. "I'm not suggesting anything different. I just need you to trust me, or I won't be able to keep you safe."

Trust him? She *knew* him. He would do anything to win, just like his grandfather. He'd proven that three years ago. Luckily for her, right now her safety meshed with his ambition. She sighed in exasperation and defeat. "When am I to be incarcerated?"

"Tomorrow morning. I tried to get you in tonight, but they're full. They're letting us have the run of the place for the next two weeks."

"Two weeks?" Two weeks sounded like forever. Then the significance of the time frame hit her. "Wait a minute. The trial date's been set?"

"Oh, I didn't tell you. It was moved forward. It starts Tuesday."

"Tuesday?" Dani said, shocked. "You mean as in Thursday—" She held up a finger. "Friday, Saturday, Sunday, Monday, Tuesday?" she continued, counting each day off on a finger. "But we aren't ready."

"I know. Tell me about it. Don't worry. We'll prep all weekend. Anyhow, the B-and-B has agreed that we can extend your stay for as long as the trial goes on. They're happy with the weekly rate we offered them."

"Weekly rate? As long as the trial goes on?" she cried. "No. This is not going to work. I'm going to see the judge and get that order vacated."

Harte gave her that smile again, the one that looked more like a smirk and made her so angry. "You can try, but ever since I passed the bar, I'm Judge Rossi's favorite nephew."

She had to fight to keep her jaw from dropping. Of course he had an uncle who was a judge. Of course he went to him for the order of protection. "So that's how you managed to get a judge's signature this time of night. Must be nice to have relatives who will skirt the law for you any time you please."

His smile faded. "I didn't skirt the law. I merely

called a judge I know rather than picking one from the phone book. You'd have done the same, Madame Public Defender."

"Fine," she said grudgingly. "You said it was a bed-and-breakfast? I guess that won't be too awful. Give me the address. I'll head over there tomorrow."

"It's on Religious Street, between Race and Orange. But as of—" he glanced at the piece of paper he held "—nine forty-three p.m. today, I'm responsible for you. So I'll pick you up."

"Okay, okay. Fine." She held up her hands in surrender. "Anyone ever tell you you're a bully?"

"Nope. Never." He cocked his hip to slide the packet back into his pocket.

Dani couldn't help sneaking a glimpse at the back side of the snug jeans before she stepped around him to open the door. "I'll see you tomorrow."

He reached over her shoulder to push the door closed, which put him way too close. She caught a faint whiff of something fresh and citrusy as she glanced up at him. She was going to have to get some higher heels. Not being eye-to-eye with him made her feel small.

"Hold it," he said. "Not so fast. I want to ask you some questions about what happened tonight."

"I told the police everything. Go read their report."

"Tell me just exactly what you were doing when the car tried to run you down."

Dani clenched her teeth. She'd seen that determined glint in his eye before—when they'd faced each other across the courtroom. He'd badger her until he got answers. With a defeated shake of her head, she walked over to the kitchen table and sat. "I'm really tired, so could we make it quick?"

"I've got no problem with that."

She rested her clasped hands on the table and stared at them. "I was late leaving the office. It was probably six-thirty, so by the time I got home it must have been around seven."

He nodded without speaking.

"I pulled into the driveway, parked and…" She paused. "I walked around to the front of the house to get the mail. The car just popped up out of nowhere. I heard the engine rev, but I didn't pay any attention to it until the sound kept getting louder and louder."

"Where were you when you realized the car was coming at you?"

"About ten feet or so from the mailbox." She wasn't happy about having to relive those moments. She'd been through them already, she'd had to answer questions about them twice for the police and now Harte was asking the same questions. She pushed her fingers through her hair. "Every single bit of this is in my statement," she groused.

"You'd already gotten the mail?"

"No. I was walking toward the box."

"So you realized it was coming at you…"

She nodded. "And I just ran. I don't even remember jumping up onto the porch."

"Sounds like it's a good thing you did."

She rubbed her wrist. "I do remember the landing. Did you look at the damage?" she asked.

"A little bit. I couldn't tell a whole lot in the dark, but

the front steps are basically splinters now." He looked at her. "Why? You haven't?"

She shook her head. "No. As soon as they were finished questioning me, I came inside, took a hot shower and tried to relax. Then I heard you sneaking around."

He opened his mouth as if to deny again that he'd been sneaking, then apparently changed his mind. "Did you see him?"

"See who? Oh, the driver?" She shook her head. "I barely got a glimpse of the car. The first thing I knew after I started running was that I was on the porch and my wrist and my left hip hurt. And my elbows and knees stung." She lifted her arm.

Harte frowned at the angry red scrape just under her elbow.

"I sat up and tried to catch the license, but the car was nearly out of sight and I couldn't make it out."

"Can you describe the car?" Harte asked.

"It was dark, maybe black."

"And the shape? The size?"

Dani closed her eyes. "It looked really big, but that might be because it was racing toward me."

"An SUV?"

She shook her head. "No. It was a—" She gestured. "A regular car. You know, a sedan."

"Have you ever met Ernest Yeoman?"

Dani shook her head.

"Myron Stamps? Paul Guillame?"

"Come on, Harte. I've answered these questions a dozen times. For the police, for the other assistant district attorney and now I've got to answer them for you? I'm tired."

"Humor me," he said. "I want you to answer as if you're answering on the stand."

Dani sighed. "I know Senator Stamps. He used to come over here a lot to talk to Granddad. They'd argue into the night. I'd make coffee for them."

"What did they argue about?" he asked.

"You know all this," she groused. "The docks. The Port of New Orleans. Granddad fought for raising tariffs and taxes. He was convinced that lowering tariffs would allow more smuggling through the Port of New Orleans."

"And Stamps argued against that?"

She nodded. "Sure. He was on Con Delancey's side."

"Lower the tariffs to boost revenue and create more jobs," Harte said.

"Not to mention creating more crime-smuggling contraband and drugs."

Harte frowned, looking thoughtful. "I've never understood that argument. Smuggling by definition is bypassing normal import channels."

"You're not that naive, are you? They smuggle the contraband and drugs in *with* the legally imported items. Sometimes inside them. Higher tariffs cut into their profits, and enforcing the higher tariffs means more port authority officers around."

Harte nodded. "I know the reasoning. So back to Stamps. You're saying he and your granddad butted heads on the issue of tariffs, even though your granddad's position had never changed? I wonder why."

"Granddad didn't like Stamps, but he was too polite to refuse to see him. He always said—" Dani stopped. As an attorney, she hated speculation and hearsay.

Harte would probably light into her if she started relating her granddad's opinion of Stamps.

"What?" he asked.

She gave a little shake of her head and made a dismissive gesture.

"Dani, tell me. Anything might be important."

"Even if defense council would cut me off in a heartbeat for hearsay?"

His eyes softened in amusement. "Tell me and let me decide."

"It could be considered defamatory."

"Then definitely tell me."

Dani covered a yawn with her hand. "Okay. Granddad said that back when he and Con Delancey faced off over the tariff issue, it was a gentleman's argument between two public servants who genuinely believed in their position. He had a very different opinion about Myron Stamps."

"Tell me."

"He was convinced that Stamps was doing it for money."

"Money? What money? Why haven't you told me this before?"

She shrugged. "Apparently, when he was first elected, Stamps was all for more stringent controls on the port. Then a few years ago he abruptly shifted positions. Granddad figured somebody got to him."

Harte took a small notepad out of his pocket and jotted something down. "Somebody as in—?"

Dani drew in a long breath. "I don't know. I hate to be rude, but I'm really tired."

He assessed her. "Sorry," he said. "I guess I forgot

that you had an exciting evening. Are you sure you're all right?"

"I'm fine. Just exhausted and a little sore. I guess I'll see you in the morning around what? Nine or ten o'clock? So you can incarcerate me."

He smiled and shook his head. "Nope. You'll see me earlier than that. I'll be staying here tonight."

"What?" She forced a laugh. "Right. Now, that's funny." She walked over to the back door and reached for the knob. But before she could grasp it, he was right there, his hand out, holding it shut.

"Stop that," she said. "Get out of the way. You need to go home. I've got locks. Those people are not going to do anything else tonight—if ever."

"You can't know that. There's no way I'm taking the chance. I told you. The order of protection names me as the responsible party. If you kick me out, I'll just sleep in my car in your driveway."

Dani regarded him. His strong jaw was tight. The irritating smile was gone and his brown eyes looked positively black underneath the dark brows. He meant business. She took a step backward and threw her hands out in a helpless gesture.

"Fine, then. Knock yourself out. I hope your car's comfortable."

His mouth curled up on one corner. "It's a Jeep Compass, so it ought to be."

"Excellent," she snapped. "I'm glad for you. Good night."

He started to say something else, but Dani lifted her chin and pressed her lips together. He inclined his head in a brief nod, shot that irritating smile at her one more time and left, pulling the back door closed behind him.

As Dani turned the lock, her hand shook. The fact that Harte was right outside her door, making sure nothing happened to her tonight, should be comforting.

It wasn't. All it did was provide an omnipresent reminder that, at least according to him, she was in grave danger.

IN THE DRIVER'S seat of his Jeep, Harte pressed the lever that slid the seat back as far as it would go. He held it until the motor whined, then stretched his legs. He had about two inches more room than he'd had twenty seconds before. "Guess that's it," he muttered. Then he reclined the seat back and wriggled his butt, settling in.

He'd bought the Jeep because it drove nicely in the city as well as on dirt roads and hiking paths. He'd never slept in it, but figured it shouldn't be too bad.

As he searched for a comfortable position, he thought about Dani. He hadn't expected her to actually banish him to his car for the night. That house was huge. There had to be at least one guest bedroom. Hell, she could have at least offered him a couch.

Still, he supposed he couldn't blame her for the way she felt about him. The first time they'd met in the courtroom, she as a brand-new public defender and he trying his first case as prosecutor. He'd reacted instantly to her tall, leggy, drop-dead-gorgeous body and eyes that caught the sun just like her hair. But she'd entered the courtroom shooting daggers from those whiskey-colored eyes.

She was undeniably Freeman Canto's granddaughter. Canto and Con Delancey, Harte's grandfather, had both been fixtures in the Louisiana state legislature. And they'd clashed on every single issue, most notably the security and tariffs on the Port of New Orleans. Canto was fiscally conservative, while Con Delancey fought to keep both security and tariffs at a minimum to help the working people. And, as Dani had said, they'd conducted themselves as gentlemen. There had been a kind of honor among politicians back then. An unspoken agreement that while the politics might occasionally get dirty, the politicians would not.

The first time he'd faced Dani across the courtroom, Harte hadn't been completely surprised that she'd shown up prepared for battle, ready to continue the feud between the Cantos and the Delanceys. Her client, the defendant, had been a woman who'd killed her husband, claiming self-defense and fear for her life. But there were no witnesses, no evidence of spousal abuse and the woman had shot the man point-blank.

As Harte fought to win his case, he'd discovered what a great defense attorney Dani was. She was passionate, a dedicated knight battling for her client.

Ultimately, Harte won the verdict, but he'd lost the respect of his opposing counsel. Later he'd found out that Dani had appealed and gotten her client acquitted.

Once he'd gotten more experience under his belt, he'd had to admit she was right. That first case had been a win for him, but it was a Pyrrhic victory. It had taken him a few years and more than a few cases to live down convicting a battered wife.

Their paths hadn't crossed but a couple of times since then, which had helped keep the instantaneous attraction he'd felt for her the first time he'd seen her at bay. But he'd never forgotten how she'd looked when she'd walked into the courtroom that first day. She'd had on a short skirt and high-heeled shoes that made her legs look a mile long. He'd never forgotten her face, her body or the unconsciously sexy, confident way she moved.

But her body wasn't all that he'd found sexy about her. She was smart and quick. Across from her in court, he'd quickly found out that as a public defender, she was as tenacious and focused as a terrier.

A cramp in his thigh interrupted his thoughts and he realized he'd been nearly asleep. Rubbing the tight muscle, he considered the irony that he and Dani were on the same side this time. Well, sort of on the same side. She still thought of him as the enemy.

His cell phone rang. It was Lucas.

"How's your girl?" his oldest brother asked.

"My *witness* is all right," Harte responded. "How were the steaks?"

"Great, as usual. We just got home."

"Really?" He glanced at the time on the display. "Late night for you, at the folks' house."

"Not my idea. Ange and Mom were exchanging recipes. I watched a ball game with him." Lucas never referred to their father as *Dad*. "I'd planned to talk to you about the info you asked me about."

Harte sat up. "What'd you find out?"

"Not much. Nothing on the record. Yeoman's got a fairly clean file. Some small-time stuff early on, but he's managed to keep his record clean for the last twenty years."

"His record. What about what's not on the record?"

"Now, that's a different story. Every detective has an anecdote about Yeoman getting away clean while one of his goons took the rap."

"Yeah, that's basically what I got from Mahoney. There's got to be somebody out there that Yeoman cheated or framed, who'd jump at the chance to get back at him."

"I called Dawson the other day and asked him what he knew. I figured he might have run into Yeoman when he was chasing down Tito Vega."

"And had he?"

"Nope, but he made a couple of calls for me."

"I hope he's careful. This is the best chance the D.A.'s ever had to put Yeoman away. We've got to be careful about where information comes from."

"Our cousin's a good investigator, kid. He knows what he's doing."

"I know," Harte said. "I'm just worried. Yeoman's hired Felix Drury as his attorney. He's a shark. He'll eat us alive if we can't vet every tidbit of evidence we present."

"You're still not sure about Dani, are you?"

With a sigh, Harte rubbed a hand down his face. "I believe she's telling the truth about what she heard. It's just hard to take in and it's going to be harder to convince a jury. She's linking a respected legislator and a renowned attorney with Yeoman, a thug and a drug dealer. She says her granddad was certain that Senator Stamps was taking bribes to push for lower tariffs on imports. If I can prove that independently, and find a solid connection between Stamps and Yeoman…"

"Are you saying you're going after Stamps?"

Harte sighed and ran a hand across his five-o'clock—or midnight—stubble. "I don't know. I need something more than Dani's hearsay about what she heard that night."

"Well, Dawson's info may help. He called a guy he uses part-time—a former drug addict who's a C.I. these days," Lucas said. "Apparently, there's been talk on the street for a long time about Yeoman's connections in the legislature. Something else that nobody seems willing to talk about openly."

"That's all well and good," Harte said. "But the fact that nobody will come forward with solid information is what keeps the D.A. up nights. Nobody's ever been able to prove anything."

"According to Dawson's C.I., some folks think that connection is Stamps."

Harte sat up, feeling his pulse speed up. "Why am I just now hearing this?"

"Because I just got it. The C.I. said to check Stamps's voting record and his bank accounts."

Harte rubbed his eyes. "I'm already on the voting records. I've got an intern tallying his position on every issue under the sun. But I have no cause to subpoena his bank records."

"You could ask him nicely," Lucas said wryly.

"Yeah," Harte responded. "I could toss a pig off a roof too, but the chances of it flying are better than a Louisiana congressman volunteering private financial information."

His brother laughed. "I've got to go. Big day tomorrow."

"Me too. I'll get with Dawson tomorrow. I hope he's got something more solid than a drug addict's report of a comment heard on a street corner."

"Good luck with that."

"Yeah, thanks. I'm going to need it."

"G'night, kid."

Harte hung up and looked at the dashboard clock, although he already knew it was after midnight. As he shifted, trying to find the most comfortable position, headlights appeared at the other end of the street. Harte crouched down in front of the headrest and waited to see what the vehicle did. It slowed down, which accelerated his pulse. Then he heard a garage door open. Peering around, he saw the car disappear into a garage three doors down. He watched until the door closed, then breathed a sigh of relief and relaxed as much as he could.

His thigh threatened to cramp again. Thanks to his long, lanky Delancey body, the Jeep wasn't going to be as comfortable as he'd hoped it would be. Still, he'd appointed himself Dani Canto's protector. A little discomfort was a small price to pay to ensure her safety.

But damn, it was going to be a long night.

Chapter Three

When Dani woke up the next morning and stretched, she yelped in pain. Every inch of her body was sore, thanks to her crash landing on her porch floor the day before. Her shoulders were tight and painful, her right knee ached and she had a headache.

She pushed herself up out of bed and hobbled to the shower. Under the hot spray, her muscles loosened and the headache eased, although the scrapes on her knees and elbows stung like fire. She blamed the sore muscles, the scrape and the aching knee on the bastard who'd tried to run her down. She blamed the headache on Harte Delancey, although, if she were truthful, he didn't deserve it.

After he'd left, she'd gotten into her pajamas and climbed into bed, fully intending to drink enough to wipe his ominous words from her brain. But the wine's taste was bitter on her tongue. She'd tried to read, tried to watch TV, even put on a blues music station, but nothing helped. So she turned out the light and lay in the dark, feeling sorry for herself.

She missed her granddad. Sure, he'd been eighty, but he'd been as healthy as a decades-younger man. In fact, he'd been planning to run for another four years in the legislature. She had been planning to have her grandfather around for another four years and more.

It hurt so much that he was gone. She wanted this trial over and done for so many reasons. It had been over a year since the night he was murdered, but every time she had to talk to the D.A.'s office, the police or a judge, all the wounds opened up again.

Now Harte was putting her into protective custody until after the trial. *She* was the one being threatened and targeted. It wasn't fair that she had to be the one locked up while the murderers were free to go where they pleased.

Under the hot soothing spray of the shower, she felt the weight of sadness and worry, heavier than ever. To her dismay, her eyes stung.

"Stop it," she told herself. She never cried. To cry meant to lose control, and she did not like feeling out of control.

Turning off the taps, she dried off, then wrapped up in a short terry-cloth robe and squeezed the last of the water out of her shoulder-length hair.

In the kitchen she put on a pot of coffee. As she waited for it to perk, she couldn't stop thinking about yesterday and her near miss. It had been almost dark when she'd gotten home. As she'd walked from the driveway to the mailbox, she'd heard a car engine rev.

By the time she'd realized the car was coming straight at her, it was almost too late. Somehow, instinct had kicked in and she'd managed to leap onto the porch. The car ripped through the wooden steps and then swerved back onto the street and took off.

It had been a close call. Too close. She shuddered,

her shoulders drawing up. With a long sigh intended to help her relax, she poured herself a mug of chicory coffee. She added cream and sugar and stirred briskly, then took that almost unbelievably delicious first sip of the morning. It was so good it gave her goose bumps.

A few more sips and she felt her courage begin to rise. Coffee made so many things better. Consciously relaxing the tense muscles between her shoulder blades, she headed toward the front porch to see what kind of damage had been done. She stepped outside and breathed deeply of the cool morning air. March temperatures in south Louisiana could be as hot as July, but they could also be fresh and springlike. This morning was leaning toward spring. But she quickly forgot about the weather as she surveyed the damage. The car had taken a huge bite out of the front-porch floor. The steps were nothing but splinters, and if she hadn't managed to clear the edge of the porch with that desperate leap, she might be just as smashed and scattered as the wood.

Shuddering at that thought, she eased closer to the porch's edge. Had the car damaged the four-by-fours that supported the front end of the porch? She took another couple of steps toward the edge.

"Dani! No!"

The sharp words shattered the quiet. Dani jerked and spilled coffee down the front of her robe. She whirled toward the voice, her heart racing with shock.

It was him! She'd been so concentrated on the damage to the porch that she'd completely forgotten about his promise to sleep in the driveway. "Stop!" he shouted.

Fury burned the shock right out of her. "You!" she

cried indignantly, flicking drops of sticky coffee off her fingers.

"Don't move!" He held up his hands in a stop gesture.

But she had no intention of budging. He was approaching fast and she was four feet above him on the porch in nothing but a bathrobe that came to midthigh—maybe. No underwear. *Oh, brother.* Her face grew warm.

"Don't come any closer!" she cried out. When he didn't stop, she screeched, "Don't!"

He stopped, looking bewildered. "What's wrong?"

"Go around back," she said, gesturing with her head. She didn't dare move anything else. Her left hand pressed the front hem of the robe against her thighs. "Go."

Harte cocked his head quizzically, then shrugged. "I will, but not until you back up carefully toward the door. The front of the porch is sagging."

"No! You first," she insisted. Her ears burned, she was so embarrassed. "Please," she begged.

His brows raised and that damnable smile appeared on his lips. "Ah," he said, his tone lightening. "Okay, I'll go. But you meet me at the door in five seconds flat or I'll come in and get you." He gave her a brief nod. "Nice robe."

She glared at him, but she still didn't dare to move a muscle.

"Go to hell," she said.

He waved a hand and headed around back.

Dani baby-stepped backward until she'd made it through the door. Then she sprinted into her bedroom to get dressed, marveling at the fact that he really had slept in his car in her driveway. The idea that he'd actually followed through with it, in some sort of quixotic effort to protect her, gave her a sense of security she hadn't felt since the night her grandfather had died.

As Harte waited at the back door for Dani to let him in, he chuckled. Once he'd been sure she wasn't going any closer to the rickety front edge of the porch, he'd paused for a second to admire those amazing legs. As he enjoyed them, she'd squirmed and turned red. When she begged him to go around to the back door while nervously tugging at the bottom of the short robe, it dawned on him why she was so reluctant for him to leap to her rescue.

She had nothing on under the robe. That thought had sent urgent, almost painful signals to his groin, signals that hadn't faded yet. He clamped his jaw against the sharp, pleasurable thrumming and forced himself to think about something miserable, like hiking in a freezing rain—or sleeping in his car. It helped a little.

He pushed his fingers through his hair and rubbed his stubbled jaw, as if that would help wipe away the sight of those forever legs. He busied himself with smoothing out the wrinkles in his T-shirt. Just as he tugged the tail down, Dani opened the door.

She'd thrown on jeans and a long-sleeved T-shirt, along with a *don't you dare mention my robe* glare. "Don't you have a home to go to?" she groused.

"Morning," he said cheerily, then pointed vaguely toward the front of the house. "Mind if I…?"

She stepped back from the door. "Down the hall on the right."

By the time he got back to the kitchen, he felt a whole lot better. He'd found a glass and some mouthwash in the hall bathroom, as well as a comb.

Dani was sitting at the kitchen table with a fresh mug of coffee in front of her. She nodded toward the coffeepot. "Mugs are in the cabinet above. Sugar's in the white canister. Cream is—"

"Let me guess," he broke in. "In the refrigerator. That's okay. I take it black." He retrieved a mug and filled it with the dark, strong brew.

"Of course you do," she muttered. When he sat, she looked pointedly at his wrinkled T-shirt. "Don't let me keep you. It's obvious you need to go home and get ready for work. I do."

"No," Harte replied, setting down his mug. "You've got to get ready to go to the bed-and-breakfast. Pack enough for at least two weeks."

Her mug stopped an inch from her lips. "I told you last night. I can't be away from work that long. I've got my own cases, people depending on me."

He drew in a frustrated breath. "Listen, Dani. This is your grandfather's murder trial. Your testimony is vital to link Ernest Yeoman directly to your granddad's murder. Do you have any idea how long the D.A.'s office has been trying to get something concrete on him?"

"You've got fingerprints from that night, right?"

"Not Yeoman's. He's got more sense than to show up at a crime scene." He looked at her quizzically. "Didn't anyone tell you about the fingerprinting results? There was one good set. They belong to a small-time burglar and general no-count named Chester Kirkle. He's got two convictions and he's on parole now. He's not going to make the most reliable witness. Our best bet is to talk him into giving up Yeoman. Then his testimony, boosted by yours about what they said, should put Yeoman away for conspiracy to commit assault with intent."

"Not murder?"

"I'm going to try for conspiracy to commit murder, but you know how unlikely we are to get it. Yeoman has an excellent alibi for the time frame."

"I know," she said, shaking her head. "I know. What are the chances this Kirkle will give Yeoman up?"

"I think once the trial date is set and he's looking at his third strike on top of parole violation, he'll flip."

She looked thoughtful. "And when he testifies against Yeoman, then Yeoman goes down too?"

"That's the plan," Harte agreed, "*if* Kirkle makes a credible witness and the jury believes that Yeoman sent him and the others to threaten your grandfather."

"Can you prove it's Yeoman who's trying to run me down?"

"I think so. I think it will be fairly easy to show him as a thug who hires thugs," Harte continued. "It matches his style."

She ducked her head and took a sip of coffee. "Beating an old man to death," she muttered.

When she looked up, Harte was surprised to see a shimmer of dampness in her eyes. The two times he'd talked to her over the past three months since he'd been appointed to the case, she'd been determined and angry about her grandfather's murder. Not once had he seen even the hint of a tear.

"Okay," she said, straightening. "I'll do whatever I have to."

He was absolutely sure that was true. The spark in her golden brown eyes spoke of the kind of person she was. If she wanted something, she went after it. She didn't sit back and wait. It wasn't in her nature.

"Look at the bright side. It's possible the trial could even be over in a few days."

She eyed him narrowly. "You don't really believe that, do you?"

He shrugged, being truthful. "No one knows anything for sure until it starts. But I can promise you this. Until the trial is over and Yeoman is in prison, you are in danger and it's my responsibility to keep you safe."

"Thank you," Dani said grudgingly.

"Have you heard who defense counsel is? Felix Drury."

"Jury Drury? I've heard he's been known to list dozens of potential witnesses on his intent-to-call list." Drury was one of the best-known defense attorneys in Orleans Parish. He was known for his ruthlessness, cleverness and charm. He'd defended some very famous and very infamous people.

Harte nodded. "He's a shark."

"Can you limit the number of witnesses he can call?"

"There's not much case law on limiting the number of witnesses," Harte said. "All I can do is discredit them or object if he tries to parade too many character witnesses in front of the jury. Of course, even if he doesn't bombard us with witnesses, even if he rests early, the jury could take forever to deliberate."

"I thought you were confident," she said, frowning.

"I am fairly confident, but there are problems. You didn't actually see the men, and you're the only witness to what they said. As you know, that can be construed as hearsay. Chester Kirkle is wavering. I think he'll roll on Yeoman. Until he signs on the dotted line, he's a wild card. So it very well may come down to your veracity versus Yeoman's reputation."

"Why is that even a question? He's a drug dealer and I'm a public defender."

"He owns twenty-three Hasty Mart convenience stores in the New Orleans area. On paper, he's a fine, upstanding businessman who made a couple of mistakes in his youth. He's known for his substantial political contributions as well as community support. And he's never been arrested as an adult," Harte said.

"Oh my gosh, the way you're talking, he sounds a lot more like a model citizen than a thug. We've probably already lost."

"Not if I can help it. I've got some feelers out about his connection with Stamps and Paul Guillame."

Dani groaned as she rose to put her mug in the sink. "So the trial could last from one day to forever. Please don't make me stay locked up until the trial is over. Why can't the police officers babysit me here?"

Harte stood too. He reached around her to set his mug down, and immediately regretted it. It put his nose way too close to her hair, which smelled like strawberries and sunshine. He backed up. "You know the answer to that," he said, his voice a bit husky from reaction.

"They know where I live," Dani responded, hoping the flutter in her pulse wasn't evident in her voice. Thank goodness he'd backed away. He'd been way too close to her as he set his mug in the sink. His arm brushing hers along with his warm breath against her hair had sent a thrill through her, a thrill she didn't welcome. She thought she'd gotten over this little crush, or whatever it was. After all, even though she'd been wildly attracted to him from the first moment she'd met him as opposing counsel, she'd quickly seen how pompous and arrogant he was, with his custom suits and his designer briefcase.

She turned toward him, forcing her mind back to the problem at hand. "How long do I have to get ready?"

"Go pack. I'll wash the mugs and the coffeepot. You can call the newspaper and the post office from the B-and-B."

"This is *so* inconvenient," she whined as she turned on her heel.

"Not as inconvenient as getting yourself killed," Harte shot after her.

Two hours later Dani pulled the crisscross strap of her purse off over her head and tossed it onto the white bedspread patterned with roses and lovebirds as Harte rolled her suitcase into the room. The entire bedroom was decorated in cluttered Victorian, just like the living room she'd just walked through. Frilly, lacy white curtains graced the windows, and every surface was covered with doilies, vases of silk flowers and filigreed photo frames.

The room was much too girlie for her taste. It was beautiful and she certainly appreciated pretty feminine things, but she limited the lace and frills to her underwear. She preferred her clothes tailored and her furnishings and décor sparse and open.

"Ugh," she groaned.

"What?" Harte said. "Is something wrong?"

She swept the air with her hand. "You tell me. Do I look like the type who would live among roses and lace?" She winced as she remembered the pink lacy panties and bra she'd donned this morning.

His gaze sharpened as if he were activating X-ray vision.

"That was a rhetorical question," she said archly. "Why am I on the first floor? Wouldn't I be harder to get to upstairs?"

Harte was still looking at her.

"That one *wasn't* rhetorical," she said.

He blinked and met her gaze. "Yeah, you'd be harder to get to, but also harder to get *out*. I don't want you stuck with no means of escape."

She frowned. "Means of escape? Really? I thought the reason you brought me here was so they won't know where I am."

He nodded. "That's true. But it's possible that someone could follow me or the police officers."

She knew she had to have a police babysitter, but him? "You?"

"I've got to prep you for your testimony. And since we're paying for this lovely place, we might as well use it. Besides, I don't want you traveling back and forth to my office—or my home." His mouth curved up in a quick, crooked smile, different from the knowing smirk he usually sent her way. It was a little comical and very charming.

Charming? *Where had that come from?* Dani shook her head.

"What?" Harte asked.

"What?" she retorted.

"You were shaking your head."

"No, I wasn't," she muttered as she grabbed her suitcase and hefted it up onto the cedar chest that sat at the foot of the bed. "I guess I've got to unpack."

"I guess you do, if you've finally accepted that you're stuck here. I can promise you that a knight in shining armor is not going to sweep in and save you from protective custody."

"A girl can dream," she said on a sigh as she unzipped the case. Her makeup kit and hairbrush were on top. She picked them up and started toward the bathroom, then turned back and looked at Harte.

"So, are *you* taking the first shift?"

"No. I'm waiting to hear from Captain Mahoney, letting me know who he's sending over. I'll stay here until they get here."

Dani straightened and propped her hands on her hips. "I don't like this. You are way too serious. Shouldn't I be somewhere farther away? Like maybe Seattle? If you're that worried about them figuring out where I am." She expected him to say no, that he was just taking precautions, but he didn't.

That worried her.

"It's possible they were just trying to scare you, but from the looks of your front steps, I'd say if you hadn't managed to jump onto the porch, you might be in the hospital, or—"

"Do *not* say smudge on the sidewalk again. I get the

picture. So when—?" she had started to ask when his cell phone interrupted her.

He held up a finger as he fished it out of his jacket pocket and answered it. "Delancey," he said shortly, turning toward the picture window as he listened. "Hello? Hello?" He walked closer to the window. "Mr. Akers, I can hardly hear you. Hold on." He looked at the phone's display and muttered, "What's with the bad reception? It was fine the other day." He stepped into the living room.

Vincent Akers was the district attorney. Dani could hear Harte trying to talk with him. After a moment, she heard him utter a mild curse, and then he appeared in the bedroom doorway. "The cell service here sucks," he said irritably, pocketing his phone. "Your day-shift officer just pulled up. I'll get you two introduced and then I need to take off." He glanced at his watch. "I've got a meeting with the D.A., I think."

"Should you call back on the B-and-B's phone and check?"

"Nah, by that time I could be halfway to his office."

"Speaking of offices, when can I get some things from mine?" she asked. "My desk is full of stuff I have to read and reports and briefs I need to write."

"I told you, the public defender's office will assign your cases to someone else. You need to worry about staying safe."

"That's all well and good, but even if somebody picks up my caseload, I still have paperwork to complete. I brought my laptop. I need that stuff."

"Okay. I'll ask the officer to take you to pick them

up. One hour, no more. And that's the last time you leave this B-and-B until I say so. Got it?"

"Yes, sir, Mr. Prosecutor, sir," she said, not even trying to hide the irritation in her voice. She heard the tinkle of the bell over the front door and sturdy footsteps approaching.

Harte turned and took a step backward. "I'm Harte Delancey."

"Field, sir," the officer said, coming into view at the bedroom door. "Ronald Field, reporting for protection duty." He stood straight and solemn, his right hand resting on the butt of his gun.

He was a medium-height officer with medium-brown hair and a medium build. He was pleasant-looking, but he didn't look as if he could do any better job of protecting her than she could herself. He wasn't in uniform, but even so, he looked spit-and-polished, from his crisply ironed shirt all the way down to his mirror-shined shoes.

As a public defender, she was no stranger to the police. But the sight of Officer Field standing in the doorway of the frilly Victorian room looking so earnest and official, despite his street clothes, and knowing he was there to spend eight or ten or however many hours every day guarding her, sent a frisson of fear down her spine.

"This is Danielle Canto," Harte said, gesturing toward her.

"Yes, sir." Field regarded Dani with a slight nod. "Ma'am. I know you, at least in the hall. I've been the arresting officer on a couple of cases you've defended."

"Oh, of course," Dani said, although she didn't recognize him. She felt her cheeks begin to warm in embarrassment. "Nice to see you, Officer."

"Thank you, ma'am."

She smiled. "Please call me Dani." She held out her hand and Field took it. He was nice, only a few years older than she.

She listened as Harte laid out the ground rules to Field about taking Dani to the courthouse to retrieve her papers—nowhere but her office, only as many papers as fit in one box or briefcase, straight back to the B & B.

"Take a different route each way and make sure you're not followed," he said. Then with a quick glance at her, he added, "And she's not to leave the house again."

She met Field's gaze over Harte's shoulder and rolled her eyes. Field's expression didn't change from quiet respect.

"Okay, then," Harte said. "Dani, be a good girl and don't give Officer Field a hard time, okay?"

She raised her eyebrows, wishing her superpower was shooting daggers from her eyes. "Watch it, Mr. Prosecutor. I could file harassment charges against you for calling me *girl.*"

"You could," he said, amusement tingeing his voice. "Anybody can file suit, but it would be dismissed as frivolous."

"I could make it stick," she retorted.

Harte's face grew solemn. "Seriously, don't give him any trouble. This is for your own safety."

Suddenly, the back of her throat quivered and she felt a twinge of fight-or-flight adrenaline course through her veins. "I understand," she said evenly, silently willing him to go away and stop trying to scare her. Because it was working. The image of the mangled porch stairs rose in her mind's eye. If the car had done that kind of damage to four-by-fours, what would it have done to her legs—or her body?

Chapter Four

"I'll call you," Harte said. "Check to see how you're doing. And tomorrow, I'll start prepping you for your testimony."

Dani nodded.

Harte headed out the door, pulling a key ring with two keys on it from his pocket. "Officer? Walk me out, will you?" he said as he passed Field. "These are duplicate keys to the front and back doors. I'm giving you one and keeping one myself. You and the second-shift officer will exchange keys. One of you will be here with Ms. Canto at all times."

"Yes, sir," Field said, turning on his polished heel to follow him.

Imperious. That was it. She'd been searching for just the right word to describe Harte Delancey. And *imperious* was perfect. He was arrogant too, and she didn't like him at all. Forget how very nice he'd looked this morning in old worn jeans and a faded T-shirt with his hair tousled from sleeping in his car and his jaw shadowed by morning stubble. Forget how easy it was to imagine that he would look just like that after they spent the night...

You are so not going there, she admonished herself,

even as she pushed the curtains aside with two fingers and watched him fold his long, lean body into his car and drive away.

She wondered why an attorney in New Orleans drove a Jeep. But it did suit him, like the jeans and T-shirt and, she had to admit, the stubble.

"Ms. Canto?"

She jumped and let the curtains drop into place. "What? Oh yes, Officer Field." She hadn't heard him come back inside.

"Do you need anything?"

She gave him her sweetest smile. "Only a ride to the courthouse."

"If you're ready to go, my car is right out front."

"The Camry?" That was the only other car she'd seen parked in front of the B & B.

"Yes. I'm driving my own car. It's not a good idea to have a police car sitting out front all day and night."

Dani grabbed her purse, its extra weight reminding her of the gun and the lock-pick kit inside it. She glanced quickly at Field. Would he be able to tell she was carrying just by how the heavy bag swung against her side? Thank goodness Harte hadn't noticed. She slung the long crisscrossed strap over her head so the bag lay diagonally across her torso and rested against her left hip. Its weight reassured her. Babysitters or not, she wanted the feeling of security and control the gun gave her until the trial was over.

Looking at the back of Field's head as he opened the front door, she still wasn't sure he had what it took to protect her, if Harte was right about the danger.

Chewing on her lower lip, she wondered how easily manipulated he was. "I'm hungry," she said. "Are you?"

Officer Ronald Field turned to look at her. "Ms. Canto—"

"Dani," she said, still smiling.

"Dani. Mr. Delancey gave me my instructions. You can order something delivered later, because right now I'm driving you straight to the courthouse and straight back."

Dani suppressed a smile as she assessed him. So, Officer Field was more strong-willed than he looked.

Chapter Five

Harte stopped outside the door of the district attorney's office to finish speaking with his cousin Dawson, who owned a private-investigations firm. "Dawson, hang on a minute," he said into his phone. "Don't say anything else. I don't want to know how you plan to get hold of Stamps's financial records. I need to be able to use the information in court, so be careful, okay?"

"No problem. I'm working on an idea," Dawson said.

"Get back to me as fast as you can. I have a feeling the judge is going to set the trial date as soon as he can—soon as in next week." Harte's phone buzzed. He looked at it. It was Felix Drury, Yeoman's defense attorney. "I've got another call," he said.

"Okay, I'll call you back."

Harte thanked him before switching to his second call. "Hello?" he said.

"Delancey, why is my client being harassed about an accident that has nothing to do with him?"

"Uh, who is this?" Harte asked innocently. Felix Drury was better known as Jury Drury, because in front of a jury he was as charming and self-deprecating as Jimmy Stewart's Mr. Smith. In person, Drury was a self-aggrandizing, annoying grouch more reminiscent of Charles Laughton in *Mutiny on the Bounty*.

"Damn it, Delancey, you know who this is. Why are the police hauling Mr. Yeoman in? He was having dinner with his entire family at Commander's Palace when your client stepped in front of that car."

"Okay, Drury. First of all, she didn't step in front of the car, as you well know. I'm not going to put up with your usual blatant rewriting of the facts of the case. Got it?" Without waiting for an answer, Harte went on. "And why am I not surprised that your client just happened to be seen at one of the busiest and most prestigious restaurants in New Orleans at the time the vehicle nearly ran her over?"

"Mr. Yeoman and I are terribly sorry about her accident, as is everyone. We do hope she wasn't injured. It would be a shame for such a lovely young woman to be hurt like that."

Harte didn't like the way Drury said that. If he were paranoid, he might construe it as a veiled threat.

Drury was speaking again. "Now, you tell your boss to lay off Yeoman. It's bad enough he's having to endure the spectacle of a frivolous trial, for a murder for which he *also* has an alibi. This treatment of a respected New Orleans businessman is approaching defamation of character."

Harte glanced at his watch and sighed audibly, for Drury's benefit. "Okay, Felix. I'll give Mr. Akers your message."

"You're a punk, Delancey, just like your father. Both of you wish you were worthy of shining your grandfather's shoes."

Harte wanted to make a smart retort, but all he could think of was *Oh yeah?* So he just hung up. He opened the door to the D.A.'s office and spoke to the secretary as he passed her desk. He straightened his shoulders, then stepped into the Orleans Parish district attorney's office. He had no doubt why Vincent Akers had called him. He was probably going to get his butt chewed for securing the order of protection without consulting him. Still, he knew he'd done the right thing.

Akers was a micromanager, too controlling to allow his prosecutors to handle things on their own. He wanted to be consulted on and approve everything they did. And that chafed Harte.

Before he even stepped into the room, the scents of breakfast tickled his nostrils. Coffee, bacon, eggs and some kind of sweet rolls. The D.A.'s breakfasts were legendary. People would come down or up from other floors to sniff and place bets on what was inside the Styrofoam container.

"Talked to Judge Tony Rossi a while ago," Akers said without looking up from a form he was signing.

Harte resisted the almost overwhelming urge to check the shine on his shoes. He didn't move a muscle. "Yes, sir?"

Akers leaned back in his leather manager's chair and harrumphed. "Are you going to pretend that you don't know what he called about?"

"No, sir."

"Then stop standing there like an eight-year-old caught with a spitball and a straw and give me the details. Judge Rossi said you didn't fill him in much. I asked him why he'd sign an order of protection without getting all the details. You know what he said?"

Harte's throat was quivering with the urge to swallow. He couldn't resist anymore. He watched Akers watch his Adam's apple move. "No, sir," he replied.

"He said, 'That's Con's grandson, Vinnie. He told me his witness was in danger, and I trust his judgment.'" The D.A. folded his hands across his large stomach. "You know what I said back to him?"

Harte sighed. He was getting tired of this game. "No, sir."

"I said, 'If he's Con's grandson, then he's a smart-ass and a rounder, but you're right. His judgment is likely on-target.'"

"Thank you, sir," Harte said.

Akers shook his head. "No," he said. "That wasn't a compliment. It was a concession. I respect Judge Rossi. What I don't respect is you using your nepotistic connections to get an order of protection late at night without consulting me first. That is not the way I run my office." He harrumphed again and patted his stomach. "Is that clear?"

"Yes, sir."

"Do you have any idea how long I've worked to nail Yeoman? He's the slipperiest snake I've ever run into in my entire career. And I've seen some slippery ones."

"I'm hoping we've got him this time, sir," Harte said.

"You better hope we do. If he's brought to trial for murder and gets away with it, nobody'll ever be able to touch him again. Do you understand what kind of a predicament you've put me in?"

"I'm just trying to protect my witness."

Akers sighed exaggeratedly. "And it's not bad enough that we may lose our last chance to nail Yeoman, we're wading into deep alligator-infested waters with Ms. Canto dragging Senator Stamps and Paul Guillame into the mix." He peered up at Harte. "By the time this trial is over, my career's liable to be too. And if mine is, so is yours. Tell me what you've found out about Stamps's involvement. And while you're at it, don't forget to include Paul Guillame."

Harte winced internally. He had an urge to tell Akers what Dani said about Stamps, but it was no more than a rumor right now. If he could get something concrete, then he'd bring it to the D.A. "Don't have anything yet, sir," he said. "I've got somebody checking out a couple of rumors for me."

"Somebody?" Akers raised an eyebrow. "Would I be correct in assuming that this somebody is also related to you?"

Harte angled his head in affirmation. "I'm hoping that with the trial coming up, there's buzz on the street that could link Yeoman with either Stamps or Paul."

"And what if the buzz says that Yeoman's buddy was Freeman Canto?"

Harte swallowed again. Of course that was the simplest explanation. Yeoman sent thugs to beat up Canto because Canto was reneging on some agreement or had failed to do something. Forget Stamps and Paul. Even if Dani really had heard her grandfather's attackers shout their names as well as Yeoman's, it could mean nothing. But he did believe Dani and he did not believe the threats the attackers had yelled while they were beat-

ing Freeman Canto to death were nothing. He lifted his
chin a fraction of an inch and challenged Akers.

"You know I have no more evidence linking Yeoman with Canto than I do with either Stamps or Paul,"
he said. "I've spent the past three months since you assigned me to the case trying to find a link while digging
my way out of the avalanche of Felix Drury's motions
and disclosure requests. We've got the fingerprint of
a small-time thug named Kirkle on the doorknob of
Canto's office, and I'm optimistic that he'll cut a deal
and give Yeoman up. But until I have that deal in hand,
all I've got is Dani's testimony. But there's got to be
something from last night—a speck of paint, a sliver
of a broken headlight—which can lead us to the car
that tried to run Dani down. I just need one tiny crumb
of physical evidence that links Yeoman to these *accidents*. If I can get that, I can make the jury believe that
he killed Canto."

Akers popped open the lid of the foam container, increasing the mouthwatering smell of bacon and biscuits.
"Are the police collecting that evidence?"

"Yes, sir. I haven't heard what they've found yet,
but they're on it."

The D.A. opened a drawer and pulled out a stainless-
steel fork and knife. "Fine. Now get out of here before
I decide to take you off this case and make you bring
Mertz or Shallowford up to speed."

"Yes, sir. There's just one more thing, sir."

Akers stared at him over his reading glasses. "What?"
he demanded as he lowered the lid of the container.

"I just got a call from Jury Drury," he said. "He ha-
rangued me about the police pulling Yeoman in for

questioning about the incident with the car and Dani—
Ms. Canto last night. But that wasn't the main reason
for his call."

Akers's expression didn't change.

"He called to let me know that Yeoman has an air-
tight alibi for last night. He was with his family having
dinner at Commander's Palace."

"Of course he was," Akers said.

Harte smiled. "That's what I said."

"Get out of here."

Harte turned and tried not to bolt out the door.

"And, Harte," Akers said. "Try not to pull the entire
Delancey clan into the fray."

He nodded as he cleared the doorway. That wasn't
as bad as he'd thought it would be. His butt was still intact and so was his case. He had his uncle Tony, Judge
Rossi, to thank for that.

BY A QUARTER to ten that night, Dani had showered and
changed into pink satin pajamas and was sitting on the
frilly Victorian bed with her mini notebook computer
on her lap, working on a report that was due the next
day. A sharp rap on the door startled her.

"Dani? It's Officer Field. Detective Kaye is here for
the overnight shift. I'd like to introduce her to you."

Detective? It was protocol for the night-shift officer
of a female witness to be female, but it was rare that
detectives took protective detail. Dani set her computer
aside, got up and, after grabbing a white shawl to throw
around her shoulders, opened the door.

Field was still almost as crisp and polished as he'd
been twelve hours earlier. Standing beside him was a

woman in her early-to-mid-thirties. Her black hair was in a long straight ponytail. She was dressed in street clothes, slim tan pants and a green shirt that complemented her dark skin. The only thing that kept her from looking like a casual friend who'd stopped by to visit was the badge pinned to her waistband and the black leather shoulder holster. Draped over her left arm was a jacket that matched her pants.

"Hi," she said, offering her hand. "I'm Detective Michele Kaye." She had a firm grip.

"Dani Canto." She searched her memory. Had she met Kaye before? "Nice to meet you, Detective."

"Call me Michele," the detective said.

"Okay, then," Field continued. "I'm on my way. Y'all have a good night."

Michele glanced around the living room, then stepped up to the bedroom door. "I need to see your room. I want to familiarize myself with it." She shrugged, adjusting the position of the holster. The gesture was intimidating. Dani decided that Detective Kaye would have no trouble handling herself in any situation.

"Ignore the mess," Dani said. She'd had Field set the boxes from her office by the bed so they'd be within easy reach. Her clothes were draped over the dainty chair that sat in front of a Victorian writing desk, and her shoes were next to the boxes.

Michele snorted. "This is not a mess. My two kids— *they* can make a mess."

"You have two children? How old are they?"

"Seven and eight." She smiled. "My mother takes care of them when I work overtime."

"I didn't realize detectives were ever assigned this kind of duty," Dani said.

"I volunteer for overtime as often as I can. It comes in handy when you're a single mother." As she spoke, she checked the bathroom, then turned her attention to the bank of windows on the far side of the room. She frowned. "I don't like those windows. They're a security risk, so large and low to the ground. Someone could climb in."

Dani swung around and looked at them. She hadn't noticed how large they were, but now, with Michele's words, the nape of her neck prickled. "Wow," she said. "Thanks for pointing that out," she finished wryly.

"It's my job. But don't worry. I'll take a spin around the house every hour or so, just to be sure there's no one hanging around. This is a pretty good area. It'll probably be fine."

"Unless Yeoman, or whoever tried to run me down, figures out where I am."

Detective Kaye nodded. "That's why we're here," she said. "Well, I'll leave you alone. I see you're working." She started for the door. "Don't worry about anything. I'll be right outside. Holler if you need me."

Michele went out and pulled the bedroom door to, leaving it ajar. Dani tried to settle back down and finish her report, but she couldn't concentrate. Detective Kaye's critical assessment of the windows had made her aware of just how big they were and how close to her bed. She set the computer aside and got under the covers, then turned out the bedside lamp.

She was almost asleep when she heard something. She froze, holding her breath and feeling a creepy déjà vu from the night before, when Harte had walked around outside her house.

She was probably letting her imagination run away with her. *Settle down.* She didn't want to get a reputation as the public defender who cried wolf on her first night.

She turned over, trying to relax her tense muscles. She sighed, closed her eyes and did her best to clear her mind.

Then the noise sounded again. Like a scrape of a shoe on a hard surface. She yelped softly, then covered her mouth with her hand. She lifted her head and peered at the windows, trying to see if she could spot a moving shadow or something.

Then suddenly, a high-pitched screech rent the air. Dani shrieked involuntarily.

Almost immediately, a knock sounded on her door and it swung open. Michele stood there, her right hand reaching for her weapon. "What is it?" she whispered sotto voce.

"I'm sorry. Something made a horrible noise outside the window. But now that I think about it, I'm sure it was cats fighting," Dani whispered, feeling silly.

Michele walked over to the windows and parted the curtains to look out. "I heard the screeching. I'm pretty sure it was cats too. But get your shoes on and go into the living room," she said. "I'm going to take a walk around the house."

"I'm sorry," Dani repeated, but Michele was already heading out the front door.

Dani jumped up, shoved her feet into her sandals and grabbed her purse before going into the living room.

She clutched the bag to her chest as she waited for Michele to return.

When the front doorknob turned Dani stiffened, but of course it was the detective.

"I didn't see anything," she said. "Not even cats. There were no footprints on that side of the house, and I think there would be, because it's been raining a little."

Dani nodded.

Michele eyed her. Her mouth twitched. "I see you're all ready to go, with your purse and your sandals."

Dani's face burned. She probably looked ridiculous, but she wasn't about to tell Michele she was hanging on to the bag because of the gun inside. She shrugged and smiled wryly. "I'm not used to being scared of anything. But I'm kind of spooked, since the prosecutor has got me guarded by police. I apologize for all the uproar over cats."

"Don't apologize. I need to know if you hear even the slightest noise. Now go on back to bed. Everything should be fine. Like I told you, I'll make the rounds every hour or so. I'll vary it in case someone's watching, but I don't think anyone is. This B-and-B is in a perfect location for hiding a witness. At the end of the street, with a vacant lot behind it. Not much traffic. I think I'll talk to Mr. Delancey tomorrow about moving you to a more secure room, though—second floor maybe."

Dani started to tell her that Harte had already dismissed the idea of a second-floor room, but she thought better of it. She wouldn't mind seeing Harte tangle with Michele. Besides, she still liked the idea of being on a higher floor. Less chance that someone could crawl in her window.

Chapter Six

The next morning, Dani woke to the sound of voices. "Granddad?" she whispered, and grabbed the covers to toss them aside, but they didn't feel right. She stared at the material. This wasn't her bedspread. She squinted up at the filmy curtains hanging at the tall windows. Then she realized where she was, and why.

The voices were still talking, too low to distinguish. She frowned, listening more closely. There was a male voice. No, two male voices. And a female. The door muffled them so she couldn't make out what they were saying. Holding her breath and concentrating, she placed the lower-pitched male voice. It was Harte.

She groaned. Why was he here? One thing she knew—it wasn't going to be good news for her. Unless maybe they'd firmed up the trial date. She threw back the covers and got up, reaching for her cell phone to check the time. Ten-thirty? Wow. She hadn't slept eight hours straight since her granddad had died.

She combed her hair and threw on jeans, a tank top and a red, long-sleeved shirt before going to the door. Harte, Officer Field and Detective Kaye all turned to look at her. Field was dressed casually today, but the paddle holster at the small of his back ruined his careful suburban image.

"Good morning," Harte said, with that smile on his face. "We've been talking about you." This morning he looked more like the man she was accustomed to seeing. He was dressed in a gray suit, a snowy white shirt and a multicolored designer tie. He was clean-shaven. Mr. Prosecutor was back.

She shot a glance at Michele, but she couldn't read her expression. She looked back at Harte. "Should my ears be burning?"

"Michele brought up the obvious security issue with the windows in your room. We won't be moving you, but I'm going to have a motion-activated floodlight installed just outside your windows. It might be inconvenient if a cat walks across the yard and triggers it, but you'll know if there's anyone outside your window at night."

She winced at his reference to cats. Had Michele told him? "Great," she said sarcastically. "I'll have warning that someone is about to crash through the windows and kill me."

Harte gave her a hard look, but Michele and Ronald exchanged a glance. Ronald's eyes twinkled. Michele's face remained immobile.

"It's the best option," Harte said dismissively.

Dani threw up her hands. "Fine. Fine. You obviously know best." She looked toward the kitchen, sniffing the air. "I smell coffee, thank goodness. Is there anything to eat?"

"I saw bagels and sweet rolls in the refrigerator," Michele said.

"The manager isn't here this week," Harte added. "Since we took over the entire house. He told me he'd left some breakfast items in the refrigerator. I feel sure you can make do."

Dani groaned as she poured a cup of coffee. Harte Delancey might be easy on the eyes, but he was really hard on the patience. And the fact that she'd gotten a good night's sleep hadn't made him any less annoying.

Harte nodded to Michele as she left, then turned to Field. "How did things go yesterday? Any problem with Ms. Canto?" he asked, eliciting what sounded like a snort from the kitchen. He ignored it.

"No, sir. We went straight to the courthouse and back. We brought two boxes of files and papers back with us."

Harte nodded. The rookie officer was impressively earnest. Harte had no doubt that he would defend Dani's life with his own if necessary. "Want some coffee? Ms. Canto and I are going to talk about the upcoming case."

"No, sir. I'll take a look around the house and up and down the street while you're here."

"Good. Thanks."

As Ronald left, Harte turned to the kitchen. Dani was dressed in the same jeans she'd worn the day before. He hadn't missed how well they fit her long sleek legs and trim, curvy backside. They looked even sexier today. How was that possible? He watched her retrieve a sweet roll from the microwave and set it on the small table. When she looked up and frowned, he realized he was staring.

"What?" she said, jerking the chair out and sitting down.

He walked over and picked up her coffee mug from the counter and set it in front of her. "Forgot your coffee," he said lightly, then turned to pour himself a cup.

"I guess Michele told you about my silly reaction to the cats?" she asked as he sat down across from her. She cut a wedge of cinnamon roll.

"Yes, but I don't think it's silly. You need to tell her or Field any time you think you hear something outside your window. I don't want to take any chances with your safety."

"Well, thanks." She gestured with her fork. "These rolls are surprisingly good. You should have one."

He tore his gaze away from her and sent a half-hearted glance toward the package. What he wanted to have was a chance to taste the little dollop of icing off the corner of her mouth. He swallowed. "I came by to tell you that the judge called me this morning. He apologized for the trial date being moved forward. Said he'd put it on the docket last week, but he'd been out of town. I'm thinking Drury must have seen the date on the docket. If he told Yeoman that the trial was moved forward, that could be why Yeoman has been trying to frighten you. You should be happy that the trial is starting. The earlier it starts, the quicker it finishes."

"I guess so," Dani said. "But that doesn't leave much time for prep."

"Right. We'll be working on that all this weekend."

"But Tuesday—I'm not sure I'm ready," she said, setting her fork down.

"Of course you are. You know the process. It doesn't

matter that you've never testified in a trial yourself. You've tried plenty of cases. You know what to expect."

She shook her head, and a couple of strands of her dark hair fell across her face. She shoved them back with an impatient hand. "I haven't been..." She paused, then started again. "I haven't talked about that night with anyone—I mean, other than the police and someone from the D.A.'s office back when it happened. Whenever I think about it..." Her voice cracked.

Harte watched her. He'd sat with lots of witnesses as they talked through their grief. Violent death was a cruel and heartless way to die. It left family and friends not only grief-stricken but guilt-ridden, wondering if they could have done something to prevent their loved one's death. He always felt tremendous sympathy for those left behind.

But the feelings niggling their way through his chest right now were more than just sympathy for Dani as a grieving granddaughter. He felt protective of her. He had an unprofessional urge to hold her close and ease her pain.

No. Not hold her close. He hadn't meant that. He *didn't* want that. He was merely concerned about her safety and state of mind. He needed to make sure that by Monday, she could clearly and succinctly describe what had happened the night Freeman Canto died. That was all.

Her voice interrupted his thoughts. He tried to concentrate on what she was saying.

"It's funny. I was okay at the funeral too. But ever since—" Her eyes filled with tears. She blinked and looked down at her hands.

Harte leaned his forearms on the table. "It's no wonder that you're upset now. You were almost run down by a car yesterday. Not to mention being uprooted from your home, which you shared with your granddad until he was murdered. I suspect that hearing those cats last night was the last straw. You're in a much more vulnerable state than you've been so far since your granddad died."

Her brows drew down. "Vulnerable state? You make me sound like a Jane Austen character. Trust me. I am not prone to fainting on couches."

He couldn't suppress a smile. "No, I'm sure you're not. Now, about the windows. I want you to pay attention to the things you hear and see while you're here. *Nothing* that frightens or startles you is silly. Tell the officers. It's their job to check out anything that looks, sounds or even smells suspicious. I don't care if you call them a hundred times about cats fighting."

She gave a small laugh. "I promise, despite the surroundings, I'm really not a hypersensitive Victorian maiden."

"You're doing fine," he said, patting her hand.

Immediately, her expression hardened and she drew her hand away. "Don't patronize me, Mr. Prosecutor." She gulped a large sip of coffee and picked up the cinnamon roll with her fingers. "So, are we ready to prep?" she asked, then bit into the gooey roll, leaving a bigger dollop of icing on her lip this time.

Harte's insides ached at the sight of her tongue slipping out to catch the sugary frosting. She was fascinating. Haughty as a runway model one second, stuffing her face like a college kid the next. He looked at a point somewhere behind her head and forced himself to ignore her unconscious sensuality. He swallowed. "We'll start this evening. Unfortunately, you don't have a lot of evidence to testify about. Not that your testimony is not important. Just the opposite. I believe we might have a chance to put Ernest Yeoman behind bars for the first time ever. I merely mean that your testimony probably won't take that long. Still, I want to make sure you're comfortable enough with what you're going to say that you come across as earnest and likeable."

"Why wouldn't I?" she retorted. "You know, every bit of what I told you and the police is the truth, the whole truth and nothing but the truth." She stuck her chin out defiantly, although since she was still chewing, it made her seem like a stubborn kid.

"Hey," he said. "I'm not questioning your honesty, but you know as well as I do that if a witness is nervous or too emotional, it doesn't matter if she's telling the truth. What matters is the jury's perception of her. And I want the jurors to see you as the grieving granddaughter who is bravely holding it together, even though her heart is broken."

"Wow. Queue the violins," Dani said sarcastically. "Think you can pull that off?"

Harte grimaced at her tone. "I'm not implying that you're not. I know how much you loved your grandfather," he said. "All I'm trying to do is—"

"Right. Save it for your closing arguments." She got up and took her dishes to the sink and turned on the water.

He sat there staring at her back. He prided himself on doing a good job of easing the pain of grieving loved ones, but somehow, he'd managed to screw this up. She sounded contemptuous, just as she'd been back when they'd faced each other across the courtroom as opponents. But he'd heard a catch in her voice.

He wished…hell, he didn't know what he wished. Maybe that she'd trust him to keep her safe and get her through the trial.

He looked at his watch. "I'm due in court soon. I'd better go." He stood and picked up his mug, preparing to take it to the sink, but she whirled and snatched it out of his hand.

"I'll do that."

He pressed his lips together. "Okay. I'll see you this evening."

"What time?" she asked, then shook her head. "Oh, right," she said sarcastically, "it doesn't matter. I'll be here."

"It depends on when the judge in my case recesses for the day. I hope it'll be by six at the latest. Want me to bring you something for dinner?"

She eyed him narrowly. "I've been craving jambalaya. And the best jambalaya in the world is Mama Pinto's."

"Where is that?"

"You've never had Mama Pinto's jambalaya? Oh, your mouth is going to thank you! It is seriously the best in the world."

"And it's—?"

"Oh, just off Tremé. It's only about three miles from here."

"Tremé? Seriously? You want me to navigate through the area where they're filming the TV series during

rush hour? It'll take me an hour to get from the courthouse to there and from there to here. And that's if
Hollywood South is done filming. If they're still on-
site, it'll be longer. I tell you what. There's a café that
makes killer jambalaya about three blocks from here
on Tchoupitoulas," he said hopefully.

"Okay, never mind," she said, her voice dripping
with disappointment.

She didn't fool him. He knew what she was doing.
She was baiting him. But that was okay. He'd virtu-
ally imprisoned her. She had a right to a little revenge.

"I'll go to Mama Pinto's. I can't guarantee what time
I'll be back, though."

"Get me some wine too, please. A good Chardonnay. I'll leave the brand to you."

"Yes, ma'am," he retorted, and touched his forehead
in a mock salute. "I'll see you tonight."

It took Harte more than an hour to drive to Mama
Pinto's, pick up two orders of jambalaya and get back
to the B & B. By the time he pulled into the parking lot,
the sky was dark with low black clouds. It looked as if
any minute they would burst open and dump torrents
of rain on the entire New Orleans area. As he reached
for an umbrella from under his passenger seat, his cell
phone rang.

"Delancey."

"Harte, where y'at? It's Dawson."

"Hey," he said to his cousin. "Just got to the B-and-
B with a delivery of jambalaya for my witness."

Dawson laughed. "Lucas told me you've got a tiger
by the tail with Canto's granddaughter."

"She's a little stubborn, but I've got it under control." *You wish,* he told himself. "Got something for me?"

"Could be. My C.I. looked up a guy he knows who used to run errands for Yeoman."

"Errands?" His brain immediately took the single word and raced through the possibilities—loan collector, drug dealer, hush money.

"My C.I. armed himself with a newspaper that had an article about your upcoming trial and used it to start a conversation about Yeoman with the errand boy at a bar. He kept buying the guy beers and finally he opened up. He ended up telling my C.I. that the biggest part of his job was delivering envelopes and packages to an aide who worked for several legislators."

Harte's pulse went through the roof. *This could be it!* If he could connect Yeoman to Stamps and bring them both down, a small percentage of the corruption in New Orleans would be cleaned up, and Dani could feel safe in her own home. Not to mention that the win could catapult his career. "Well?" he said.

"Well what?" Dawson responded. Harte could hear the amusement in his voice.

"Come on, Daw. Did he say who the legislators were—and what was in the packages?"

"Nope. He didn't. But my C.I. gave me the errand boy's name. Well, *gave* isn't quite the right word."

"I'll pay you back. Just let me have it. This could be huge."

"I tell you what. Sounds like you're pretty busy with your witness, so while you're babysitting her, I'll have a talk with the guy and see what he's willing to spill and how much it will cost."

"Thanks, Dawson. But remember, anything you find out has got to be able to be confirmed. I can't use unverified information. I definitely owe you one."

"You definitely do." His cousin hung up.

It had started to rain while they were talking. Harte grabbed his umbrella and hurried inside.

What he saw when he entered surprised him. Dani and Michele were sitting at the kitchen table, mugs of coffee in their hands, laughing. They looked up in unison. Dani's smile faded and Michele set her mug down and stood.

"Hi," Harte said, amazed at how effectively he'd doused their good time just by walking in. "Don't stop on my account." He set the food and wine on the kitchen counter and took off his damp coat and tie. "Where's Field?"

"Today is his wedding anniversary. He left early and I'm covering."

Harte frowned. "He didn't tell me that."

"It's not a big deal, sir. One of us will be here twenty-four-seven."

Harte wasn't sure he liked not knowing exactly who would be here at any given time. He nodded reluctantly.

"I was just about to do my walk-around," Michele said.

"Take your slicker or an umbrella," Harte advised.

Dani and Michele both looked toward the front window.

"Wow," Dani said. "It got dark out. The weatherman said it was going to rain, but this looks ominous."

"Yep," Harte agreed. "I just heard on the news that

there's a tornado watch and a severe thunderstorm watch for the entire area. They're warning about hail and funnel clouds."

Michele grimaced and looked at her watch. "Mom was going to take the kids to a school play at seven. I need to call and tell her not to go out."

"That's probably a good idea," Harte commented, just as a low rumble sounded in the distance.

Michele took out her phone and looked at the display. "I don't have any service." She stepped over to the window. "Still none. That's odd. My cell service is usually excellent."

"Try the landline," Dani said, pointing to a table by the sofa.

Michele stepped over to the phone and dialed. She stood there a moment, then pressed the disconnect button, listened, then dialed again. Finally, she set the receiver on its cradle with more force than was necessary.

"That phone doesn't work?" Dani asked.

"It works, but all I'm getting is that fast beep, you know?"

"It means all the circuits are busy," Harte said. "Try mine."

"Thanks," Michele said. She took his phone and walked back over to the window.

Dani turned toward her bedroom. "I'll check mine too." She ducked into her room and then came out again. "How long is this storm supposed to last?"

"They couldn't say. They seemed worried that it might stall over the gulf because of a low front. If it does—"

Dani blew out a frustrated breath.

"What's wrong?" Harte asked.

"Nothing," she said shortly. "I just don't like storms."

Harte heard Michele talking. "Mom? Hello? Mom!" She listened for a few seconds, then handed his cell phone back to him. "Thanks, but you're not getting any service either."

"My phone's showing no bars too," Dani said, watching the display as she moved toward the window, then across to the kitchen area. She stuck it into her pocket.

"Your mom wouldn't take the kids out into a bad storm, would she?" she asked Michele.

"No, but it might not be bad over there yet, and I doubt she's been listening to the weather. She likes to play games with them, rather than just sit and watch TV." She looked at her phone one more time. "She heard me at first, because I heard her say *Michele?* She's going to be worried now."

"Harte, don't you think it would be okay if Michele ran by to check on her kids while you're here?" She turned to Michele. "How far away do you live?"

"Ten to fifteen minutes, but no. This is my assignment. I'm not supposed to leave my post until I'm relieved."

Harte felt Dani's gaze on him and tried to ignore it. He agreed with Michele that she shouldn't leave her post.

"Harte—" Dani started.

"Okay, okay." He didn't like it, but he supposed he could be flexible. After all, he was planning to be here for another couple of hours anyhow. Besides, he wasn't happy with the lack of cell service.

"I tell you what," he said. "As lead prosecutor on this case, I'm relieving you for one hour to go pick up a squad car. I'd like to have one here in case we have a problem. Even if we lose electricity, we'll have the police radio and a means of transportation that won't get stopped."

Michele looked blankly at him for an instant. "I'm not sure I understand—"

"Detective, you should pick up a squad car. If you swing by your house on the way, I don't think it would be out of line."

Michele's face lightened as his meaning sank in.

"I'll be here for a couple of hours. But don't delay. Try to beat the storm."

"I will," Michele said. She grabbed her car keys and headed toward the door. "Back in less than forty-five," she called over her shoulder.

"That was really nice of you," Dani said, sending him a smile.

"Yeah. Shocking, isn't it?"

"I didn't say that."

"Not out loud."

Dani propped a hand on her hip. "I'm beginning to think that this is not going to be a fun evening."

"Depends on your definition of *fun*," he said, gesturing toward the bag with Mama Pinto's on the front. "I rode all the way back here with the smell of the *best jambalaya in the world* filling my car. I'm going to eat. All I can say is it better be worth the trip."

"Oh, right," Dani exclaimed. She took the bag from him and peeked inside, inhaling deeply. "Mmm. That's Mama's jambalaya all right. Thank you," she said.

He angled his head. "Your wish is my command," he said solemnly.

"And I thought chivalry was dead," she murmured.

"I occasionally slay dragons too," he shot back as he picked up his briefcase and set it on the kitchen table. "We'll get started with the prep after we eat."

"After *we* eat?" she echoed, clutching the bag tightly.

Harte saw the twinkle in her eyes. First time he'd seen one there. It made them appear amber. He liked it. He wanted to see it again. "Hey, I got two orders, even though one looks like enough to feed a family of four."

Before he'd finished, she'd dug into the bag and pulled out the two cardboard containers. She shoved one toward him and opened the other, then dug into the bag again and tossed him one of the two plastic forks she found.

He picked up the fork, but he wasn't as interested in his jambalaya as he was in watching her. She opened the carton and dug into the mound of rice and shrimp and sausage. She shoved a forkful into her mouth and closed her eyes as she chewed.

"Best thing I ever ate," she mumbled, closing her eyes. "Mmm."

Harte swallowed hard. The look on her face made his mouth water, but not for food. A spear of pure lust shot through him. He was hungry for her. Grimacing, he forced down a few mouthfuls of jambalaya, then pointed at the bottle. "Want some wine?"

She looked up. "Will you help me drink it?" she asked.

He shook his head with a wry smile. "No. I'm working." Not to mention that he needed to keep his head clear around her.

"Well, I guess if you're working, so am I." She looked longingly at the Chardonnay, then turned her attention back to the food. Fifteen minutes later, Dani moaned and leaned back in her chair, stretching her arms over her head and arching her back. "Oh, I ate too much. Now I'm sleepy."

He tried to look away. He really did. But the red shirt had fallen away and her perfect breasts strained against the thin cotton of the white tank top she wore underneath, outlining her nipples clearly. He didn't think he'd ever met another woman who was so unconsciously sexy. And that was part of what turned him on. She had no idea how just looking at her affected him.

Shifting subtly, trying to tamp down his physical reaction, he reminded himself that she was his witness, and therefore his responsibility. He had vowed, to her and to himself, to keep her safe.

She caught his gaze and quickly adjusted her shirt so that it covered the revealing tank top, but her eyes stayed glued to his and something glinted behind them. Was it interest? Maybe even desire?

He busied himself with closing the cartons and putting them in the refrigerator. "Want a glass of water?" he asked.

"Sure, thanks."

He filled two glasses and held one out to her.

As she reached for it, a crack of thunder split the quiet. She jumped, nearly turning the glass over.

Chapter Seven

Harte caught Dani's glass just in time to keep it from turning over. "Hey," he said. "It's okay. It was just thunder."

"I know," she snapped. "It startled me, that's all."

He studied her closely as she took a deep swallow of water. Her hands were trembling. She really was afraid of storms.

"Are you going to be able to concentrate?" he said.

"Of course," she replied, her voice sounding slightly defensive. "Why wouldn't I?"

"If the storm passes directly over us, it could get nasty. We might lose power."

"I'm fine."

"Okay. That's good, because we've got a lot to cover."

"A lot to cover? I thought you said my testimony wouldn't take long."

"It won't. Not your direct. But with Jury Drury sitting first chair on the defense side, there's no telling how long he'll try to drag out the cross-examination. He's a master at rattling witnesses. He'll be on everything you say like a vulture on roadkill. Make you doubt what you heard with your own ears. I want to try to give you some defense against that."

Dani groaned. "As you pointed out yesterday, I've questioned and cross-examined my share of witnesses. I know what to expect."

"I know. But this time you're the one testifying. Keep in mind that your goal is to put away the scumbag who caused your grandfather's death."

"I'm not likely to forget that," she muttered.

Harte grabbed his briefcase and pulled out the Canto file. During the three months since Akers assigned the case to him, he'd familiarized himself with the specifics, including the autopsy report, Dani's witness statement and the transcripts of all the interrogations of suspects. Plus, he'd had the dubious pleasure of reading and responding to the mountains of motions filed by Drury.

But during all that time, he'd only talked to Dani twice. He remembered his dad telling him something his grandfather had said. *"Criminal law's nothing like television. It's ninety-nine percent paperwork and one percent court drama. So if you're in it for the limelight, find yourself another career."* Lucky for Harte, he didn't mind the paperwork.

"Okay. You pretty much know what to expect. So let's start with you telling me what happened. Start from the beginning, as if I've never heard it before. You've never testified on the stand, right?"

Dani nodded. "That's right."

"Keep in mind that facing a jury as a witness is very different from facing them as an attorney."

Dani bristled at Harte's tone. Now that he was talking about the trial and her testimony, he'd switched to his imperious prosecutor's voice. She didn't like it. It made her feel as if she were back in the courtroom, facing off against him.

Her immediate instinct was to shoot a cutting response at him, but it was beginning to dawn on her how hard it was going to be to sit in that witness box and talk about her granddad's murder in front of a judge, a jury and the man responsible for his death. So she bit her tongue and nodded again.

His brows twitched, but he didn't comment. Had he expected a retort? "Okay," he said. "Go ahead."

For a second, she wasn't sure how to begin. "I've thought about that night so many times you'd think I wouldn't have any trouble describing what happened." She rubbed her temple.

"Why don't you start with what you were doing that day?"

"Okay." She nodded. "That was the day of the City Hall Awards Banquet."

"That's right," Harte commented with a grimace. "The annual rent-a-tux rent-a-crowd."

"Exactly," she said with a smile that lightened her expression and put a twinkle in her eyes. "I was going, of course. I'd even bought a new dress. But I caught a stomach bug. I ended up throwing up all day. Granddad brought me some crackers and ginger ale—" She had to swallow hard before she could continue.

"So I'd finally gotten to sl-sleep—" Her breath hitched. "Oh, this is awful." Her fingers massaged her temple. "Let me start over."

"No," Harte said. "You're doing great."

She shot him a skeptical look. "Anyway, I woke up hearing voices." She shifted in her chair. "They were yelling. I heard one of them say, 'You'll do it or you'll regret it,' and Granddad yelled back, 'You sons of bitches can go to hell.' That was just like him. He didn't suffer fools gladly."

Harte nodded and smiled back at her. For some reason his smile made her feel better.

"I was groggy and weak, so at first I didn't pay much attention. I figured it was one of his friends and they were arguing about politics. That wasn't unusual. He had guests several evenings a week. I used to scold him about not getting enough sleep." She sighed. "If I'd gotten up then—" Her heart ached with a hollow, sharp pain.

"Hey, don't go there. Just stick with the facts. Stay on point. You're fine." He laid his hand on top of hers where it rested on the table and squeezed it.

She looked down, surprised at the gesture. It didn't bother her. Just the opposite, in fact. His large, warm hand felt so good, so comforting, over hers. She longed to turn her hand over and clutch his. She wanted, needed, comfort so badly. But she'd already discovered that she was much too vulnerable to his good looks. She pulled away.

"Watch out," she said. "The jury might think you're fraternizing with your witness." She aimed for a smile and a light tone. When his gaze snapped to hers, she realized she'd failed. She'd meant it as a joke, but now, her gaze caught by his, she felt something flare between them. Something hot and intimate. Much more intimate than the touch of a hand or a glance should be.

A flash of lightning and its accompanying clap of thunder made her jump, and that quickly, the spell was broken.

Harte withdrew his hand with a quick smile. "You're right," he said. "I'll have to watch it."

A chill slid through her—was it from the thunder or the absence of his warm hand on hers? She shivered and glanced up at the kitchen clock. "I wonder if Michele's made it home. The storm is getting worse."

A second flash and rumble proved her right.

"I'm sure she's fine," Harte said. "She'll be back soon."

Another time, Dani might resent Harte's carefully patient tone, as if he were trying to calm a screaming child. But right now he was her only port in the storm—literally. And he was being quite nice.

He pulled his cell phone out of his pocket and checked it. He shook his head.

"Still no service?" she asked. In the distance, a high-pitched wail signaled that emergency vehicles were responding to calls.

"Not even one bar. When I was trying to talk to the D.A., I had two bars and it still kept dropping the connection. I hope the storm hasn't knocked out any towers." He sighed and pocketed the phone. "So. Your grandfather and whoever was in his study were yelling."

She cleared her throat. "Then I heard noises—grunts and crashes, like furniture being knocked over or things being thrown. I didn't know at the time, but now I know they were hitting him. When I think of those awful sounds, I—" She stopped. She had to swallow a couple of times to get rid of the lump in her throat. "There was one guy. He was louder than the others, sounded like he was in charge. He's the one who started naming names."

"What names did you hear?"

Dani looked at Harte blankly for a moment. Her head was filled with the awful, sickening sounds she'd heard that night. The dull thud of fists hitting flesh. The crash of a body falling against a table or the floor. Sounds that would always haunt her dreams.

"Dani?" Harte said. "What names did you hear?"

"Yeoman, Senator Stamps and Paul Guillame. All that's in my statement."

"I know. But remember, I asked you to tell me about the night as if I'd never heard it before."

She sighed. "I heard 'Mr. Yeoman sent us,' and—"

"Okay, hold on a second," Harte interrupted. "One of the men said, 'Yeoman sent us'?"

"He said, 'Mr. Yeoman sent us.'"

"You're absolutely sure? It couldn't have been 'Mr. Yeoman said' or 'Mr. Yeoman should'?"

Irritation burned in her stomach. "You know it's not either of those. He said, 'Mr. Yeoman sent us.'"

Harte studied her for a moment. "Okay. Don't forget that I'm asking you these questions for the jury. What else did they say?"

"I couldn't understand everything. The next thing I could make out was something about Senator Stamps, and—" She stopped. Just like that night, the exact words the men had said eluded her.

"Can you tell me specifically what they said when they mentioned Stamps's name?" Harte prodded.

"They didn't *mention* Stamps's name. They yelled it."

"Okay," he said with exaggerated patience.

She closed her eyes and forced herself back there. Creeping quietly across the hardwood floor toward Granddad's study, her stomach queasily protesting, listening to the awful sounds and trying to remember where her cell phone was so she could call 911. "It was like 'Senator Stamps warned or armed or aimed.' I was groggy from nausea medication and terrified, because I couldn't figure out what was happening."

Harte's mouth thinned. "That brings up a good point. Where were you that night while all this was going on?"

"I was trying to get to the telephone in the living room."

"And where was your grandfather?"

"In his study, on the other side of the house."

"That distance has been measured. From the door of your bedroom to the door of Freeman Canto's study is sixty-two feet. Are you telling me that you could hear and understand what the men were saying?"

She bristled. "Ye-e-es." She drew out the word sarcastically.

"Dani, you're supposed to be answering as if you were on the witness stand. You're the prosecution's main witness. As an attorney you know better than to get defensive. Remember that it's your job to give the judge and jury an accurate recounting of the events that led up to your grandfather's death."

The control she was holding on to with such desperation cracked and her eyes filled with tears. "This is a lot harder than I thought it would be. I'm talking about hearing men beating my grandfather to death while I was three rooms away."

Harte's gaze seemed to soften. "It'll be even harder

when you're on the witness stand," he said gently. "How many phones are there in the house?"

"Besides the one in the living room, there's one in Granddad's study. Then there's my cell phone, which was in my purse on the hall table, and Granddad's, which I believe was in his pocket." She pushed her chair back from the table and began pacing. Her path took her toward the front room where the rain was pounding the picture window. "And you don't have to remind me that it will be harder. I know that."

Harte continued with his questioning. "Now, if you were frightened, sick and medicated, how can you possibly be sure the name you heard was Stamps?"

"I know what I heard. He didn't just say Stamps, he said Senator Stamps. And I heard the name Paul Guillame too and he's Stamps's political adviser."

"Again, Ms. Canto, you've admitted that you were medicated. In fact, you really can't testify to what the men said, can you? They could have said William or DeYoung or a dozen other names, right? It might not have been a name at all. It could have been anything."

Dani spoke clearly and calmly. "I was there, and I know what I heard. I can't tell you exactly what they said about Senator Stamps or Paul Guillame, but I am absolutely certain those names were spoken that night, along with the name Mr. Yeoman." She glanced at him sidelong. "And don't think for a minute that I don't know who Paul Guillame is."

"Objection. Irrelevant."

"No, it's not. Tell me, counselor, is it going to impact me that my attorney is related to one of the people whose name came up while my grandfather was being beaten to death?"

Harte's mouth thinned. "The D.A. has considered that and is not concerned. We're marginally related at best. He's like a third cousin."

"So Akers asked you about it."

"I'm your attorney. Don't even suggest that I don't have your best interests at heart. But please, by all means get all this hostility out before you actually go on the stand. And don't forget that it's not going to be me badgering you about what you heard. I'll let you tell the jury what happened in your own words. It's going to be Drury who'll be hitting you with the tough questions. He's a snake. Don't let him upset you. Think about what you tell your own witnesses. They lose credibility if they let the opposing attorney get to them."

Dani tried to compose herself. Everything Harte said was true. But the renewed pain of her grandfather's violent death, combined with the storm outside and the fact that she had to rely on Harte Delancey, her courtroom nemesis, was about to undo her. "I apologize," she muttered.

"Let's get back to the question at hand. Isn't it true that you're *not* certain about the names you heard? That you're merely desperate to find someone to blame for your grandfather's death?"

"That is *not* true. And of course I'm—" She stopped. Her breath caught in a sob. The tears she'd been trying to hold back stung her eyes. She blinked fiercely. She would not cry!

"Okay, okay," Harte said gently. He sat back. "Don't

worry about not being absolutely sure about Stamps and Guillame. As long as you're positive about Yeoman."

She sniffed. "But I am sure—like ninety-nine percent. About Stamps and Guillame, I mean. I'm definitely a hundred percent about Yeoman. That guy said his name twice, or maybe three times."

"Okay. That's good. When you're certain, be sure the jury knows you're certain. Now, go on. You said you heard violent noises."

She nodded. "They must have been hitting him. I heard him fall, and one of them said, 'Do you understand Mr. Yeoman's message?' But Granddad didn't answer. Then I heard them say, 'We better get out of here. The granddaughter will be home soon. And I think he's hurt—bad.'" Her breath caught again and her hand flew up to cover her mouth.

"It was so awful," she mumbled from behind her hand.

"Come back over here and sit down," Harte said. "Want some coffee?"

She shook her head. "No. I'm fine. I just can't help thinking of Granddad. They *murdered* him. He must have been so scared in those last minutes—" She stopped and tried to suppress the little sobs that kept quivering in her throat. "And I wasn't able to help him. By the time I got to his study, the men were gone."

"They didn't pass you as they left?"

She shook her head. "The study has French doors that lead to the outside. That's how they got in and how they left."

He studied her for a few seconds, then turned his attention to his water glass, tracing a finger down the side. He spoke without looking up. "You know, my grandfather was murdered too."

Dani was surprised. He didn't seem like the type to share his personal life casually. Certainly not with a witness—or a rival.

She nodded. "I'd heard that. He was killed by one of his employees?" She looked at him, expectant, but apprehensive. Was he about to try to give her encouragement by relating some anecdote about bravery in the face of tragedy? Or how Con's wife testified, head held high, even though she was heartbroken?

"He was murdered by his personal assistant, Armand Broussard."

"I've heard that name," she said. She waited for a few seconds, but he didn't explain why he'd brought up his grandfather. "What are you saying?"

He shrugged. "Just that we have something in common." He grimaced, then tilted his head. "I never got the chance to know him because someone murdered him. He died the year I was born," he said quietly.

"The year you were born?" Dani said. "I'm sorry. It's awful that you never got to know him."

Harte met her gaze, and his dark eyes, which normally caught the light like brown bottle glass, were soft and sincere. "What you've been through is worse. You had your grandfather with you for your whole life. I can't even imagine how much you must miss him."

One of the tears that kept gathering in Dani's eyes slipped down her cheek. To her surprise, Harte reached over and stopped it with a finger. She barely felt his touch, but somehow, it acted like a current of electricity, sizzling through her, creating heat in every inch of her. She stared into his eyes, wondering what he would do if she leaned over and kissed him. Then wondering what she would do if he kissed her back.

For a split second, their eyes held; then Harte blinked and cleared his throat. "So, do you think you're ready for Jury Drury?"

Dani moistened her lips. "I'm sure I'm not," she said with a tiny, ironic smile.

"You just do what the oath says you should. *Tell the truth, the whole truth and nothing but the truth.* I'll object to everything I can think of if he tries to bully you."

"He's going to rip me to shreds, isn't he?"

"I don't think so," Harte said. "I hope not."

She pushed her fingers through her hair and took a long breath. "I'm going to end up looking like an idiot and a liar to the judge and jury."

"No, you're not. You'll come across as earnest and sincere and heartbroken. Between us, we'll make sure the jury sees your honesty and integrity. I know you don't think so, but I'm a good prosecutor."

She studied him. "Oh, I know you're a good pros—"

Just then the wind picked up, flinging rain like gravel tapping against the big picture window in the living room.

Dani jumped. She drew up her shoulders and braced for more. Sure enough, lightning flashed as a sharp crack rent the air. She swallowed a shriek and vaulted up out of her chair.

"Hey," Harte said, rising. "It's okay."

"The storm's right on top of us. Do you think it's a tornado?" she asked tightly.

"Hopefully not. I'm thinking it will blow over soon. It should be moving north."

Dani nodded as she rubbed her arms. "I hope so."

He smiled that crooked smile. "Trust me," he said. "So, I'd like to keep going if you're up to it."

"I'm fine. Let me just get some water. The jambalaya made me thirsty."

"Yeah," he said, following her as she stepped over to the sink. "Me too."

As Dani reached for the tap, a huge burst of bright white light blinded her, a deafening explosion split the air and everything went black.

She screamed and flung herself toward Harte. Caught off guard, he stumbled backward when her weight hit him. "Dani—?" he started.

Her almost silent whimper cut him off. Her hands clutched at the front of his shirt. Instinctively he folded his arms around her. Her body trembled violently.

He breathed deeply and nearly groaned at the sweet melon scent of her hair. That delicious fragrance combined with the pressure of her body so tight against him ripped away at his normally rock-solid self-control. The soft firmness of her breasts, the slight bump of her hip bones, the feel of her warm breath on his neck, were as tantalizing as he'd known they'd be. He squeezed his eyes closed. He could learn to love the feel of her body pressed against his. He pulled her closer.

After a moment he turned his head and looked out the kitchen window. He couldn't see a thing. Not a pale porch bulb of a neighbor's house. Not a streetlight. Nothing.

"The lightning must have blown transformers all

over the area," he muttered. "There are no lights as far as I can see."

She nodded and more of the sweet scent of melon tickled his nose. He clenched his jaw as his body reacted. Damn it, he was on the edge of some very dangerous territory.

A vision of them together in bed taunted him. He struggled to banish it.

The only reason she threw herself into his arms was that she was terrified by the lightning and the darkness. She was seeking safety. If she had the slightest notion of his unprofessional thoughts, she'd be away from him like a shot and any trust he'd managed to build with her would be gone.

"Hey," he said, peering intently at her. He could barely make out her features in the darkness. "It's just a storm, that's all. You live in south Louisiana. It's not like you haven't been in a storm before, right?"

She stiffened and pushed away. "Right," she said shakily, then cleared her throat. "Sure. I'm fine. I've got a flashlight on my key ring. It's in my purse in the bedroom—"

"Hang on. I'm sure there are candles around here somewhere," he said. "Check the kitchen drawers." He turned and reached out for a drawer handle, found one and pulled, then searched inside. "Ow!" he exclaimed. "Be careful. I just pricked my finger on a knife."

"Is it bad?" she asked, sounding more like her old self.

"Nah." He stuck his fingertip in his mouth for a second, then continued searching. His hand closed around the distinctive shape of a lighter and next to it, the waxy tapered length of a candle. "Here we go," he said as he pulled them out.

He thumbed the lighter and lit the candle. The flickering light gleamed eerily as it reflected in her wide eyes. Her mouth was set in a tight line.

"Here," he said. "Take this. I'm sure there are more. I'll see if I can find something to hold them."

She held out her hand, her eyes glued to the flame.

Outside the thunder rumbled loudly and lightning flashed, lighting up the windows for a split second. She flinched and scrunched her shoulders. She was definitely afraid of storms. He felt a different emotion take hold of him. An urge to shelter her, protect her, hold on to her and reassure her that everything was going to be all right. It surprised him that he felt so protective toward her. She was one of the strongest, most determined women he'd ever met.

He touched her sleeve and felt her stiffen. "Storms really bother you, don't they?" he said gently.

She tried for a casual shrug, but her shoulders moved jerkily. "I'm fine."

"No, you're not. Tell me why storms scare you."

She sniffed in frustration. "Why storms scare me. Well, my father died in a tornado when I was seven. Maybe that's why."

"That's an awful thing for a little girl to go through."

She shrugged and the candlelight outlined her sad face in shadows. "I had this image of the tornado as a big whirling monster that ate everything in its path. When it storms like this, I can't wipe that image out of my mind."

Thunder rumbled again and she hugged herself.

"Don't worry," he whispered. "I'm right here."

Her gaze snapped to his, and her chin lifted. "I said I'm fine."

He considered what he'd been thinking about her seconds before and amended it. She was one of the strongest, most determined and most *stubborn* women he'd ever met.

He shrugged and turned his attention back to the drawer, looking for more candles. He found a few that had been burned down at least halfway. Those would be easier to set up. He lit one and began dripping wax on a saucer he took from the drain board.

"I have to get my purse," Dani said.

Harte nodded, still busy with the candle. He got it stuck to a saucer with wax, then started on a second one. "Now we've got several candles," he called. "This should last us until they get the power back on—"

A crash drowned out his words. His head snapped toward the window. Was that glass breaking? Or just the noise of the thunder?

"Harte!" Dani's panicked voice came from across the room.

"Dani?" he asked. He stuck a stubby candle and the lighter in his pocket as he hurried toward her.

"What was that—?"

He saw her and halted. Something wasn't right. The way her body was lit—the way shadows were flickering, almost dancing, as if tossed around by a fire.

A split second later, he knew what was wrong, but that was a split second too late. Dani had figured it out too. She was screaming and pointing behind him. He turned, already certain of what he would see.

In the middle of the hardwood floor, in front of the big picture window, surrounded by broken glass that glinted red and yellow and orange, was a bottle belching flames from its mouth. Flames that licked at the curtains and crawled across the floor.

Chapter Eight

As Harte watched the flames spread, another bottle sailed through the window and bounced and rolled. The first one was a Molotov cocktail. This one was a smoke bomb.

Yeoman's men. It had to be. Had they followed him from the courthouse through all the traffic? He should have been watching, should have been aware that he could be followed. His Jeep wasn't exactly the standard for the courthouse parking lot. They must have been waiting outside for the right moment.

He lunged toward Dani, grabbing the candle out of her hand and blowing it out. "They're trying to burn us out," he said. "I'm calling 911." He snatched his phone from his pocket, but he still had no service. He thumbed the three numbers anyway, but the phone just made a pinging noise and went back to the default screen. He dove toward the landline phone.

"How'd they find us?" Dani croaked.

"Get into your room. We'll go through the windows. My car's parked on that side." He grabbed the phone to dial 911, but the line was dead. The smoke from the bomb was filling the air as he ran toward the bedroom behind Dani. He'd break the tall windows and make a run for his car.

He hoped whoever was out there didn't have the house surrounded. The only thing that might save them was the darkness and the cover of the driving rain. Right now, though, lightning streaked the sky directly over their heads.

Just as he made it through the bedroom door, the biggest flash lit up the sky. It outlined two dark figures in the yard, moving toward the house. Dani was standing in front of her dresser, picking up something. He grabbed her by the hand. "There's someone out there. We've got to head for the kitchen."

She pulled away. "I need my purse!" she cried.

"It'll just get in your way!" he countered, but she grabbed it. As soon as she grasped the handle, he jerked her back out into the living room.

"Come on!" he croaked, coughing with every breath. The Molotov cocktail had burned itself out, but clouds of smoke still rose from the smoke bomb. Beside him, Dani was coughing and choking too.

He knew their only chance now was through the kitchen. He'd inspected the bed-and-breakfast thoroughly before he'd booked it. The manager had gladly turned the keys over to him and left to visit his grandkids in Baton Rouge. On the key ring was the master key to the house and another, smaller key. It went to a storeroom off the kitchen that opened onto an alley.

The manager had passed right by the door, but Harte had insisted on checking it out. The storeroom was small and dark, filled with cleaning supplies and boxes. It had an identical door on the other side of the room that led outside. On the outside, the door was finished just like the rest of the house. At a glance, it was impossible to tell it was a door.

All of that slid through his mind in the three long seconds it took for them to cross the living room. By the time they reached the small door, both of them were coughing constantly.

"Where are we going?" Dani asked, hanging back as he unlocked it.

"This goes to the alley. It's our only chance."

"What happened?" she cried. "How did they find us?"

"I don't know. I'll go first. Make sure they're not out there waiting for us." He unlocked the door to the outside and slipped through. With any luck, the men hadn't noticed the delivery door. They'd be guarding the front and back, poised to grab Dani when she was forced out by the smoke and flames. With a little luck, he just might get her out alive.

Harte pressed himself flat against the clapboard wall of the B & B. The rain was punishing, but the narrow overhang of the roof kept the worst off him. It didn't help with his vision, though. The veil of falling water obscured everything beyond a couple of feet. And if that weren't bad enough, it turned to steam as soon as it hit the hot asphalt. Everything was enveloped in swirling gray. Harte couldn't see anything or anyone. And he could barely hear through the rain's dull roar.

Dani touched his arm. "Harte?"

He held out his hand. "It's okay. Come on," he said as loudly as he could to be heard over the rain, "but be quiet."

She took his hand and stepped through the doorway, ducking her head and hunching her shoulders against the rain. She clutched her purse tightly. "Is it safe?" she asked.

Harte squinted at her, blinking against raindrops. "No, but it's the best chance we've—" He stopped. "Shh. Hold it," he whispered. Sure enough, he heard shouts coming from the front of the house.

He tugged on her hand. "Come on. We're going that way, up Race Street." He gestured in the opposite direction. "Can you keep up with me?" he asked.

"Yes," she said firmly.

He looked her up and down. She had on sneakers, thank goodness, and that huge purse was draped across her body like a messenger bag.

He plunged into the gray sheet of rain with Dani right behind him. He didn't want to run. They were too handicapped by the rain and the nearly impenetrable darkness. Of course the bad guys were handicapped by the downpour as well, but judging by the two men they'd seen and the shouts he'd heard, he feared that he and Dani were outnumbered by at least four to two.

All he could do was trust his instincts and try to get Dani to someplace safe.

He moved as fast as he could, tugging her with him until, out of nowhere, he stepped into a pothole. "Ahh!" he cried as his leg collapsed beneath him. He winced as pain shot up his leg from his ankle. He flexed it gently. To his relief, he could move it.

"Harte!" Dani knelt beside him as he tried to push himself to his feet. But when he put his weight on the ankle, a sharp throbbing stabbed him to the bone. *Damn it*. It was sprained. He knew from the first- and second-aid preparation courses he'd taken as a precaution for solo backpacking trips that he needed to wrap it as soon as he could. But right now he had no choice but to grit his teeth and bear it.

Dani touched his foot with her hand. "Is it broken?" she asked.

He grabbed her hand. "Get up. We've got to go." He knew the ankle was just sprained, not broken, but it hurt like a son of a bitch even so.

He pulled her to the edge of the alley. The rain was in his eyes, soaking his clothes and shoes. He tried his best to see whether there was a vehicle waiting for them on the far side, where the alley opened out onto Orange Street.

As far as he could tell, both the alley and the street beyond it were clear. He wiped his face on the drenched sleeve of his white shirt. It didn't help.

He headed across, pulling Dani with him, doing his best not to limp. A pair of glowing orbs was visible in the distance.

Headlights.

Dani saw it too. She squeezed his hand. "Harte! A car!"

"Hurry, before they see us." The vehicle was approaching much faster than it should have been, considering that the driver had to be barreling blindly through the rain.

They headed across the street and ducked under an overhang. Without the rain beating down on them, they both leaned gratefully against the side of the building, trying to catch their breaths.

Suddenly, the whole street lit up as another flash of lightning ripped through the sky, followed by a deafening roar. The rain, which was already a downpour, now fell in sheets.

"Harte—" Dani cried.

He blinked as he desperately tried to see through the beating rain. It was dangerous and stupid to stumble blindly around without knowing where they were headed.

He'd studied the streets near the B & B, but the combination of the rain and the darkness was doubly disorienting, and there was no hope of reading a street sign from more than a few inches away.

"Harte!" She tugged on his shirtsleeve and stood on tiptoe to get close to his ear. "Look. The headlights aren't moving."

He focused on the pallid, blurry spots of the headlights. They were still. He blinked and looked again. The vehicle was still moving, but more slowly. Then he noticed dark shadows in front of it, heading in their direction. But he couldn't tell how many. Two? Three?

"It's them!" Dani cried.

Harte tightened his hand around her wrist and jerked her with him as he ran unevenly, gritting his teeth against the pain in his ankle.

He spotted a darker rectangle in the midst of the gray. The entrance to the alley? God, he hoped so. If he was wrong, they'd be sitting ducks. He sped up, tightening his grip on Dani's wrist.

But moving forward through the rain was like pushing through a maze of heavy drapes while fording a stream, because the water rushing around their feet was

at least three inches deep, making the roads slippery.
And the pain in his ankle wasn't helping. He stumbled
and his fingers slipped off Dani's wrist.

That quickly, she was gone.

Dani lost her footing when her hand slid out of
Harte's grip. Her knee hit the wet pavement, hard. With
a small cry she tried to regain her footing. But the road
was too slippery; the rain pressed on her shoulders like
a heavy hand and she was quickly losing strength from
fighting it.

Where was Harte? She squinted through the rain
and held her breath, listening. The drumming roar of
the rain was confusing and disorienting. It was impossible to tell where any sound came from.

Straining, she thought she heard Harte's voice calling her name. But she couldn't tell for sure. Heading in
what she hoped was the right direction, she was tempted
to call out, but what if it wasn't him? Was she heading toward Harte or was she about to plow right into
her pursuers?

She wiped her face on her sleeve, for all the good it
did, and pushed her heavy, soaked hair back.

At that instant, the roar in her ears changed in pitch.
She squinted, as if that would help her see. A dark rumble rose from beneath the rain's din. The sound was not
thunder, but mechanical, rhythmic. Like a car engine.

Frightened by the closeness of the sound, she felt the
hairs on the nape of her neck prickling. She blinked,
trying to see. Why didn't Harte call out again? She
couldn't tell which way to run. The rumble grew louder,
seeming to surround her.

Lightning flashed. She swallowed a shriek and barely

stopped herself from diving to the ground, but from what little she could see around her, she was in the middle of a street, completely exposed. Thunder cracked and roared. She moaned in fear and frustration as she trudged on.

Pushing against the rising, punishing wind, she squinted, looking for anything she could use for shelter. A dark building loomed just ahead. Her pulse jumped in excitement.

She trudged toward it, hoping to slip into an alley or a corner where the car couldn't go, praying that she could find Harte.

As she wiped rain off her nose, she thought she heard his voice again. But then a car door slammed right behind her. That sound was unmistakable—and way too close. Terror crawled up her spine and twisted her insides. She had to run. Lowering her head, she pressed forward, her legs beginning to ache with the effort of pushing against the wind and rain. She prayed she was going in the right direction.

The rain, the lightning and her imagination were distorting everything—what she saw, what she heard. She squinted against the gray rain. She could no longer see the building she'd been headed for.

Her toe struck something and sent her sprawling. Her hands took the brunt of the fall, sliding and scraping across rough wet concrete, and her shin banged painfully against a hard edge. She bit her cheek to keep from crying out.

She'd tripped over a curb. Behind her, heavy footsteps reverberated across the ground. She didn't dare turn around to see, but she knew from the sound that they were almost on top of her. With a great deal of effort, she managed to get her feet under her and gain some traction. Just as she straightened, a bright flash of lightning lit the street. This time she couldn't resist. She turned to look.

A large dark form barreled toward her, too big and broad to be Harte. In the same second, she heard Harte's voice clearly.

"Dani!"

But it was impossible to pinpoint where it had come from. Directly in front of her? Ahead and to the left? She heard the man chasing her and wondered if she had time to dig her gun out of her purse. But he was too close. So close she could see color beginning to seep through the gray. The dark blob turned to a dull tan, and as he lumbered toward her she realized that it was a raincoat with the collar turned up. Although she'd already figured out that it wasn't Harte, still her throat seized, cutting off her breath.

She tried to run and almost fell again when she put her weight on her knee. "Harte! Here! They're after me!" she screamed. She didn't care if the man in the raincoat heard her. He was so close that she imagined she could hear his heaving breaths over the downpour. Letting Harte know her location was her only chance.

"Harte!" she shouted again, but her voice was gobbled up by thunder. Then a strong hand grabbed the back of her shirt and jerked her off her feet.

Chapter Nine

Harte heard Dani's terrified scream, cut off by thunder, but he couldn't tell where she was. He'd been retracing his steps ever since he lost hold of her hand. She should have been only a few feet behind him, if she'd stayed put. She must have gotten turned around and been moving away from him all this time.

He heard another short cry. Had they found her? He pushed forward, praying that the shriek he'd heard had just been her startled reaction to the thunder and lightning.

Then he saw it. A big black shadow, rising out of the mist. The car. He slowed down, cautiously keeping an eye on it. Then he detected another difference in the constant gray of rain and wind. He wiped his face, then blinked. He saw movement. Something large and brown and vaguely human shaped. It had to be one of Yeoman's men.

Did he have Dani? Harte couldn't tell. He moved slowly and steadily toward the man, hoping not to attract notice. But then he caught a splash of red—her shirt. Adrenaline burned through him like flaming jet fuel.

The man did have her. He was dragging her toward the car.

Harte had only one chance and it was a slim one. Balancing himself on his right foot, he dove, aiming at the man's knees. He hit what felt like solid rock. The impact rattled his teeth and echoed in his head, but the man fell like a dead tree, slamming into the pavement.

Harte ducked and rolled out of his way. He came to rest not ten inches from the front fender of the car. It was smashed and the headlights were broken—damaged, no doubt, from ramming Dani's front porch. Glancing over his shoulder, Harte saw the big man flip over onto his stomach. He waved his arms and legs like a turtle, trying to get his hands underneath him. Too soon, the man managed to get to his hands and knees. He shook his massive head and made a noise that echoed through the pounding rain like a lion's roar. Then he propelled himself forward.

Harte scrambled to his feet. The goon had brute strength going for him, but he was about as graceful as a bull elephant. Harte heard his sawing breaths coming closer and closer.

Harte waited until the last possible second, hoping that the other man was as disoriented by the rain as he was, before diving out of the way. Luckily, the brute had built up enough momentum that he couldn't stop. He obviously counted on Harte to break his fall. He hit the ground, hard.

Harte regained his balance and looked inside the attacker's car. It was empty. Dani wasn't there. Hot fear pulsed through him. Where was she? Did one of the other men have her?

And where were the other three men?

Were they on foot, sneaking around to ambush him,

or had they taken Dani somewhere? As he turned, he caught a glimpse of a dark figure rising from behind a trash receptacle. Another man rose right beside him. Before he could react, both men lifted their arms and he heard the unmistakable crack of gunfire muffled by the rain. Before the shots faded, he heard Dani scream behind him.

"Dani!" he yelled, whirling and spotting a splash of red through the gray curtain of rain. It was Dani! She was on the ground, several feet away from the car. His gut clenched. Had she been hit?

He sprang toward her, wrapping his fingers around her upper arm and yanking her upright, quickly scanning her clothes for blood. He didn't see any. "Are you hit?" he yelled.

"No!" She shook her head. "Are you?"

Behind them, he heard car doors opening and closing. He tried to count, but the sounds were too muffled by the storm. Maybe two, maybe three. The men had gotten back into the car.

"They're in the car. Run!" he shouted before pumping his legs, pulling her with him. Behind them, more gunshots rang out and he heard men shouting. He pulled her behind a parked van.

"Get that shirt off!" he cried.

"What? My shirt?"

He turned her around and grabbed the collar, jerking it over her head. "It's too bright."

After tossing it over a nearby parking meter, Harte pointed toward a narrow alleyway in front of them and yelled in her ear, "Through there!" Grabbing her arm, he tightened his grip. He wasn't going to lose her again.

Dani half ran, half stumbled alongside Harte. The only thing that kept her from collapsing onto the drenched pavement was the painful grasp of his hand on her arm—the same arm the thug had bruised when he'd grabbed her.

She could hear the pop-pop-pop of gunfire behind them, and her shoulders tightened reflexively. Then she heard the deep revving of a car engine. Harte had stunned her attacker enough to make him let go of her, but they were in their car now, and it would be no time until they caught up with them again. She could barely catch her breath in the rain, and in only her white tank top, the chill had long since seeped under her skin. She gritted her teeth and concentrated on staying on her feet. As Harte led her into the dark recesses of the alley, she glanced around in trepidation. She hoped he knew where he was going.

The overhanging roofs gave a bit of protection from the rain. Once they were safely underneath, Harte slowed to a walk, then to a stop.

Dani wiped her face and squeezed water out of her hair as she gulped in huge lungfuls of air. All at once, a massive shudder shook her, a delayed reaction to the brutish thug's hand on her. Between that and the cold, she couldn't stop shaking.

"Harte, are you shot?" she panted. She didn't see any blood, but he hadn't answered her when she'd asked before.

Beside her, Harte leaned against the building's wall. He shook his head, breathing hard. After a few seconds, he straightened and looked toward the entrance of the alley, listening. "Come on," he said. "We've got to keep going."

"Where?" she asked as he grabbed her hand.

A bit of brightness behind them rose through the gray like a hazy sunrise. "It's the car," he said. "Move!"

But as he moved into the alley, he saw that it was a dead end. A high wooden fence stretched between the two buildings. They were trapped. Twisting back, Harte could see the headlights. They'd blocked the entrance of the alley. He saw two men climbing out, then a third.

Without waiting to see if a fourth man got out, Harte pushed Dani behind him so his body would shield her as he desperately searched for an escape. Even if they could climb the fence, they'd be sitting ducks. Then he saw a door set into a side wall. "This way," he said. "Stay behind me."

He rattled the doorknob, then stepped back and rammed the door with his shoulder. Nothing happened. He took two steps back, prepared to ram the door again, but Dani grabbed his arm.

"Get out of the way! I've got this!" Dani cried. She grabbed the lock-pick set from her purse and unsnapped the cover. Her hands were soaking wet, just like the rest of her, and shaking with cold and fear, but she managed to pick up the right tool. She shouldered her way in front of Harte, bent over the doorknob and after a shaky false start, got the pick inserted into the lock.

Harte grabbed her upper arm. "Dani, what are you doing? They're coming. Get behind me."

Gritting her teeth, she worked the pick.

"Dani!"

"Wait," she snapped as the tumblers slid. "The door's

open. Let's go." She opened the door and grabbed his arm, pulling him inside. She kept her grip on the knob as Harte stumbled in behind her, then slammed the door shut and turned the dead bolt. They were inside and, at least for the moment, safe from the faceless men pursuing them. Collapsing back against Harte, her eyes closed, she gasped for breath. She'd done it. She'd picked the lock. She couldn't count the number of times she'd picked all the locks in her granddad's house, learning the feel of the tools and the faint differences between tumblers sliding apart and slipping back together. But she'd never dreamed she'd actually use her knowledge in a life-and-death situation for real.

Her pulse was racing so fast that it echoed in her ears. Harte wrapped his arms around her shoulders from behind, pulling her closer against him. His chest rose and fell against her back. His breath was cool across her wet forehead. With a sigh, she let herself relax against his long, lean body. Through their wet clothes, she felt the heat of his body envelop her. A shudder, equal parts cold, fear and desire, shook her.

"Dani?" he whispered.

She went still. Did he want her to move? She hoped not, because she didn't want to leave the heat of his body. She was soaked, and while April in New Orleans could hardly be called cold, even in the rain, she felt chilled to the bone.

As she waited to see what he was going to say, she concentrated on the feel of him pressed against her. Warmth wasn't all she needed from him now. She greedily soaked up the feelings of safety, comfort and a deep, rich yearning she'd never felt before.

He was silent and still for a long moment. His breath had calmed, and she could feel his heart beating fast but steadily against her back. Or at least she imagined she could.

He lowered his head and whispered in her ear, "How the hell did you do that?" She felt his lips graze the sensitive skin of her ear, and her insides quivered with longing. It took her a moment to figure out what he was talking about.

"Oh, the lock," she muttered; then deliberately, she turned her head so that her mouth was close to his. "I picked it," she whispered.

He made a small noise like a gasp as her mouth brushed his. "You what?"

"Picked the lock. Granddad gave me his lock-pick kit when I was ten. He said, 'You never know when you might need to get through a door.'"

She felt his chest rumble with laughter. "That's illegal."

"So sue me," she said lightly, then turned in his arms, rose on her tiptoes and kissed him. It was a tentative brushing of lips against lips, but it sent desire arrowing through her, all the way down to her toes.

Harte lifted his head slightly, and Dani moved with him, straining upward, keeping her mouth against his. For a moment that seemed suspended outside of time, he didn't move, and then she felt him relent. It was a subtle relaxing of his tense muscles, a tiny dip of his head as he took the kiss to the next level. She felt his tongue touch her mouth, felt his arm slide from her shoulders down her back to pull her even closer...

She lifted her head to meet his deeper kiss, just as

an odd sound broke through the steady drumbeat of the rain.

Harte stiffened—he'd heard it too.

Her heart skipped a beat. "Do I hear shouting?" she breathed.

He nodded. "Right outside the door," Harte whispered as the noise suddenly stopped. He straightened slowly, his hand still around her waist. "Move away—without a sound."

She opened her eyes for the first time and met a solid wall of darkness. She held out her hands in front of her, trying to keep her balance. Total darkness was so disorienting. She felt as though a single misstep would send her tumbling into a bottomless pit. She wanted to close her eyes again. She wanted to be back in Harte's arms.

Finally, slowly, she became aware of a faint lessening of the total dark. She searched, making herself dizzy, until she found its source—small windows set high in the walls of the warehouse. At last, she had something she could look at to maintain her balance. She took one cautious step, then another. She braced herself, not wanting to crash into something.

By her fourth step, she'd nearly convinced herself that she could see vague shadows in the darkness. Whether they were real or figments of her imagination, being able to focus on something made her feel better.

Then her fingers touched something. She gasped. "There's something here," she whispered to Harte.

"Keep going, slowly," he whispered back. "What does it feel like?"

"Paper?" she said, but that wasn't quite right. It was too hard. "No. Plastic?" she guessed.

She started to take another step, but Harte laid a hand on her shoulder from behind.

"Wait," he said, stopping.

"What is it?"

"Shh."

She held her breath, but didn't hear anything. "You heard them, didn't you?" she whispered.

She felt Harte shake his head. "Not yet. But they will be here soon," he said grimly.

"Maybe they doubled back to look at the building. We don't know how many doors there are." She paused. "Or if they're all locked."

Suddenly, the door they'd come through rattled. The men were trying to force it open. Then a ferocious pounding filled the air. They were kicking the metal door.

"Keep going," he said. "We need to get away from there, and fast. I need to see how many other entrances there are."

His words were cut off by a sharp, ricocheting sound. "They're trying to shoot the lock. They gave up on forcing the metal door open."

"The lock's a Schlage," Dani said. "It'll take them forever to break it by shooting at it."

"It's a what?"

"A Schlage. The strongest and most reliable padlock in the world. Granddad had Schlage locks on every door. When you've tried to pick one, you develop a healthy respect for them."

Several rounds fired within a few seconds. Each

one ricocheted just like the first. Then they heard more shouting.

"Maybe one of them caught a ricochet," she said hopefully.

"Maybe it's the boss, telling them to surround the building," Harte replied.

"Surround?" she said in surprise. "How many men do you think are out there? I only saw three."

"I think there are four, unless there's another vehicle. I don't think so, though. I can't believe these guys can still maneuver that car out there, with all the wind and rain. Come on. We need to find a place to hide."

"Why can't we just wait here until they give up and then sneak back out this door?"

"If I were the boss, I'd find the freight door and try to ram it with the car." He took her hand and started forward, into the blackness.

As soon as she put out her hand, it bumped a solid, rounded surface in front of her. "Oh, wait. I've got a flashlight," Dani said, fishing in her purse. "I forgot about it."

She felt him shrug. Then he said, "You've got a lot of stuff in that purse, don't you?"

She couldn't help chuckling. "You have no idea."

"What does that mean?" he asked.

She pulled the flashlight out and turned it on. The narrow beam shone on a massive, gaping red-and-blue mouth lined with dozens of sharp white teeth. It loomed over her, poised to rip her apart. She stared into the gaping maw, a shriek ripping its way past her tight throat.

After a moment of paralyzing fear, she whirled and grasped at Harte's shirt as she tried to suck air into lungs that felt collapsed with terror. She held on to him with all her might.

Harte pulled her close and took the flashlight from her numb fingers. A noise like laughter rumbled up from his chest. *Laughter?* Carefully, she turned her head enough to peek back at the thing that had nearly attacked her.

Harte shone the flashlight's beam over the monster's dreadful eyes, gleaming white teeth and garish slashes of color. Her knee-jerk reaction was to bury her face in the hollow of his shoulder. But there was something familiar about the garish face. Her cheeks began to warm as she figured out what she was looking at.

Harte laughed out loud. "I've heard about these, but I've never seen one," he said, chuckling. "We're in a warehouse used to store Mardi Gras floats."

She unclenched her fists from his shirt and turned around. Slowly, with Harte shining the flashlight around, the nightmarish bloody beasts morphed into the familiar fiberglass, crepe paper and feather decorations she'd seen in every Mardi Gras parade.

The awful mouth with its razor-sharp teeth that had threatened to devour her belonged to a colorful Chinese dragon head mounted on the front end of a brightly painted double-decker float dripping with gold, purple and green Mardi Gras beads.

Next to the dragon was a gigantic leprechaun face topped with a kelly-green hat. She remembered seeing both floats in last year's parade.

Similar garish and vaguely disturbing shapes stretched beyond them until they melted into the darkness. Even though she knew what they were now, the back of her throat still fluttered with fading terror and she couldn't stop shivering. "This can't be Mardi Gras World?"

He shook his head, still chuckling. "No. You've seen Mardi Gras World, right? It's a museum. This is just a storage warehouse."

"Stop laughing," she snapped. "I was scared."

"Sorry," he responded, but the amused tone was still there. "Shh," he said. "Listen."

She did. The shooting and banging had stopped. "I don't hear anything."

"I think they've abandoned that door," he said.

"You think they're looking for the freight door?"

"It's what I would do. If I only had four men, I'd leave one at the door we came in and the rest of us would look for the best way to break in…" As he talked, he fished his phone from his pocket and flipped it open. "I've still got nothing." He pressed a couple of buttons. "Can't call out or send a message."

"The storm must have knocked out a bunch of cell towers."

Harte nodded. "If we can't call for help, they can't either. Let's go," he said. "I want to see where the freight door is—and how many other doors there are. Then we can plan how we're going to get out of here." Glancing around, he continued. "If we're careful, we can use the floats like a maze. There must be thirty in here, maybe forty."

"That's thirty or forty too many for me. They're creepy."

"Come on," he said, leading the way into the darkness lit only by the flashlight's narrow beam. She followed his winding trail through the dozens of floats, giving the huge fiberglass monster heads as wide a berth as she could while still keeping up with him.

He stopped abruptly and she almost ran into him.

"Here's the freight door. It looks pretty sturdy and it's on the opposite side of the building from the door we came in." He glanced around. "They're going to use their car to break it in, I'll guarantee you. Come on. Let's circle around this side of the building." He gestured. "Stay away from both the freight door and the door you opened."

They made their way diagonally away from the freight door. When they reached the wall, Harte slid along it, feeling for a door. Dani stayed behind him.

"Here," he said finally. "If I haven't totally lost my bearings, I think this door is just about halfway between the freight door and the one we came in and on the opposite wall." He caught her hand and drew it toward him. "Feel the lock. Is it like the one you picked?"

"It feels like a Schlage. It's got a turn bolt on the inside, just like that one. All we should have to do is turn the latch and open the door."

"Great," he said.

"Do you want me to open it now?"

"Hang on a minute and listen."

Dani heard pounding and shouting and an occasional gunshot. "Won't the police hear the gunshots?"

"In a storm like this? I'm guessing the only reason we can hear them is something about steel and echoes. That's not my area of expertise. But outside, in the rain and the thunder? I doubt that noise they're making will carry for twenty-five feet."

"How long is it going to take them to break in?"

She felt his shoulders move in a shrug, and a small thrill slid through her. Now that she'd kissed him, she was reacting to his every slightest move. He was tall and graceful and rock-hard. His skin was like silk over steel. Everything about him radiated warmth and safety and a sexuality that drew her to him like a moth to a flame.

She shivered. "Will you hold me for a minute?" she asked.

For a brief, heart-stopping moment, he hesitated. Then he slid his arm around her shoulders. His wet shirt against her thinly covered breasts caused goose bumps to rise on her skin. She felt a fine trembling in his muscles.

Was he chilled in his wet clothes, or was he as affected by their closeness as she was? She hoped he was. At that instant, he bent his head and laid his cheek against hers. With a sigh, she lifted her chin slightly, so that her lips brushed his skin.

"How's your ankle?" she whispered, looking up at him. His face was barely visible in the almost pitch-black. Light from the small windows glittered in his deep brown eyes. His breath drifted across her sensitized lips, making them tremble with the need to feel his mouth, his body, pressing against her.

"Harte?" she said, hearing the question in her voice and wondering if he would hear it and understand it. She felt odd, almost weightless, as if she were floating. She ached with wanting him, and that frightened her. Because he wasn't interested in her at all, except as his witness. The thoughts flitted through her head in the space of a single breath.

"What is it?" he answered, his voice unsteady.

A niggling question at the edge of her brain almost brought her up short. What was she doing? Harte Delancey was the last person she should be having sexy fantasies about. Sure, she'd been fascinated by him and his good looks from the first moment she'd faced him across the courtroom, but his superior attitude had been a turnoff. She'd decided back then that she was only interested in him because of his notorious legacy and their grandfathers' feud. That was still the only reason for her interest, right? That and the fact that he was breathtakingly handsome.

Enveloped in his arms, with the citrusy scent of his shampoo and the warmth radiating from his body, she knew she was kidding herself. She couldn't deny how much she desired him. He was so much more than arrogance and a pretty face. He was strength and confidence and compassion. And she needed all three.

Despite the pounding rain and the men trying to kill her, all she wanted to do was to stay here, wrapped in Harte's gentle yet sensual caress. Longing sent a shiver through her.

He pressed his lips to the corner of her mouth. "Are you cold?" he whispered, his breath tickling her skin.

"No," she whispered on a sigh. Heat flowed like lava through her entire body. Out to her fingertips and toes and back, swirling through her to her core. She bit her cheek to keep from moaning with pleasure.

He lifted his head slightly and even in the dim light she could see that his firm, wide mouth had softened. Was he really about to kiss her right here in the middle of running from people who were trying to kill them?

She should say something. Should stop this. Because all they were doing was seeking comfort in a dangerous situation. The men outside were a danger to her, but so was Harte. And right now she wasn't sure who frightened her most.

By the time she'd decided that it would not be in her best interest to kiss him, his lips were trailing across hers.

She reacted with a tiny gasp and he took the opportunity of her parted lips to kiss her—really kiss her. Then he dipped his head a little more and tasted her mouth. His tongue urged her lips apart and he deepened the kiss.

Her reaction was so immediate, so intense. It scared her. She had to regain control. Didn't she? Because if she didn't, she was going to sink into him, take his kisses and give them back. She was going to beg him to make love to her.

Harte shifted and her taut, sensitized nipples pressed into his flesh. Electricity sang along her nerve endings, centering in the most sensitive part of her. And that quickly, the desire spread through every inch of her body. The tips of her fingers and toes, the hairs on her neck, the skin on the insides of her wrists—all were now erogenous zones, waiting for his touch to ignite their fire.

"Harte—?" Her breath caught.

He froze. "Listen."

She held her breath, but couldn't hear anything except the rain and the quick, excited beating of her heart. After a couple of seconds she heard it. A faraway whining sound, like a car engine revving, came from the far end of the warehouse. "Is that—?" she started.

"They're going to ram the freight door with their car."

The engine noise grew louder and tires screeched; then the air was split by a deafening crash. Harte was still as a cat waiting for its prey. Another crash, much louder than the first, echoed through the warehouse.

"It's working," he said, setting her away from him. "The car's ripping a hole in the freight door."

Just then a third crash, louder and longer than the other two, echoed through the warehouse. As the squeal of tortured metal faded, the sound of voices became evident, echoing clearly off the metal walls.

"Son of a— What the hell is all this?"

"Hey, look! Mardi Gras floats!"

"Must be fifty of 'em—"

"It'll take hours to search all—"

"Just torch the whole—"

"Hang on! That ain't what Mr.—"

"Smoke 'em out, or let 'em burn up."

Dani's hand tightened on his arm. "They're going to burn the warehouse down," she whispered anxiously.

Harte pressed a finger against her lips. The men were still talking.

"How're we—?"

"Get over here and listen—"

Then the voices died down.

"We've got to get out of here," Harte said. "These floats will go up like dry kindling, and fiberglass fumes are toxic." When he stood, the dim light angled harshly off the rigid line of his jaw.

"Let's go. Are you sure all we have to do is turn the bolt on the door?"

"I think so. It looks just like the other one," she responded.

On the other side of the warehouse, the voices rose again and a small orange glow pierced the darkness.

"Wow! They sure burn fast—"

"Get outta the way!"

"Careful or—"

The glow steadily got brighter. Just as Harte had thought, the floats were catching fire with incredible speed. Within seconds, the glow had quadrupled in size and he could see smoke and smell the harsh fumes.

Chapter Ten

Harte moved toward the door with Dani right behind him. On the other side of the building, a roaring whoosh of air indicated more floats going up in flames. The acrid fumes grew worse. Dani coughed, and the sound echoed off the walls.

"Listen!"

Dani clapped her hand over her mouth.

"You!" a loud, gruff voice said. "Go around. They'll be smoked out in no time. Find the doors! Don't let them get away."

Harte reached the door and flipped the lock. He stopped, trying to get his bearings. If they were on the opposite side of the warehouse from the door they'd come in, then which way should they go? His best guess was to the right.

"Harte?" Dani sounded nervous.

"You stay behind me and follow me. I'm turning right. But keep up. I may have to change direction. If there's someone outside the door waiting for us, you stay inside until I can take care of him. Understand?"

She looked as though she wanted to say something, but she didn't. She nodded and covered her mouth again, coughing as quietly as she could.

He turned the bolt and pushed on the door, opening it a crack and checking to be sure the coast was clear. The only thing he saw through the silvery haze of rain was the dark, wet alley. Carefully, he pushed the door wider and stuck his head out. Nothing.

He slipped through the door with Dani right behind him. The alley was somewhat protected from the storm, but he heard the wind. It roared as it whipped around corners and flung rain at awnings, street signs and shutters in all directions. Paper and trash swirled and flapped against curbs and walls.

"Stay right behind me," he told her. They hugged the wall of the warehouse until they reached the street. He stopped Dani with a hand, then pressed himself against the building. He peeked out, trying to see both ends of the street without exposing himself.

So far they were in the clear. "Looks like we beat them here. But they're going to be right behind us," he said, pointing to the right. "This way."

Dani started to move, but Harte stopped her. He leaned close to her ear. "The wind is worse than it was," he said. "Hook your fingers into my belt. If you lose your grip, *do not move*. I'll find you."

She nodded and he felt her fingers slide beneath the waistband of his pants. He wrapped an arm around her and hooked a finger through one of the belt loops of her jeans. "Okay," he said. "Ready."

When they emerged from the alley and onto the street, the wind nearly knocked Dani's feet out from under her, but she held on to Harte's belt. He braced himself, tightened his grip on her belt loop and turned as directly into the wind as he could. He had learned on a winter hike in the Rockies that when his back was to the wind it was more difficult to maintain balance and control.

Once they were clear of the alley, the wind, rain and thunder quickly drowned out any other sound. Harte was acutely aware that a vehicle could be upon them before they could hear its engine. He trudged on, favoring his strained ankle and trying to ignore the prickling at the back of his neck. He wanted to put as much distance as possible between them and the men who were chasing them.

He was pretty sure the warehouse was west of the bed-and-breakfast. At least that was the direction he'd started out. He had a good sense of direction, but the combination of the darkness, the wind and the rain were playing havoc with his usual calm assurance.

He knew he was disoriented by the rain, but his best guess was that the wind was coming from the south, since that had been the projected path of the storm. That meant if they kept facing into it, they'd be moving farther away from the bed-and-breakfast.

The pelting of the rain on his face and hands stung like blackberry briars, making it hard to keep his eyes open. Dani was having the same problem; plus, with her eyes closed, the wind was pummeling her, causing her to stumble.

Harte pulled her close to his side. He wiped his face with the soaked cuff of his shirt, not that it did much good. Lowering his head, he continued on.

Then everything stopped. Harte had been leaning so far into the wind that he almost toppled forward. He stood still, looking around and listening. Amazingly the wind had suddenly calmed, the rain had stopped and the thunder had quieted. The silence was eerie, intense, as if the storm were holding its breath.

"What happened?" Dani asked.

"It's the eye of the storm," he replied, and started walking again, urging her along with him. "We need to take advantage of it. Come on!"

Without the wind and rain fighting them, it was much easier to walk. Harte blinked and used his drenched shirt cuff again to wipe his face. Looking around, he saw that most of the buildings were old, with fading paint and unreadable signs. Several appeared abandoned. He didn't recognize anything. He looked up and down the street. He needed to find a corner. If he could just get to a street sign, he'd know where he was, he was sure.

"Let's go this way," he said to Dani, pointing to the left. They'd only gone a few steps when she grabbed his arm.

"Listen," she hissed.

Harte stopped. At first he didn't hear anything. He held his breath.

"Is that voices—?" Dani said, her tone rising in a question.

"Yeah. Hurry!" He'd glanced at the buildings, hoping he'd recognize the street. Now he looked at them again, assessing which one would be best for them to hide in.

It was impossible to tell what most of the buildings were. Office buildings, probably. Harte grimaced. They'd be dry, but what could they offer other than shelter? He'd passed four seemingly identical facades before, tucked into the corner of one of the buildings, he saw a sign for a diner. That could be a little better. The diner would have food—and knives.

Then, in the distance, obscured by the damp haze that still hung in the air, he saw an old, distinctively shaped sign, rocking lazily back and forth on the chains that held it suspended above a set of glass doors.

He blinked, then squinted. It was an Rx sign. A drugstore. His heart skipped a beat. Considering the predicament they were in, hiding out in a drugstore would be like taking shelter in Santa's workshop. If they could get inside, they might be able to find more flashlights. Maybe even some dry clothes.

"Drugstore," he said to Dani, pointing toward it as he picked up his pace.

Then, as suddenly as the storm had quieted, it started up again. The sky dumped rain as if by giant bucketfuls. The wind blew it into their faces like tiny, stinging darts. Thunder rumbled in the distance. Then a blinding flash of lightning lit everything, and Harte read the faded words on the sign. Delaughter's Drugs and Sundries.

He bent his head toward Dani's ear. "When we step onto the street, the wind's going to blow us sideways. Walk steadily and deliberately. Be careful. The water looks like it's about four inches. It's flowing fast. If the wind doesn't knock you off your feet, the water will." He wrapped an arm around her waist. "Ready?"

She nodded. They stepped into the street. Dani faltered, but caught herself with Harte's help. When they were about halfway across, a harsh scraping noise rose above the roar of the rain and wind. Harte turned. A metal street sign, battered into a twisted mess by the punishing gusts of wind, was tumbling down the street, directly at them.

Harte threw himself to the pavement with Dani in his arms. "Hold your breath!" he yelled in her ear as he ducked his head and covered her head with his hands.

He cringed, praying the sharp-edged runaway sign wouldn't hit them. A rush of air on the nape of his neck and a discordant twang told him the sign passed way too close over them. A few inches lower and its jagged edges would have sliced right through them. He looked up in time to see one sharp edge of the piece of metal cut a fallen tree branch in half and not even slow down.

It took him a couple of seconds to calm his labored breathing.

Dani still lay beneath him, not moving.

"Dani?" he said, loosening his hold on her.

She took a gasping breath. He rolled off her and helped her up. Then they ran toward the drugstore.

Without even checking his stride, Harte used his forward momentum to kick at the glass entry door until it cracked. He half fell against the door when his ankle gave way, but he caught himself. Gritting his teeth, he kicked again and again, until the glass in the lower half of the door shattered. He reached in and unlatched the door from the inside. He pushed it open and pulled her inside, then closed it and latched it, for whatever good it would do, now that the bottom half was gone.

"Stay down," he ordered Dani as he quickly assessed the interior layout of the store. Directly in front of them was the cashier's cage, which was encased in a thick glass that Harte figured was bulletproof. Perfect. He guided Dani around behind the cage and they collapsed onto the floor with their backs against the wall, their shoulders touching. Harte felt Dani shivering.

"How're you doing?" he asked.

She nodded as she pushed wet hair out of her eyes. "I'm okay," she said, flinging water off her hands. "I used to think that walking in the rain was fun." He took a good look at her face. She was pale, but she seemed to be fine. He breathed a sigh of relief. They'd made it.

"Stay here. I'm going to check the street." He got up, wiping water off his face and head. Now that he had Dani in a safe place, he wanted to make sure they hadn't been followed. He didn't think so, but in truth, it had been impossible to see well enough to be sure.

He positioned himself with his back in the corner between the front window and the wall and surveyed the street. Everywhere they'd been, once the storm started, the streets had been deserted. Not even a dog or a cat. New Orleans people and animals knew better than to fight a storm.

The street was flowing with water, and the rain was still coming down. The sky above the tops of the buildings seemed to be almost constantly lit with flashes of lightning. This was the worst kind of spring storm, and like many of them, it was caught right over the Port of New Orleans. Harte hadn't seen or heard any tornadoes, but he knew this kind of storm could spawn them—sometimes by the dozen. They'd been lucky so far.

After he'd done his best to scan every corner and alley and scrutinize every shadow, he headed back behind the cashier's counter and sat down beside Dani.

"There doesn't seem to be even a rat moving out there. We should be okay here for a while," he told her, brushing water off his face again, then leaned his head back against the wall. When he closed his eyes, he could see the metal sign, tumbling toward them. That had been a close call. Too close. He didn't have to work hard to conjure up a vision of that piece of twisted steel slicing through them. He shuddered. At least they were finally safe. For now.

DANI COULDN'T REMEMBER ever being so tired or scared in her life. Not even on the night her grandfather was murdered. She'd been scared in the B & B when the lights had gone out. And she'd been afraid when the men had started burning the warehouse floats. But neither of those things had compared with the terror that had overwhelmed her when Harte had suddenly grabbed her and dove to the ground with her in tow. She'd had no idea what was happening. She'd heard the metallic whistling of something passing over their heads. At first she'd thought the sound was bullets, whistling close by her ears, but it droned on for too long. Then she'd heard a harsh screech in front of them. The whole while, she'd scrunched her shoulders, expecting some kind of blow at any second. When Harte rolled off her, and she'd raised her head, she'd caught a fleeting glimpse of a bent, jagged-edged sign as it disappeared into the gray distance.

She shuddered now, recalling the sight. "That sign. It b-barely missed us," she muttered, shuddering.

Harte didn't answer.

"You saved my life—again."

Drops of water from her hair dripped down the back of her neck. She didn't want to move, but the chilly drops were tickling her back. She gathered her hair in her hands and squeezed it, shivering as the water ran in rivulets down her neck and between her breasts.

Her eyes burned and her throat clogged. She felt tears welling. She'd been a hairbreadth away from death three times within a week. Harte shifted, then turned on the flashlight. The beam was weak and pale.

"Oh no, the battery's nearly dead," Dani said.

Harte turned his gaze to hers. His eyes twinkled in the pallid light. "But we're in a drugstore."

She got it immediately. "And drugstores sell batteries," she said, her mouth turning up in a smile.

"Right." He stood, shining the flashlight's beam around.

"They're usually close to the register, aren't they?"

"Yep. Here we go." He walked out of her sight and after a moment she heard paper tearing. When he came back and sat down, he handed the mini-flashlight to her. Then he tore more cardboard.

"What's that?" she asked, shining the beam on what he held.

"A bigger flashlight." He finished inserting the batteries, then turned it on.

Dani shielded her eyes. "Ow, too much. We've been in the dark too long."

"Watch this." He clicked a button and the intense brightness went away and a softer, more diffuse light replaced it. "And this." Another click and the light turned red and bright again.

"A triple-duty flashlight. Nice," she said as he switched it back to the soft light and set it on a shelf just beneath the counter. "Does it do any more tricks?"

"There's a button that will make it flash. And I found this." He held a tiny disc between his first finger and thumb. He pressed it.

"A laser beam. What are you going to do with that?"

He shrugged. "Who knows? It's neat, though, isn't it?"

She chuckled. "It is neat." She flicked her light on and off, then stuck it into the pocket of her jeans.

"We should be all set," he said. Then he put his light on the soft setting and pointed it at her face.

"Hey," she protested, squinting.

"You're kind of cute with your hair all wet and your raccoon eyes."

She swiped a finger below her eyes. It came away smudged with black. Great. Her mascara was running and she didn't have any makeup in her purse. Gun—yes. Makeup—no.

An odd little hiccup bubbled up from her throat, followed by another one and another. Tears ran down her cheeks, but she wasn't crying. Not exactly. She was laughing—kind of. She put her knuckles against her teeth. Was she becoming hysterical?

Harte frowned. "Are you okay?" he asked.

She shook her head and tried to stop the laughter that was bubbling up from her chest, but she couldn't. "I—I'm sorry," she stammered. "I—can't seem to—help it."

"It's okay," he said softly, wrapping his arm around her and pulling her close to his side.

She shivered at the warmth of his body.

"Now, what's so funny?"

"When you called me raccoon eyes, my first thought

was that I don't have any makeup in my purse." She could barely talk for the spasms of laughter.

Harte smiled. "Hard to believe, given the size of it."

She sniffed.

"You know, people react in different ways. Just let it out."

Her throat and chest quivered with the strange half laugh, half sob for a few more seconds. Then suddenly, it stopped. Dani hiccuped one more time. "That was weird," she said.

Harte's arm tightened around her shoulders, urging her to relax. She gave in and let herself sink into his side. She felt him put his lips against her hair, felt them move as he murmured gentle, comforting words. She couldn't hear everything he said, but that was okay. It was his strength, his warmth, his closeness that mattered.

Her muscles, cold and tired, twitched shakily. Each time her arm or leg jerked, he laid his palm on the twitching limb and rubbed it.

In an odd way, it reminded her of when she was a child. Tears choked her throat again. She coughed. "When I was little, my granddad would rub my legs when I woke up crying with the leg-ache," she said.

"You always lived with him after your dad died?"

She nodded. "My dad died when I was seven. So Granddad raised me."

"Where was your mom?" Harte asked, his breath stirring her hair.

"Gone. Since I was three."

"I'm sorry," he said.

Dani shook her head, but when she opened her mouth

to say, *It was a long time ago,* the words wouldn't come out. A little sob erupted from her throat, and tears filled her eyes. "Damn it," she muttered. "This is ridiculous. I never cry."

"Hey," Harte whispered, putting a finger under her chin and lifting her face to his. "Give yourself a break."

"A break? It's so stupid to cry. It doesn't help anything." She blotted her cheeks with her palms. "It's humiliating."

"I don't know a handful of people who could have dealt with everything that's happened as well as you have." His mouth quirked upward. "And you pick a mean lock."

"I do that," she said, trying to smile. A sob, like a tiny hiccup, escaped her lips.

"Shh." Harte touched the corner of her mouth with a finger, then bent his head and brushed a kiss across her cheek. It was so light it seemed hardly more than a breath.

But it was enough to reignite the fire he'd stoked inside her earlier, when she'd dared to kiss him. She felt the exquisite longing rise and flare again. She wanted to turn to him, open to him and beg him to wrap her in those strong, warm arms and make love to her. Her rational mind knew that giving in to the urge would be a big mistake, for so many reasons. She and Harte Delancey were at opposite ends of every spectrum she could think of—political, financial, social. He was ambitious, probably hoping to be D.A. one day. She'd become a public defender because she wanted to help people who would otherwise have no one on their side.

The only thing the two of them had in common was

the enemy that was after them. And while joining forces to fight a deadly enemy made good sense, it also made for strange bedfellows. Right here and now, though, she didn't care. She wanted closeness. She wanted comfort. She wanted assurance that no matter how desperate the situation, the two of them were still alive. And she wanted to feel something besides fear, at least for a little while.

He was unaware of the argument going on inside her, but he was not unaware of her. She knew it, and she used it. Turning, she settled closer into his arms. Reaching up a hand, she slid her fingers along the line of his jaw and back to caress his earlobe. His mouth was firm yet gentle as she touched her lips to his. Ignoring the voice in her head that was telling her what a bad idea it was to kiss him, she leaned in farther, opening her mouth to taste him better. The feel of his lips and tongue was so sweet and at the same time so titillating that hot new tears sprang to her eyes and her breath caught in a sob.

Harte froze for an instant, then pulled back. "Dani, I don't—" He stopped. His chest was heaving.

"No, I'm sorry. It's just everything." She felt tears welling up in her eyes. She willed them to stop, but it didn't help. They spilled down her wet cheeks, scalding them. "I promise you," she said with a choked laugh. "I almost never cry."

Harte sat back and held out his arm. Instinctively, Dani moved closer. For a brief moment, he didn't move, just sat there, his arm resting across her back. "I believe you," he said softly. "Makes my eyes red and gives me a headache."

He ran his palm down her bare shoulder to her upper arm. "You're cold."

"Not so much now," she murmured as she nestled into the shelter of his arm. "How do you stay so warm in nothing but a shirt?"

He shivered and laughed ruefully. "I don't."

"But your skin—it's always warm."

"Maybe warmer than yours. But that's because you're so skinny you can't hold any heat."

Dani chuckled as her tears dried on her cheeks. "Please. Don't try to butter me up. I am not skinny."

"No. You're not. At least not everywhere," he acceded. His palm caressed her shoulder and arm, sending shivers not caused by the temperature through her.

She snuggled a little closer to him. "Oh, I've never felt so helpless in my life," she murmured. "Except maybe the night Granddad died." That thought closed her throat and made her eyes sting. "Here I go again," she said, blotting the tears from her cheeks.

"Hey." He slid his fingers under her chin and urged her head up. "It's okay. No need to cry," he said, his thumb brushing across her cheek; then he pulled her closer.

His lips pressed against her forehead—warm, firm, steady. "No need to cry," he whispered again, the comforting words penetrating her heart and lighting all the dark, scary places inside her.

Right now he wasn't her rival or her attorney. She didn't want to put a name to what she was feeling right this minute. All she knew was that he was her port in the storm. He was strength and warmth and safety, and she needed that. She lifted her head, seeking more. His mouth moved from her temple to her cheek and then to her lips.

She moaned quietly.

He made a sound in his throat, bent his head and covered her mouth with his. This time it was no gentle, comforting kiss that made her question her reaction. His tongue slid along her parted lips and farther, to explore the inside of her mouth. The sensation turned her blood into molten lava that flowed through every part of her, changing her smoldering longing into searing desire.

He whispered her name as his fingers slipped up the nape of her neck and through her hair to cradle the back of her head. He went further, deepening the kiss, invading her mouth in an erotic mimicry of lovemaking. The sensual stroking of his tongue sent shivers of desire down, down, all the way to her core, feeding a hunger that nearly consumed her. She wanted him—needed him. She kissed him back greedily, amazed that his straight, firm mouth could feel so supple and gentle and at the same time so demanding.

She breathed in his scent, felt the rough stubble on his cheeks scrape her skin. He was deliciously male, solid and strong in a fascinating way that was so different from her own body. His arms and chest felt like steel wrapped in silk. Just as she reached up to wrap her hands around his neck and pull him closer, greedy for more of the breathtaking desire, he froze.

"What?" she said against his mouth, her heart jackhammering in her chest. "Did you hear something?"

"No," he rasped, his voice hoarse with emotion. He pulled away from her and leaned back against the wall.

"Then what? Is it me?" She winced as soon as the

words were out of her mouth. Even if that was why he had pulled away, she didn't want to know.

He gave his head a shake and rose to his haunches. "Harte?"

"Don't make something of nothing. You're soaking wet and you haven't stopped shivering. I'm pretty miserable too. We need to find some dry clothes and see what else is around here that we can use."

Dani wanted to tell him that yes, she was chilly, but her shivering was caused not by the weather, but by his kiss, his scent, the warmth of his skin. But before she could speak, he was pushing himself to his feet.

"And we can't forget that those guys are still out there, looking for us. Thank God they no longer have a car. But there are four of them." He turned his attention to the front windows for a moment, then wiped his face.

"I'll go see what I can find," he said in what she thought of as his prosecutor's tone—formal, a bit detached, professional. He could have been talking to anybody. Anybody except the person he'd just shared a hot, erotic kiss with.

It was clear as glass. He was sorry he'd kissed her—and she was very sorry about that.

Chapter Eleven

Harte cursed himself silently but fluently as he clenched his jaw and forced his breathing under control. How had he let that happen? Being so close to Dani was too enticing. He was apparently not capable of controlling himself around her.

He'd promised himself that he'd protect her. As her attorney, it was his duty. And in no dictionary did any definition of the word *protection* include seduction. He'd gotten her into this dangerous situation, and there was no way he was going to allow himself to be blinded by his raging attraction to her. Her safety, her life, depended on his self-control. It was important that both of them understood that.

He took a deep breath and turned back toward her, digging deep inside for the strength to face her dispassionately.

"Dani," he said tightly. "Your safety is my responsibility. If I'm going to protect you, you're going to have to help me. We need each other's warmth and support, and it's natural that our closeness might lead to—tension."

He stood and looked down at her, his expression grim. "But I can't let anything happen between us. If

I let my guard down for even a minute, it could get you killed."

Mortification flooded her face, and her cheeks flamed. His heart ached to pull her into his arms and assure her that he desired her, but it was better for her to think he didn't want her than to risk her safety.

"I'm aware of the danger," she said archly.

"I know you are."

"And I understand what you're saying. I suppose you're right. It is the normal male reaction—"

"That's not what I said."

Dani held up her hand. "It's all right. We're in a deadly, dangerous situation and the only way we're going to survive is if we can depend on each other to be strong. I didn't mean to distract you."

"Damn it, Dani. I'm trying to keep us alive. This is not personal." Hell. That hadn't come out right. He'd gone about this all wrong, and she was not helping. If she'd just stop and think, surely she'd realize what he meant. Irritation flared inside him.

"Just try to stay focused, okay?" he said, and turned to shine the flashlight toward the main floor of the store.

Dani could see the muscle in his jaw working. His chiseled features looked sculpted in marble. She watched as he withdrew, physically and emotionally. His back was ramrod straight, the muscles knotted. His whole body exuded intense control.

What she'd told him was true. She knew he was right. They had to stay focused. Distractions could be deadly. Harte might have lost his focus for an instant to indulge his lust, but now Mr. Prosecutor was back.

"I'll be right back," he said, just as lightning flashed and thunder roared.

Dani jumped and gasped. "Where are you going?" she asked anxiously.

Harte heard the apprehension in her voice. It reminded him that, as brave as she'd been, she was deeply afraid of storms.

"I just want to check things out." He turned to look out the glass front of the drugstore as another bolt of lightning flared. The thunder seemed to be roiling continuously. The rain and wind made it almost impossible to see anything, and all the lightning did was to brighten the grays.

"I don't think they will suspect that we're here. I couldn't see inside from out there."

She turned to look, and cringed when a flash of lightning flared, followed immediately by a clap of thunder. "Why isn't the storm moving away?"

"I guess that low front stalled it."

"I guess." Dani's voice was a mixture of apprehension and weariness.

Harte picked up the big flashlight and shone the narrow beam on the signs about the aisles of shelves. "Batteries, aisle four," he read. "Stationery, toys, paper towels. Looks like we've got all the comforts of home." He turned the flashlight in the opposite direction. "Ah, kitchen," he said, and headed in that direction.

"Kitchen?"

"Sure. I want some towels to dry off with. As soon as I get them, I want to find an elastic bandage."

He grabbed some dish towels. "These should work," he said, and tucked them under his arm.

Dani was reading the signs on the other aisles. "Look, Harte," she cried. "T-shirts."

They picked out long-sleeved T-shirts that read The Big Easy. "And hoodies!" Dani cried. "Ooh—fleece."

His heart twisted painfully in his chest at the look on her face. She beamed as if the fleece were golden. It took all his self-control not to hug her tight and promise her he'd make it his personal mission to see that she never felt cold again.

"Here," he said, spotting fleece throws. He grabbed two. "These will be good if we get chilly."

"I wish they had pants," she said wistfully. "Although these jeans are hard enough to get on and off dry. I'll probably never be able to peel them off soaking wet."

Harte couldn't help looking as she held up a pink hoodie with a graffiti design, measuring it against her. *Tight* didn't begin to describe her jeans, now that they were wet. They looked as though they'd been painted on her sexy hips and legs. He loved her body. It was curvy in all the right places and in precisely the right amount. He swallowed hard and did his best not to get lost in an image of her wiggling her way out of those wet jeans.

"Harte, look!" she cried.

He turned. She'd gone to the end of the aisle and was reading the signs farther along. "Scrubs and socks—and oh, thank God, underwear."

She ran. When he caught up, she handed him a pair of scrubs. "Here's a pair of XL for you and a medium for me." She headed up the aisle to a display of socks, boxers and briefs and panties. She grabbed a package of cotton panties and one of socks, then paused. She looked up at him. Her face held a pained expression. "We're looting, aren't we?"

"I guess so, in the strictest sense of the word. But I'll bet the owner wouldn't begrudge us these few items, under the circumstances." He gave her a small smile. "If it makes you feel better, I'll send him a check when we get out of here."

"When we get out—" she echoed, then turned toward him, doubt and fear darkening her eyes. "Swear to me that we will get out of here."

"Of course we will," he said, unable to resist reaching out to touch her cheek and berating himself for his weakness. A fluttery feeling rippled in his chest when her head inclined toward his hand. "As soon as we've rested for a few minutes, we need to get out of here and get as far away from this area as we can. As soon as I figure out what street we're on, I'll be able to find a police station."

She lifted her head and gave him a searching gaze. "A police station. Really?"

"Really," he assured her. He wished he was as confident as he sounded. "Now we need to get out of these wet clothes."

A sudden blast of wind rattled the windows and doors and made the roof creak loudly. It roared like an oncoming train. Dani threw herself into Harte's arms with a small shriek. He held on to her until the noise died down.

"I'm so sorry. I'm trying not to react every time it thunders," she said as she picked up the items she'd dropped.

"You're doing real well."

"You don't think that was a tornado, do you?"

He shook his head. "It sounded more like straight-line wind. But I wouldn't be surprised if some of the damage we've seen and heard has been from tornadoes. These spring storms can spawn them."

"I know," Dani muttered.

Harte cringed, his heart aching with understanding. Her father had died in a tornado. Of course she was terrified that any wind and rain would turn into a deadly funnel cloud. He shouldn't have gone on and on about them.

"There's the pain-relief aisle. I need an elastic bandage for my ankle. Then we can check out the back." He grabbed a bandage and headed toward the back of the store.

"There," he said, pointing toward a door that said Employees Only. When he opened it, he found a dark, musty storeroom with shelves groaning under the weight of boxes and bins of all shapes and sizes. There was a door marked with an Exit sign.

Throwing the latch on the exit door, he eased it open. The rain was still coming down in buckets, and the alley behind the store was running at least six inches deep in water. He set his jaw and stuck his head out, wincing at the chilly wind that blew rain in his face. He'd almost dried enough that he didn't feel waterlogged. He wasn't anxious to get out into the rain again. But he'd needed to check out their means of escape. "We can get out this way if we need to," he said, closing and latching the door.

Dani sighed. "Okay. Can we go back inside the store?

It's chilly out here. And look." She pointed. "The roof is leaking like a sieve."

"Sure, go ahead," Harte said. "I'll change in here. Take some of these towels."

"Stand over here near the door while you're changing," she said. "Otherwise your clothes will be wet again before you get them on."

She left and Harte quickly shed his shirt and peeled off his jeans, remembering what she'd said about hers. She was right. The wet denim felt like duct tape as he peeled them down his legs. He dried off quickly and donned the scrub pants. Then he sat on one haunch as he quickly and efficiently wrapped his sore and swollen ankle and pulled on clean dry socks. But once it was wrapped, he found that he couldn't get his shoe back on. He tried the bandage alone, but no. It was still too large. Finally, sighing with frustration and the anticipation of more pain, he unwrapped his foot and tossed the bandage aside. He was able to get the shoe on over a dry sock. Just as he reached for the long-sleeved Big Easy T-shirt, he heard a crash and a scream.

Grabbing the flashlight, he bolted through the door and almost ran headlong into a shelf. Careering around it, he sprinted to the front of the store. "Dani? Dani!"

He heard her whimper.

Turning toward her voice, he saw the narrow beam of her flashlight canted across the floor, illuminating a pale body sprawled on the floor. "Dani!"

She was sprawled facedown on the floor with her wet jeans and a pair of white panties tangled around her feet, and scrubs and hoodie in a pile beside her. She was wearing nothing but the T-shirt. *Nothing* but the T-shirt. Her pale, shapely backside was bare.

He blinked and clamped his jaw tight. "Dani—" he said, and started to bend down. Thank God there was at least one part of his brain that was holding on to rational thought, even though the rest of him was reacting to the exquisite sight of her beautiful, bare body.

"No!" She turned her head and looked up at him, horrified. "Get away!"

He froze.

She wriggled as she tried to pull the tail of the shirt down to cover her butt. She wasn't successful. "Go—somewhere, please," she begged. "Don't look."

Harte didn't know what to do except turn his back. "Are you hurt?"

"No," she said shortly.

He heard fabric rustling and a couple of quiet groans of frustration.

"So you tripped over your jeans when you tried to take them off?" he asked, trying his best to sound serious and supportive, although in a different situation, it would be really funny.

"Don't you dare laugh at me. I swear I'll—" She yelped in pain.

Harte whirled. She was holding her left wrist. "What is it?" he asked. "Your wrist?"

"Don't look," she cried. "Turn around!"

"I need to look at your wrist."

"It's fine," she said. The stubborn tightness of her voice was in sharp contrast to the mortified and pain-filled look on her face. She raised her gaze to his. "Please."

He turned his back again. While he waited for her to dress, he occupied himself by trying, without much success, to banish the vision of her exquisite curves. He heard her moving around. Then she bit off another gasp of pain.

He almost turned around, but he restrained himself. "Be careful with your wrist. If it's broken—"

"I am," she grated. He could practically hear her jaw clenching. After a few moments, she said, "Okay. I'm dressed."

He turned around and looked at her. But she was looking at the pile of clothes on the floor, and her face was turning bright red.

He looked down to see what was so embarrassing for her. There, nice and white and pretty, were the cotton bikini panties she'd found on the store shelves. He stared at the dazzling white scrap of fabric lying on the drugstore floor, every bit as mesmerized as she'd been, and certain he was thinking the same thing she was. He raised his gaze to hers and felt himself grow hard at the thought that she had nothing on under the thin cotton scrub pants.

She swallowed audibly and drew in a long breath.

Harte waited, wondering what she was going to say, because he had no idea what he should do.

"I—guess I forgot something," she said hoarsely.

Harte felt his face burn. He let go of a huge breath that he hadn't realized he was holding. "Yeah," he said, his gaze flickering toward the panties, then back to meet hers. "Yeah."

After a long moment, he cleared his throat. "Let me see your wrist. I need to make sure it's not broken."

"Okay," she said meekly.

He realized he was still holding the flashlight, so he set it down on the counter. It was on the soft-light setting and he aimed it toward the wall, hoping the light and its reflection would help him see. Swallowing hard, fighting for control over his libido, he bent down next to her and gently took her forearm in his hands and examined it closely.

While he studied her wrist, Dani took the opportunity to study him. With his head down, his profile was lit by the faint light of the flashlight. He was undeniably good-looking. She already knew that. But she hadn't realized just how classic his features were. His nose was long and straight, his mouth was firm, his jawline was chiseled. And those eyes—she could actually see the shadow of his lashes on his cheek.

"How'd you hit it?" he asked as he used her flashlight to inspect the wrist bone.

"Hmm?" Was it fair for one man to be so beautiful from so many different angles?

"Dani?"

She blinked. What had he said? "What?"

"Are you sure you're all right? You didn't hit your head, did you?"

"No, I didn't hit my head. I think my wrist hit the edge of the counter when I tripped. And it was already sore from when I jumped up onto the porch."

He nodded. "It's a little red, but I don't see any swelling or discoloration."

His touch was so gentle, his voice so kind that it made her want to cry—because apparently, she was going to cry about *everything* from now on. And once they managed to get away from these men who seemed determined to kill them, she could tell she was in for a long jag.

With a quick shake of her head, she bit down on her cheek and blinked away the stinging behind her eyelids.

"Does it hurt when I move it?" he asked, manipulating it tenderly.

"No," she said. "It really doesn't hurt any more or any less. It just aches."

"It's probably strained. Try getting up. See if you can put weight on it."

She stood without a problem. "It's fine," she said, but when she looked up at him, she found that he'd stepped close, ready to catch her if she faltered.

"Are you sure—?" He stopped talking when their gazes met. His mouth was less than an inch from hers. She looked at his lips, then back up into his eyes. His gaze was dark, his eyes smoky. "Dani—" he started.

At that instant, the front windows rattled and something crashed into the door. Dani screamed just as Harte caught her in his arms and dove to the floor.

Chapter Twelve

A roar like a freight train filled the air, and the windows rattled more loudly. Dani lay shielded by Harte's strong body. His hands covered her head protectively, and his cheek rested against hers. His long, rock-solid thighs were splayed across hers, his hard, heavy arousal pressing against her belly.

The wind roared and whistled, slinging trash and shingles and tree branches against buildings. She lay there, shielded by his body, as the tornado—because she knew without a doubt that it was a tornado—passed over them. Finally, the deafening noise died down.

Harte wasted no time pushing himself off her, and she knew why. She'd felt his arousal. Her cheeks grew warm. No matter how he felt about her, she knew he did desire her. He just didn't want to.

"That was bad," she whispered.

"Stay still," he said. Without looking at her, he rose and looked out the windows. He whistled under his breath. "Lots of damage," he said. "I see a couple of bicycle tires, twisted spokes." He craned his neck. "I think that big crash was a screen door hitting the windows. There's a huge crack in the window on the left.

I'd expect the bulletproof glass to stay intact, but I'm amazed that all the windows didn't shatter."

"That was a tornado," she said, wishing she could stop imagining deadly funnel clouds roaring toward them, sucking up everything in their paths. When the wind had been at its worst, it had sounded like a freight train.

He yawned exaggeratedly, popping his ears. "I think so. It's so quiet it feels weird."

"I don't hear any sirens."

Harte shook his head. "With this much debris and damage everywhere, the city will be focusing all its manpower toward clearing major thoroughfares and routes to hospitals for emergency vehicles."

"At least we're all right."

He nodded as he pulled his cell phone from his pocket and checked it. "Hey! I've got bars!" he exclaimed. "Two bars."

Dani's heart leaped into her throat. "Call 911!" she exclaimed.

He paused in the act of pressing a button. "They can't get to us. They probably can't keep up with the injuries in the busier parts of the city. I'm calling Lucas." He pressed a button and listened. "Oh, come on," he muttered. Then his eyes lit up. "I'm getting through."

Dani's eyes stung. Finally, this awful nightmare would be over.

"Lucas!" Harte yelled. "Lucas, can you hear me?" He stepped out from behind the counter and moved toward the front of the store, checking the signal every few steps.

"Yeah, it's Harte. I know, the connection does suck,

but listen…" He paused. "Lucas? You still there?" Then he walked the line of the windows, from one side of the store to the other.

Dani held her breath, as if that would help hold together the fragile connection.

"Damn it, don't fade on me now," Harte said, then spoke loudly and distinctly. "Lucas, we're at Delaughter's Drugs, near Religious. Repeat—Delaughter's Drugs. Pursued by armed men. Repeat—armed men." He listened for a few seconds. "Lucas?" Then he threw his head back and growled.

"Do you think he heard you?" Dani asked.

Harte was frowning at his phone. "I don't know."

Dani fished down into her purse, her fingers brushing the cold steel of the SIG as she searched for her phone. She knew she needed to tell Harte about the gun, but she'd waited too long. She had no doubt how he'd react, and she dreaded the prosecutorial lecture she'd have to endure when he found out she'd been packing this whole time. She found her phone and pulled it out. It showed one bar. "Let's send a text." If the phone managed to get the text sent, then Lucas would at least see it once service was restored.

Harte nodded. "I'll send it to Lucas and Ethan." He quickly entered a message. In Delaughter's Drugs near B & B, hiding from armed men. Send help! He pressed Send and pocketed his phone. "Give me yours. I'll send the same text. That'll be two service providers—two chances for it to get through."

Another loud rattling of the windows announced the wind picking up again. Harte grabbed Dani and pulled her down behind the counter. "We need to be careful.

One of these gusts of wind is likely to throw something hard enough at those windows to break them."

They sat together, shoulder to shoulder. Dani closed her eyes, basking in the heat Harte's body gave off and trying to pretend that she didn't want him to pull her close and make hot, sweet love to her. But as much as she wanted him deep inside her, she craved his warmth and strength surrounding her even more. When he held her in his arms, she felt as if nothing could harm her.

"Harte? Where do you think they are—the men?"

She felt his shoulders rise and fall. "No telling. I tried to keep up with which direction and how far we ran from the warehouse. I think we made it about ten blocks. That's a big circle they've got to search."

"And you're sure they were sent by Yeoman?"

"Don't know who else it would be. Like I said before, I think Stamps would have more sense. Yeoman, on the other hand, deals in physical force. It's what he knows."

"It doesn't make any sense. Why would he think killing me would solve his problem?"

Harte assessed her. "You're the only person who can connect him with your grandfather's murder. In his world, shooting you is the easiest way to get rid of you. It's incredibly hard to prove somebody shot somebody without an eyewitness."

She shivered and Harte immediately put his arm around her.

"Cold?"

His heat soaked into her, making her feel aroused and languid at the same time. "A little," she said, "but mostly, I can't shake the feeling that they're right behind me, breathing down my neck." She shivered again.

"Should we be doing something—getting farther away maybe?"

Harte didn't speak for a moment. He ran his palm up and down her arm. "I wondered about that. If Lucas or Ethan gets my message, they'll come here." He settled back against the wall and tightened his hold on her. "Look at it from those goons' point of view. They're looking for a needle in a haystack. And that car can't be drivable after they rammed it into that freight door three times."

"So they're on foot, just like us. I guess that's a good thing."

"And like I said, they've got an awfully big area to search, and they have to search every building on each and every street."

"They know which door we went out."

"Yeah, but we made at least two right turns. We couldn't see anything, which means they couldn't either. If they'd been able to see us, they'd have shot at us."

The wind rose again, whistling around corners and roaring past the broken door. "Here we go again," he said. Rain pelted the glass windows, flung there by the whipping winds.

"Those windows are going to break eventually," she said.

"They might," he agreed, "but that's why I put us here in the cashier's cage. It's metal, bolted down and we've got bulletproof glass protecting us." He gave her arm a reassuring squeeze.

"Okay," she said, not sounding convinced.

"Hey," Harte said. "Trust me."

She snuggled in closer to his side. Harte held her

and listened to the storm. He could feel the tension in her stiff limbs, her fingers that were curved into a fist against his skin, her shaky breaths.

Lightning flashed almost continuously and the roar of the thunder and wind was near deafening. Above their heads, a vicious screech overrode the sound of the storm.

Dani jumped. Harte cupped the back of her head and pressed it to his chest, resting his cheek against her hair. "It's okay," he murmured, although he doubted she could hear him. "It's going to be okay."

He risked a glance upward, fully expecting to see that part of the roof had blown off, taking the ceiling with it. The screeching had sounded like nails being ripped out. But the ceiling appeared intact. With all the rain and wind, they'd know soon enough if the roof was damaged.

Then, as quickly as it had started, the roaring stopped. The lightning was no longer continuous and the thunder seemed farther away.

Dani didn't relax a bit. Now that things had calmed down, he could feel her trembling.

"Listen," he said. "I think the worst is over." He took his hand away from the back of her head and touched her chin. "Look at me, Dani."

Slowly, haltingly, she raised her head. "I—I'm sorry," she muttered.

"For what? For being scared? I was scared too."

She shuddered. "Not like me." She sighed. "My father died more than twenty years ago and I'm still acting like a child."

After a long time, she lifted her head. Harte looked

down at her. "You okay?" he whispered, giving her a little smile.

She nodded, then dropped her gaze to his mouth. "Harte—?"

He looked at her parted lips, her soft whiskey-colored eyes.

"Dani," he said, "I don't think—"

"Don't think," Dani whispered, and brushed his lips with hers. She meant that admonition for herself as well as him. He'd held her and sheltered her. He'd protected her from the storm.

Sighing, she kissed him again. This time she touched his mouth with the tip of her tongue.

She wasn't thinking about what would happen once they were safe. Right now she wanted him with an ache that had been growing ever since he'd kissed her that first time.

He didn't move a muscle.

She withdrew and turned away, pressing her knuckles against her teeth. A short unamused laugh escaped her throat. "Sorry," she said tightly. "It takes me a while, but eventually I get the picture."

He closed his eyes and shook his head.

She cleared her throat. "I apologize. I guarantee it won't happen ag—"

He pulled her back to him. His mouth came down on hers hard, his tongue parting her lips.

Dani gasped as he deepened the kiss. The ache inside her turned to a tingling thrill that surged through her like a lightning bolt.

He moaned deep in his throat and lifted her onto

his lap. The only thing between them was two layers of thin cotton.

"Still think I don't want you?" Harte muttered against her lips as he pushed his fingers through her damp hair and kissed her again, more fiercely than before. "Don't ever make that mistake again."

Any doubt she might have had disappeared into a silver haze of desire. His arousal pressed insistently against her, stirring her blood to a fever pitch as he slid his hands under the T-shirt and pushed it up. She raised her arms so he could pull it over her head.

His hands moved on her skin, trailing sparks like a wizard everywhere they touched. Her waist, her rib cage, the soft skin beneath her breasts. Finally, with exquisite slowness, he trailed his fingertips over the swell of her breasts until she arched, pressing them into his hands.

He skimmed his thumbs across her nipples. They puckered immediately and throbbed, they were so sensitive.

His kisses were sweet and erotic at the same time. One instant his tongue sparred with hers in a sensual dance that almost sent her over the edge. The next, he withdrew, only to return and plant light, unbearably sweet butterfly kisses onto every square millimeter of her mouth, cheeks and eyelids.

Just as she thought she couldn't feel any more turned on, he bent his head and took a nipple into his mouth. He teased it with his tongue, then grazed it lightly with his teeth. A tight, choked scream erupted from her throat. Every touch sent electric shocks across her nerve endings from her fingers to her toes to her very core. He licked the tiny nub until it was wet, then lightly blew on it until Dani thought she would scream with pleasure. Then he turned to lavish the same attention on the other breast.

"Harte," she rasped. "I can't stand any more—" Her words were cut short by his rumble of soft laughter.

"You're going to have to," he said. He ran his palm down her body to the drawstring of the scrub pants. He untied it, then slid the material down over her hips and past her knees. She kicked them off, leaving her completely naked.

She didn't care. She twisted until she straddled him, then leaned down and gave him back the kisses he'd given her. Putting her hands on his bare chest, she used her fingertips on his nipples, teasing them to instant arousal and drawing a pained moan from his throat.

"Do you like that?" she asked as she teased the erect tips unrelentingly.

"No—" he gasped, taking hold of her wrists. His arousal pulsed against her, belying his words.

Harte arched, thrusting upward in unfettered response to her playing with his nipples. It was an unfamiliar, slightly uncomfortable sensation, and yet each touch arrowed straight down to his throbbing arousal.

She peered at him from under her lashes, a seductive smile on her face, and then twisted her wrists out of his clutches. Placing her palms on his chest, she bent and kissed him again.

"Slow down," he muttered, "or it's going to all be over."

"I don't want to slow down," she whispered in response. "I want you in me, now."

"Too soon," he protested. "You're not ready." As he spoke, he slid his hand down over her belly to the slight rise of her mound.

"Yes, I am," Dani gasped, so turned on by the twin pressures of his hand and his arousal against her that she could barely breathe, much less speak.

When he curled his fingers into the patch of hair that hid her sexual center, then slowly, gently, slid a finger between her soft, sensitized folds, she cried out, certain she was going to faint. He pressed into her, testing her readiness to receive him.

Her thighs tightened involuntarily, whether to hold on to the sensations he was stirring or to slow down the inevitable explosive conclusion, she didn't know. She was becoming lost in erotic ecstasy.

"Yes, you are," he whispered.

In answer, she lifted herself and guided him into her. He pushed carefully and steadily until he was buried inside her. She moaned and threw her head back, losing herself in a climax that went on and on.

Harte felt Dani's delicately intense contractions, and they triggered his own. With his breaths sawing in his throat and his muscles and sinews straining, he came, driving into her welcoming body as she met him, thrust for thrust.

Finally, drained, he collapsed back against the wall and Dani melted, as if boneless, atop him.

Chapter Thirteen

After a long time, Dani felt Harte lift her off him and set her gently down on the fleece blanket, then stretch out beside her. She didn't open her eyes. She didn't want to face reality yet. Her entire being was still floating on an ethereal cloud of fantasy.

A fantasy where there were no storms, no thunder, no soaking, pounding rain, where the sun was warm and bright, where no bad guys were chasing her and where the man with whom she'd just shared sweet, erotic sex would still want her once the danger was over. But trying to preserve the fantasy was a fruitless effort. She could feel reality hovering, looking for a way in. The reality of their separate lives—hers as a public defender who had to live on a government salary, and his as an assistant D.A. who was wealthy in his own right. They lived and worked in two different worlds.

Harte spread something over her, the pink hoodie maybe, then slid his arm under her head and shifted so she could rest her head on his shoulder. It helped a little. But reality was still out there, lurking.

She had to open her eyes sometime, and when she did, she'd be defenseless against the surge of regrets that were waiting to hit her. How many mistakes had

she made when she let that one careless second pass—
that one instant during which she could have made the
decision *not* to kiss him?

First and foremost, she'd exposed herself to him—
physically, yes. But also emotionally. The thing she'd
vowed not to do. For her, sex was not a casual romp.
It was too intimate, too exquisitely satisfying, to take
for granted. She never took it lightly and she'd never
had regrets.

Until now. Once they got out of here, she knew she'd
never be able to face Harte in court again. She could
picture him now, standing before the judge in one of his
impeccably tailored suits, with his expensive briefcase
and a knowing smile as she walked into the courtroom.
Her face burned just thinking about it.

She might have been able to work with him if all
they'd done was kiss. She'd still be fascinated by him,
still be amazed at how one person could be so unrelentingly gorgeous and sexy. But now they'd made love,
and Dani knew she'd never be the same. What had
been a silly office crush was no longer silly or just a
crush to her.

She'd just put herself on a fast track to a broken
heart. And she didn't even want to think what her
granddad would say if he knew. She moaned silently.

"Dani?"

Harte's soft voice startled her. Her eyes flew open
and met his dark gaze.

"Hey," he said, smiling. "I guess you were asleep. I
thought you said something."

Dani lifted her head from his shoulder and scooted

backward, holding the hoodie in place over her breasts and thighs.

He leaned up on one elbow.

"No, no," she said. "I didn't say anything." She wanted to sit up, to take some sort of control, at least of her body's position, but the hoodie wasn't big enough to cover everything she wanted covered. Any move she made would expose something.

"So I did wake you," he said. "Sorry."

She kept shaking her head. "You didn't wake me at all. No. I was awake already. I didn't go to sleep. I was just—" She stopped, clamping her jaw. She was babbling. "I need to—get dressed.

Harte held her gaze for a beat as something shadowed behind his eyes, and then he nodded. "Sure. Give me a second." He rolled away and sat up with his back to her, straightening and tying the drawstring waist of his scrub pants.

Without turning around he said, "I'm going to take a look around. See how much more damage the storm has done. See if anyone's moving around outside."

Dani's face burned like fire as she looked around for the panties she'd forgotten to put on earlier. She'd let him take all her clothes off, strip her naked. And he'd never even dropped his pants, just opened them. Like a quickie. She grimaced and her hot face got even hotter.

To him, she'd been a quickie. Mortified, her cheeks burning and her eyes stinging, she glanced over to be sure he wasn't looking, then pulled on the panties and grabbed the scrub pants. She held the hoodie against her breasts as she took off in the direction of the storeroom.

Harte shook his head as he heard her padding quickly

toward the back of the store. He'd never claimed to understand women. The things they did never ceased to befuddle him.

Sex with Dani had been better than he could have imagined. Her body was exquisite. Sleek and smooth, enticingly curvy where a woman should be. He'd been entranced with the mix of eagerness and shyness she'd displayed. Then there was their lightning-fast, nearly simultaneous climax. Her immediate, sensual response had surprised him.

His own hair-trigger climax had blown his mind.

Both of them had collapsed afterward, drained. He'd felt sapped, and had basked in the afterglow with Dani's soft hair against his shoulder and chest as her soft breaths echoed in his ear. He'd thought she was basking too. But despite her seeming boneless as she'd collapsed against him when he'd pulled her close and rested her head on his shoulder, she'd acted embarrassed and escaped as soon as she could.

She didn't strike him as one of those women who was embarrassed about her body. Shy maybe. He shrugged. That could be it, he supposed.

Now that she had run to the back of the store, he came back around the counter and looked for the long-sleeved T-shirt she'd found for him. Then he remembered. It was in the storeroom. He'd dropped it when she'd screamed.

Not wanting to disturb her, he headed toward the racks of T-shirts to find another one. Just as he got to the rack, she opened the storeroom door and came out. She was dressed in the scrub pants, the Big Easy T-shirt, the pink hoodie and her wet sneakers. She stopped short when she saw him. Her gaze skittered down his torso to the drawstring on the scrub pants, then back up.

She blinked. "Here—here's your T-shirt." She held it out for him.

"Great, thanks," he said. He took the shirt by the tail, shook it out once, then pulled it over his head and down. A slight shiver went through him. He ran his palms down each sleeve, then down his torso. "That feels good," he said, meeting her gaze.

She looked away. "These wet shoes don't."

"Yeah," he said, looking down at his own wet loafers. "I know." He patted the pockets of the scrubs. "Where's my phone?" he muttered. "I must have left it in my jeans."

She moved out of the way of the storeroom door. "Your jeans are on the floor," she said, then headed toward the front of the store.

Harte quickly retrieved his phone and followed her. "Damn it," he said when he checked the display. "No reception."

Dani pulled her phone from her purse. "Oh, I have a voice message," she cried.

Harte moved to where he could look over her shoulder. "From Lucas?" he asked.

"Don't know. I'll put it on Speaker." She pressed a button on the phone and they listened.

"We're sorry, you cannot access voice mail at this time. Please try again later."

"Great," Harte said, checking his display again. "Yep. Zero bars. I thought maybe since the storm had passed over, we'd be able to call for help."

Dani dropped the phone back into her big purse.

She raised her head, then suddenly moved away from him. It was as if she'd just realized how close he was standing to her. She still hadn't looked directly at him.

For once, he was sure he understood *this* woman perfectly. She regretted sleeping with him.

"Listen, Dani—"

"So, what now?" she interrupted, and immediately bit her lip. Her cheeks turned pink. "I mean, now that the storm is over, should we get out of here? Try to get to a police station or something?"

Harte turned to look out the front windows. "Yeah. The sun's going to come up soon. I'm going to go out and scout around."

"Then I'm going with you," she said.

"No. It's too dangerous. We could run into those men any second."

Dani propped her hands on her hips. "Exactly. Or a utility truck or a policeman. You'd have to come back and get me. That's just dumb."

Harte winced. She was right and she knew it. He could tell, because she gave a little nod of her head. Not much, just enough to say *So there*.

"Get ready to go," he said, then pointed his finger at her. "But I'm checking around the building first. You're not stepping one foot out of here until I'm sure the coast is clear."

"You're not going out there unarmed."

"What do you suggest I use? Your lock picks? Or maybe a water gun from the toy aisle?" he shot back.

With a look designed to wither him where he stood, she dug into her purse and pulled out—

"What the hell is that?" he snapped, staring at her hand.

She gave a short laugh. "It's a gun," she said with mock patience. "A SIG Sauer, to be specific."

"Where'd you get that?" he demanded. "Have you had it this whole time? Banging around in that—" He gestured. "Do you know how dangerous that is?"

She flushed, but not with embarrassment. She was angry. He could tell by the fire in her eyes and the lift of her chin.

"Yes," she snapped. "I know exactly how dangerous it is. Granddad gave it to me *and* taught me how to use it and care for it. You don't think for one minute that he would be so careless as to give me a weapon without making sure I could handle it?"

"How would I know what your grandfather would do?" Harte said irritably. "I do know this. Apparently, he skipped some basic precautions—like having enough respect for your partner to inform him that you're *packing* sometime within, say, the first eight hours or so of running for your lives."

Dani's face drained of color.

He realized immediately what he'd said. "Dani—I wasn't trying to insult your granddad—"

"You go to hell," she grated, then turned and stomped away. Her slender shoulders in the too-big hoodie were stiff and straight; her walk was regal.

Harte sighed in frustration and wiped a hand across his stubbled cheeks and chin. He'd crossed the line with his rude comment about her grandfather.

Hell, he'd crossed more lines in the past few hours than he ever had in his life. Insulting Freeman Canto wasn't the worst thing he'd done by far. No, the worst was forgetting his vow to keep Dani safe. He'd given in to the explosive attraction between them and taken advantage of her.

And now they were back to square one. Just like the day they'd faced off in court. Rivals, even enemies, in every sense of the word. The fragile trust he'd built with her by vowing to keep her safe had been strained by their lovemaking, but now he'd shattered that trust. And it could get Dani killed. Because they were going to have to make a run for it.

He glanced at his watch. Almost six o'clock in the morning. Any minute now the sun would start lightening the sky. That was good and bad. They'd be able to see street signs and landmarks, but it also meant they'd be visible. Reluctantly, he had to admit that he was relieved that they had a weapon. But they needed more than one.

What kind of weapon could he find in a drugstore? Pepper spray or a knife? He hoped like hell the men chasing them would not get close enough that Dani or he would need either of those.

"Harte!" Dani cried.

He rushed toward the front of the store and saw Dani crouched down behind the counter. "What is it?" he hissed.

She gestured at him. "Down! Get down! I saw something moving out there. I think it's them," she whispered urgently. "What are we going to do?"

"You saw them? What did you see?"

"I noticed the three-way flashlight was still on. I reached across the counter to turn it off and I saw dark shapes moving across the street."

The flashlight. It had been on the soft setting, but

still. What a stupid, potentially fatal mistake. From the street, the faint light probably looked like a beacon—the only speck of brightness in the unrelenting gray. He'd led their pursuers straight to them, because he'd let himself get distracted by his desire for Dani.

"At least you got it turned off."

"They must have seen it," she said shakily. "They know where we are."

"Not for certain. And we don't know for sure it's them." He laid his hand on her forearm. "But if it is, it won't take them five minutes to find the back door. Follow me and stay down."

They headed to the back, keeping low. When Harte opened the storeroom door, he saw that part of the roof had blown off and several pieces of rafters and broken plywood boards had fallen. He was glad they hadn't stayed back there.

"Stay here. I'm going to check and see if the coast is clear."

"Take the gun," Dani said, pressing it into his hand.

"No," he protested. "I'm not that good a shot."

"We know they have guns," she countered. "If they're already back here, this gun may be our only chance. If you won't take it, then move. I'll go out and see if the coast is clear."

He took it reluctantly, felt for the safety and thumbed it off. "What size magazine do you have in it?"

"Seventeen shots."

He nodded, then, bracing himself, pushed the door open—or tried to. It felt stuck. What the hell? His pulse hammered. Had they already made it around back and blocked the door? He pushed harder and heard a scraping sound. Through the tiny crack he saw a purple glow. Early dawn. The sky was just bright enough to make the shadows darker.

He slid the door open a bit more, grimacing at the noise made by whatever was blocking it. He was pretty sure he knew what it was. It was big, and had a distinctive hollow sound as it scraped on the ground. It was a plastic trash can—the thick, industrial size.

Finally, he'd managed to move the can enough so he could look around. Then he ducked back in. "I don't see anything. We need to run while we've got the chance."

"Okay," Dani said. "Which direction?"

"Straight back, between the two buildings right behind here. I've got to find the name of that street. Then maybe I can figure out where we are."

She nodded.

"Ready?" he asked.

"Ready."

Dani held her breath as Harte pushed open the door and went through it. She held on to the edge of the door for a couple of seconds. Once it closed, it would lock and they would have no place to hide. They could be picked off like plastic ducks at a carnival.

Harte gestured for her to wait. He quickly surveyed the alley, then moved forward cautiously. "Now," he whispered.

Dani felt a prickling on the nape of her neck. It reminded her of when she was a child and had to go into a dark room. Just like back then, and in the dark Mardi Gras float warehouse, she felt as if monsters were breathing down her neck.

In front of her, Harte's wide shoulders gave her a

measure of confidence. He believed they'd be fine, and she realized *she* believed him. She trusted him.

Ten minutes before, when he'd tossed out that unkind remark about her granddad, she'd painted him with the same brush as his father and grandfather. Everything she'd ever heard about the Delanceys depicted them as ambitious, ruthless and violent. Con Delancey had died violently, and Harte's dad, Robert, was rumored to have as violent a temper as Con.

But every time they were in a dangerous situation, Harte had protected her, so she felt confident and, yes, safe, as she stepped off the concrete stoop into the ankle-deep water that covered the pockmarked and cracked asphalt. Immediately, the cold water seeped through her already damp sneakers to soak her feet. Grimacing, she ignored it and followed him.

Just as they reached the center of the alley and Harte pointed to the left side of the building in front of them, Dani heard a noise. She couldn't tell what direction it had come from.

Harte's head snapped to the right. He'd heard it too.

Before she could even begin to decide how to react, he'd grabbed her upper arm and pulled her forward and down behind a stack of tires.

A loud pop echoed in her ears as she dropped to her knees, her fall partially broken by Harte's body. Her brain clicked into instant-replay mode and she realized that just prior to the pop, she'd heard a zinging sound near her ear—way too near.

"Are you hit?" Harte demanded, his hand still on her arm in a punishing grip.

"No," she panted. "You?"

He gave a negative jerk of his head. "Go!" he said. "Run to that alley and keep running."

"Not without you."

Another bullet whistled past them, then another.

"Dani, go! I'm right behind you."

She met his gaze and saw his steely determination. "I swear!"

With a horrible sense of foreboding, she ran. Behind her, Harte fired three quick shots, covering her.

"Harte, run!" she cried. She reached the building and ducked behind it, pressing her back against the wall. If she angled her head, she could see Harte.

He was inching up from behind the tires to check the shooter's position. When he did, a shot rang out, but to Dani's surprise, it ricocheted off the wall close to her head, sending shards of plaster flying. She ducked back.

"Bastard," she heard Harte growl; then he vaulted up and ran, firing rapidly.

Dani backed up as Harte rounded the corner of the building and slammed back against the wall. "You okay?" he panted.

"Yes."

"I know where we are. Through this alley is Tchoupitoulas Street," he said, pressing the back of his head against the wall and angling around to fire off another couple of rounds, then ducking back. "Did you see the words painted on this building? This is the back of La Maisson Restaurant. La Maisson fronts onto Tchoupitoulas and it's only about three blocks from my great-aunt Claire's house."

Gunshots peppered the corner where he'd just leaned out.

"Go through there. At the end of the alley, go left. Don't look back. I'll catch up." He leaned out and fired again.

Dani ran as fast as she could, her sneakers squeaking on the asphalt. She heard footsteps behind her and prayed it was Harte and not one of the goons who were trying to kill them.

The air was filled with gunfire. Her neck prickled, her scalp burned and her lungs felt strained to the point of bursting, but she didn't dare stop.

She heard a short, pained groan behind her and the footsteps stumbled unevenly. She dared a glance backward in time to see Harte regain his footing. "Harte—" she gasped.

"Don't stop!" he shouted.

Sirens suddenly wailed behind them, and then Harte caught up with her. He passed her, pointing at a blue building. "Through that alley," he shouted, and slowed down. "Go!"

She ran past him and into the alley, but she had no idea which way to turn out the other end, so she slowed to a stop.

The siren changed to short blasts. Maybe they'd caught the men.

Harte ran around the corner a few seconds later. He leaned against the wall, his chest heaving and sweat dripping in rivulets down his face. "Aunt Claire's house is right behind here. White with green shutters. Come on."

Dani frowned at him. Something was wrong. "Harte—?"

"Move! No time to talk." He took off down the alley and she followed.

Then she saw it—the blood on his shirt. "You're bleeding!" she cried.

He didn't acknowledge her. He just kept on across the street, dodging tree limbs and trash and torn roofing shingles, then bounded up a set of stone steps to ornate double doors with stained-glass sidelights and transom.

He turned the handle and pushed against the door, but it didn't open. He hammered on the wood with the gun. "Paul!" he cried in a strained voice. "Open up! It's Harte."

Chapter Fourteen

Harte pounded on the door again. "Paul!"

Before the word was out of his mouth, the door flew open and Harte's cousin on his grandmother Lilibelle's side, Paul Guillame, stood there, surprise and anger on his face. "Harte? What the—? Do you know what time it is?"

Harte pushed past Paul with Dani in tow. Paul's strident voice penetrated the haze in his brain. "Good Lord! You're bleeding! Is that a gun?"

"He's been shot," Dani cried. "We need to get him to a doctor."

Paul sent her a quizzical look, then turned back to Harte. "Who is this? And what's going on?"

Despite the seriousness of the situation, despite the bullet wound that hurt like hell, Harte shook his head at Paul's blithering. But the black at the edges of his vision was growing and he knew he'd pass out if he didn't sit or lie down. "Shut the door, Paul. We've got dangerous men after us."

Paul's black eyes widened, showing white all the way around the irises. "Dangerous men?" He craned his neck around the door, then pushed it closed and locked it with shaking hands. "Why did you come here?"

While Paul was talking, Harte felt Dani's hand on his good arm. She pulled him through the foyer and into the large, too-warm front room. A fire was blazing in the large fireplace. He was already feeling light-headed from loss of blood. The heat made him feel as though he couldn't get a breath. He stopped for a moment, leaning against the faux-finished walls of his aunt Claire's house, trying not to pass out.

"Not in there!" Paul cried, hurrying toward them as Dani guided Harte toward an ornately carved sofa upholstered in ivory. "Take him to the kitchen. Through there." He gestured in a shooing motion. "Put him in one of the kitchen chairs."

Harte let Dani guide him through open French doors that separated the living room and dining room and on past the huge mahogany dining table into the dark kitchen. He sank into a chair with a pained sigh. His pulse was racing and he thought he could feel blood pouring out of his wound. There was a towel on the counter and he got his feet under him and reached for it, but Dani put her hand on his chest and pushed him back into the chair.

"You sit right there," she ordered him. "And give me that!" She took the SIG out of his hand, thumbed the safety on and shoved it into her purse.

She straightened and turned to Paul, who had grabbed a candelabra in his hand—a real silver candelabra sporting eight blazing tapers. "Where's your phone?" she demanded.

Paul set the candelabra in the middle of the wooden kitchen table. "Does it look like we have any of the conveniences?"

Harte squeezed his eyes shut, trying to get rid of the odd haze that was enveloping his brain. He dug out his phone and flipped it open. "Still no bars," he said, hearing the strain in his voice. "And I'm about out of battery too."

Dani had sat down next to him and was trying to pull the material of his shirt away from the bullet wound in his upper chest. "I need a first-aid kit," she commanded.

Paul gestured vaguely with his right hand. "It's up there—in the cabinet above the sink," he said.

"Get it, please," she said archly. "Hot water too, and cloths."

Harte winced as another square inch of material tore away from the dried blood at the edge of his wound. He could barely swallow. He needed fluids. Blinking against the haze that seemed to be growing denser every second, he saw that Paul held a highball glass in his hand. "Hand me that drink," he said.

"This is my Pimm's and lemonade," Paul said, glancing at Harte, then at Dani. "That's the last of the ice." With a shrug, he handed it to Harte.

The glass was about half-full and dripping with condensation. There were three tiny, melting ice cubes floating in it. When Harte wrapped his fingers around it, a chill slid through him. He turned it up and drank. The cool liquid burned his throat as rivulets of water dripped down his chin and neck. He shivered.

By the time he'd drained the glass and wiped his face with his wet hand, Paul had set a plastic box and a couple of kitchen towels on the table and was running water into a bowl. Dani grabbed scissors from the first-aid kit and started cutting Harte's shirtsleeve off. "He needs more water," she said.

Paul picked up the glass and went to the sink.

"Just wrap it—stop the bleeding," Harte protested. "Paul, give me your car keys. We've got to get to a police station."

"Harte, for crying out loud," Paul snapped as he set the glass down in front of Harte. "Don't you think if I could move my car we'd be in Biloxi—or Jackson—right now?"

"Why can't you?" he asked.

"A branch fell right across the driveway."

Harte took a drink of water. "How big is it?"

"It doesn't matter," Dani snapped. "*You* won't be moving it." She dipped a towel in the tepid water, then laid it like a compress over his wound. The little bit of heat felt wonderful and awful at the same time. He groaned.

Dani spoke as she pressed the compress tightly against his shoulder. "So, how big is the branch?" she asked Paul. "Could you and I move it?"

Paul's eyes widened. "Certainly not. It's huge—more of a tree than a branch."

At that instant, Harte saw movement in the dim candlelight of the dining room. "Who's there?" he demanded. Asking the question seemed to use up all his air.

Dani shot up from her chair and pulled the gun out of her purse. He heard the safety click.

"What are you doing?" Paul cried. "Put that gun away. Myron, you might as well come out. Harte, you've met Senator Stamps," he said. "We were having a business discussion over dinner when the storm hit."

Myron Stamps stepped out of the shadows and into the flickering circle of candlelight.

"Stamps?" Harte almost laughed at the irony. "Where's your car?"

Senator Stamps shrugged. "Behind Paul's in his driveway. You wouldn't get very far, even if you had a car," he said. "There are trees and billboards and who knows what other debris all over the streets. It's awful. Our city isn't ready for more destruction and tragedy."

Dani was wrapping gauze around a makeshift compress she'd placed against the wound in Harte's shoulder. She paused and turned to look at the senator.

"Really?" she said archly as she ripped the gauze off the roll. "You're practicing sound bites for a new campaign already?"

"Young woman," Paul said. "I don't know who you are, but you are out of line—"

Dani broke in. "You don't know who I am?"

Harte grunted as she tied the loose ends of the gauze.

She stood. "Well, let me introduce myself. I'm Danielle Canto. I know *he* knows me," she added, indicating Stamps.

Paul turned his gaze full on her for the first time. "Oh," he said. "You're Freeman Canto's granddaughter?" He took a pair of glasses from the pocket of his lounging jacket and peered through them without putting them on. "Oh yes, I recognize you now." He turned to Harte. "I'd heard you were handling Freeman Canto's murder, but, Harte, what has this person gotten you into?"

"Hey!" Dani took two steps to plant her feet directly in front of him. She stared up at him, her chin thrust out. "How dare you! I'm the person who heard my grandfather's murderers threaten him using your name—" She pointed a finger at him, then at Stamps. "And yours."

"Dani!" Harte cried, forcing himself to his feet and grabbing her arm as his cousin's face went deathly pale and Stamps made a growling sound deep in his throat. He knew why she was so upset, and he couldn't blame her, but he had no idea what Paul or Stamps would do, and he was too weak to defend her if her accusations made them violent.

Dani whirled.

Paul cried, "Oh—no, no, no. I had nothing to do with all that. It was all between Yeoman and Myr—"

"Shut up!" Stamps yelled, lunging at Paul.

Paul screeched and hopped aside as Stamps, with too much forward motion to check himself, barreled into Harte, then stumbled over him and plowed into the side of the stainless-steel refrigerator.

Harte fell on his left shoulder. He felt gauze and tape tear. Blood, hot and wet, immediately soaked the bandage. Cold sweat popped out on his forehead and trickled down into his eyes. He blindly struggled up into a crouch, but nausea enveloped him and he wasn't sure he could stay upright. As the red haze of pain faded from his eyes, a black halo started closing in around the edges of his vision.

Just then a deafening crash thundered through the house. Paul yelped as the front door shattered.

Men spilled through the opening, kicking splinters and planks of wood aside. The flickering light from

the candles and the fire reflected redly off the metal
of their guns.

A deep voice shouted, "You! Go around!"

"Dani, watch out!" Harte yelled. He grabbed the
edge of the kitchen table and tried to lift it. Dani immediately saw what he was doing and ran to help him. The
two of them upended the table with a bang. He crouched
behind it. Dani threw herself down beside him.

"What's going on?" Paul cried from behind the corner wall that opened onto the dining room. "Do something!"

Out of the corner of his eye, Harte saw Stamps open
the refrigerator door and hide behind it. Beside Harte,
Dani pulled out her gun.

"Give it to me," he said.

Dani gave Harte a sidelong glance. He was pale
and his lips were pinched and white at the corners. He
looked as if he would pass out any second. "Not a
chance," she snapped. "You're wounded. Switch sides
with me."

"Dani—"

"Do it!" she hissed, and crawled behind him. "Move,
Harte! I mean it. And stay down."

She saw the irritation and resignation in his eyes
as he acquiesced. It hurt him that she wouldn't let him
protect her, she knew, but she didn't have time to argue
or persuade. He was wounded and too weak to handle
the gun, and she had to be able to aim and shoot with
her right hand.

She clicked off the safety and sat up and held her
gun in her right hand, steadied by her left. Carefully,
she eased her head up enough to get a glimpse of the

men. She needed to see their positions and, if possible, get a look at their armament.

There were two of them casting about blindly, working to get their bearings in the dark living room after being outside in the brightness of the rising sun. The one on the left was the brute who'd grabbed her. She could tell by his size and the tan raincoat. She aimed low and fired. He yelped and went down.

She ducked back behind the table.

"Paul!" Harte yelled. "Get out the back and go for help!"

"What?" Paul's mouth fell open. "Me?"

"Hurry!" Dani snapped. "One of them is going around the back."

"I can't!" Paul gasped.

"Watch out," Dani cried. "Duck!"

Sure enough, a firestorm of bullets peppered the walls, the tabletop and the stainless-steel refrigerator.

Paul cowered farther into the corner. With a moue of disgust for the man, she popped up again and fired off four quick bursts.

"Damn," she whispered. She could tell from the weight of the weapon that the magazine was almost empty. Why hadn't she counted how many times Harte had fired it? She slung her purse off over her head. "Get my other clip!" she told Harte.

She fired again, and again the men responded with a burst of pistol fire. As the noise from the explosions faded, she thought she heard police sirens. She exchanged a quick glance with Harte.

He handed her the fresh clip. When she took it, she felt the sticky slickness of blood on it.

Harte's blood. Her pulse pounded in her throat as she ejected the nearly empty magazine and inserted the new one, then braced herself to rise and fire again. If she didn't keep up a barrage of bullets, the men would rush them and kill them. She'd hit the brute who'd grabbed her the night before, but she wasn't sure she'd hurt him.

She glanced behind her. Paul was still tucked into the corner and Stamps was still behind the refrigerator door. She didn't see a back door. She'd just have to deal with the third guy when he showed up.

As she turned back to shoot another round at the men in front of them, a gun fired behind her. She jerked in surprise. Before she could distinguish where exactly the shot had come from, Paul let out a tortured cry and fell to the floor.

She turned her head, preparing to whirl and take out the shooter, but Harte yelled, "Got him!"

"No! Harte!" she cried, but it was too late. He had vaulted up. She heard a thud and two grunts and knew he'd connected with the shooter.

Don't you dare get killed after all we've been through, she thought desperately as one of the men in front of them angled around the French doors and fired directly at her. She ducked behind the table, heard the bullet zing past her ear, then rose and shot several rounds at the open doors.

A startled cry told her that one of her bullets had found its mark. Suddenly, the staccato yelp of police sirens sounded, deafeningly loud, and a bullhorn roared.

They heard a voice, accompanied by more short bursts of the siren. "Police! Drop your weapons! Drop them! Now!"

Dani rose slowly, her gun at the ready, and pointed toward the two men. The man in the tan raincoat, the goon who had grabbed her in the alley, was on his knees. He dropped his weapon and leaned a hand against the wall. His pant leg was soaked with blood.

The second man stood, feet splayed apart, his gun aimed directly at her. Blood dripped from his left hand. She straightened, her barrel pointed right at the space between his eyes.

"Drop it," she growled, just as two uniformed policemen appeared at the front door.

"Drop it!" they shouted in unison. "Now!" One officer advanced as the other continued to shout.

"Drop it and hit the floor," the advancing officer yelled. "Do it or I'll shoot."

The first officer stepped past the brute and kicked his gun at least four feet across the living room floor. He stopped just out of arm's reach of the man who was still aiming at Dani. "Drop it or you're a dead man," he said.

The shooter jerked, startled that the officer was so close to him. He let the gun dangle by the handle from his hand. The officer grabbed his arm. The gun hit the floor and the officer slammed the man against the wall and cuffed him.

Dani gasped for air. Had she been holding her breath or had fear sucked all the oxygen from her lungs?

At that instant, a tall man with blazing blue eyes and an NOPD badge pinned to the waistband of his jeans stepped into the room, breathing hard. "Where's Harte?" he demanded.

Dani was wondering the same thing. She turned

around and what she saw shocked her. Harte was on the floor, holding someone in a half nelson. That someone was grunting and snuffling like a pig headed to slaughter. To her surprise, she realized it was Myron Stamps.

"Lucas," Harte wheezed as he let go of Stamps. His pale face and labored breathing told her there was something terribly wrong.

The detective stepped past Paul, who was writhing on the floor whimpering, and grabbed hold of Stamps's collar.

"Gun!" Harte rasped.

The detective dropped the man like a hot potato and put his foot on his neck. "Don't move," he barked. Bending, he wrenched the gun from Stamps's hand.

As he cuffed the senator, he glanced at Harte. "How you doing, kid?" he said.

"He's shot," Dani cried. "He's bleeding." She crawled toward him on her knees.

From the corner of the kitchen came a whining voice. "Lucas, help me. I'm shot too," Paul squealed. "I think it's serious."

Lucas. The detective was Harte's older brother. "How'd you find us?" she asked.

Lucas knelt next to Harte. "Got your messages and went to the drugstore. Then I heard gunshots. I called for the closest police cruiser."

"Thank goodness you got here," Dani said as more sirens filled the air.

Lucas jerked his head in the direction of the sound. "That's the EMTs," he said shortly. "I was afraid they wouldn't be able to get through. Kid? How'd you get yourself shot?"

"I'm okay," Harte said weakly, lifting his head. "Just my shoulder."

Dani crawled over to him and cradled his head. "It's not his shoulder. It's his chest. See?" She showed Lucas the bandage. "He's lost so much blood."

Harte shook his head. Then it hit her. Lucas was his oldest brother. He was the one Harte had told her gave him such a hard time for becoming a prosecutor instead of a cop. Harte didn't want to look weak in front of him.

No danger of that, she thought. He'd taken care of her, saved her more times than she could count and fought off the men who were trying to capture her or, worse, kill her. Even after taking a bullet in the chest, he'd still fought to keep her safe.

She looked up at Lucas, who met her gaze. She saw in his expressive face that he was thinking the same thing. Then he leaned over his younger brother. "Somebody get those EMTs in here now! My brother's been shot."

Harte lifted his head. "Paul's wounded," he gasped, "and Dani took down at least one of the shooters."

"Yeah," Lucas said, frowning. Then he added louder, "Get the damned EMTs!"

Chapter Fifteen

Dani wanted to go to the hospital with Harte, but the police had a different idea. After she was examined and released by the EMTs, she was taken to the police station, where she spent all the rest of the morning and a large part of the afternoon being questioned and writing out and signing her statement. Someone had found her a clean set of scrubs and a blanket to wrap up in, but she still had on her wet sneakers.

She glanced at the clock over the door for what had to be the two hundredth time. It had been over an hour since anyone had even peeked in to see if the room was free. Had they forgotten about her?

She picked up the foam cup that held what might have passed for coffee two hours ago, but was now sludge. One whiff and she set it down and pushed it as far away as she could.

At that instant the doorknob turned. It was Lucas. He had her purse in tow. "I gotta say this is the biggest purse I've ever seen."

"Thank God you're here," Dani said. "I can go now, right? I need to see Harte. How is he?"

"He'll be fine," Lucas said. "I've got an officer waiting to drive you to a hotel."

"You mean to my house."

"No," he said evenly. "I mean to the hotel. You're still under an order of protection until the trial is over, and it's been delayed."

"Delayed?" She wanted to cry. She was exhausted and filthy and sleepy and hungry. The pallid vending-machine ham sandwich and watery soda she'd had who knew how many hours ago were long gone.

Lucas nodded. "The D.A. is assigning another prosecutor to handle the trial, and he or she will need time to get up to speed."

"Why another prosecutor? You told me Harte was going to be fine." She grabbed Lucas's arm. "Please. Is he okay?"

Lucas narrowed his eyes. "He *is* going to be fine. They're giving him blood. As soon as they can, they'll get him into surgery. Apparently, the bullet hit the top of his left lung."

"Oh no," she said. That was why he'd sounded wheezy, why he'd struggled so much to take a breath. "But they can get it out. Just go in and—" she put her thumb and forefinger together "—pluck it out. Right?"

Lucas looked somber. "They think so. It's pretty close to his heart."

"Close to—?" Her pulse pounded in her throat. "Have you seen him? Talked to him?"

"They've got him sedated. They don't want that bullet to move."

"Oh," she moaned, sinking into a chair. She pressed her palm against her chest. Her heart felt as though it was going to burst wide open, it was hurting that much. "I didn't know how bad he was hurt."

"Hey," Lucas said, rubbing his forehead. "The doctors know what they're doing."

His tone didn't match his reassuring words. She looked up at him. He looked exhausted. His hair was furrowed and sticking up as if he'd run his fingers through it multiple times. He had a smudge of dirt on his cheek and a scrape on the knuckles of his left hand. But what frightened Dani was the look on his face. His brow was furrowed and his mouth was grim.

"You're worried," she said.

He met her gaze. His mouth curved upward slightly, in a duplicate of Harte's crooked smile. The sight of it made her heart ache.

"I am," he said, "but Harte is tough and stubborn. A little thing like a bullet won't stop him. It wouldn't dare."

Dani smiled back at him, even though her eyes were burning. "You're right about that. He is pretty stubborn," she said.

"He comes by that naturally."

She studied him for a brief moment. "You and he don't look much alike. I mean obviously you do, but—"

"That's because he took after the French side of the family, and I got the Irish genes." As he spoke, he opened the interrogation room door for her, then closed it behind them. A young uniformed officer was waiting outside the room.

"Dani Canto, this is Officer Roebuck. He'll take you to the hotel."

The officer nodded. She acknowledged him with a brief nod of her head. "Officer, will you be my day-shift babysitter?"

"No," Lucas said. "You won't have a guard during the day. Just at night."

"So I'm in less danger than I was?" Dani shook her head. "How exactly does that work?"

"The men who chased you are in custody, for one thing."

Dani pushed her tangled hair back from her face. "Good," she said tiredly. "So, Officer Roebuck, shall we go?"

"Yes, ma'am," Roebuck said. "The car's out front." He stood back to let her precede him.

Dani turned back to Lucas. "Can we swing by the hospital to see Harte?"

Lucas shook his head.

"Lucas—Detective, I need to see him." She bit her lip, doing her best to look him in the eye, to appear strong and capable, not small and scared that she might never see Harte again.

"I told you, he's sedated. They're not letting anybody see him right now." Lucas looked past her at Roebuck and nodded.

"Ma'am?" Roebuck said. "We need to get going."

Dani couldn't tear her gaze away from Lucas. "Please don't lie to me," she said. "It's too important."

He glanced at Officer Roebuck and nodded toward the door. The officer walked toward the exit door to wait. Once he was out of hearing, Lucas stepped close to her.

"Harte is unconscious. They're taking him to surgery any minute now. It's going to be touch-and-go. If the bullet shifts, it could go into his heart. My parents are there with my sister, waiting."

Dani pressed her lips together, working to stay calm. Her heart was threatening to burst again. She could barely breathe, her throat was so tight. But she heard Lucas loud and clear.

Harte is in critical condition. He needs his family.

"I understand," she said hoarsely, then grabbed his shirtsleeve. "Please, when you can, have someone call me?"

"Okay," he said gently. "As soon as I can." He turned and walked toward another detective who was obviously waiting to talk to him. She saw him rub the back of his neck as he spoke to the other man.

Dani squeezed her eyes shut. She couldn't wipe away the vision of Harte's soft, dark gaze as he'd lowered his head to kiss her, or the pinched pallor of his face as he'd looked up at his big brother and tried to pretend he wasn't bleeding to death.

They'd been on the run together for less than twelve hours. But she didn't think she could live if he died.

ETHAN DELANCEY DIDN'T like hospitals. People died there. He paced back and forth between the window and the door of the private room where his youngest brother lay—too quiet, too pale, too still.

He stopped and looked at Harte for what must have been the twentieth time. How the hell had this happened? He and Lucas and Travis were the ones who flirted with danger. It was cops and soldiers who took their lives in their hands, who went out there day after day to try to make the world a safer place. They understood the risk. They dealt with it.

Harte hadn't followed in his brothers' footsteps. He'd

taken a different path—the path of their dad and their notorious grandfather. He was a *lawyer*. Lawyers didn't get shot.

Ethan walked over to the bed. He felt so damn helpless. Reaching out, he straightened the tubes that fed oxygen through Harte's nostrils. Then he brushed thick dark hair off his brother's forehead.

Behind him, he heard the room door open. He turned. It was Lucas. "Hey," he said.

"How is he?" Lucas asked, closing the door and coming up beside Ethan.

Ethan shook his head. "No change. Didn't the doctor say he'd be awake by now? It's been almost twenty-four hours since the surgery."

Lucas nodded. "The surgeon said they wanted him to sleep as much as possible. That's why they kept him in the ICU for twelve hours."

Ethan rubbed his temples and flopped down in a hard vinyl chair near the bed. Lucas leaned against the wall near the window. He crossed his arms.

"You look pretty scruffy," Ethan observed. "What's the latest?"

Lucas sighed and rubbed his jaw, his palm scraping like sandpaper across the stubble. "When did I talk to you last?"

"Yesterday, after you got Dani to the hotel."

"You mean Saturday."

"No, I mean yesterday. You'd talked to Paul, but you said Stamps had lawyered up."

"Right. After I got Paul's statement that it was Stamps who'd shot him, I talked to Stamps's lawyer. That was a massive waste of time. She claimed he was sedated after the traumatic events and couldn't be questioned."

Ethan laughed. "Seriously?"

"I'm thinking she's setting him up for an insanity defense."

"What about Paul?"

"I asked her what their response to his accusation would be, and she wouldn't talk about it." Lucas shook his head. "I'm trying to get a court order to test for gunshot residue—"

"Talk about a waste of time," Ethan put in.

"I know. Stamps, sedated or not, will have hosed himself down by then."

"What do you think about Paul saying Stamps shot him?"

"That's odd too. Paul was nearly hysterical at the scene, screaming that Stamps had tried to kill him. I've got several witnesses that heard him. But later, after he was discharged from the emergency room, he said it was an accident. Said Stamps was firing wildly." Lucas sat on the small couch under the window and leaned forward, elbows on knees.

"I thought you told me—"

"That Stamps only fired one shot?" He nodded. "That's right. I did."

"And you've got the gun," Ethan said, glancing over at Harte's pale face. "A senior senator shooting people, our distant cousin somehow involved—what the hell did the kid dig up?"

"Well, he was right about one thing. Ernest Yeoman is in it up to his neck. And he's not going to walk this time."

"The D.A.'s probably over the moon. So the no-necks Dani shot are Yeoman's men?"

Lucas nodded smugly. "They weren't carrying any ID, but here's a shocker. They were both in the system."

"Yeah? Who were they?"

"Couple of small-time crooks. You know how it goes." Lucas pulled a small notebook out of his pocket. He flipped a few pages. "One of them was Chester Kirkle, the guy who left the fingerprint on Canto's office door the night he was killed," he said.

"Right. Harte was hoping to cut a deal with him. I thought he was remanded."

"Somehow, this past week, he got himself a decent lawyer and made bail. No information where he got the money." Lucas rubbed the back of his neck.

"Do you think he's still willing to cut the deal?"

"Oh yeah. I dangled aggravated assault three over his head."

That surprised Ethan. "A. A. Three? Can you make that stick?"

"Hell yeah," Lucas said, gesturing at Harte. "The D.A. authorized it. They wounded a public official with a deadly weapon, threatened a second and were fleeing from law enforcement. And one or more of them may have been involved in the murder of Freeman Canto."

Ethan smiled. That was what made Lucas one of the best detectives on the force. Better even than Dixon Lloyd, Ethan's partner. He gave Lucas a tip of an imaginary hat. "Good job. What'd they cough up?"

"Get this. Kirkle's playing the deal card. Says he had Harte's promise of a deal if he talked, so now he's singing about Yeoman. He claims Yeoman sent them to *persuade* Canto to reverse his position on tariffs and one of the goons got too rough."

"What do you think?"

"I'm inclined to believe him. If he rolls on Yeoman, the D.A. and a lot of other people will be ecstatic."

Ethan looked at Harte again. "One of them shot Harte," he said, hearing the catch in his voice.

Lucas heard it too, because he sent him a sharp glance, then stood and walked over to the bed. He touched Harte's hand where the IV tubing snaked out from a white bandage with a tiny spot of blood on it. "I know," he said. "I'd like to bury both of them, but they're punks. Nobodies. We need to get Yeoman if we can."

Ethan didn't say anything. He and Lucas stared at their baby brother for a moment. Finally, Lucas patted Harte's hand and turned toward the door. "I've got to go. I'm going to run home and shower, then—"

"Good," Ethan interrupted. "It's about time."

Lucas shot him a warning look. "Then I'm heading over to Impound. The vehicle is a Lincoln Town Car and it's totaled."

"They used it to break down a freight door at that warehouse where Harte and Dani were hiding, right?"

Lucas nodded.

Ethan shook his head. "I can't wait for Harte to tell us how he managed to keep away from them all night long."

"I know. So the crime scene guys collected paint and glass fragments from the vehicle that rammed the warehouse freight door and ran them. They matched the glass and paint the car left at the scene at Dani's house."

"They used the same car? That's amazing."

"You want amazing, guess who owns the car."

"Not Yeoman—" Ethan said.

"It's registered to the general manager of the Hasty Mart Corporation."

Ethan was stunned. "Are you kidding me? Yeoman's got to be smarter than that. Otherwise, how has he managed to stay out of jail all this time?"

"I don't know," Lucas said, rubbing a hand down his face. "Maybe it was his henchmen who were too dumb to change vehicles. All I can say is thank God for stupid crooks."

Ethan laughed. "Way to go. That plus Dani's testimony should nail the SOB."

"It should." Lucas sighed. He looked at his watch. "What are you doing the rest of the afternoon? Is Mom coming over?"

"She said she might be here around six, after she fixes dinner for Dad." Ethan stood and stretched. "I think I'll stay here until she gets here. I've got a feeling the kid might wake up soon."

"All right, E. Call me if he does, okay? And try to get some rest."

Ethan nodded and held out his hand. Lucas took it and the two shared a quick, awkward man-hug.

Once Lucas was gone, Ethan thought about turning on the TV, but he wasn't in the mood for seven million channels and nothing on. So he yawned, then sat back and closed his eyes.

Rest sounded good. He had been up all night sitting with Harte, and was exhausted. Lucas, on the other hand, had worked the crime scene, and was about to head back out for a third shift with no rest.

Lucas had always been a superhero in Ethan's eyes.

Chapter Sixteen

Harte's whole body hurt worse with every move he made. They'd been running for so long that he and Dani were both exhausted. He glanced back to check on Dani, but suddenly, darkness enveloped everything.

"Dani?" he cried, but she didn't answer. "Dani, answer me."

Nothing.

"Dani!" She was gone. His biggest fear had come to pass. He'd failed to keep her safe.

"Hey, kid? Wake up."

Harte heard someone. Was it Dani? God, he hoped so. But the voice sounded far away. Indistinct.

"Harte? Are you trying to wake up?"

The voice beckoned him. But the closer he got to it, the more he hurt. Who was trying to keep him from finding Dani?

"Leave me alone. I've got to find Dani."

"Harte, it's Ethan. Talk to me, kid."

Ethan? Harte felt as though the bottom had dropped out from under him. He opened his eyes to slits, which made his head hurt. Everything was an ugly, dull blue color.

"Ethan?" he rasped as his brain slowly began to process what his senses were taking in. A small TV on a stand was suspended from the ceiling in front of him. Under it, a whiteboard held a sign in big letters that read Today is_____. There was nothing written in the blank. His nostrils burned with the mingled smells of disinfectant and rubbing alcohol, and he could hear a continuous hiss-pop, hiss-pop.

From somewhere, a different voice spoke. "Everything all right? Does Mr. Delancey need ice water or towels?"

"No, thanks."

Then everything coalesced in his brain. His eyes flew open wide. "Oh no," he moaned. "Not the hospital."

His brother Ethan's face moved into his field of vision. "Can't understand a word you're saying," he said, smiling. "Want some water?"

Water sounded wonderful. Harte licked his lips, or tried to. They were so dry they barely moved.

Ethan held a big cup and guided the plastic straw into Harte's mouth. When the first splash of cold water hit his tongue, the chill shot all the way through him. He shuddered, then greedily sucked up more.

"Whoa," Ethan said, taking the cup away. "The nurse said you could have a *little*."

His lips still felt parched, but inside, he was feeling much better. He tried to push himself upright, but that turned out to be a bad idea.

"Ahhh!" he growled, and collapsed back into the soft bedclothes. He muttered a few choice curses, which actually seemed to help.

"Nice," Ethan said, pulling a chair up beside the bed. "Good thing Mom's not here."

Harte growled again. "Am I in a hospital?" he asked, trying his best to control his thick tongue.

"Okay. What I think I heard is *hospital*. So yes, you're in the hospital."

Harte's eyes were still burning, so he closed them. "What am I doing here?"

"Good. You're getting better. You and Dani Canto were attacked at the B-and-B, so you ran and hid all night through that mother of a storm. Somewhere in there you got shot. Then you ended up at Paul's house with the bad guys on your tail. Paul took a bullet and a couple of your pursuers were shot. The cavalry arrived and saved the day. You had surgery and voilà, here you are."

"Not quite all that happened," Harte muttered between gritted teeth. "Where's Dani? Is she all right?"

Ethan nodded, his expression turning more serious. "She's fine. The EMTs examined her at the scene and released her. You, on the other hand, have a great big surgery to recuperate from. By the way, the nurse also told me you'd be too drowsy to make sense." Ethan's frown faded. "I see she was right about that."

"I'm fine," Harte muttered. The nurse was correct. He could barely hold his eyes open and he had to concentrate like mad to keep up with what Ethan was saying. But there was no way he was going to let his older brother know that.

"Fine," he repeated, looking out the window. He couldn't see anything but sky and the top of a portion of the New Orleans skyline. He didn't even try to figure out what direction the window faced. "What time is it?"

"Six-twenty."

He stared at his brother, then blinked and gave his head a shake. "Six-twenty?"

Ethan's mouth turned up. "Twenty minutes after six."

"P.m.?" He reached up to rub his forehead, where the groggy haze seemed centered, and discovered that his hand had an IV hooked up to it. He growled.

"Here," Ethan said, picking up the cup again. "Drink some more water before you fall asleep."

This time, he reached for the cup, but the IV tubing that was inserted in his hand got caught in the bedclothes. Ethan untangled it and handed him the cup.

Harte sipped slowly. His stomach didn't feel great, but the water—a little water—helped. "Thanks," he said.

Ethan took the cup from his hand and set it down on the rolling table. "You're going to fall asleep and spill that all over yourself."

"Six-twenty," Harte said thoughtfully. "I've been here all day? When can we leave?"

Ethan shook his head indulgently. "Not so fast, kid. You haven't been here all day. You've been here since Saturday morning. Today's Sunday."

Harte stared at him in horror. "Sunday? What happened to Saturday?"

"You spent a lot of Saturday unconscious. They sedated you so they could give you blood. Then they took you into surgery. The doctor said you wouldn't remember anything, and I guess he's right."

"What about—the—trial?" Harte was having a lot of trouble staying awake.

"The trial's been set to start Thursday."

"Okay. I can be—ready by Thursday."

Ethan laughed. "Oh, trust me, kid. You will not be ready by Thursday. The D.A. has got another prosecutor working twenty-four-seven to get up to speed."

"What?" Harte tried to sit up, but couldn't. "My case!"

"Hey," Ethan said, patting the sheet near Harte's hand. "You don't need to worry about the trial. You just need to rest and get better." He stood. "I'm going to go tell the nurses that you're awake, then I'll head out. Mom will probably be over later to see you."

"Wait," Harte said. "Where's Dani? She been here?"

"Nope. She's in protective custody, remember? She's not allowed to go anywhere."

"I want to see her. Make sure she's all right." Harte tried to sit up. He put most of his weight on his right arm. With a lot of effort and a lot of pain, he managed to scoot a little more upright in the bed.

"Hang on," Ethan said with an exaggerated sigh. "You're going to rip out all of the doctor's pretty stitching." He leaned over and pressed a button on the console that hung from the bed rail. The head of the bed rose, pushing Harte into a more upright, seated position.

"Thanks," he said. "I need to see Dani."

"She's just fine. If you're going to be stubborn, I'll call the head nurse. I think she was a drill sergeant."

"Call her."

"Harte, you haven't seen this nurse—at least not that you remember."

As if she were summoned by Ethan's threat, the door to Harte's room opened and a large, imposing woman in white slacks and an incongruous lavender scrub shirt with pink puppies and kittens on it entered. She had an IV bag in her sizeable hands.

"Mr. Delancey, you're awake." The nurse leveled a glare at Ethan, then the badge pinned to his jacket pocket. "And *you* are still here." Stepping around the bed and past Ethan, she replaced the nearly empty IV bag with the new one and adjusted the flow.

Then she inspected the IV cannula in Harte's hand, walked around to the other side of the bed and looked at the large bandage that covered from just beneath the collarbone to his upper abdomen. Then she lifted her head and peered through the lower half of her glasses at the LED screen of the heart monitor mounted above the bed.

"How are you feeling?" she asked, her voice gentler than her physical presence might suggest. "Having any pain?"

He gave a halfhearted right-shoulder shrug. "I'm okay," he said.

She looked up at Ethan. "I'm going to give him a dose of morphine. I'd suggest you go interrogate somebody who's up and around." When she glanced back at Harte, he saw a fleeting glint of amusement in her eyes. "My patient here needs to rest."

"Yes, ma'am," Ethan said, rolling his eyes in Harte's direction. "I'll be back later, kid." He stood, leaned over and planted a kiss on the top of Harte's head, sent a quelling look at the nurse when she grinned at his sentimental gesture and left.

"There you go," the nurse said as she pressed a button on the IV flow meter of a second bag that was piggybacked into the first. "A nice little boost of morphine."

"Not too much," Harte murmured. He could already feel the drug doing its job.

"You aren't getting too much. You're getting just the right amount. You'd better sleep while you can. Tomorrow morning, your nurse is going to make you get up and walk."

"How soon can I get out of here?" he asked.

"I'll let you and the doctor talk about that." She nodded toward the door. "So, I suppose that was your brother? Nice guy. You and he must be close. You look like twins."

"He wishes he was as good-looking as me," Harte muttered, unable to keep his eyes open any longer. He heard the nurse chuckle as she went out of the room.

Chapter Seventeen

Dani sat in the courtroom, waiting for the judge and jury to enter. The jury had reported about an hour ago that they had reached a verdict.

The judge entered and, in doing so, stopped the idle chatter in the courtroom. He stepped up behind the bench and spoke to the prosecution's attorneys and then to the defense's, ensuring that they were ready to proceed.

"Bailiff, you may bring in the jury," the judge said.

"Your Honor?" asked Natalie Shallowford, the attorney the D.A. had assigned to take over for Harte. "May I approach?"

The judge nodded and so she did so, along with Felix Drury, the defense attorney. After a short, quiet conversation, the judge nodded and the two attorneys returned to their seats.

Dani heard the door to the courtroom open and saw the judge nod to whoever had come in. Most of the observers turned around, then started murmuring.

The judge pounded his gavel. "Quiet!" he demanded. "Welcome back, Mr. Delancey."

Dani's heart pounded. She half turned, but because she was just behind the prosecution's table, she couldn't see at first. Then she heard footsteps and a slight metallic creaking sound.

Natalie Shallowford opened the gate and a court officer wheeled Harte Delancey, in a wheelchair, through the gate and over to the prosecution's table.

Dani looked at him for the first time since he'd been taken away by ambulance almost a week ago. He was pale and drawn, and his eyes had circles under them. His arm was in a dark blue sling. Her heart squeezed with compassion. He'd come very close to dying, she knew. Lucas had told her it had been a long surgery to remove the bullet that had clipped the upper edge of his lung, near his heart.

Once the bullet was out, Lucas had told her, everything was fine and he would recover quickly. But he didn't look recovered yet. She wasn't sure why Lucas had let him come to court. It would be exhausting for him.

The jury came in and the judge quickly ran through their duties and responsibilities. Then, finally, he asked for the verdict.

The foreman stood. "As to count one, murder in the first degree, we the jury find the defendant, Ernest W. Yeoman—not guilty."

Dani's heart sank. *Not guilty.* She'd expected it, but the two words still cut like a knife.

Ernest Yeoman, standing behind the defense table, pumped a fist in the air. Felix Drury, his powerhouse attorney, laid a subtle hand on his arm. Yeoman straightened as the foreman continued.

"As to the second count, conspiracy to commit murder—"

Dani braced herself. Based on the way the trial had gone, she figured aggravated assault was the best they could hope for.

"We the jury find the defendant, Ernest W. Yeoman…" The foreman paused. "Guilty."

The courtroom was suddenly abuzz with whisperings, mumblings and a few shouts, gasps and cheers.

The judge banged his gavel and the din quieted as the foreman went on to read guilty verdicts for conspiracy to commit aggravated assault on two public officials and conspiracy to kidnap a public official.

It took Dani a split second to process everything the foreman had said. They'd done it. Yeoman was going to prison. Based on the verdicts, it sounded as though he'd be in prison for a very long time.

She felt light-headed. Then she realized that quite a bit of the noise in the courtroom was coming from the defendant's table.

Yeoman was up in his attorney's face. "What the hell?" he shouted. "You incompetent son of—"

The judge pounded his gavel. "Silence!" he snapped. "Silence. Guards!"

The guards were already on Yeoman. They grabbed him and cuffed him. All the while Yeoman continued to curse Drury.

Felix Drury, on the other hand, had abandoned his attempt to quiet his client. "Your Honor! Your Honor! May I approach the bench?" he shouted over his client's curses and the gallery's whispers and mumblings.

The judge was ignoring Yeoman. He looked at Drury over his glasses. "No, you may not." He banged the gavel again and shouted, "This court is adjourned." He thanked the jurors, then stood and left the courtroom.

Natalie Shallowford turned to Dani. She smiled and held her arms out.

Dani came around through the gate and hugged her. "Great job," she said. "Thank you so much."

"Oh, honey, Harte had all the paperwork in order. And your testimony, not only about the night of your grandfather's death, but your ordeal the night of the storm, cinched it."

"Oh," she said, gripping the bar that divided the courtroom from the visitors' gallery. She covered her mouth with her hand.

"Dani, are you okay?"

She nodded. "I am. For the first time since the night Granddad died, I'm okay." She blinked away the burning behind her eyelids. "He's really going to prison."

Natalie squeezed her shoulder. "I'm so glad. And don't forget, the three men who attacked your grandfather are going to prison too, on plea agreements."

Dani nodded. "Thank you again, Natalie."

Natalie waved a hand, then turned to pick up the piles of papers and cram them into her briefcase.

Dani turned toward Harte. Her knees felt weak and she had to grasp the back of a chair to steady herself. She hadn't seen him since the EMTs had put him in the ambulance at Paul Guillame's house. She'd been locked up in that damned hotel room while he'd lain in the hospital fighting for his life.

He looked so awful. Pale and thin and—almost breakable. And it was her fault. He'd protected her and doing so had nearly killed him.

He smiled the crooked smile that made her heart hurt. Somehow, she managed to walk up to him, even though her knees still felt boneless.

"What are you doing here?" she asked. "Your surgery was only four days ago." A movement to Harte's left caught her eye. It was Lucas, approaching. She turned an accusing gaze on him. "He shouldn't be here," she snapped.

"Yeah? Try telling him that," Lucas shot back. "I'll be outside." He put his hand on Harte's shoulder. "Try not to undo all the work the surgeon did, okay, kid?"

Harte gave him a brief nod. "I wanted to be here," he said. His voice sounded hollow. "So, Natalie did a great job. Congratulations. Yeoman's going to prison."

"She said you did all the work," she responded.

He shrugged, then winced. "So you can go home now. No more 'incarceration.'"

"Yeah. I'm not even sure I believe Yeoman's really going to prison yet. It's a lot to process." She gestured toward Harte's arm. "So how—how are you doing?" she asked, working to keep her tone light.

An odd expression flickered across his face. "I'm doing okay. Mom's taking care of me."

She noticed his hand was white-knuckled on the chair arm. "I'm glad," she said. "Let her spoil you."

"I don't have much of a choice right now."

She nodded, looking at his hand, wanting so badly to touch it. "Lucas told me that the surgery was touch-and-go—" Her voice gave out. She cleared her throat. "I mean—"

He inclined his head. "It was, although I didn't know it until it was all over. The first thing I remember after they put me in the ambulance is waking up in the hospital. Ethan was there, looking exhausted and worried."

"Everybody was worried about you."

The crooked smile played about his mouth again. But the smile didn't reach his eyes. "I know," he said. "A lot of people came by—and called."

Dani winced. "I wanted to call. I asked Lucas about you, but he said your family was there. And that's who you needed. You needed to rest and get better with your parents and your brothers around you." The more she said, the lamer her excuses sounded. But what was she supposed to say?

Get well soon? Thanks for keeping me alive and for taking a bullet for me? By the way, did the mind-blowing sex mean anything to you?

She'd been his star witness. He'd taken care of her, protected her, made sure the bad guys didn't kill her. He'd have been here in the prosecutor's chair, fighting for justice for her granddad, if he'd been able. But it was over now. He'd done what he had to do. He'd go back to being a prosecutor and a Delancey, and she'd go back to being a public defender.

"Dani, it's okay. I understand. We Delanceys can be intimidating."

She shook her head. "You almost died. You needed your family. Besides, I was in good hands with Natalie. She's a good prosecutor. Not as good as you, I didn't mean that. I mean, you're both good."

Harte grimaced at Dani's words and her tone.

She continued, talking too rapidly. "So the judge didn't talk about sentencing. When do you think it will be?" Her hands twisted in her lap.

He put his hand over hers to still them. "Dani, stop."

She looked up, a faint panic showing in her eyes. He had no idea if she was afraid he was going to say something intimate, or afraid he wasn't.

"Tell me what's the matter?" he asked warily.

Her hand squeezed his. She closed her eyes. "I—I'm not sure. I know Yeoman's going to prison. I know you're going to be okay. I should be happy to get back to my normal life."

She straightened and looked at him, uttering a short laugh. "I thought I was afraid of storms. But that was a childish phobia. When I saw you lying on the floor bleeding, when I thought we were going to be killed and I couldn't do anything—I realized that is real fear. Fear of how easily all this—" She waved a hand. "Our lives can be cut short. That's a fear I'm not sure will ever go away."

Harte's throat tightened. The pain of his wound didn't hurt nearly as much as seeing her like this. She had learned a horrible lesson, and it had destroyed her last childish belief—that fear was all about oneself, and there was always a stronger person who could wipe it away.

"I know," he said. "When I felt the bullet hit me, I was sure that was it. I was dead."

She made a strangled sound.

"But that didn't scare me nearly as much as the thought that I'd be leaving you alone." He closed his eyes. "I've never been that afraid before."

"You thought of me?" she said. Her tone was reverent.

"Of course I did. If I could, I'd make sure you never had to feel afraid again." He squeezed her hand.

"There's nothing I'd like better," she murmured.

"Do you mean that?" His voice was subdued. He pulled her hand toward him and pressed her fingers against his lips.

She swallowed, her gaze on his lips against her knuckles. Then she looked at him. "Except maybe to make sure you're always safe."

He smiled at her. To his surprise, her eyes immediately welled up with tears. She swiped at them as if they were flies.

"I swear to you I never cry," she said, sniffling.

"Yeah, right," he said as he leaned toward her, pulling on her hand. She sat forward and kissed him gently on the lips.

He wanted more, wanted to pull her to him and kiss her hard and long. He wanted to do more than kiss her, but every time he moved, his bound shoulder seized in pain, reminding him of how close that bullet had been to his heart.

Dani pulled her head back and looked at him. "So, what now?" she asked.

"What now?" He smiled at her. "I'd like to pick you up and carry you off to my bed. But I don't think that's going to happen for a while." He shifted in the chair and winced. "The best I can offer you right now is the opportunity to lie beside me and watch me sleep, occasionally fetch me a glass of water and help me get to my feet when I need to."

"That sounds wonderful, as long as you promise to slay dragons for me."

"That, my lady, is what I live for."

* * * * *

A sneaky peek at next month...

INTRIGUE...

BREATHTAKING ROMANTIC SUSPENSE

My wish list for next month's titles...

In stores from 21st June 2013:

❏ Carrie's Protector – Rebecca York

& For the Baby's Sake – Beverly Long

❏ Outlaw Lawman – Delores Fossen

& The Smoky Mountain Mist – Paula Graves

❏ Triggered – Elle James

& Fearless – HelenKay Dimon

Romantic Suspense

❏ The Colton Ransom – Marie Ferrarella

Available at WHSmith, Tesco, Asda, Eason, Amazon and Apple

Just can't wait?

Visit us Online

You can buy our books online a month before they hit the shops! **www.millsandboon.co.uk**

0613/46

Special Offers

Every month we put together collections and longer reads written by your favourite authors.

Here are some of next month's highlights— and don't miss our fabulous discount online!

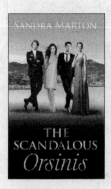

On sale 21st June

On sale 5th July

On sale 5th July

Save 20%
on all Special Releases

MILLS & BOON®
Book Club

Join the Mills & Boon Book Club

Want to read more **Intrigue** books?
We're offering you **2 more** absolutely **FREE!**

We'll also treat you to these fabulous extras:

- **Exclusive offers and much more!**

- **FREE home delivery**

- **FREE books and gifts with our special rewards scheme**

Get your free books now!

**visit www.millsandboon.co.uk/bookclub
or call Customer Relations on 020 8288 2888**

BS/ONLINE/l1

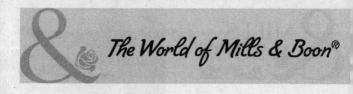

The World of Mills & Boon®

There's a Mills & Boon® series that's perfect for you. We publish ten series and, with new titles every month, you never have to wait long for your favourite to come along.

Blaze®

Scorching hot, sexy reads
4 new stories every month

By Request

Relive the romance with the best of the best
9 new stories every month

Cherish™

Romance to melt the heart every time
12 new stories every month

Desire™

Passionate and dramatic love stories
8 new stories every month